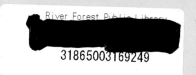

MY
FATHER,
THE
PANDA
KILLER

MY FATHER, THE PANDA KILLER

JAMIE JO HOANG

CROWN BOOKS
NEW YORK

CONTENT NOTE: Certain passages in this book contain depictions of abuse, violence, suicide, assault, and death.

Readers may notice honorifics like O instead of Cô or name spellings like Hương as opposed to Hướng that may not be familiar. Vietnam has many different dialects; from north to south, the way we speak and spell can deviate. My family is from Đa Nẵng and Vũng Tâu, respectively, so I stayed true to our regional dialect and spellings.

All rights reserved. Published in the United States by Crown Books for Young Readers, an imprint of Random House Children's Books, a division of Penguin Random House LLC, New York.

Crown and the colophon are registered trademarks of Penguin Random House LLC.

Visit us on the Web! GetUnderlined.com

Educators and librarians, for a variety of teaching tools, visit us at RHTeachersLibrarians.com

Library of Congress Cataloging-in-Publication Data
Names: Hoang, Jamie Jo, author.
Title: My father, the panda killer / Jamie Jo Hoang.
Description: First edition. | New York: Crown Books, 2023. | Audience: Ages 14 and up. | Audience: Grades 10–12. | Summary: Told in alternating voices, seventeen-year-old Jane rails against her family's Vietnamese culture and struggles with a perpetually angry father, whose traumatic journey to the United States as an eleven-year-old refugee is revealed in flashbacks.
Identifiers: LCCN 2023009872 (print) | LCCN 2023009873 (ebook) | ISBN 978-0-593-64296-2 (hardcover) | ISBN 978-0-593-64297-9 (library binding) | ISBN 978-0-593-64298-6 (ebook)
Subjects: CYAC: Fathers and daughters—Fiction. | Vietnamese Americans—Fiction. | Refugees—Fiction. | Boat people—Vietnam. | LCGFT: Novels.
Classification: LCC PZ7.1.H5978 My 2023 (print) | LCC PZ7.1.H5978 (ebook) | DDC [Fic]—dc23

The text of this book is set in 11-point Adobe Caslon Pro and 11-point Whitney.
Interior design by Megan Shortt

Printed in the United States of America
10 9 8 7 6 5 4 3 2 1
First Edition

For my family

THIS BOOK IS NOT
A HISTORY LESSON.

CHAPTER 1
JANE

Angry. I'm angry that I'm thinking about my mom again. It's the last thing I *want* to be thinking about. But here I am.

My mom left us when my brother, Paul, was three, almost four, or maybe he was four. Actually, he must have been four because the week after she left, he started preschool. Whenever I think about that week, I wonder what must have been going on in her head as she packed my lunch, knowing she wasn't coming back. Did she think about us? Were we the reason she left? Was I not helpful enough, not smart enough, not clean enough? Did I need too much? Did I annoy her? Why was she so unhappy? Was it us? Did she not want to be a mother? Or was it something else or someone else? A scandalous love affair with some shop patron? If so, had I seen this man before?

Because the thing is, I never heard my parents fight.

They weren't in love or anything stupid like that. I didn't grow up believing in fairy tales or princes or *equality*. My family is old-school—as in America in like the fifties, except it's 1999. My father is the head of the household. He controls every aspect of our lives, from the finances to our daily schedules, and no one—not even my mother—ever argues with him. So, we might be American, but we're certainly not *Americanized*.

Surprised. I was surprised she left. I *am* surprised. Not that she wanted to go or thought about it, but that she actually did it, and if I didn't have a stomach full of resentment, I might have even admired her for it. But I was fourteen, and all I really felt was abandoned. Left to fend for myself and Paul at a time when my classmates were gushing about who might ask them to homecoming. The bitterness, even three years later, is strong. As for Paul, he was too young to really understand anything, so he probably assumes she died.

That day, the day she left, I knew something was wrong when my dad picked me up. My dad *never* picks me up from school. That he even knew where it was is perplexing. Since kindergarten, not once had he ever attended an academic function. Education was my mom's domain. She never cared to check my homework or report cards; no, my enrollment was about being free of me for seven hours a day, five days a week.

My suspicions grew when he told me to walk to and from school for the next week. We didn't live far, and to be honest, that was the greatest thing I'd ever heard. *A full two miles to walk untethered to my parents?* My preteen self did celebratory cartwheels all the way home. But this guttural, sinking feeling—intuition, I guess—was there also. I knew something wasn't right.

To this day, I have no idea where Paul stayed during that first week. I just know that eventually, he came home. My dad must have closed up shop to come get me, but I couldn't be entirely sure because he dropped me off at home alone and went back to work. I hate to say it, but my biggest concern at the time had been that I had no idea how long it would take to walk to school. It didn't seem far, but having always been a passenger in the car, I couldn't gauge the distance on foot.

What I did know was that I couldn't be late. So, the next day, I woke up at 4:00 a.m., ate rice and eggs with scallion, made an American sandwich with bread, ham, and mayo, stuffed chips into my backpack, and left the house.

I sauntered past three blocks of apartments before reaching the busy Chapman Avenue, where I patiently waited for the white walk signal even though there weren't any cars around. After the light, I continued past CVS Pharmacy, three small shopping plazas I hadn't even noticed before, and McDonald's. When I checked my watch, it was already 4:15 a.m. I picked up my pace but still felt like I was walking too slow. Valentino's Pizza, aka the $7 pizza place, was so far away that I couldn't see its signpost. My shins began to ache, and panic set in. Where was the park? Had I made a wrong turn? I hadn't made *any* turns, so that wasn't possible. Still, I doubted myself. The park that I thought was just around the corner was in fact seven stoplights away. Images of Safeway, Del Taco, and the hot dog stand I'd wanted to try since it opened six years ago flashed through my mind. Immediately, I started sprinting toward school.

My heart was pounding, my legs felt weak, I couldn't get

enough air, and just before I thought I would pass out, a horn blared behind me.

Bleary-eyed, I looked over at the car and jumped away from the curb. It took me a moment to realize it was my dad. I don't know when he woke up or how he knew where to find me, but there he was.

"What are you doing?"

I stared at him, dumbfounded. "I think I'm going to be late."

"Do you know what time it is?"

I shook my head.

"Get in the car."

I opened the door and climbed in.

"It's only four twenty-five in the morning. Why did you leave so early for?"

"Because I didn't know how long it would take, and I didn't want to be late."

"How long you think it takes to walk to school?"

I didn't have a good answer.

It didn't dawn on me then, but when I look back at that morning—and I look back pretty often—I'm fairly certain that my dad must have followed me from the moment I left the house. He must have lain awake while I got ready and waited for me to leave before tailing my every turn. Maybe he panicked when he saw me running. Maybe he thought I was running away. Maybe he thought I was leaving the same way my mother had.

But I wasn't. The thought hadn't even occurred to me. And actually, I find it insulting. I am *not* like my mother. I would never leave Paul alone with my dad. She is a coward. A heartless, non-motherly bitch who I swore would no longer occupy my thoughts. I wasn't going to be like those weak-ass kids whose parents ruined them—who had to go to therapy because Mommy left. People leave, life is shit, and some of us don't have time to sit on a couch and talk about our feelings.

Anyway, instead of driving me to school, my dad pulled into Callahan's, a diner I hadn't even known existed until we parked—and walked inside. We never ate American food. Maybe McDonald's on the rare occasion my mom wasn't able to cook, but never any food as fancy as Callahan's. The booths were soft, faux leather, and there were packets of jam, salt and pepper, three different kinds of syrup, saltine crackers, and sugar on every table. And there weren't just a few booths either but rows and rows of them.

Once seated, I scanned the enormous menu. There were eggs and pancakes and waffles and burritos and ice cream sundaes.

"What do you want to eat?" my dad asked.

"I don't know. What are you having?" Honestly, I was more concerned with the prices.

Everything looked good but also really expensive.

"I think I'll have the steak and eggs," my dad said, pointing to the picture. In my memory, his English is impeccable. I found the steak and eggs on the menu and checked the price: $12.99. So, I knew whatever I ordered had to be less than $12.99. That seemed easy enough.

When the waitress came over, my dad pointed at the picture, and I gave her my order. "I'll have the pancakes and eggs."

"Anything to drink?"

"Do you have beer?"

The waitress frowned, which, in hindsight, isn't at all unusual. Who comes to a diner at dawn with their daughter and orders a beer? But this is normal. Dad has a beer with every meal, and while he is a lot of things, he isn't a drunk. "No, we don't serve alcohol here," the woman said. I wanted to punch her in the face. How dare she talk down to us like that? Who the hell did she think she was? A stupid, dumb waitress is what. Fuck her.

My dad, though, didn't even flinch. He just said, "Okay, water then."

"Same," I cowered. "Nhà hàng này vắng huh?" I said, looking around at the empty restaurant.

"Because they don't serve beer." My dad laughed, echoing my thoughts. I laughed too.

The waitress rolled her eyes. "One steak and eggs and one pancakes and eggs coming right up."

I'm ashamed to admit that I was so enamored by the biggest stack of pancakes I had ever seen that I forgot all about why we were there at 5:00 a.m. on a school day. The sweet, fluffy pile reached the edges of the plate and stood nearly four inches tall. My dad seemed pretty content, too, so I'm not sure why, between mouthfuls of pancake smothered in all three kinds of syrup, I decided to drop a bomb: "Is Mom gone?" As soon as the words left my mouth, I regretted them. We aren't a family that discusses problems, and I was never included in any decision-making, ever. I shouldn't have opened my mouth, but I did. Gripping my fork tight, I dropped my fist to the table and braced for impact.

"I think so." He said this without any emotion, then took a gulp of water.

Did she take Paul? I wanted to ask. But I had already tiptoed so close to the line with my dad that I decided not to press it. Paul wasn't with my dad when he picked me up, so I assumed she took him with her. He was her favorite anyway, being the boy and all.

"Okay," I simply replied. And it *was* okay. Lots of kids got along just fine without a mom. We were a team now.

I think about that morning a lot, the morning my father followed me to school. Over and over again, I imagine him waiting for me to leave the house, watching me turn the corner, getting into the car, and slowly following me. One block, two blocks, ten blocks . . . past all the darkened landmarks, until he sees me running.

I think about this when I'm standing at the end of another beating I'm receiving for reasons I don't fully understand. I play the moment over and over in my mind to soften and dull the pain. I do it because, in this memory, I know. I know that my father, for all his faults—and he has many faults—loves me.

CHAPTER 2
PHÚC

"Sit still. Both of you. Mr. Rogers needs some blanket too."

"You're acting weird," Paul says.

"I need to tell you a story, and it might take a while, so get comfortable," I reply.

"Why? What's the story?"

"Can you please sit still? Every time you shift, I lose my concentration, and if you break my concentration, I'll miss key details and then you won't understand what I'm trying to tell you. It's about Dad."

"Can't we just watch a movie?"

"Shhhh. There is a small town in the center of Vietnam called Đà Nẵng. That's where our family is from. . . ."

Phúc awoke, staring at the bunched-up mosquito netting hanging from the ceiling. The cascade of white was made of fine mesh but did little to protect him from bites. His two sisters, Linh and Uyên, lay beside him, huddled around Linh's daughter, baby Thi. He listened as their shallow breaths glided across the quiet air. On a normal day, outside his window, he'd hear the rattling of baskets clanking against squeaky handlebars, motorbikes roaring then easing off the gas while deftly avoiding potholes, and the occasional whipping of large blades cutting through the sky above. Typically, the city was alive with movement. But on April 30, 1975, there was no rain, no wind, no airplanes or helicopters; there was only a hollow silence.

For months on end, whenever school was canceled, Phúc gathered sand alongside our grandma, Phúc's mother, Bà Nội, who was determined to rebuild her courtyard. A tall woman, she stood stiff like an evergreen but moved with the steadfast determination of a turtle. Bit by bit, she would rebuild her home time and again despite the constant destruction. Having embraced her role as primary caretaker in the house, she bathed, cooked, cleaned, and fixed anything that needed mending. The courtyard, destroyed long ago by an explosion in the middle of the night, was just one of those jobs.

Phúc was slim in stature, but his scrawny arms and legs had begun to gain some muscular definition. On his bike, he carried three bamboo buckets, two dangling from his handlebars and the third resting on the back edge of his seat with a rope tied to his waist to keep it from slipping. Bà Nội carried an even heavier load of two larger buckets strapped to a bamboo stick that stretched across her shoulders. With half the courtyard already rebuilt, this was a well-established routine, and Phúc expected this day to be no different—but things *were* different. Instead of preparing to join him, she sat glued to the radio.

"Are we going?"

"Bring back eighteen buckets, and you can go play for the rest of the day."

Phúc didn't wait for additional instructions. He immediately left the house before she could change her mind. His bike hitched as the bent chain hopped from one gear to the other, but Phúc didn't care. Pedaling as fast as it would take him, he raced through the streets to the beach, shoveled sand into his buckets, and quickly pedaled back. He repeated this six times, determined to get it done before midafternoon. Phúc was so focused on his task that it wasn't until his sixth and final run through the alleyway of mud-brick homes and dirt roads that he noticed the chaos.

Furniture was carried from deserted homes, and the anguished cries of shattered hearts cut at Phúc's ears. Old men looked on, dazed. Something was very wrong. Frightened, Phúc dropped off the last of the buckets and pedaled toward his quiet hiding place. When explosions shook the earth, as they often did, Phúc would run. Not because there was anywhere safe to go but because instinct told him it was better than standing still.

Vietnam was on the precipice of change and no one knew what to expect.

Abandoned motorbikes siphoned of their gas lay scattered everywhere, blocking the path up the hill. With no city lights, darkness quickly enveloped the land. But Phúc didn't need light to guide him—he knew the route by feel. At the base of the hill, with his body covered in a mixture of sweat and humidity, he hopped off his bike and ran to an outlook with only his wooden flute strapped across his back.

In the jungle, vines grew around the oldest and thickest trees, and naturally, this was Phúc's favorite place. Here, the plants' abundance and dense nature made it impossible to know where one began and another ended, which meant you could cut, bomb, or chop away at it, and it would inevitably grow back. Finding one's way through the forest was no easy task, which, of course, only made the place all the more special.

At the entrance to Phúc's favorite and secret spot—an unmarked, unremarkable place, nowhere special in the landscape—he looked around to be sure no one else was watching. Phúc could feel the earth open up to him. There, at the edge of the jungle, with plants and bamboo marking the border between humanity and nature, Phúc waited for stillness. When he felt the coast was clear, he crouched down, pressed his palms flat on the ground, inhaled one long, deep breath, and ran.

Like Moses parting the Red Sea, he sprinted forward, and the bright green foliage recoiled to the side, revealing a path. The plant that covered this hidden passage was found all across Vietnam. To the locals, it was aptly named the shy plant, because when you touched it, its leaves would clamp shut. Not aggressively like those prickly plants that capture insects, but rather like a startled cat retreating underneath the couch.

At the top of the hill, Phúc looked back to make sure the leaves uncoiled, concealing the trail behind him. Once sure he was alone, he walked to the plateau's edge and looked down at his village. Even though Phúc was a child of war, meaning he was born during wartime, he didn't really understand what the war was. The same explosions that rocked the ground under his feet also caused bodily harm so painful that death seemed preferable, and that was normal. His classmates showing up to school with shrapnel stuck in places too precarious to remove, and metal raindrops blasting through hands that would later be amputated on the plastic rugs of Phúc's living room floor, was normal. Phúc's father, Ông Nội, was an uneducated medic learning on the job, and these broken people, held down by grown men struggling to sedate their thrashing bodies, were his patients.

That Phúc himself had no physical scars was actually something of a miracle. The name *Phúc* means *luck*, and he was given that name because following the births of his brother and sister, his mother had three miscarriages. It was thought that she might never bear any more children. Phúc's birth meant the family's fortune was turning. When his younger sister, Uyên, was born two years later, Phúc's name took on an even stronger meaning. True to his namesake, he became the family's lucky charm. And Phúc grew up during a time when luck wasn't to be taken for granted.

Phúc didn't believe in luck, though; he knew his time would come eventually. He knew better than to trust the stillness of the earth. Beneath his feet, tension filled the soil, so that even though there was no physical quake, its touch sent chills up his spine.

From this seemingly safe vantage point, he had watched over the years as the continually changing landscape evolved from green leaves and cream-colored structures to large burning banana leaves in darkened black holes and back again. This vicious cycle of growth and destruction was routine. Build up, burn down, build up, burn down. Đà Nẵng was volcanic— eruptions and quakes caused by bombs came without warning and destroyed everything they touched. Build a courtyard wall, watch it crumble, rebuild, feel the earth shake, and see a neighbor's house reduced to rubble.

Phúc didn't know how to process what he saw. He didn't understand why he felt uneasy in the quiet. He only knew what was familiar, and that was his flute. He never had any formal training, but he didn't need it. Once his lips hit the smooth bamboo, he let the notes find him.

On that hilltop, Phúc would release soft, melancholic sounds and then listen as they caught the wind and floated on the wings of a long breeze. Out into the ocean and back again, through the forest and to his heart. On good days like this one, when the pops of raining sand were more phantom than real, Phúc would sit beneath an 800-year-old banyan tree, unaware of its symbol as the mother of Đà Nẵng. As protector of the land with its vast interlacing root system that stretched unseen beneath the entire city, Vietnam's soul lived in the rings of her trunk. For a few moments, he swayed with the wind, listening to the sounds of the earth before curling his lips around his flute once again and playing a soft melody all his own.

As his music passed through the forest, the vines came to life with dance. Offshoots of greenery would move along Phúc's legs and body, slithering around his waist and up across his shoulder blades until they reached the end of his flute, where there was nowhere else to go. The flute, carved from nature's own elements, would sway about as if lifted by its own spirit, with the gentle, trailing plant creating a sweet flutter after every note.

Whenever Phúc could get away, he would come here for hours, rain or shine, because in Vietnam, the weather added to his song. Without an accompaniment of instruments, he relied on Mother Nature to provide elemental sounds. A breeze was not just a breeze; it was an enchanting whistle. And raindrops plinking on the leaves, stones, puddles, or even Phúc's own plastic sandals worked like a smattering of xylophone keys. When combined, the instruments weaved a texture impossible to replicate. It was of no consequence that Phúc had no musical education. No matter how many times he tried to recreate the same song, Mother Nature played it differently.

To the west were lush mountains where rice grew along switchbacks, and to the east was the vast Pacific Ocean. Here, people connected to the land. They walked with bare feet so they could feel the earth. They dressed in loose fabric so they could feel the wind. They touched the soil, and it became a part of them. No one wanted to leave, and yet they couldn't stay.

CHAPTER 3
JANE

My father is the reason I avoid Vietnamese people at all costs. My father is the reason I purchased blue contact lenses from Samar Mhaskar, who stole them from his ophthalmologist father. My father is *not* the reason Jackie Nguyễn and I are best friends. Jackie and I are the double Js. We're friends, despite us being Vietnamese, because our names both start with the letter *J*, which ordinarily wouldn't mean anything, but *because* we're Vietnamese, it means everything. It's a symbol of how whitewashed our parents want us to be.

Of all the names they could've chosen, our parents decided on ones that begin with the letter *J*, which happens to be one of only four letters in the English alphabet with no counterpart in Vietnamese—the other three letters being *F*, *W*, and *Z*.

They wanted us to be American so badly, they gave us names beginning with letters they couldn't pronounce. Hardly any more evidence is needed. Luckily for all of us, Jackie and I are more than happy to oblige. We avoid other Vietnamese people, especially the fobby ones. *FOB* stands for *Fresh Off the Boat,* and it's what we call Vietnamese people who immigrated to the US recently. Their accents and their clothing (brand-name shirts and sneakers that are *just* slightly off—Adidas = Addidas, Nike = Ike's, Fila = Fifa) make it easy to peg them. A FOB is the last thing either of us wants to be.

Both of us speak English like white people, and it hurts our ears to hear Vietnamese people butchering the language.

I speak Vietnamese, but not as well as I understand it. Before my mom left, we attended family gatherings every few months and someone would inevitably comment on how I spoke Vietnamese with a strange accent. Apparently, my dad's central accent and my mom's southern accent merged in my head, and both sides had a hard time understanding me. After my mom left, I sort of stopped speaking it altogether. I didn't see the point.

Jackie and I are a duo in a group of four. Carly and Mirabelle make up the other half of our group, but it has always been us two and them two. I have my broken-heart friendship necklace to prove it. Jackie is my other half. This has been our dynamic since middle school when the four of us sat together at the very top row of the Villa Park Middle School Amphitheater during lunch.

And when our middle school filtered into El Dorado High, our group moved from the amphitheater to a walkway just outside the quad area where the popular kids congregated. None of us were popular, but we had each other.

Jackie is the yin to my yang and has been since the fourth grade when, after three days of playing on the swings at recess with the class twins, Sarah and Zoe, the two of them abruptly decided they didn't want to be friends with me anymore. A new girl, Raven, had taken my place in their trio, and apparently, there wasn't room for four. My fatal mistake, I later learned, was talking about my Vietnamese heritage. They asked me what kind of food I ate, and when I gave a boring answer of rice and eggs, I could tell they were disappointed, so I started listing off the things I knew would gross them out. I told them we ate lots of fish, like the *whole* fish, including the eyeballs, and when they began laughing, I took that as a good sign, so I continued. Beef tongue, duck blood on sesame rice crackers, dried squid, the list goes on. I brought up everything and anything I thought might entertain them, and then they ditched me as friends.

I guess I should thank them for the early lesson on "fitting in" because I never made *that* mistake again. I went hungry for weeks after that because I was too ashamed of the rice and Spam, fried rice, or rice with dried shrimp that my mom usually packed in my lunch to eat. I even tossed my favorite sweet green sticky rice balls and the sweet soy milk I'd begged her to buy.

And then Jackie showed up.

Her family had recently moved up north to San Jose from Orange County, and just as I was about to dump the contents of my lunch into the trash bin, she put a hand out to stop me.

"Hey, if you don't want that, I'll trade you." She was wearing a neon-green shirt with a frog on it over a gray skort and had half of her jet-black hair up in a high ponytail. She was so cool.

"What do you have?" I asked. She showed me her Lunch-ables with Oreo cookies in the corner. "The cookies too?"

"The whole shebang," she said.

We swapped, and I watched her scarf down my entire lunch like it was her last meal on earth. "I haven't had this stuff since we moved up here. Seriously, I don't know how these kids eat that garbage every day."

"You don't think it's weird to eat rice at school?"

"What? Who says it's weird? You can't possibly tell me you think that junk tastes better than this sweet, sweet sticky rice?" She had a point. I thought about telling her how the other kids stopped being my friends because of the food we ate, but I was too embarrassed at my own inability to stand up for myself.

"My mom started buying me that crap after she saw some other moms in the grocery store stacking their carts with them. I prefer rice: cơm chiên[1], cơm cháy[2], cơm tấm[3]. Give me rice all day, any day." She gulped down the last of the soy milk, making loud slurping sounds as she squished the carton to get every last drop. One would think her love of Vietnamese food would equate to a love of Vietnamese people, but one would be wrong.

When my mom left, I blamed myself. Sometimes I still do. A single word uttered in a particular tone, the one that tells me I'm in trouble, can drop me right back into that mindset of self-hate. Jackie never lets me wallow in it, though. She's full-blown confidence. "No. No, no. Nope. You're not doing this, Jane.

---

1   fried rice
2   burnt rice
3   broken rice

She's not worth it. You are beyond amazing and fuck her for not knowing it," she'd say, forcing me to look at her and then repeat the mantra.

I don't know what I'm going to do without Jackie. Like, part of me is seriously considering staying back and attending San José State University. If I do, I'll start college with my best friend *and* I won't have to tell my dad, or Paul, I'm leaving. But Jackie would never let me do that; she didn't even let me apply as a backup.

When I showed Jackie my acceptance letter to UCLA, as expected, her reaction was larger than life. This is why I love Jackie. She isn't afraid to be herself, unlike me. She has always been like this—an external force who says the things I am scared to admit. Who gives me permission to be angry about things I mostly feel guilty about.

Jackie always has my back, like the time she saw the faint bruises on my thighs just before winter break and asked me what happened. I sighed and told her I had put off doing the dishes because I was finishing homework, and when my dad called me to do them, instead of coming right away, I said, "Hold on."

"That's it? What the fuck?" Jackie was incredulous.

"I know." I knew Jackie would understand. Her parents are from the same motherland.

Punishment there is different. To them, a pathetic slap on the wrist or time-out is why wayward American kids have no respect for their parents or elders. My dad loves to remind me of this, often laughing at me for crying before he even hits me. I hate crying, but I can't control the impulse. My dad is cruel because Vietnamese people are cruel. Still, it felt unfair. Jackie not defending him, or her own parents, helped unburden me of the heavy weight of my anger.

Because I'm a spineless chicken, I've kept the letter taped to the back of my desk for the last three months. I'm too afraid to tell my dad I got into UCLA. Instead of acting like an adult and saying what I want, I've mapped my escape route to college via public transportation. It requires five buses, two trains, and nine hours, but I can do it. Except I don't want to leave that way. No, I'm *afraid* to leave that way. I can't imagine what that would do to Paul.

My hands tingle just thinking about the weathered and crumpled envelope I carefully tore open so that I could preserve one of the few pieces of mail ever addressed to me. That letter was, and still is, the single most valuable thing I own. It's my ticket out.

My ride into another life. University of California, Los Angeles, a partial scholarship, and the offer of a student job on campus to help supplement the rest of the costs. Luckily, I was rejected by Berkeley, which would've been only a two-hour drive from home, meaning I'd be forced to come back on weekends to work.

I plan to tell them.

I'm going to tell them.

I'm worried about the family business. Well, I am a little worried about it. Paul will probably have to start working. Yet another reason he is going to hate me if I go. He'll be eight in November—young by most people's standards but older than I was when I first started unpacking boxes in the shop. If my dad and I did it together, he and Paul can too.

He's smart for a seven-year-old or maybe just smart in general. I don't hang with many seven-year-olds. What I do know is that he can read our dad better than I can because he somehow manages to avoid getting hit. That's not true. He does get hit—just not as often as I do. Still, it's the real reason I don't want to leave him.

But I also can't stay.

I need to be brave for just one more summer. This last summer is the only thing that separates me from a life of possibility. I just need to survive it. And decide to go. Survive and decide. I can do this. And not cave. This is the critical part. I cannot cave.

Paul is tough. If he can suffer through the four years it'll take me to finish college, he could move in with me then. We could start fresh. Away from home. Away from family. Away from anyone Vietnamese. Still, I'm scared to tell him because I know he's going to wonder if I haven't become exactly like our mom.

It's 5:03 a.m., and I've officially been awake all night. My alarm will go off at precisely 5:05 a.m., giving me ten minutes to shower, fifteen to get dressed, and another fifteen to make eggs and toast for myself and Paul. Paul will then wake up right before I leave to say goodbye. He's never actually said it, but I'm pretty sure he's afraid I'm going to leave one day and never come home. His fears are not unfounded—obviously.

I turn my alarm off before it has a chance to make any noise and get up. Lifting my heavy head off the pillow, I undress groggily in the bathroom and hop into the shower. The scalding-hot water provides instant and satisfying relief. I feel like I could stand here for days.

Over the past few months, I've been trying different tactics to ease Paul into the idea of me leaving. I ask him a series of questions like, "Hey, Paul, how would you feel if I went to a sleepover at Jackie's house?" Or, "Hey, Paul, wouldn't it be awesome if you had your own room?" But he goes quiet and says nothing at all. Or he shrugs in that way we both do when we know it's not up to us. But the message is clear: he doesn't want me to go.

Popping my head into the room we share, I whisper loudly, "The eggs are still warm. Eat them, and then go back to bed." When he doesn't move, I ruffle his hair playfully and give him an over-the-blanket hug before going to work.

As the door closes, I watch him climb up on the stool to eat in the dark, knowing he'll make sure to do the dishes and reset his alarm for 9:00 a.m., before our dad wakes up. In our household, no matter how tired you are, you do not sleep in past Dad. Nobody is as tired as he is, and sleeping in is the quickest way to get an early morning beating.

I'm tired when I arrive. The signage might say LIQUOR STORE, but it's really a convenience store that happens to sell liquor. We're a local joint, so what the sign reads doesn't really matter; the people who live here know what we are. I pick up the empty wrappers, random takeout, and plastic cups that somehow always appear overnight and toss them before walking to the front to unlock the doors. Lately, my brain just won't shut off. It plays and replays hundreds of scenarios of me leaving for college with different outcomes, some hopeful, some awful, and all terrifying. If I ask Dad too early, I risk the possibility of him changing his mind. If I ask at all, I risk having to enact a plan resulting in not being able to see Paul ever again. There is no scenario in which it goes smoothly, and knowing that makes me anxious, which in turn means I'm awake for more hours than any living human being ever should be. So, my patience is virtually nonexistent when I happen upon a man sitting against the iron pull-out gate of our shop. It's bent inward against his weight, and this would normally be a mild annoyance, but because I'm so tired, it might as well be the end of the fucking world.

"You can't sit here." My pitch is just a notch below yelling. I don't want to have to repeat myself, even though I know thinking that is a self-fulfilling prophecy in this case. He doesn't move.

"Hey."

He stirs.

"Get up, or I'm calling the cops. No loitering."

He stares daggers at me as he stands, moving at the speed of a sloth. Before I have a chance to step back, a smell is kicked like sand into my nostrils: it's the familiar spicy stench of someone who hasn't showered in days, maybe months.

He knows me. He's seen my face before. We've had this same interaction at least three other times this month, yet he acts as though this is his first offense. As though he's never seen me before. His disheveled blond hair swings sideways and then back over his eyes while he struggles to stand.

I feel bad. Of course I do. I mean, I'm a freaking human. But he needs to skedaddle.

With the man now sufficiently far enough away from the shop, I scan the perimeter to make sure no one can sneak up on me, uncurl my balled-up fists, and, with mildly trembling hands, open up for business.

One fucking summer. I just need to get through one last fucking summer.

CHAPTER 4
PHÚC

When the news broke about a boundary being drawn, Phúc's family had no idea. They weren't tapped into the main line of communication, and they weren't educated enough to understand the ramifications of what it meant. So, even if they had heard of it, maybe on the radio, they didn't understand it. In any case, they weren't going to move to the North just because the government decided to cut itself up. Their home and their livelihood were in the State of Vietnam, so they remained in the State of Vietnam.

As a new government, new currency, and new leaders who were friendly with the Americans emerged, the fight for country began. For the Vũ family, though, it was simpler than that. Their only objective was survival. For twenty years, they lived this way. This was true for everyone except Phúc's older brother, Long.

Long emerged from the womb as a ball of fire.

Hot-tempered, he would not be stopped from joining his friends at war. He developed a friendship—probably through one of the many tunnels that ran deep underground from North Vietnam into the South—with someone in the North, probably Bà Nội's sister, who still lived up there. It's all speculation and gossip, though, because even today, only the Việt Cộng know where those tunnels begin and end. Whatever the circumstances, Long smuggled himself across the border, forged documents, and proclaimed to be a northerner. Again, it was probably as simple as this: Long wanted to be with his friends, his friends joined the army, so Long joined his friends. *Long* means *dragon* in Vietnamese, and, true to his namesake, once he learned to breathe fire there was no stopping him. Born in 1955, Long left home at just sixteen years old.

For Grandma and Grandpa, his defection was an embarrassment. Rumors rolled in, permeating the neighborhood with toxic whispers, and Long was immediately denounced. It wasn't a loud proclamation. The family simply stopped discussing him. Phúc was out a brother, and that was that. Still, seven-year-old Phúc missed Long and continued to ask for his whereabouts. He was told they didn't know. Phúc pressed on.

"Anh Long ở đâu rồi?" Still nothing. Maybe no one knew.

After hours of pestering, Bà Nội snapped, "Đừng hỏi nữa." Her stern tone told Phúc she was serious, he better not ask again, but the flick of her wrist shooing him away concerned him more than the reproach. He knew the truth. This gesture was Grandma's attempt at downplaying her own worries.

No matter; Phúc idolized his older brother, who had always jumped when Phúc was afraid to, who spoke with conviction when Phúc was stunned mute by fear, and who was in every way the man Phúc wanted to become. He heard the rumors. Whispers among neighbors turned Long into a kind of legend—good or bad, though, was still to be determined. But Phúc remained loyal.

For months, Phúc listened as his parents peddled false narratives around town to counteract the truth. Long died in an explosion . . . was sent off to live with relatives in Vũng Tàu . . . joined the Republican army . . . drowned in a boating accident . . . The story was forever changing. But it was his sister's words that cut him deepest. Reeling from her husband's departure to fight for the south, she was cold and callous about the truth: Long was a traitor.

As the war dragged on and recruiters came looking for new soldiers to join the army, it became a constant worry for the family. Would any of the neighbors give them up? What would the Army of the Republic do when they discovered the truth? More important, how much would it take to pay them off?

When the Army of the Republic asked about Long, Ông Nội told the soldiers that he believed his son was dead. He explained that Long had a mean streak, that he wanted to fight for his country, and he ran away. He didn't mention which side he ran away to fight for. The family had no idea if he was still even alive. They heard the grumblings of betrayal, but they had so many reasons to believe differently. Why would the Việt Cộng trust Long? He was no one special. He had no combat experience. So why wouldn't they just shoot him for trying to be a spy? Or to make an example of him? It was entirely possible that Long was just a stupid teenager whose body now lay in a mass grave of likewise rebellious teens.

Phúc never believed this, though. His brother was scrappy and sharp. Nothing like how his parents described him. And their betrayal only made Phúc's allegiance stronger.

The soldiers left the family alone after that. But this visit scared them by bringing the possibility of persecution right to their doorstep. So, that night, though it broke Bà Nội to do this, she put her son's photo next to their other deceased ancestors. Back then, superstitions were as sacred as religion. Even though she believed putting Long's picture on the ancestor wall was basically signaling to the universe that she accepted her son's death, she had to do it. There was no other choice.

When a regime falls, there is this image of the winning side marching in on big tanks and seizing everything immediately, but that's not what happened in Đà Nẵng. It took weeks before Phúc ever saw their presence, and when they eventually arrived, it wasn't on tanks but in haphazard caravans with valuables strapped to the rooftops. They were looters in uniform who moved from house to house touching the wives of their enemies, ripping walls and furniture apart in search of jewels, burning money, and leaving behind a yellow slash across each door to mark their progress.

For weeks the military men swept through the community. One family tried to barricade their doors closed, and the entire village watched as a pistol was held at the temple of the oldest son in the house and the trigger pulled. The boy, a kid just a year older than Phúc, was shot point-blank for his father's defiance. The message was clear: Do you value your belongings or the lives of your loved ones? For most, those who had lived on rations for years, giving up what few valuables they had left meant further starvation and eventual death anyway, so even though they knew the price, some of them chose to play the odds.

As homes around them were ransacked, the Vũ family's door remained untouched. The entire town was burning, yet they seemed to be cloaked in invisibility. But why? Their walls were made of the same sand-brick as the neighbors'. As far as status, they were neither the richest nor the poorest. If anything, they should've been a primary target because Grandpa technically worked for the Army of the Republic of Vietnam. But maybe no one knew that. Maybe the records had been destroyed.

In the days and months that followed the fall of Saigon, Phúc naively thought he would see his brother again. The war was over, and there was no reason they couldn't be brothers again. He had been gone for just over four years. Four years couldn't possibly change a person that much, could it? Four years wasn't enough to erase eleven years of brotherhood—of family. Phúc believed this. He really did.

"Vũ Đoàn Thái, get out here!" a voice yelled from outside.

Phúc began to shake. The voice was curt, extremely rude, and arrogant. All signs of bad things to come. And more confusing still was this soldier looked exactly like Long. Much to everyone's dismay, his long-lost big brother stepped forward. He was older, taller even, and more . . . not sophisticated—robotic. He had the commanding presence of a general or a lieutenant, someone of high ranking. He stood with his back straight, his posture perfectly stiff.

"Anh Long!" Phúc stupidly called to his brother. "Anh Long về rồi!" Phúc was so overcome with emotion that he shouted Long's return loudly before running, arms outstretched, toward his big brother.

"Đứng yên," Long barked, the palm of his hand stretched forward in front of Phúc. Phúc stopped, following his orders. Confused, he looked up at his brother, who ignored him completely. Closer now, Phúc noticed the men behind him. Like a flock of migratory birds flying in formation, his comrades, with duplicate faces of stone, stood rigid and still behind Long.

His brother wasn't *acting* like a general, he *was* a general, and the men behind him were waiting for his order.

Ông Nội emerged, quiet and peaceful like a monk, with Bà Nội following suit. Behind them, Linh's shrieks of anger followed by Uyên's careful cries could be heard. Bà Nội must have forced them to stay in their room. Phúc's sisters would not be greeting their brother today.

"Quỳ xuống." Long's voice was firm and confident in a way that showed this wasn't rehearsed—it was practiced. As he spoke, spit flew like sparks from his lips.

Ông Nội moved farther into the courtyard, but not before putting up a hand to stop Bà Nội from following him through the entryway. In the courtyard, he knelt silently. Tethered by an unshakable bond, Bà Nội also slid to her knees in place, watching as Ông Nội's thighs shook involuntarily with fear.

"Father, do you know what my superiors are saying about you? They're saying I can't be trusted," Long said, circling the weathered figure of his father.

Standing not two feet from Long, Phúc kept waiting for his dad to stand up, to slap Long across the face and ask him who he thought he was talking to.

But Ông Nội kept silent for a long time before asking, "Why did you come home?"

This was not the right thing to ask, and his question was met with a backhanded slap across the face.

"Dã man." This would've been insulting to say to a peer. To his father, though? Unfathomable. With the flick of two fingers, Long was given a long metal chain that he wrapped around his palm like gauze. The metal locks crushed together, then ripped taut as Long's hand swung backward, and the chain whipped across Ông Nội's face.

Grandpa dropped to the floor. Phúc quickly scrambled backward as he watched the large gash that cut across Ông Nội's cheek and nose peel open like a bleeding red flower.

At the sight of blood, Grandma shrieked and cried out, "My family is broken!" Tears fell from her face as she knelt in the doorframe. "What is my son doing? What is my son doing?" she repeated in a dazed chant.

The chain loosened until it hit the ground and metal scraped against dirt following Long's movements. As he adjusted his grip, Phúc saw the slightest of movements, an opening of his palm. Then, like a boxer who's just heard the starting bell, Long whipped his father once, twice, three times. Six. Ten. Fourteen. Too many times to count. Too many times.

Long's eyes glistened as they flickered past, his body like a hawk circling its prey. Phúc looked on, paralyzed with fear. *Say something!* Phúc screamed to himself. No sound left his mouth. Instead of standing up for his father, instead of taking the beating in his place, Phúc cowered in the corner, hiding his eyes, shielding his ears, and waiting for it to all be over.

Finally, it was Bà Nội who stepped in. Amid the chaos, she had retreated into their home, but now she moved with the same purpose and determination she had when rebuilding her courtyard. Slow but steadfast, she walked over to her elder son and stared him dead in the eye, daring him to hit his mother. At her feet, Grandpa lay motionless, his face turned into the gravel dirt, the brown linen of his shirt melting into his open wounds.

"Đủ rồi." Her words were even and firm, like a referee who's let a fight go on too long. With two hands, she offered Long a small bag of jewels and money. Phúc watched as Long took the neatly folded stack—which was more cash than Phúc had ever seen in his life—flicked open a lighter, held the money to the flame, and lit it on fire.

"Số tiền này không có giá trị." Their money no longer had value. Flipping a coin into the air, he let it land in the dirt. This was the new currency. The burning bills fell at Phúc's feet, and he closed his eyes, waiting for his brother's wrath to turn to him. Feet shuffled, the chain slid backward, and when Phúc finally had the courage to look, he saw his mother helping his father to his knees.

"Dạ." His body was weak, but Ông Nội spoke in a tone Phúc had only ever heard him take with his grandfather—a voice of deference.

Power made Long fierce. It emboldened him to strike a man Phúc would never even dare raise his voice to. But Phúc saw something else that day. Through the armor and the projected hate, he saw a flash of sorrow, a twitch of remorse, an imperceptible loosened grip on the chain. Long hadn't wanted to beat his father. He hadn't wanted to burn their savings. He was not a monster. He was just doing what he had to do. By beating him, he saved their lives.

CHAPTER 5

JANE

Stereotypes aren't true—except when they are. And when they are, they're annoying as hell. Vietnamese people often get lumped with Chinese people, and their stereotypes become ours. Like the overachieving student thing. You know the type. The two-year-old who reads physics books, plays the piano, and speaks Chinese (or in our case, Vietnamese) as fluently as they speak English, if not better. Take me, for example. I *am* a straight-A student, but I *do not* have a mother who pushes me to excel. And not because she left—she was just never interested in my studies at all.

It makes me wonder if, in trying to make up for this, I'm too tough on Paul. He's smarter than I am, but his intelligence also makes him lazy. When I quiz him on his vocab, and he knows all the answers, I have to find more complicated words for him to learn.

"Don't." I stare.

With one hand holding a bowl of eggs over rice, his other reaches for the handheld *Columns* video game tucked away in one of the small cubbyholes beneath the shop's register. I swear he's going to go blind from staring at that tiny screen for hours on end.

"But it's the weekend," he whines.

"Define *ambition*."

He sighs. "The strong desire to achieve something."

"*Continent.*"

"Any of the seven big landmasses on Earth."

"*Privilege.*"

"Having the time to annoy your younger brother on the weekend."

"Funny. Thirteen times twenty-six."

Paul laughs. "Even you don't know the answer to that!"

I relent. "Two hours. Then it's studying. Okay? Finish your food first."

Holding the bowl to his face, he scoops what's left of his breakfast into his mouth, grabs his game, and turns it on.

"Hey, nerd, make some room. I'm coming in."

I look up to see Jackie's face pressed against the cloudy bulletproof (in theory) window.

Jackie is wearing jeans, a white tank top, and a color-block jacket with the sleeves pushed up to her elbows. Her hair has a faint purple streak in it and is tied up with a scrunchie into a high ponytail. She is cooler than I am in every way.

"What are you doing here?" I ask, suddenly feeling self-conscious in my "work uniform," which consists of high-waisted jeans, an oversized gray T-shirt, and maroon Vans sneakers. Despite being best friends, Jackie has never, not once, come to hang at the store. When we were kids, I asked my dad if she could come play with me, and he agreed, but her mom said she'd rather I come to their house—something I couldn't do because I was always working. Neither of us ever mentioned meeting up outside of school after that.

"I brought coffee."

"We have coffee," I say.

"That's Vietnamese coffee. This is Starbucks," she says, handing me a mocha Frappuccino she knows I never would've paid for on my own. I don't spend money on frivolous things like overpriced coffee.

"Seriously, what are you doing here?"

"It's our last summer," she says. "If you can't come out, I'm coming here."

"And your mom's okay with this?" When she hadn't accepted my first invitation, it didn't take long for me to realize that her mom didn't want her daughter coming to this part of town. I wasn't mad about it; I was grateful she didn't make Jackie stop being friends with me. That's something my parents absolutely would've done.

"Jane, I have a car. I go where I want." She smiles. She isn't fooling anyone, though. Jackie is as much a Goody Two-shoes as I am.

I look down at Paul, who is sitting in the only other space inside the cramped cashier's box. He's engrossed in his game. "If you're done eating, take these bowls to the office, and you can play there for the next two hours."

Paul beams with delight. The tiny office next to the bathroom has a small cot, a desk, overflow products, and surveillance video stuff. It's my favorite part of this place for one reason: no customers.

I unlock the door to the register, aware that Jackie is probably not allowed back here, but I can't exactly leave her standing outside like a patron, so it hardly seems like I have a choice.

"Hi, Jackie. Bye, Jackie," Paul says as he slips through the door.

"Make sure you lock it," I shout after him. He gives a thumbs-up high in the air so I can see as he sprints away.

"Welcome to my humble abode," I say, wishing I had used some of the countless hours I've spent daydreaming while trapped here to make the place less dingy.

Jackie appears to be unfazed by the cracked and blackened tile floor, the crumbling faux-leather chair wrapped in tattered plastic, or the old camping chair—the kind with no legs and a back that requires a human to sit in it to stay propped up. She hands me my drink, slides into the camping chair, leaning into the wall so that the seat almost looks comfortable, and says, "I take it you still haven't told Paul?"

"You know I haven't," I say, glaring at her. She looks at me with an arched eyebrow, and I don't even bother trying to out-stare her. "He's going to hate me. Why prolong the misery? If I tell him later, he'll have less time to make me feel guilty."

"You already feel guilty. You gotta do it, Jane. It's mean not to."

I know she's right, but I don't know how to go about it. Our family doesn't share stories or talk about personal problems. My dad never sat on the edge of my bed to ask me how I might feel if he left me alone at the age of eleven to work the register while he smoked outside with my uncles. This type of conversation is so the opposite of how we are. Just the thought of him trying this makes me uncomfortable. I either take care of a problem myself, or I ignore it.

"I haven't even talked to my dad about it. If he says no, there might not be a point in telling Paul."

"Um, no. If he says no, you pack a bag, and I drive you to college. Period."

"You know it's not that easy."

"Sometimes, actually, it's exactly that easy," she says. When I don't say anything, she adds, "Part of being an adult is doing things your parents don't like."

"Yeah," I sigh, because I know she's right, but I still don't know if I can do it. I don't know why it's so hard for me to rebel. Other kids do it all the time, but I'm just so . . . scared.

The back door opens, and my spine sharpens as I jump from my seat to stand. I'm not sure why I feel the need to do so, but sitting doesn't feel right when I'm pretty sure I'm about to be in trouble.

"Go," my dad says. On Saturdays, when my dad gets here, we leave to go grocery shopping and clean the house.

I stand there frozen, unsure of what to do because I should

tell him Jackie's here. Saying it before he sees her is definitely the better route (well, the best route would have been to ask permission first, but that ship has sailed). Somewhere in the back of my mind, though, I'm hoping to avoid a confrontation altogether by crossing my fingers and hoping he just doesn't see her. But then Jackie stands up.

"Uh—" is all I can say before Jackie cuts me off.

"Chào Chú Phúc!" she says spritely.

I see his eyes go wide with suspicion before he recognizes her. "Chào con." He nods. "Your parents finally not scared to have you come here, huh?" He laughs. Any other person would read this as a scoff, but he's actually joking.

"I got keys, so . . ." Jackie smiles, and he laughs too.

"Good, they worry too much. What is there to worry about?" It's not really a question, and neither of us answers. Without any kind of salutation—those are reserved only for adults—my dad goes to the office.

I turn to Jackie. "We're going to the store, but then I'll just be home cleaning if you want to come over?"

Leaning down to pick up her bag, Jackie tosses it across her body before saying, "Can't, church lets out in like fifteen minutes."

I laugh. "I see your rebellion is going well for you then."

"Part of growing up is picking your battles. Sometimes the path of least resistance is the way to go."

"Have you been reading self-help books or something?"

"Buddhism. Instead of going to church, I'm still being indoctrinated, just not by my parents' religion."

"Clever," I say.

"Same time next week?"

"Sure."

Playing the piano is a Chinese, not a Vietnamese, stereotype. Or maybe it is a Vietnamese stereotype, and my mom just didn't fit it. Despite my mother *not* guiding my education, I do take piano lessons—more on that later—but it wasn't my mother who made me. And those straight As I got were not because anyone pushed me to do well in school either. Actually, that's not true. The white kids who always copy off my tests motivate me to do well. I want them to like me, and them liking me is contingent on my having the right answers—enough to get them a B, anyway.

The honest truth: I'm not that smart. I study a lot. And by "a lot," I mean, from the moment I wake up to the moment I fall asleep, I think of almost nothing else. If other kids are studying for one hour, I study for two. If I finish all my schoolwork, there are flash cards with SAT words I'm trying to learn. Or extra-credit books that I read. I love extra credit, not because I like doing the extra work but because it gives me a buffer in case I bomb a quiz or a test. But make no mistake, I never understand stuff the first time around. Still, the stereotype of Asians being smart is like a jacket I can't take off. Some people got varsity jackets for playing sports. *I* got jacketed as the person you could copy off of.

A stereotype that *is* true, though, is this: Vietnamese families do not talk. It's not that we sit around the table in silence, but our conversations are . . . shallow. They revolve around what time I need to be at the store, when I need to pick up Paul, what needs to be restocked, which pipe burst in the back, who shoplifted and needs to be ousted the next time they come in. Like right now, as I swap places in the cashier booth with my dad, I say, "Ba, is there anything you want me to get at the store?"

"Get some snacks."

"Dạ," I say. Amazing. We have a shop full of American chips, nuts, crackers, you name it, but he wants almond cookies, durian wafers, and shrimp crackers. I add those to a running mental list of what I know we're low on at home: eggs, soy sauce, green onions, beef, chicken, ramen, a couple TV dinners, soup, spaghetti, and milk.

The phone rings and my dad answers. "Hello?"

Someone on the other end of the line speaks and he breaks into a wide grin. "Ah! Má!" He turns to me and hands me the receiver. "Say hi to Grandma before you go."

"Chào Bà Nội! Bà Nội có khỏe không?" I ask. She tells me she's well and I stay awkwardly on the line, waiting for her to ask for my dad back. Thankfully, that's the next thing she says, and I pass him the phone. Phone cards are expensive, so I never have to stay on the call longer than a few minutes.

After grabbing my purse, I poke my head into the office and say, "Hey, I've got to go to the store. Get up. C'mon, let's go."

"You said two hours. It's only been one," Paul complains, but he's already shutting off his game.

"I know, I'm sorry. You can play the other hour when we get home."

At the store, I grab a cart and Paul climbs onto the front. While I shop for the things we need, I zigzag through the aisles like we're on a roller coaster.

"Eggs, two cartons!" I say as I wheel him up to the eggs, but before he can reach for the item, I spin around in a circle. He laughs. "C'mon, two cartons, and make sure you don't drop them!"

"You drop it, and we're dead meat," he says, doing an extremely poor impression of me as he hops off the cart and carefully grabs one carton at a time. Even playing a game, he knows to be careful and not do anything that might get us in trouble with Dad. I roll my eyes, even though I think it's funny, as I take the cartons from him and place them in the basket. Paul is so freaking lovable, I can't imagine why anyone would leave him.

When I was in kindergarten, Ronan, this chubby kid who always carried a tattered gray elephant head attached to strings of threadbare gray fabric, came running to class, screaming, "I'm gonna have a new baby brother!" The teacher spent half the morning talking to him, and us, about what a big responsibility it was to be an older sibling. Ronan nodded along or occasionally rolled his eyes because he'd probably already had this conversation with his parents. And I probably thought, *Why would they tell you that? That's grown-up stuff.*

But I would later look back on that day with anxiety, trying to recall all the things I was supposed to know about having a baby brother. Because how I learned I was about to be a big sister was, well, a little less straightforward.

There was no discussion about learning how to share or accepting new responsibilities. No one asked me if I wanted a little brother. No one asked me how I would feel about sharing my toys or if I thought I'd be a good big sister.

We weren't at home nestled on a comfy couch or in a doctor's office or anywhere that made sense to reveal such information to me. I caught on while standing in the checkout line at the grocery store—*this* grocery store, two aisles over, cashier number 5—where I was secretly coveting the Reese's Pieces Minis candy packets.

My mom, who rarely spoke to strangers, was humming a tune to herself and putting our meat and bread on the conveyor belt when the cashier asked how far along she was.

"Six month."

"Me too," the cashier gushed. She stepped back from the register to reveal her round belly. "Boy or girl?"

"Boy."

"Me too!"

To my immature ears, their conversation sounded a lot like a game of Go Fish, and I giggled.

"Well, aren't you going to be the best big sister?"

I nodded, eager to please. If she thought I was going to be a good big sister, then I certainly wanted that too. The woman had kind eyes, but I wasn't used to anyone looking at me so directly and so intensely. I immediately dropped my gaze to the floor.

That's when I felt my mother's hand grab my chin and force it up so that I was looking directly at the cashier. "Don't be rude, she asked you a question." She spoke in Vietnamese, so no one else would understand, but her tone was clear enough that the cashier jumped to my defense. "Oh, don't worry. I was so shy when I was your age too." She laughed.

"Do babies cry a lot?" It was all I could think of to say. I didn't have a reference point for what questions you were supposed to ask about babies or what I was supposed to say about having a baby brother that would show what a good person I was. The moment was so unexpected that the words came out loud—a shout, really. I didn't want to talk to this woman. My mother looked down at me sharply, and I knew I was in trouble. I felt such disdain for this stranger, with her stupid, peppy attitude and arrogant, baby-carrying face. Of course, the woman couldn't have known, but her question and my ornery answer were about to earn me a beating. Mom and I both knew that punishment would be swift when she told my dad I had been rude in public. And I *was* punished, but that's not what sticks with me about that day.

I remember the cashier totaled our purchase and said, "It's going to be $25.73 today. You must be so happy."

"Yes. So happy."

So happy. This was the first time I'd ever heard my mother use the word *happy*. Honestly, up until this point, I didn't know there *was* a Vietnamese word for *happy*. But Paul hadn't even been born yet, and he already made her happier than I ever could.

So, I resented him.

I also resented the fact that no one had bothered to tell me— that I had discovered it only after a stranger in a supermarket had asked. And I used that resentment to create a divide between myself and Paul. Instead of being excited, I shunned him. Rather than think about all the things we'd get to do together, like play games or share in the misery of having tyrannical parents, I ignored him. He wasn't even born yet, but I wanted nothing to do with him. I acted like I didn't care if he existed.

It didn't help that after I became aware of Paul's existence, *everything* seemed to be about him. Aunts and uncles would call, and my mother would be on the phone for hours talking about how great it was that they were finally having a boy.

Okay, the stereotype of Asian families wanting sons more than daughters is real.

In the entirety of my life, the whole nine years up until that point, not once did my mother ever say something complimentary to me. When strangers said I was cute, she would lift my hair, scoff, and say, "With hair as dirty as this?" When a teacher remarked on my ability to subtract single-digit numbers, my mother laughed as though it was the least a five-year-old could do, because when she was my age, she was doing real work like washing clothes along the embankment or separating fish into piles to be sold at the market or sun-dried and fermented.

That I could do simple arithmetic was, to my mother, laughable.

This disdain for everything I did and her love for my perfect unborn brother made me really resent him. I said snide things to him in my mind. I wished for six fingers, a lopsided head, and other deformities. I cursed him every day—that is, until he was born. And then our mother treated him the same way she treated me, like a burden.

He cried a lot, more than is normal, but I was ten at the time, so I didn't know. *Babies were annoying because they cried, and they pooped*—that was the extent of my knowledge. I ignored his cries and focused on my schoolwork. But one night, he cried for seven hours straight, and I couldn't take it anymore. Despite my jealousy, I went to him. He was on the floor in the living room, screaming at the top of his lungs, his tiny fists shaking with fury, and there was my mother, sitting on the couch with a vacant look in her eyes.

Annoyed, I picked him up for the first time. I found a pacifier on the floor, and when I stuck it in his mouth, he immediately stopped crying. Given the force with which he seemed to be sucking on the nipple, I decided to find him some food. To be honest, I've never understood the point of a pacifier. Isn't sucking a biological instinct because we need to eat? Sticking a piece of plastic into a kid's face rather than just feeding them makes no sense. In the fridge, I found bottles of milk. My mother couldn't be bothered to pick up her son, but she somehow had the sense to breast-pump. I grabbed one, swooshed it around, and nervously pulled the pacifier from Paul's mouth. He immediately started screaming until I stuck the bottle in, and that's when I realized what my mother was doing. She was starving my baby brother.

Unsure of what to do, I borrowed a book from the library called *A Guide for First-Time Parents*, where I learned about burping, warming the bottle, sanitizing the nipples, and how to treat a diaper rash. It was here that I discovered the point of pacifiers. Apparently, babies don't know how to "pop" their ears and relieve the pain by swallowing or yawning, and sucking on a pacifier helps. Also, my mother breast-pumped, I learned, because women's boobs hurt if there's milk in them and they don't pump—the book went into horrifyingly graphic detail about this.

Anyway, I was so busy being the parent that I didn't realize my mother had gone back to her regular life. Every day when I came home from school, Paul would be in the same position—on the floor crying—while she finished getting dressed before heading off to god knows where. It would take her another three years to actually leave, but as far as I'm concerned, she abandoned Paul long before she was physically gone.

As a newborn, Paul was small and soft, and though he cried a lot, he also smiled a lot—mostly in his sleep. I had so many questions that I knew would go unanswered. What was he dreaming about? What good feelings did he already know about, having only been in this world a few days? Was I happy once too? Had the womb been so comfortable and safe that I had had dreams of happy things too? Or were those thoughts only reserved for the boys? Yes, I really thought that. At the time, I was looking for anything that would explain my situation. I'm still looking for answers as to how I ended up here, in this ass-backward family—struggling with how to leave for college.

"Pick a candy bar. Just one," I tell Paul as we reach the checkout counter. I watch his eyes go wide as he scans his options. He's going to hate me when I tell him I'm leaving. Maybe after I earn my degree and start making some money, I can bribe him into loving me again.

CHAPTER 6
PHÚC

"Did Bác Long really hit Ông Nội?" Paul asks.

"What did I say about asking questions?" I say.

"Well, if he could hit Grandpa and he's the son, why can't I hit Dad?"

His question throws me. He has a point. "Because that was Vietnam and this is America," I say, though I'm not fully convinced of my own answer. "Now shhh . . . no questions until the end."

News in those days, especially news of the personal kind, was like a game of telephone—hardly reliable.

Thanh's boat sank.

Thanh's boat made it to Australia.

Thanh's boat got stopped by Thai pirates.

No one has heard from anyone on Thanh's boat.

Khánh made it to California.

Wasn't Khánh on Thanh's boat?

There was no database of people to search through. The census that would later calculate the 3.1 million lives lost during the war and subsequent mass exodus didn't exist yet. But people felt the loss of their loved ones. Mothers knew their sons were gone. Fathers knew their daughters were lost. Because of this, Grandma and Grandpa made a strategic choice about escaping and sent their kids off separately instead of all in the same boat. Trust was not built: it was gauged by intuition—and hope. Every person they encountered was a potential threat. The priest who organized the trip, the captain, or the other passengers could purposely or inadvertently lead the Communists to their escape boat.

After Long's return home, things settled into a new, disquieting normal. The downstairs room, which was now Long's, became off-limits even though he didn't have much—just three identical uniforms on hangers and a drawer of casual clothes. A maid was brought to live with them. Bác Loan was a live-in helper whose uniform consisted of a simple brown button-down and matching loose cotton capris with an elastic waistband. She didn't speak much except to answer directions, but she loved the family like they were her own. And she tended to Grandpa's wounds with herbal remedies only a military nurse would know about. The family was careful never to speak ill of Long or the Communist regime in front of her, because though she had a kind disposition, she could not be trusted. No more neighborhood houses were ransacked. No more fighter jets were seen in the sky. No more explosions. There was still gunfire, though. And executions. So many executions. Anyone convicted of supporting South Vietnam was shot dead and left there for family members to bury, if they dared. Families wanted to bury their loved ones, of course they did, but they were afraid of looking like sympathizers.

Phúc envied his sisters for their bond. Linh, at nineteen, was a natural-born leader. After Long left, she swiftly stepped into her role as the elder sibling, but Phúc loathed her attempt to replace his brother. Uyên, two years behind Phúc, was quiet and reserved like a monk. Even at nine, Uyên often moved behind Linh, clinging to her dress like a permanent shadow.

Lose a war, and people quickly repatriate—that's the job of the new citizen. Long's return meant that the family kept the house, whereas many others were forced to leave— pushed into the streets with nothing but the clothes they wore. Overnight, everyone loved Hồ Chí Minh. Hồ Chí Minh was a great leader, the rightful leader. The Army of the Republic was defeated because they did not believe in Vietnam enough. That's what the kids were taught, anyway—until they shut the schools down.

By May 1976, the countryside still had no music. People moved about in hushed fear as families planned escape routes. The Americans were gone, but signs of their occupation still littered the landscape. A full year later, the scenery becoming quite pretty. Ships that sank close to shore had transformed into colorful anemones. Life grew around and through the crashed airplanes, burnt helicopters, broken tanks, army boots, and helmets. And refugees used these markers to help each other navigate their escapes.

On the eve of June 17, 1976, 414 days after the fall of Saigon, Phúc was woken up in the dead of night. He rubbed his eyes several times to get them to adjust, but even after a few minutes, he could barely see. He had never known the world to be so dark. Bà Nội quickly gave him pants to pull over his shorts and a long-sleeve shirt to button over his nighttime T-shirt. Straightening his clothes, Grandma said, "Watch for these lines, inside are pieces of gold. Only if you desperately need it do you take it out." Phúc reached down to touch his pants, but she slapped his hand away. "Don't give anyone a reason to think they should cut off your ankles." He stood up straight. The only other thing he was allowed to take with him was his flute.

"If they ask where you're going, tell them you're visiting your uncle. If they accuse you of escaping, ask them, 'With what? A flute?' If they threaten to shoot you, tell them who your brother is."

The instructions were vague, but there wasn't time to ask questions. In the hush of night, the two of them began to walk. With only cracks of moonlight leaking through the thick jungle and Bà Nội's memory to guide them, they moved steadily toward the ocean. This was the same jungle covered in landmines that Phúc had been strictly forbidden to enter. Beneath his feet, Phúc could feel the damp mud squish under his weight. Every step potentially his last. Every step toward the unknown. Every step away from his family.

In preparation for the journey, Grandma had dimmed a flashlight by leaving it on for several nights. When they came to an area so dense that Bà Nội couldn't see the small hand that clutched her own, she turned it on. Slowly they continued forward until her faded light landed in front of a fighter plane partially swallowed by the mud. After a quick look around, she reached into the cockpit and produced a small bag. This fallen plane was both a marker and a storage place for supplies. They pivoted ninety degrees east and continued past torn parachutes hanging from burnt and hollowed tree trunks, rusty metal chains, and blown tires. Every step was wrought with fear, but Phúc's body pressed forward despite his heart begging him to retreat.

"Sình, sình, sình . . ." Phúc repeated this word over and over again as a way of manifesting it. If he said *mud*, it would appear beneath his feet. Mud was good, mud was ideal. In this situation, mud was better than gold. Mud meant life.

Wet leaves brushed across his face, arms, and legs. A snake hissed from one of the trees above, spiders scuttled up dried bark, a rat raced across Phúc's open-toed sandal, and crickets bounced against his legs as he walked. A mosquito that he dared not kill drew fresh blood from the back of his neck. The distance, which was probably no farther than his eight-block bike ride to school, might as well have been the distance from Earth to Saturn—impossible.

Bà Nội's hand dug deeply into Phúc's shoulder, forcing him to a halt. The sun had begun its slow ascent and shapes were taking form. Not good. The night was his cloak, and daylight was about to strip him of his camouflage. Those seconds moved like hours, ticking slowly as she stood still next to Phúc's racing heart. *We've been caught. The Communists are coming.* Phúc's knees shook and started to buckle before he heard it, the low whistle of a familiar tune. *Kìa con bướm vàng, Kìa con bướm vàng.*

"*Kìa con bướm vàng*
Kìa con bướm vàng
Xòe đôi cánh
Xòe đôi cánh
Sorry, bro, I don't remember the rest. It's a kid's lullaby."

Tweet, tweet, tweet, tweet, pause, *tweet, tweet, tweet, tweet,* pause, *tweet, tweet…* This repetition of the first stanza hung in the air as Bà Nội and Phúc tried to discern its direction.

"Use your flute, blow the sound, thit, thit, thit, *the*, thit, thit, thit, *the*, thit, thit. Quietly."

Phúc's hands trembled, causing the first few notes to fall flat. He tried again. This time, soft notes fluttered outward.

Silence. Maybe they hadn't heard it. Maybe he needed

to blow louder. Bringing the flute to his lips again, he took a deep breath, filled his lungs with courage, and was about to blow when soft beeps could be heard pushing through the cold morning air.

Turning to their left, where the sound originated, they saw it—a speck of light in the distance.

Darkness, then three quick beams, so tiny they could've come from stars in faraway galaxies—if those were things that floated toward the sea in the middle of the night. Three clicks of the light, then darkness, three clicks, darkness, this repetition was his guide.

"You'll go alone from here," Bà Nội said, strapping the cloth bag full of food onto Phúc's shoulder before nudging him onward. "Đi, đi."

Fear gripped his ankles as Phúc walked forward, every step feeling more cumbersome than the last. At the water's edge, he looked back toward his mother for reassurance, but the space she had occupied just moments earlier was already empty.

In the distance, the speck of light appeared again in a continuous, foreboding loop. Adrenaline propelled him into the cold oceanic water. With every silent stroke, he reminded himself to trust. Trust that his mother knew what she was doing. Trust that his boat would make it. Trust that he would be one of the lucky ones.

Breathless, he surfaced, slowly sipping air so as not to make a sound despite his burning lungs. Up ahead maybe forty paces, the light was brighter now. Its source, a thin hand flicking the silver flint wheel of a lighter. Flame, flame, flame, darkness, flame, flame, flame, darkness.

He reached the boat's edge but was told to stay put. Slowly, the two men on board scanned the shore while Phúc waited. He tried not to think about what might lurk in the water beneath him.

"Đưa tay đây." The high-pitched whisper came from a man whose arm was extended toward him. Phúc recognized him as a fisherman whose boat Ông Nội had once helped fix. Phúc reached up and grabbed the man's arm. He felt his body scrape against the boat's wooden side as he was hoisted on deck before being quickly shooed toward the engine room. Through a small entryway and down a few steps, Phúc found thirty-seven people crammed into a space meant for eight.

For a while, nothing happened, but then the small engine rumbled to life, and the boat began to cruise. Water rushed against the sides. No one spoke. No one locked eyes. Everyone prayed. Everyone except Phúc. He sat on the bottom step of the stairs. The last to arrive, he found this to be the only surface left unoccupied. Curling up into a ball, Phúc pressed his chin to his knees and tried to think of brighter days. Running through the hills and ancestral cemeteries with his friends, eating sweet rice in a hammock, skipping stones along an alleyway, racing up his mountain. "I am safe, I am safe, I am safe," he whispered. He pleaded for safety, but it wasn't a prayer; it was a chant meant to convince himself that he would survive.

In the darkness, Phúc searched for familiar faces and,

surprisingly, found that there were many. No one with whom he was particularly close, just villagers he had seen around. Like Quốc, a classmate who used to get in trouble all the time for having a dirty or torn sheet of paper. Paper was scarce back then, so students wrote on a single sheet and erased it day in and day out. They weren't friends, nor were they enemies—they were classmates. There was also the local butcher and his family, and a few of the upper-class families huddled together, clutching their things tightly to their chests. A couple in their early twenties—the wife looked pregnant and pale. A dressmaker and her son, no father. And others who Phúc had seen around, a cousin of a cousin, perhaps, or some other more distant relation.

As Phúc turned his attention back to Quốc, it dawned on him that he was the only person on the ship traveling alone. Everyone else had family. He searched again. There was an uncle, a notoriously mean drunk, who would shove Phúc's head and demand he get him another beer. Dressed in a silk shirt and black slacks, he looked like he was trying to fit in with the wealthy group.

Phúc gazed down at his own muddy and drenched cotton drawstring pants and pit-stained shirt and knew his uncle would not be an ally on this journey. In fact, he should be avoided at all costs.

Knock.

Knock, knock.

Knock, knock, knock.

"Im lặng!" someone whispered loudly. But it was hard to

be quiet amid panic. The knocks continued, then more rapidly. A gasp. Then screaming. People were bleeding.

"Gunfire," a solemn voice said to no one in particular. It wasn't a scream, nothing like what you'd expect. Just a voice acknowledging circumstance. Like a reporter talking about the aftermath of a catastrophe. Except they were still mid-catastrophe. Bodies slumped. More screams met by more bullets.

CHAPTER 7
JANE

This isn't good.

There's a commotion in the living room. He sounds drunk. Or maybe just angry. He's talking to someone. *That* person is drunk. I don't know who.

The front door shuts. It never slams. He's never been one to punch walls or break things.

I don't move.

Footsteps pound heavily on the carpeted stairs. I'll know if they move past me. I'm hoping they move past. My hands are squeezed so tight the nails I consistently neglect to trim dig into my palms as I count to ten. I do this even though I know my balled-up fists will not protect me.

This could all blow over in ten seconds. That's all I need. Just ten seconds.

One.

Two.

Three.

Four.

Five.

Six.

Seven.

Silence.

Fuck.

My bedroom door opens and I shut my eyes.

Something hard presses against my back.

"Get up."

Thump. The impact is harder this time, and I can feel my organs vibrate as they bounce forward and back, following my body's natural momentum. It's the sole of a shoe.

The next kick is unmistakable. The slam reverberates all the way through my chest and hangs there a moment before I remember to breathe. I scramble to my feet, but I am prepared to fall backward. My feet are planted exactly two inches in front of my bed, right by the strategically placed Barbie doll I put there to mark the exact spot my heel needs to touch so that I'll land without hitting my head or knocking into my desk. I know what's coming. I'm prepared. My body tenses as its only form of defense, and I wait.

"Get dressed. I'll be in the car."

This is unexpected. His tone is unagitated, calm even, like he's not mad, except that I know he is. There's an edge to that tone, moderate as it may be, an edge that warns me not to do anything stupid—like ask him why he's upset. Instead, I stand still, waiting for the expected. A slap across the face, a shove onto the floor, or worse. But that's it. He leaves the room, and I quickly scramble to get ready.

Paul.

He's awake. Obviously. But I've taught him the art of pretending to sleep, and he's perfected it. It's one of my prouder achievements. Whatever he hears, he doesn't move. And he won't for many minutes until he's sure that we've gone.

As fast as I can, I change into jeans and a T-shirt. Yesterday's filth clings to my skin despite my change of clothes, but I ignore the sticky feeling as I rush to the car, where he is impatiently drumming his fingers on the sill of the open window. I quickly get in before he starts backing up with my door still ajar. Using both hands, I shut it, and we peel out of the driveway. There are hardly any other cars on the road at this early hour on a Saturday, and my dad takes the liberty of driving in two lanes while speeding down residential streets. It's frightening how fast he's going, but I keep my mouth shut.

One hundred yards from an intersection, the light turns green, but the car in front isn't paying attention, and my dad ultimately has to slam on his brakes. This jolt causes the psychology textbook that I've stored beneath my seat to slam against my heel.

It's summer, so nothing is technically due, but I have no intention of going to college unprepared. My plan had been to read a textbook a week until school begins. Except that, lately, it's been impossible to concentrate. I'm used to being interrupted during my studies by customers in the store, but in the past week, I've had to read and reread entire sections because all I can think about is the conversation I still haven't had. Though *conversation* seems too light a word for the life-altering moment I'm preparing for. It's nerves. Or maybe it's fear. I'm worried my dad will tell me no. I'm worried I'll actually be okay with that outcome, that I will slide into the reprieve it would give me from the guilt I know I'll feel if I leave.

As we pull into the parking lot of the store, I am both relieved and nauseous—the latter having only partly to do with his erratic driving. Jackie is supposed to come back today, and I really want to hang with her, but I have to tell her not to come. When my dad is in a bad mood, he doesn't like surprises.

"I need to work in the back. Watch the register." Before turning to leave, my dad looks at me for a moment. For a second I think he can sense that I'm waiting for him to leave. He has this uncanny ability to know when I want privacy and then to not give it to me.

This time, though, there's something he needs to do, so he leaves. As soon as he exits, I pick up the phone and dial Jackie's house. I twist the phone's cord around my hand, stretching it tight so that it leaves red indentations on my skin. The phone rings and rings, which means someone is on the phone and won't click over, or they're asleep like normal people would be at six in the morning. I hang up,

"Pack of Marlboro and whatever beer you have on sale," a voice says, startling me. The woman's bloodshot eyes stare at me hard as the smell of weed wafts toward my nostrils. (If bulletproof glass doesn't protect against odors, how am I supposed to believe it'll stop a bullet?) She tosses a twenty-dollar bill toward me. It's crumpled and warm, like she's had it tightly balled up in her fist since the moment it met her hand. Her boyfriend moves to the refrigerated section.

"I don't know which one is on sale, so you'll have to bring it to me."

"Jesus, you don't know your own inventory? Just charge me for the cheapest beer and I'll go get it after. What the hell kind of shop are you running?" Her pushy attitude puts me on high alert. In the liquor store business, *pushy* means they're up to no good. If she's yelling, it's because she's the distraction. The real action is going on at the drink coolers.

The kind where assholes like you aren't allowed in, I want to say. Instead, I raise my pitch and play dumb. "Actually, I'm underage, so I'm not even allowed to handle the beer. You're welcome to wait two hours for my dad to return if you'd like."

"Frank, grab the beer and bring it here!"

Frank returns with a can of Bud Light, and I ring it up.

"That'll be $11.89."

"Twelve dollas? That ain't right."

"Well, it's $3.70 for the can you put on the counter, $7.40 for the other two bulging in his jean pockets, and 79 cents for the Milky Way bar. Am I missing anything else?"

The lady looks at me suspiciously. Our register is one of those old grocery store registers that went through several generations of owners before we picked it up at a thrift store. Most of the buttons don't function, including the one for the number 5. Anytime I need to use the five, I replace it with nine and subtract four in whatever decimal place the five is in. We have a roll of white paper at the top left, making it appear as though a receipt is printing, but there hasn't been ink in the machine for—well, ever. We just re-feed the old tape in the machine over and over into the register, because, for whatever reason, the machine doesn't work without it. We don't give receipts, though. There are no returns here. And our clients aren't exactly the type to return beer.

"Plus the Marlboro," the woman sneers.

"Right, sorry. Red, gold, or white?"

"Red."

I reach behind me without turning my head and grab a pack of red Marlboro Lights from the shelf. Customers often steal things when you look away from them, so I've learned to find things without having to turn around.

"Okay, that'll be $17.62." I make change from the register.

"What's this? I gave you a fifty."

"No. You didn't. You gave me a twenty, which I put on the top of my register in plain sight of my fancy camera over there, so do what you gotta do, lady."

"Okay, geez. You don't gotta be rude about it. Bitch."

The couple leaves and I open my shaking fists and press my fingers onto the counter. After years of doing this, I still feel the hairs on the back of my neck stand in anticipation of a fight. Well, that, and I know I'd be fucked because I actually forgot to leave the bill on top like I was supposed to.

I try Jackie again.

"Alô?" Jackie's mom answers.

"Chào Bác, is Jackie home?" I ask.

"She left already, call again later, okay?"

"Dạ," I say, and bow my head slightly even though she can't see me. I hang up. Crap.

A young white guy with green eyes and a jacked body (which I can see because he isn't wearing a shirt) walks in as I drop the phone onto its base. If he hadn't defaced his body with tattoos that I assume are gang-related but could just be masochistic art, he could be the guy on the cover of a *Soap Opera Digest*. He saunters over to the Flamin' Hot Cheetos, looks directly at me, grabs them, and makes a run for it.

"Hey!" I shout, unlocking my door and darting after him.

As I exit, I notice my dad standing off to the side, smoking with the lady who just tried to rip me off. He looks at me like I'm an idiot and says, "What are you doing standing there? Go after him!"

I make a half-assed attempt at following the guy to his car, which is behind the building, knowing I'm not going to catch him.

He knows it, too, because around the corner, he is already walking with his legs pressed outward, barely keeping his pants up. How guys can walk, never mind run, in pants like his always amazes me.

"Hey, asshole, get back here!" I yell.

The "getaway car" is a black Mustang with several large dents along the passenger side. Waiting inside the car is his friend, an equally shady human, who starts laughing as the Cheetos Stealer hikes his jeans up, bolts toward the car, and jumps through the window as he flips me off with a wink. They speed off laughing. I memorize the license plate: A254BBC.

Just because there won't be consequences for the Cheetos Stealer does not mean there won't be consequences for me. To anyone else, a bag of chips getting stolen probably isn't a big deal, but to my dad, it's a lack of respect. No one ever steals when he's behind the register—at least not that I'm aware of. If the guy hadn't run, I doubt my dad would have even noticed the bag was missing, but we're past that now. I need to go and face the consequences, but I stall by slowly walking around the parking lot. It's futile. I know I'm in trouble now. Oh god, I'm on the verge of tears, and it hasn't even begun yet.

I retrace my steps to the entrance of the store.

But then I spot it. The bag of Flamin' Hot Cheetos.

The guy must have dropped the bag, or it fell out of his baggy pants. I jog to the edge of the sidewalk, begging God for it to be real. *Please don't let it just be an empty bag. Please.* I pick it up and feel the weight of a full bag. Victory. I know it's just a bag of chips to anyone else, but in this moment, I feel like a boxer who just secured the World Heavyweight Championship title. I won. Cheetos Stealer: 0; Jane: 1.

"I got it!" Returning to the store, I make sure not to sound overly boisterous despite the karate chops and kung fu flips going on inside my head. And no, I don't know martial arts—those, too, are stereotypes.

"Good."

Good. That's a compliment. He doesn't make a show of it, but my dad is proud. I mean, he actually said *good*, and it really does *feel* good. I smile to myself as I head toward the cleaning closet with a light skip in my step.

Moments like this are usually a turning point. He loves it when karma comes around, and we get to witness it for a change—hence the *good*. It's a big deal. It means whatever pissed him off this morning is dissipating.

"Dang, girl, I didn't know you could run like that," Jackie says. She stands near the register with two mocha frappes in hand.

I look to my dad, who comes in behind her. "Is it okay if Jackie stays here for a little while?"

"Okay," he says, but then adds, "Make sure you mop the floors."

Jackie follows me as I open up the WET FLOOR signs so I can mop.

"It won't take me long, five minutes tops." I unlock the register room for her to sit in.

"Uh-uh, girlfriend. You're not locking me in there alone."

I look up at her and laugh. "It's the safest place in the building."

"Nah. I'm good, I'll just sidestep you. Plus, I only have an hour, so let's talk about that hottie you just chased down like a teenage superhero vigilante."

"You're crazy," I laugh. In the bathroom, I fill the industrial yellow bucket with soapy hot water, lift the mop up and down to soak it, and then drop it in the metal wringer. I'm about to pull the red handle down when I hear myself scream, "Ah!"

"What? What happened?" Jackie asks, eyes wide as my dad fills in the other half of the doorframe.

"Spider," I say, moving backward. Jackie shudders and follows suit, darting away from the bathroom hallway altogether.

Cupping the daddy longlegs into his hands, my dad brings it to me as I jump back into the wall.

"Girl as big as you, scared of a tiny spider. Here, look," he says, pressing it toward me again. "It's nothing." Outside, I hear Jackie gasp. She's as scared of spiders as I am.

I scrunch my face and press my lips tightly closed, wishing I could press deeper into the wall. He laughs before squishing the spider in his hands and washing it down the sink. I hate it when he does that. Spiders are my worst nightmare. I'll take a rat infestation over spiders any day.

After he's gone, Jackie whispers, "Oh, hell no, that's jacked up. That's like child abuse right there. I swear only Viet people do that to their kids."

I shudder. "One day I know he's going to actually throw it at me."

"My mom is the same way. She's always making fun of me for not wanting to do disgusting things like, oh, I dunno, twist the neck off a duck so they can make some nasty dish with the blood—blech!"

I laugh because I've definitely seen my dad do that. "Just stand over there and let me do a sweep real quick."

Vietnamese people are so gross, I think as I mop the floors. Wiping away a streak mark left by the Cheetos Stealer's black sneakers, I imagine myself running after him and jumping in his car. He smiles at me and takes my hand, causing it to tingle. Immediately we're a couple. The girls at school would go nuts if they saw that he was my boyfriend.

"Oh my god, Jane, you're totally having dirty daydreams about that guy. I can see it on your face. Should I leave? Give you and your imaginary boyfriend some privacy?" She laughs.

I flush, and then gush, "I was just imagining myself jumping into his car and speeding down the coast. Then going to the mall to walk around and running into Sarah, Zoe, and Raven, but pretending not to notice them looking at us. I am totally cool and unfazed by their mad-dog, jealous stares—at me, the girl they were too good for, who snagged the sexy, older bad boy."

"I see someone is still holding a grudge over being dissed in the fourth grade," Jackie says. "Remind me never to get on your bad side."

I ignore her dig. Karma seems to be taking its sweet time, seeing as how they went from ditching me to being popular members of the student body . . . Whatever. I continue, "I know they'll all be wondering how it happened, how we became a couple, and they'll never know, because we're not friends. I mean, the guy was really cute, right?"

Jackie laughs. "Honestly, though, it's just a bag of chips. Is that worth chasing him down the street? What if he had a gun or something?"

"If people think we won't chase them, they'll come in and just take things all the time," I say, repeating what my dad used to tell me when I whined about having to run after the kids who pickpocketed candy. I didn't understand why I could eat whatever I wanted of the inventory but had to run after someone who took something. Couldn't we just pretend I ate it? I never said this, though, because in my family that's akin to talking back, and the price for talking back is a thousand times worse than just running after the thief.

"So you're telling me you have to risk getting shot at over a bag of Cheetos because of your dad's ego?"

"You watch too much *Law & Order*. Not everyone wants to kill us. It's like a game we play with each other. They try to steal things, I chase them. Sometimes they win, sometimes I win. It never ends in being shot at." As I say these things, part of me wonders if I believe them. I'm not used to questioning things. I'm used to just doing as I'm told.

"Why don't you call the cops?"

I laugh. "And say what? This guy stole a bag of chips? If you call them for everything, they won't show up for anything." We learned this the hard way when a Latino-looking guy with a swastika on his forehead (yes, both things were true) came in and took two cases of beer. "We called the cops since we had video footage and figured his face should make him pretty easy to find. The cop who showed up looked at the footage and said, 'What do you want me to do about it? You people need to learn how to take out your own trash.'"

"What? They can't say that!"

I look at her, amused. What planet is she on? They're cops; they can say whatever they want. "Anyway, after that, my dad decided we would only call the cops if someone was bleeding."

Jackie looks at me wide-eyed, and I say, "Don't worry, if anything happens, I promise to sacrifice myself first."

"That's comforting," Jackie says sarcastically, and we both laugh.

CHAPTER 8
PHÚC

"Che lỗ!" But no cover would be strong enough.

"Cắm lỗ!" But no plug would hold.

"Đình!" But Đình was gone.

"Anh!" But her husband was gone.

"Em!" But his wife was gone.

"Quốc!" But Quốc was fading.

Struck still by fear, Phúc watched the chaos in horror, his eyes begging for the blood not to be real, for the bodies to start moving, for his own legs to do what his brain was commanding. *Stand up. Stand up.* A stream of whipping air flew past his temple, slicing him above his right cheek. Despite knowing he was in imminent danger, his body refused to move. Then he locked eyes with Quốc.

The moment happened slowly. Quốc's body lay still, his face contorted in fear. His schoolmate, the one who caught dragonflies using paper cups, looked down at the hole in his stomach and must have felt the impact, but the realization that he was hit took a little while longer. And before his expression could change, he was passing on to the next world. Phúc had known classmates who died and adults who died, but until this moment, he hadn't witnessed the transition from here to *not here* in real time.

Water poured in through the bullet holes.

One inch.

Two inches.

"Nước ngập," a woman said. Her voice was hoarse and panicked, but at a distance—like this was a movie, and she was watching someone else's boat begin to flood. The rising tide jogged Phúc from his daze, and he unceremoniously moved bodies out of the way. He was too late, but still he tried, using clothing, bags, socks, anything he could find to plug the holes. The ship took on more and more water, and he knew it was only a matter of time before the whole vessel was sunk. His only shot at survival now was to jump and hope he could make it back to shore.

Calf-deep in water, Phúc scrambled toward the staircase, passing lifeless bodies that appeared empty of spirit but could have been stiff with shock. Phúc was too scared to check.

"When you get off the boat, swim away from the sun." The godlike voice speaking to him came from behind. Phúc turned back to find that it was Quốc's dad, crouched in the corner with his arms wrapped tight around his dead family.

"Đi Bác," Phúc urged, pulling at him to get off the boat, but the man ignored him. He wouldn't let go.

"Xin lỗi."

"Xin lỗi Anh."

"Xin lỗi Chú."

"Xin lỗi Bà."

I'm sorry, or perhaps more accurately, *I beg of you to forgive my fault,* became Phúc's mantra as he climbed past acquaintances he barely knew—but who shared with him one of the most traumatic experiences of his life—and jumped off the sinking ship and into the open water.

In the daylight, Phúc saw that they hadn't made it far from the shore. The boat was still in the shallows. So shallow, in fact, that Phúc's feet hit the sand when he jumped off the ship and into the water. No wonder they hadn't sunk. The boat was already at the bottom.

From the water, Phúc couldn't see the camouflaged gun barrels hidden behind the splintered tree trunks or in the green leaves perched high above. They had no reason to care for any survivors, but by some miracle, they didn't shoot. Maybe it was because he was so young, maybe it was the shell-shocked look on his face, maybe they figured he was a dead man walking, but each of their trained guns passed the duty onto someone else, and ultimately no one shot.

Exhausted, he crawled farther onto shore. He lay there awhile, tears and salt water streaming down his face. When he finally looked up, it was into the black sole of a Việt Cộng military boot.

The hard rubber rammed into his face, knocking his back molar loose.

"Please stop. I've been kidnapped!" The lie fell from Phúc's mouth like vomit he needed to expel—and tasted like it too. "Cô Lệ wanted a child to help her gain sympathy from the Americans, and she tricked me into following her!" More lies—these worse than the previous. He hadn't been kidnapped and certainly not by Quốc's mother. But in the three seconds he had to come up with a plausible excuse, this was what slipped loose.

"Lies." The accusation, or in this case the truth, was hurled at him with a punch in the gut to match.

"No, I was kidnapped. My brother is Lieutenant Colonel Long Vũ." Phúc didn't actually know if Long was a general because he didn't know what rank that was. All he knew was the title, lieutenant colonel.

This stopped the men. Phúc wouldn't know it for many years, but he was wrong. His brother was not a lieutenant colonel; he was a đại tá, a senior colonel, which was an even higher ranking.

"Hồ Chí Minh is my leader." The flicker of doubt that crossed their eyes was enough for Phúc. He began shouting at them with indignation. *"Tìm anh con đi!"* This command was bold. Phúc had no idea how capable these men were of doing what he said, of confirming his brother's identity. But what worked in Phúc's favor was their fear. If they asked and Phúc was right, the fact that they had beaten a general's brother would be met with consequences. Better not to ask.

"Why would they kidnap you?" the guard asked skeptically, but his demeanor suggested he bought the excuse. Phúc didn't answer.

After a moment of silent deliberation, the higher ranking of the two men nodded back, indicating that Phúc could leave. He scrambled to his feet, and, despite the raw ache of his broken ribs, Phúc bowed low in deference, faltering slightly as a pin-sharp pain shot through his chest. Then he walked away quickly, knowing that at any moment a bullet could pierce his back.

There was no way for Phúc to know where his lie would lead. His mother had often warned him of the ripple effects of a lie. That it could begin small, like a wayward ember drifting from a flame. On its own, the spark would likely extinguish, but give it a chance to land in nature's tinder nest and watch it ignite a devastating fire.

So, Phúc waited. And two days after his failed escape, he heard the consequence of his lies—a shattering scream from the neighborhood. The sound began somewhere deep in Bà Hương's belly and roared agonizingly loud as it spread. Initially, Phúc didn't pay it any attention. The gut-wrenching cries for loved ones had been a regular hum in the neighborhood. Over time, the once excruciating sound dulled to white noise because this tune had played on an unrelenting loop for as long as Phúc could remember. This time was different, though. This time, the screams were directed at him.

"You killed my husband. You killed my husband. You killed my husband." Her tone shifted dramatically from sorrow to incomprehension to anger. This fluctuation in her wail was the outgrowth of the deepest kind of pain. Bà Hương lived four streets over, and she repeated this cry all the way to Phúc's doorstep.

"First my son, then my grandson, now my husband. You murdered my husband, you murdered my husband, you murdered my husband," she screamed, her voice hoarse from crying.

Bà Nội came to Phúc's defense immediately.

"Không," she countered softly. "No," Grandma repeated. "No, it wasn't us. It wasn't us. It wasn't us. It wasn't us." Bà Nội shook her head in repetition with the words. Bà Hương wasn't the only person she was trying to convince. "It wasn't our family." Except it was.

Phúc couldn't have known that those guards would investigate his story and discover Quốc's entire family had fled. Because of this, they brought his grandfather to the street and executed him. Just like that. No trial, no defense, no mercy. The man's son, Chú Khoa, Quốc's dad, was accused of kidnapping a Việt Cộng official's brother and holding him as ransom to get through government checkpoints. The story didn't make sense. *Why would they kidnap an official's brother?* the neighbors argued. *Please, have mercy,* they begged. *He's just an old man,* they reasoned. None of it mattered. Quốc's grandfather was blamed for not imparting better morals upon his son, and he was shot dead. In front of everyone.

No one said anything to Phúc. No police came to question him. No investigation was opened to look into his allegation. He told a lie, and a man was murdered.

The whole town knew the rumors were true, but no one confronted him. Maybe they understood he hadn't meant to hurt anyone, that he was just a kid, that he was afraid too. But really, they only worried about themselves. If this harmless old man could be executed because of a lie a little boy told, the same could happen to them. Instead, the neighborhood treated Phúc differently, with hushed voices, no eye contact, and purposefully expressionless faces. And no one dared accuse him of murder.

Even so, Phúc expected a swift beating from his father. A caning of epic proportions. The punishment of kneeling on the sharp skin of a durian peel. Or a beating like the one Long had given to his father. But nothing came. No one told him that what he did was wrong, no one accused him of murdering an innocent man. No one mentioned the incident at all. And neither did Phúc.

Long came and went with irregularity, often being gone for months at a time. And with scars not quite healed, Ông Nội and Bà Nội bickered about whether it was safe to stay.

"If he wanted to kill us, he would have already," Bà Nội argued, though her tone was far less assured than normal.

"Even if he is our loyal son, do you really think the Việt

Cộng will just let the other kids roam free?" He shook his head no. "Look around the town. Have you seen little kids running around?"

"Maybe Long can keep them free."

Maybe seemed to be the only answer to every question. Maybe they were safe now, maybe their son hadn't betrayed them, maybe the Việt Cộng really would unify the country. Or maybe this was just the beginning, and the worst was yet to come.

A full year passed before it was time to go again.

The meeting point was different. Instead of on the water, Phúc was instructed to enter the church, kneel to pray, and wait. The exterior was plain with cracked edges like wrinkles on what was once a new worship hall. The Communists were atheists, so churches weren't the safest place to meet, but Catholics were stubborn. After forty minutes of kneeling alone in the church with anxiously trembling legs, a priest entered, looked at him with no expression, and walked away. Phúc followed him to the rectory, where a group of thirty or so had been waiting. A few people paced back and forth while others lay napping on the floor. They all moved about so methodically, and their belongings were arranged in a way that told Phúc they had been there awhile. The way they bore daggers into his eyes suggested they had been waiting for *him*.

The room settled, and everyone turned to the priest. The instructions were simple: Don't travel in groups. Keep off the main roads. Walk facing away from the shoreline. Overshoot the meeting spot and backtrack if you have to. Whatever you do, do not lead the Việt Cộng to the ship. There will be other boats if you miss it, just come back.

The next part was the same trek he had made with his mother, except this time Phúc was alone and aware of the thirty-one other people who would be aiming for the same direct route to the ship. Earlier that morning, Bà Nội had dressed Phúc in the same clothes he had worn to escape the first time. "Remember this: If someone asks you to work, you work. It doesn't matter what. You do it," she said with her pointed finger an inch from his nose. He tugged at the sleeve where she had sewn a gold bracelet inside the seam and lightly kicked the hem of his pants where three more gold necklaces were placed. "Protect the seams," she said, as if he needed reminding of what valuables were inside.

This time Bà Nội didn't walk with him through the forest because it was too dangerous. It was better for him to walk alone. A kid wandering alone is not suspicious. This was the safest way.

CHAPTER 9
JANE

Cậu Hòa and Mợ Bích are coming for dinner. They are not immediate family as far as I know. Close friends, maybe. Though, not that close since I've never even heard of them. Family visiting is not usually an issue, but I've been told I need to prepare food. Again, not a big deal—if you know how to cook. I haven't cooked a proper meal since my mom left. And even when she forced me to help her, I barely paid attention. How was I supposed to know that she had been planning to leave?

In our neighborhood, there is only one Vietnamese grocery store, so here I am. It's a grungy place called SJ Market. The cheap signage, made of white acrylic with red letters taped on top, is emblematic of everything one might find inside. Two decades behind its American counterparts, the store resembles a Vietnamese night market crammed into a Sam's Club warehouse. Long fluorescent bulbs hanging precariously above without any covers make the whole place come together because, as it turns out, bad lighting is pretty universal to grocery stores. The shopping carts are a mishmash of colors with broken or missing child seat covers. Rust spots and bare metal with remnants of what used to be plastic coverings are what's left of the handlebars. They are the type of cart I imagine you'd find at a grocery store version of Goodwill—if that were a real place. Boxes of canned goods, ramen packets, and various other products line the aisles, waiting to be shelved. An aroma of salty sea air mixed with rubber permeates the store, and the scent is most potent in the seafood area itself, which is displayed like a self-serve buffet of various fish on ice.

Memories of my mom come rushing at me. There's the seafood counter where I would watch in disgust as my mom picked her fish using a plastic bag as a glove, placed it on a plastic tray, and passed the tray across a tall glass counter to be cleaned, descaled, and cut.

This part of the store is unsavory, rancid, and utterly Vietnamese. Not one person in the store speaks English, including the Mexican butchers behind the counters who respond to inquiries in Span-amese (Vietnamese with a Spanish accent). It shames me to know they speak my native tongue better than I do, so I avoid eye contact with them when I make my request in broken Vietnamese.

Back when I came with my mom, my job consisted mainly of being a human bag stand. I would pull a bag off its roll, lick my thumb, peel it open, and wait for her to drop in celery, lettuce, tomatoes, cilantro, jalapeños, bean sprouts, and whatever else she needed for the week. My mother moved swiftly through this section, and it was sometimes hard keeping up because the bags would stick together or rip under the weight of her produce selections. Leave it to her to try and fit fifteen tomatoes into one flimsy bag.

Here alone now, though, I see so many ingredients I don't know how to cook with. Slowly, I grab scallions, onions, cilantro, and tomatoes. I don't yet have a dish in mind. I just know these are things I've eaten. I pass through the vegetable section and try my luck in the frozen section. Bad idea. Nothing is labeled. I'm just supposed to know what it is based on looking at it, and everything looks the same in vacuum-sealed bags covered in freezer burn.

Next aisle.

Ah, here I know what I'm doing. The sweet aisle is the aisle I know best. Fresh soybean milk, strawberry Pocky sticks—all things we could eat straight from the package. Almond cookies, mint Tết candies, chocolate Hello Panda bears, a tin of sweet flaky egg roll cookies, and White Rabbit milk candy for Paul. I start to grab a few packages but stop myself. *What am I doing?* I can't serve them cookies. Soup. I decide on white rice with sour soup and a fried fish for the center of the table.

Back in the fish aisle, I'm ten again, and my mother is right in front of me.

"Wait," she says. *"Come here, you need to learn this."*

My mother pushes me toward the slimy fish that I typically avoid.

"*Now?*" *I whine.* I couldn't help it back then, and my relationship with the fish hasn't changed since she left. I want to shake myself of the memory, yet I cannot escape it.

She doesn't say anything. Instead, she stops abruptly, turns to me, and waits. The look on her face tells me I will apologize immediately. I will not ask again to deviate from her plan, or I can all but guarantee I'm not getting those snacks. And if she's in a foul mood, I might also be in for a stick lashing.

I watch myself shift my feet and say nothing, knowing that the next words that exit my mouth better have the sound of deference with a slight uptick of joy. And they do. But now, I can see that I was bold back then. I knew what she expected, and yet I resisted. I want to hug my younger self. I'm proud of her.

"*Sorry.*" *I don't make excuses. She doesn't care.* I hate that I knew this as a ten-year-old. I hate that her one look can make me feel so insignificant—so small.

I follow this memory to the raw fish buffet and unconsciously shift my breathing from my nose to my mouth to dampen the smell of oceanic salt from an early morning fisherman's pier— the kind covered in seagull and pigeon shit.

"*Do you know how to pick fresh fish?*" *she asks, daring me to reply disrespectfully and already knowing the answer.*

Forcing a smile to disguise how annoyed I am, the corner of my mouth actually twitches when I say, "Pick the ones that are still moving?" I know it's probably the wrong answer, but I don't want to give her the satisfaction of simply not knowing anything. It's my best guess based on my mother's previous lesson on how to pick crabs.

84

"*No. Look here.*" *She points to the eye.* "*You see how this one is glassy and wet? That means it's fresh. When it's frozen or old, the eye is dry and sunken in.*"

I stare down at the fish and quickly avert my gaze now as I had then. I don't like staring at it. Back then, it felt improper and invasive to stare at the dead—it still does. A cold breeze passes under my chin, and my head turns as it had when she grabbed my face, forcing me to watch.

"Look." This new voice is unfamiliar and distant. I turn to find a mother peeling a banana for her toddler, but I'm so deep into my memory that when I return my gaze to the freezer, in the aluminum frame of the icebox, I see myself again. I'm concentrating hard on the white edge of the cooler to keep from crying. I wish my mom were here.

Pointing to a previously used plastic bag within arm's reach, my mother continues her lesson. "*We need one of these for the hot pot,*" *she says, handing me an empty tray.*

The display is exactly as it had been all those years ago, down to the placement of fish. They are arranged so that their tails are at the top and heads at the bottom because the mouth is where you grab hold. I see slimy black ones with what seem to be mustaches, flat red fish, and the kind I'm now standing directly in front of, cá bớp. Beneath the $3.79/LB. price tag is the name, cobia. Since it's more than a foot long, I attempt to pick up the fish by its belly with one hand, but it slips. I try two hands with the same result.

And then I hear her again. "*Grab it by the mouth.*"

Reluctantly, I reach for the mouth and stick my fingers in.

The slippery insides of the fish make me want to vomit, but I have a firmer grip than I did at ten years old, and I'm able to get it onto the tray in one motion.

Carefully, I add my tray to the line.

"Clean, descale, and cut?" the Mexican butcher asks me in Vietnamese.

"Clean, descale, no cut." I understand Vietnamese better than I can speak it.

"Toss the head and tail?" he asks. I want to say yes because I know myself, and I won't eat the head or the tail, but I know if my dad doesn't see those parts in the soup, he'll call me spoiled and ungrateful. Refugees do not waste food.

"No. Keep the head and tail." I say the words as though they are familiar, but they're not.

"You got it, pretty lady," the man responds before grabbing the tray and getting to work behind the counter. That part, I do understand. I scrunch my nose in disgust, but no one notices. They used to say this to my mom all the time, *pretty lady*. It's not quite as gross as when construction workers holler at you, but, still, don't they know how young I am?

At the far end of the butcher's counter is the frying station and I order a flash-fried fish to go. And then I remember something else.

"Why do you think that is the good fish to eat?" my mom asks me, her tone softer now.

"Because it's fresh, not frozen."

"None of these are frozen, so why that one?"

I shrug.

"Big eyes. The bigger the eyes, the more curious the soul. Fish are like people, and you become what you eat. You want to see the world, you eat fish with big eyes."

"Is that why you like to eat the eyeballs?" I reply in disgust. My younger self is hilarious.

Was I really ever that carefree?

"Exactly." She smiles.

I look down at the dirty plastic bag in my hand, which I had just used to successfully pick up my fish.

"Leave it," I hear, only now the command is formless and far away.

Reluctant, because I still think this is unsanitary and gross, I shake the bag loose and leave it at the edge of the freezer cubby. The butcher shouts my number. As I walk away, I notice another woman slide her hand into my used bag and deftly gather her own fish.

Back home, I unpack the groceries and restock the fridge. When I'm done, I peel open the flimsy paper lid of a Cup O' Noodles foam cup and fill it with boiling water from our dispenser before replacing the cover and laying my chopsticks on top. For so long, I haven't wanted to look at my mother with any sort of kindness or reverence. But remembering that trip, remembering her better, more motherly moments, feels somewhat cathartic now.

Sitting alone at the kitchen counter, I watch her imprint move throughout our home.

On the floor of the kitchen, my mother sits atop a thin layer of newspaper with the only round, wooden cutting board we have, and with the practiced boredom of an assembly-line laborer, she prepares the fish. I do the same.

"Why don't you ask the butcher to cut it? I saw him do it for other people." I'm squatting beside her, wanting to poke the fish's eye but afraid she'll chop my finger off with how quickly she's slicing.

"They never cut it right." She makes a clean slice just below the fish's gills. *"Can't waste food,"* she continues.

From the fridge, I unpack the fish I just bought, and, using the counter instead of the floor, I copy her movements.

"I mean, we're not gonna eat the head," I hear myself say.

"Why not? The head is the best part."

"Because it's gross."

There it is, a cackle of untempered joy. Proof that I brought joy if also misery. I remember this part in repeated astonishment because it was rare to see her laugh. *"Hurry up and eat so you can come help me."*

My mother guts the two-foot-long fish with the precision of a sous-chef at a fancy restaurant.

She isn't like those white Betty Crocker moms who have twenty different knives that are each designed for cutting specific things, or a countertop full of mixers, blenders, deep fryers, slow cookers, grinders, coffee makers, nor any other easy-prep cooking tools. On some level, I always understood that her tendency toward suffering came from something more profound. Because she had suffered, there was honor in suffering. The more difficult a task, the higher the achievement, even if an easier way leads to the same result. Like every boat person, things happened to her that I could only guess because she, like my dad, never talked about the past unless she was yelling at us for being spoiled or ungrateful. Maybe she had a valid reason for leaving us. Maybe she wanted me to learn how to pick fish, but she was also telling me something else. Maybe she wanted to teach me something about humanity and choosing glassy-eyed, fresh people to surround myself with. Because that was what she had planned to do. Maybe, in a way, she was telling me to leave too.

Or maybe she was just a selfish bitch.

The meal I've prepared doesn't look right, but it's edible. I know this because I tasted it, and I'm not dead yet. Two large, steaming bowls of sticky white rice flank two bowls of canh chua, and in the center is the toasted and crunchy flash-fried fish that completely wrecked the kitchen with oil splatter. If my canh chua is inedible, at least they have the fried fish. I only made canh chua that one time with my mother, so it's possible I've omitted a few ingredients. I cooked the tamarind in boiling water to create the broth, added pineapples, half of a tomato, bean sprouts, and a spoonful of fish sauce. When I hear Cậu Hòa and Mợ Bích arrive, I toss in the fish, lower the flame, and set the table.

My dad ushers them inside with a big smile. "Mời vào, mời vào!"

They pat each other on the back with an awkward sideways embrace that in no way resembles a hug.

Cậu Hòa, a severe-looking man who stands a good six inches shorter than his wife, kicks off his shoes and follows my dad through the living room with his wife lumbering behind. "This apartment is so big. Much bigger than the apartment you shared with eight people," he says. He's jovial and a breath of fresh air in our home, yet there's something familiar about him too.

"Where are the kids?" my dad asks, but I'm already clearing the two extra bowls.

"They're at Anh Dao's house." I guess their kids didn't want to come hang at our ghetto apartment. Can't say I blame them.

"Chào Cậu," I say. I bow, and my long black hair falls beside my cheeks. "Chào Mợ." Saying hello is just about the only time my Vietnamese sounds halfway normal.

"This is your eldest child?" he asks, addressing my dad as though I'm incapable of speaking.

"Jane is the first, and Paul is my second." We're introduced in order, me first because I'm the oldest and then Paul.

When Paul is called over, though, he bows his head but addresses them improperly, saying, "Chào Chú va Cô." This is probably the most annoying part of the Vietnamese language. Everyone is addressed based on their relative age to our dad. And "age" isn't measured in years lived; instead, it's based on their relationship at the grandparent level. Basically, it's complicated, and no seven-year-old should have to know it.

"Chào Cậu va Mợ," our dad snaps, and Paul immediately

repeats the greeting and bows extra low, which makes all three of the adults burst into laughter. I don't get the joke.

"Okay, it okay," Mợ Bích says. It's the first thing she's said since entering the house. Spotting the kitchen, she gently pulls my shoulder toward it. "Let me help you." Oh god, she's expecting me to show her around the kitchen.

"I . . ." My Vietnamese isn't as strong as it once was, and I flounder. "I made the canh chua, fried fish, and rice already." I'm hoping that if I tell her it's all prepared, she won't ask to enter the kitchen. I haven't cleaned up yet and it looks like a war zone.

Mợ Bích briskly moves to the table, tastes my soup, carries the two bowls to the stovetop, and pours them back into the pot. She flicks the heat on high, digs around our smattering of spices, adds pepper and a squeeze of lemon, and deftly chops scallions with my dull knife. After adding them and stirring it for a minute, she feeds me a spoon to taste.

"Good?" She smiles.

"Good." I beam. Not just good—like, *really* good.

She pours the now-steaming soup back into the two bowls, and we each carry one to the table.

My dad looks at them and asks jokingly if my food was inedible, but Mợ Bích is gracious.

She blames it on herself and her fickle taste buds needing the soup to be scalding hot. She doesn't mention the added ingredients.

"Mợ Bích taught you mom how cook," Uncle Hòa says. She

did? I had assumed my mother learned to cook from her own mother. Not this woman I'd never even heard of until today.

I glance at her for confirmation, and she nods but says nothing more. If she thinks positively or negatively about my mother, it's impossible to tell from her even expression.

Scooping rice into the bowls, I pass the first bowl to my dad, but he quickly pushes my hand toward Cậu Hòa, so I serve him first, then my dad, Mợ Bích, myself, and Paul. In that gesture of him pushing my hand, I am meant to understand the hierarchy of the table.

Looking downward, I notice Paul's bouncing legs. "Go pee," I say, and he quickly beelines it for the bathroom.

"What a good big sister," Mợ Bích says, stroking my hair. "How old are you this year?"

"Seventeen."

"Do you plan to go to college?"

When I don't answer, she plows ahead.

"It's still early, maybe you haven't heard back. My daughter, Cathy, is going to Cal State San José—engineering. Very good at math."

I think it's the tone of her voice. The assumption that I'm not smart enough to get into college that causes me to blurt, "I got into UCLA."

"Oh! Good for you! I hear that school is very famous," she says. She's impressed and not in that catty way some Vietnamese people can be when they've underestimated you. Instantly, I regret saying anything—for multiple reasons.

"The orientation is in August. August seventeenth, is that okay?" I ask, turning to my dad.

"Okay." *Okay?* I'll find out if he really means it later.

"Brother, you raised such a high-achieving daughter and all by yourself. Cheers," Cậu Hòa says.

They clink beer bottles, but my dad only shrugs. "If this works, it could be a good thing for both our families." I have no idea what he's talking about. Is he selling the liquor store? I'm about to ask when he adds, "But we never know, right? Maybe she fails all of the classes."

Annnnd I shut my mouth.

Paul returns from the bathroom, plops down again, and starts slurping his food.

I do my best to contain my excitement. I'm going to college. Me. Jane Vũ will be part of the incoming freshman class of 1999. And for the rest of the meal, I sit diligently watching for empty rice bowls and quickly standing to refill them if needed. I'm in a daze imagining things I shouldn't, like how my dorm room might look and if I'll like my roommates, when something in their conversation pulls me back to reality.

"Quốc, he used to steal a bunch of yogurts from his mom's shop and we would sell them for five đồng. It was a good business. I bet he's a banker now." Mợ Bích continues to reminisce, but my dad doesn't respond.

"Quốc is lost," he says as he sips his beer, then stares at the label as though it were animated. And then he does something he's never done before—he elaborates. "Bullets were flying and I knew I needed to move but I was shocked still. And I saw Quốc, his body was stiff but his face was full of fear. There was a hole in his stomach. That was the first time I saw someone alive become a ghost."

"When his grandfather was taken, I thought it was just a random excuse . . . ," Mợ Bích says with a look of horror on her face.

My dad doesn't answer. He stares at the beer, its label now peeled and shredded on the table, and takes a long swig.

Then, as if realizing she's said the wrong thing, Mợ Bích hastily adds, "Surely you don't think it's your fault? The Việt Cộng didn't need to torture his grandfather. Don't confuse their mistakes for ours."

My dad's only response is to tsk his tongue and shake his head, like he's not sure what he believes.

As I listen to this story, two things occur to me. Quốc is Paul's middle name. Did my dad name him after this kid who died during his first escape? And whoever this aunt is, she knew my dad before they came to America—a cousin maybe?

"Let's leave the past in the past," Cậu Hòa says. "Today we're celebrating a successful business partnership."

They cheer and start talking about the miles and miles of empty land driving from Denver to California. My aunts and uncles will do this a lot. The few I've met, anyway. They'll talk about people I've never heard of and things that happened before I was born. I'll get little snippets of information about old class-mates, neighborhood pranks and games, or sometimes updates on where some people are now, like one lady from their village who I guess works in Washington, DC, doing naval intelligence. When they stop talking, I know it's because they hit on something tragic. What I don't know is if they're stopping for my benefit or their own.

Because they clam up about it, I don't bother asking. I mean, if I did ask, they'd probably just laugh at me. But hearing about this little boy makes me consider my dad, somewhere between Paul's age and mine, having to watch a classmate die and then get on another boat to try escaping all over again. Seems surreal.

Later, after they've gone and I'm cleaning up, I consider asking my dad about the stories, but I don't know how. The best I can muster is to ask how they're related to us.

"Cậu Hòa is your mom's brother. Mợ Bích live in my neighborhood," he says.

I knew it! I mean, I didn't, but something about him felt so familiar. They have the same stout and rounded physique, chubby nose, and short arms. I think it was the way he chewed, with his mouth open and only on one side, like he was perpetually trying to push food out to prevent it from being stuck by his left cheek.

The answer only leads to more questions, like, did he and my mom meet through this aunt? If not, when did she teach my mom how to cook? I can't ask, though; we haven't talked about my mom since the day she left, and it's too risky of a subject to bring up. Especially because my dad is in a particularly good mood. So I pivot instead and ask about college. "Should I complete the financial aid forms? For school?"

"Okay." He nods, and that is a big freaking win. I finish

wiping down the counters for the third time because now would not be a good moment to mess up, and only after my dad has gone to bed do I go to my room and open the FAFSA application.

"I'm going to sleep now," Paul says.

In my haste, I hadn't checked to see if he was still awake or not. I should've also checked to make sure he brushed his teeth, but we're past that now. "Okay," I say, watching as he turns away from the bright light of my computer screen. And then I remember that Paul still doesn't know, and that telling him may be scarier than telling my dad.

CHAPTER 10
PHÚC

One of Bà Nội's favorite stories to tell Phúc was about the Man on the Moon. This ancient folklore had been passed down from generation to generation as a means of explaining the mysteries of the moon, but Bà Nội's reason for telling Phúc the story then was a personal one. Using a crudely drawn map that she'd bought from a local cartographer, she unfolded the paper to show Phúc.

"Việt Nam ở đây." Her finger pointed at a blob the shape of a worm with a diamond for a head. *Vietnam is here.*

She explained to him that Vietnam was a small country, a tiny speck on the planet, but that it was an unconquerable land filled with precious minerals and other earthly treasures. And the reason all these different countries wanted to occupy it was because of its resources. Bà Nội felt that even though we'd lost the war, Vietnam's unification meant the country, as a whole, won.

At the time, Phúc didn't understand that what she meant was the Vietnamese spirit never dies. Whether we win the war or lose it, we're all still Vietnamese. The essence of the land runs in our veins, and the water we drink, which falls from the sky and collects minerals on its way down from the mountain, nourishes *us* because we are Vietnamese. She made sure to emphasize that the Americans had to add medicine to their canisters, little pills that chemically changed the water, because drinking from the streams made them sick.

"This water is the bloodline of Việt Nam," she said, placing a glass of water before him. Phúc took a drink, and she nodded in approval. Because he drank it, Vietnam would always flow through his veins. If Phúc survived, he would embark on an unknown journey to places she could only imagine, and she wanted to make sure he knew where his roots were. *Leave if you must, but don't forget who you are.*

"A long time ago, there lived a man, his wife, and their only son. North Việt Nam is home of the giant mountains, the tallest, most vibrantly green mountains on all of the earth . . . ," Bà Nội began, pointing to the area inside the diamond.

The man, a rice farmer, owned all the lands in northern Vietnam. Miles and miles of these lush hills were covered in switchbacks upon which rice fields grew. The moist climate meant that, year after year, rice patties bloomed, and grains could be picked. For a long time, the locals believed that it rained so much because the Vietnamese people were blessed by God. This man, the rice man, represented God's generosity.

He was a hardworking man, up at sunrise and still working

long after sunset. He planted, he sowed, he churned, and he picked each and every grain of rice he harvested.

The man farmed day and night, doing backbreaking physical labor, but it wasn't enough. He could barely feed his small family. As the years dragged on, his body gave way to age. The harvesting became more and more difficult, and his resentment toward God mounted. At first, he grumbled about it at breakfast, then gradually at both breakfast and dinner. Eventually, he grumbled about it all day, to others and even sometimes just muttering to himself.

Until one day, during a uniquely dry season, a bright white light flashed across the dull sky, and within seconds, red flames engulfed the hills. Running after his beloved crop, he swatted at the fire, but to no avail. His entire harvest for the year was scorched. "Enough!" he yelled to the skies.

How could any god be so cruel to a man as hardworking as he? "What do you want from me? You need me to suffer more? I've suffered enough!" he yelled.

Silence.

Louder this time. "You expect us to believe in you and yet you are nothing but a farce! Look at me, hurling insults, because you don't exist. You hear me?! You fake, worthless deity!"

He watched the fire ravage his crop until at last he fell to his knees, wearied. And instantly, the flames disappeared. The bright red fire that just a moment ago had covered the land in flickering orange and yellow light was extinguished and replaced by gray ash. There were deep, dark holes where the crops burned most intensely and lighter shades of gray ash on the periphery. He looked around and saw that everything was gone. In fact, *all* color had disappeared from the world entirely. In a panic, he searched for his wife, his children, his home, but like everything else, they were gone. All he had left was a world shaded in monochrome. In complete disbelief, he wandered the desolate area, walking for miles and miles in search of life.

Then, finally, as day turned to night and he laid his head down to rest, he saw above him, high in the sky, a bright blue and green planet. He looked up at the earth and back at his feet, surrounded by gray. Earth, gray, earth, gray, and after a moment, he understood that his lack of piety and gross unappreciation for Earth's abundance had gotten him thrown off the planet. The rice man now walked the moon.

When Phúc tried leaving Vietnam the second time, he was not the same timid kid. His hands were stronger, his feet sturdier, and his breath even. He was not a boy anymore; at thirteen, he was a man. Kicking off his sandals, Phúc let his feet sink into the mud. Just as he had done his whole life, he would navigate to the ocean alone—via instinct. While the others hunched over and moved cautiously together, he stood up straight and walked. And with every milestone—a shoe, a helmet, an airplane, an upside-down bucket—that he remembered passing the last time, his confidence grew. He was going to make it.

He found the boat without incident, and they quickly moved away from shore. Phúc might not have believed in his personal luck, but he figured the odds of sinking twice must not be that high. He was wrong. The odds were extremely high, if not practically assumed, and his confidence was short-lived when ten minutes later, the boat slowed to a stop, and the engine sputtered and died. Not good.

"Im lặng. Đừng nhúc nhích," the captain hissed from above. Quiet he could do. Not moving an inch, though? Impossible.

For a while, nothing happened, then heavy boots dropped on board. One set, two sets, three sets, four? Once they began walking, it became harder to count. Soft hands dropped over children's mouths, silent prayers began, hope turned to fear, and everyone froze, listening silently to the exchange:

"Chỉ một chiếc thuyền tôm thôi." But it wasn't just a shrimp boat.

"Giấy phép." But there were no licenses for stowing away refugees.

Silence.

"Bắt gì tốt khong?" But he wasn't really asking about the catch.

"Không đặc biệt, quá nhiều cá mập trong nước." And that was true: the catch wasn't special, and there were a lot of sharks in the ocean.

A sinister and throaty laugh came from the main Việt Cộng patrolman—the leader of the group. Heavy footsteps moved to the galley entryway, where another soldier came down and looked Phúc directly in the eye, then called up to his boss,

"Nets, baskets, and the general stench of shrimp." His voice was nasally and high-pitched; he was a boy not yet through puberty. The thirty-two passengers below deck appeared to be invisible. Still, no one moved, and if they breathed, it was inaudible. Overcome with anger, Phúc dug his fingernails into his calves.

Over two years had passed since Long had come home. Men were sent to fix the courtyard; beautiful, antique, hand-carved pieces of furniture arrived unannounced to the house; and a toilet was installed. Long might not have been physically present, but his presence filled the atmosphere. And all this time, Ông Nội found it within himself to not be angry. He even joked about the scars from his beating making him more handsome.

"This here? This scar is my beauty mark. I tell you, in all of Việt Nam, no one has one like it," Ông Nội would say to his friends. But it wasn't a beauty mark, it was a scar that ran much deeper than the surface. Ông Nội walked with a hobble, trembled as he fed himself, and took sips of air rather than deep, pain-filled breaths. And no matter how much Ông Nội tried to downplay it, Phúc knew what happened. He saw it with his own eyes, and there was no reconciling this egregious mistreatment as anything but evil. And as Phúc cowered below deck on the shrimp boat, staring at the yellow star on this boy's uniform, his anger grew. He wanted to lunge at him and choke him until his soul left the earth as retribution. He wanted to plunge his fingers in the kid's eye sockets and drain the life out of him. He wanted to break him. To do to him what the war had done to his family.

No one else dared to make eye contact with the boy, only Phúc, who stared angrily, silently threatening him to shoot. *Go ahead, try to kill me,* Phúc thought. But the guard misread Phúc's expression. He saw fear in Phúc's eyes, not hatred, and he nodded at him in recognition. He bowed in a silent apology because in any other circumstance, they might have been friends. Maybe the soldier saw himself in Phúc, or maybe he was sad because he had seen the bodies of other refugees wash up on the shores, bloated and lifeless. Whatever the case, the two maintained locked eyes as an older patrolman came into view. The captain of the ship rushed over and slipped a thick gold bracelet into the man's hand, shaking it vigorously. The older patrolman stuffed the bracelet into his upper breast pocket as though it were nothing more than a handkerchief decorating his uniform. This was just one of many "gifts" he would confiscate today. Unlike his younger counterpart, this general had no shame, guilt, or remorse for the impossible situation he and his comrades were leaving the refugees. Of course he didn't, he was a Communist, just like Long. The image of Long in an identical uniform standing over their broken father wrapped itself around his brain like a scalding-hot cloth, and he dug his nails even deeper—so deep that he broke skin and caused a thin line of blood to trickle down his leg. Its warmth was surprisingly soothing.

Unlike the captain of the first boat Phúc boarded, this one

had scheduled checks with the Communists in advance. They were bribed up front and again on the vessel so they would let the ship pass through their checkpoints. Of course, Phúc didn't know this, and it would take another fifteen years before he learned who was responsible for the boat's safe passage. That gold bracelet, which at the time felt significant, was nothing compared to the loot they were collecting from other ships. Some other boats were stripped so bare that heading farther out to sea was nothing more than a suicide mission. It wasn't just jewels and gold they took, but fuel, water, and grain—the basic necessities.

Not all the Việt Cộng found it easy to execute people. Not all of them were murderers. Some of them were worse. Some were cowards. After they stripped the vessels of everything, they might wave them through, appearing benevolent but knowing the passengers would die at sea of starvation or dehydration, or at the hands of vicious Thai pirates. Or the boat might drift with the current back into Vietnamese waters, where their fate became someone else's problem.

That first night, after the boat burned through its initial batch of fuel, Phúc climbed on deck, looked up at the sky, and thought about the man who lived on the moon.

CHAPTER 11

JANE

Hope is bullshit.

Hope is the thing little girls who live in big houses behind big gates get to have because their parents shield them from the harsh realities of life. For the rest of us, though, hope is a dream crusher. Even the word *hope* irks me.

Hope *can* be a good thing; deep down I think I know that. But for me, it's dangerous because it's so reassuring and big and *distracting*. Hope blinds me from disappointment when I'm dumb enough to let my guard down, and *that's* a real problem. Hope makes me giddy, and when I'm giddy, I do stupid things like forget to clean the fridge or move the laundry from the washer to the dryer. And missteps like that have painful ramifications.

Despite knowing all this, I am awake at 5:03 a.m. Although I've told myself I'm just going through the motions, I still imagine crossing the threshold into the theme park.

We're attempting to go to Disneyland. Again. For the

fourth time. The first time was canceled because the van's radiator started leaking. Bác Luy asked a friend who worked as a mechanic to fix it, and my dad helped. The trip was rescheduled for the following Saturday, but then Bà Huỳnh, my grandmother's sister, whom I hadn't even known existed, passed away and everyone had to attend her prayer service in Sacramento instead of going to Disneyland. That's right, not a funeral, a *prayer* service. Because Bà Huỳnh died in Vietnam and none of us could afford (or maybe weren't allowed) to go, we had a liturgy here. No casket. A few hysterical criers. A full rosary. Then, finally, a feast cooked in both the kitchen and on electric burners in the garage. Most of the day was spent with Paul sulking and wondering why we needed to pray on the exact day we were supposed to be at Disneyland. I mean, he had a point. She died on a Tuesday; shouldn't we have prayed on that day? No. Because that would make sense and therefore isn't at all in line with our family motto of suffering at all costs. When in doubt, choose the option that involves maximum suffering.

Most recently, the trip was canceled because the bathroom at the store exploded, and disgusting sewer water threatened to drown our entire business. This might have been understandable if the toilet hadn't clogged three times the previous week and wasn't patchwork fixed. I knew it at the time, and I had meekly pressed my dad to fix it, but he didn't listen. So that's how Paul and I found ourselves clearing the bottom shelves of product (lest they become contaminated by actual shit) instead of eating cotton candy and hurtling through Splash Mountain.

It's cold when I step out of the shower and stand in the

fogged-up bathroom wearing just my towel. I stay here a minute, shivering, despite knowing that it's only going to get colder as the steam escapes through the bottom of the bathroom door. Finally, I pat myself dry and get dressed, and the blast of cold air washes over me as I walk back to our room and gently shake Paul's feet to wake him. "Go take a shower."

Paul turns over, rubs his eyes, and drops his feet off the bed, forcing himself awake. My wet hair drips down the back of my favorite top, a feather-gray T-shirt with a neon-pink cassette tape that says "pop mix" on the title bar. I had rolled and ironed the sleeves the first time we were supposed to go to Disneyland, and it's been sitting in my closet ever since. I might have jinxed myself by putting it on, but I figure not putting it on could signal to the world that I really want to go and am trying to trick it. So, I'm wearing it. Weird logic, I know.

The night before, I purposely let Paul stay up past his bedtime so he could go right back to sleep and only endure half a shitty day rather than a full one if this whole thing falls apart.

"Disneyland day," he says, stretching his arms upward.

"Maybe. The bathroom is still warm, go shower."

He walks away, eyes still shut, and like clockwork, I hear the toilet flush first, then the shower spring to life. Smiling at his predictability, I stuff my emptied backpack full of snacks and grab my molecular biology textbook and *Tiger Finds a Home* for Paul. He loves this book. We've read it a thousand times, but it's still his favorite. Sometimes I make him read to me, other times I let him make up his own animal adventure stories. It's not Disneyland, but we make do.

The squeak of brakes can be heard outside as a vehicle parks in our driveway. Through the window, I spot a shiny, not exactly new, 1987 Toyota minivan as Paul exits the bathroom.

"C'mon." I pull him downstairs and nudge him toward the car, where Dad is already greeting Bác Luy. Inside, Bác Luy's wife sits with a cooler at her feet in the second row with Stephen, the youngest. Becky and Vicky have picked their corners in the rear.

"Can I sit by a window? I get carsick," I lie. Vicky, the younger one, moves over without acknowledging me, and I get in, making myself small.

Before my mom left, we used to hang with this family all the time. They would come to the shop, and my mom and their mom would make food. Bác Luy and my dad would drink in the shed, and Becky, Vicky, and I would play cards together. But after my mom left, the family stopped coming over. Only Bác Luy still comes to visit with my dad. So, even though we've known each other since we were kids, we're virtually strangers. I would much rather be going on this trip with Jackie and her family.

We wind through residential streets for a few minutes, and I notice that Bác Luy drives with only his right hand. Whether he's turning left or right, it's all done with one hand, not the proper two hands on the steering wheel we were taught in driver's ed. I watch and think, *This must be why people think Asians are bad drivers.*

I glance over at Vicky and Becky, who are staring into keychain electronics with screens the size of a quarter and only three buttons. Some kind of animal is moving back and forth along the bottom of the screen.

"What is that?" I ask, leaning over to get a better look at the digital dog running across Vicky's toy.

"Have you never seen these before?" Becky asks. "Everyone has one at my school."

"What does it do?" Honestly, I'm not that interested. I'm never going to spend money on something like this, so there's no point in learning about what it is, but I don't feel like reading my book.

"Did you see the Tamagotchi Erica had? Oh my god, it was so cute," Vicky says to Becky. I choose not to take offense at her complete disregard for my question and awkwardly say nothing, wondering if pretending to read would be better than pretending to be interested in their stupid game.

"No, but Grayson spent all of lunch Friday showing me his T-Rex Giga Pet," Becky replies. Before my brain can stop my mouth, I hear myself ask, "So they're all different animals?"

Silence.

Before this car ride I was pretty sure I didn't like either of them. Now I'm certain.

"Animals, babies, they have a bunch of different ones," Vicky finally says, leaning toward me so I can watch her digitally feed her fake puppy dog. "See, every hour or so, your virtual pet will ring, and you have to feed it so that it'll grow."

"What happens if you forget?"

"It dies, and you have to start all over again."

So, it's a pet that you have to take care of, but it's digital, and if you forget to feed it, it dies? The idea is so dumb that I have no idea what to say.

"Well, there's other stuff too, like playtime and games," Vicky says as she leans away from me. This is obviously not a topic we're going to bond over.

"Can I try?" Paul asks Stephen, who is so short and quiet, I forgot he was even there. Stephen is small for his age, even by Asian standards, and wears thick Harry Potter glasses that make him look seventy-five rather than seven.

"No," he says flatly.

Vicky averts her eyes as she slouches lower in her seat, pretending not to hear the exchange. Since she's older, she's obligated to share her toy with Paul, but, like her brother, she doesn't want to.

Becky nudges her. "Let him try."

"Why don't you give him yours?" Vicky says.

"Ey," their mother says, and the girls instantly shrink inward. I know that tone. It's so familiar, a part of me almost wants to come to their rescue—*almost*.

"Fine. Here," Becky says, shoving her game at Paul.

Paul takes it but doesn't know what to do. He presses the buttons, but the screen doesn't seem to change. I watch him closely, in part because I want to see how it works, and because I should make sure he doesn't break it. But I also don't want the girls to think I'm interested in their toy anymore, so I opt for pretending to stare past Paul at the buildings beyond his window.

Becky looks on irritably. "You need to clean the poo," she says.

Paul continues to press buttons until a shower icon appears and he's able to clean up the poop. The virtual pet then goes to sleep. Paul, thinking it's broken, shakes it while pressing down on the two end buttons until the game beeps several times and shuts off.

"Oh my god, what did you do?" Becky yells this time. She snatches the game from Paul's hands. "You reset my game, you little brat!"

"I—" Paul sputters, "I was just trying to get it to wake up."

"*So you reset it?!*"

"What happened?" I ask, trying to divert her attention and calm her. The last thing we need is for Becky to throw a bitch fit and have my dad turn us all around.

"Paul just ruined my game," Becky whines.

"Who told you to play with her game?" my dad snaps, directing all blame at Paul.

I can't help springing to Paul's defense even though I know it might further inflame my dad. "She let him. It was an accident." I hate that there's an undertone of begging in my voice.

"I didn't think he would break it," Becky huffs. I want to knock her teeth out.

"Ey." Becky's mom hushes her. "What did I say?" The adults always say things like this. The question is purposely vague, but everyone knows what she means. She likely had a conversation with them about sharing before they arrived at our house.

"Is it broken?" Dad asks Becky. My pulse quickens at the question. I open my mouth to answer "No" before Becky can lie, but then I shut it, afraid to make things worse.

Finally, after what seems like an eternity, Becky relents. "No."

"Ey ya, all this fuss over nothing." Becky's mom laughs. Bác Nguyệt is doing the same thing I am: placating my father so he won't turn us around. Bác Luy is my dad's elder (at least by greeting, but also probably by age), so even though Bác Nguyệt is younger and a woman, she has power, and, at this moment, I love her.

"The kids are probably hungry, Nguyệt, give them some snacks," Bác Luy says.

"If you kids can't get along, we can turn around and go home," my dad warns. There it is—the forever threat. One misstep and everything falls apart.

I knew it. I knew it was too good to be true. I knew we'd never make it all the way there. They never had any intention of taking us to Disneyland. I bet they don't even have the money and will use this as an excuse to make us miss it. The thoughts come quicker than I can counter them, and hot tears threaten to surface. My fists shake with rage even as my facial expression remains stoic. *Don't you dare cry.*

I turn to the window and swallow my feelings. I'm not upset. I expected this. I can't be mad. I did not hope for anything, so there's nothing to be disappointed about. It's fine. I'm fine. Life will go on.

The dark black hole in the back of my mind opens up.

I watch as my faint reflection in the window stamps itself on corporate buildings, concrete parking lots, malls, and fast-food restaurants as we whiz by. I'm technically the one moving, but it feels the opposite. I see myself, with my long, jet-black hair, uneven bangs, and no real style, stuck in the same place as the world passes me by. I'm an empty, blank page. I have no distinctive personality, no voice, no real sense of being. This is the face of a girl whose mother leaves her. For a fleeting moment, I imagine that the giant semitruck hurtling toward us in the oncoming fast lane suddenly swerves in our direction and smashes through the median. As it does, we're tossed about in chaotic slow motion, and when I'm found in the wreckage, they struggle to distinguish any unique physical identifiers. I die knowing I came and left and had no impact on the world at all.

Gently—self-consciously—I lift my finger to the window and press against the cold glass.

After a second, I release it and see its imprint overlaying the passing outside world. Opening my mouth, I exhale a warm breath and watch a cloud of condensation collect around the fingerprint, then recede back into nothingness.

"What are you doing?" Vicky is staring at me oddly with an expression that is a mixture of concern for my mental sanity and wonder.

"Nothing." I wipe my fingerprint away with my sleeve, let my eyes lose focus, and stare through the window, not really looking at anything anymore.

When our van pulls through the parking kiosk, I can hardly believe my eyes. We pass flags marking different parking areas. Alice, Goofy, and Mickey are full, but we find a spot in Minnie—Minnie, aisle 17.

I crouch toward the sliding door from the back corner and my legs wobble a little from sitting for so long in the van. I tighten my backpack on my shoulders, check to make sure Paul has his stuff, and then offer to help unload the car. I will not get in trouble today.

As we make our way to the entrance, I finally let myself succumb to feelings of excitement. Throngs of other families crowd toward the gate, many dressed in Mickey Mouse shirts, hats, and cotton sashes covered in Disney pins. At the ticket booth, Bác Luy and my dad fight to pay for the tickets.

"Let me pay," Dad says in Vietnamese as he reaches for his wallet, but he can't find it.

Frantically, he begins checking all his pockets.

"You won't find it," Bác Luy smirks. He looks misplaced in his shorts, sneakers, knee-length socks, button-down shirt, and zip-up hoodie. And my dad's not much better with his bright white polo shirt, tan cargo shorts, and matching knee-high socks. Actually, I'm surprised they aren't wearing their old, never-before-washed fisherman's hats that they typically sport on swap-meet outings. When Bác Luy turns, I see a scar that runs the length of his calf and notice a slight stiffness to his gait.

"I invited. I pay." Bác Luy thrusts Dad's wallet, which he had palmed earlier, back into his hand. He was always doing that, pickpocketing my dad when he knew my dad would try to pay. I've always wondered how he became so good at it, but I don't dare ask. Bác Luy slides a thin stack of pre-counted hundreds toward the cashier. I am glad for that. I don't know how we could've afforded it at $39 per ticket. In return, he receives eight beautifully decorated tickets with the Disney castle printed in color on thick, glossy card stock. I want one *so* bad, and am flabbergasted when he actually hands me one—my very own entrance ticket.

My ticket is ripped perfectly along the perforated lines as I cross through a turnstile. Everything is so bright and vibrant that it feels like it's two steps away from tipping into horror movie territory. Off to my left, a kid screams at the top of his lungs while his mom frantically searches the back of his stroller for the item that will quell his screeching. A few feet away, another kid decked out in Mickey Mouse gear licks a huge rainbow-colored lollipop. She's wearing a lanyard that is so shiny, a sparkle of light follows her every move.

When the screeching boy's mother finally emerges from the depths of the stroller's undercarriage, she grasps an identical lanyard, which, when swiftly dropped around her son's neck, instantly transforms him from a demon into a giddy, cherubic child. The little brat's ignorance makes me want to slap him. And not lightly. How else will he learn to be grateful for the things he has?

I look over at Paul. He's about the same age as this kid, but he's patiently waiting for the adults to tell him what's next. He doesn't beg or ask for candy. He's not whining about all the shiny objects in the windows that we're never going to buy.

I turn away to find my dad admiring the Mickey Mouse–shaped topiaries surrounded by pink and orange flowers that have been arranged in precise order and somehow bloomed uniformly.

The sheer number of flowers covering the small hillside aston-ishes me. For the first time, I realize that in the entirety of our apartment and store—and among everything we own—there is not a single living plant.

We squeeze together for a photo using a disposable camera Bác Nguyệt pulls from her purse.

Becky and Vicky huddle with a map in their hands.

"Okay, let's just go in order. What side should we start on?" Vicky asks Becky. They were smart enough to grab the map after passing through the ticket counter. I was worried it would cost money, but now I wish I had taken one too. I see another map sticking halfway out of Becky's mini backpack, and I consider stealing it. Based on the way she flippantly folded and shoved it there, I can tell it's of little value to her.

"You're just scared of the Matterhorn," Becky teases, and jabs Vicky lightly in the side.

Instead of laughing, Vicky sharply draws a breath. I turn to look. I know that sound.

"Sorry," Becky whispers.

Vicky has a bruise just beneath her rib cage. I can't see it, but I know it's there. I look at her, hoping she'll catch my sympa-thetic eye, except my face must be contorted into a smirk because when she looks at me, her eyes are stiff and icy.

"Let's go the opposite way from everyone else. The lines will be shorter," Vicky says, already walking in the direction she wants to go.

Up ahead, the whitest woman I've ever seen glides toward us in a sparkling blue dress. She has bright blond hair, white gloves, a freshly powdered face, and bright red lips. She looks exactly like the cartoon Cinderella. My insides flutter as I watch her float past.

"You want to take a picture with Cinderella?" Becky asks, catching my stare. I can't tell if it's a serious question or if she's making fun of me.

"What? No," I lie. "I was just wondering what she really looks like 'cause she has so much makeup on."

"I'm sure she's all pimply and red-faced like all the other white girls," Vicky sneers.

"Yeah, that's what I was thinking." That and how I can be like Cinderella in my next life.

On Splash Mountain, we climb into giant floating logs that bump against the green plastic river basin and listen as the loud-speaker blares, "For your safety, please keep your hands and feet inside the cabin at all times." The cart has two compartments, so my dad, me, and Paul are in the front and Stephen, Bác Luy, and Bác Nguyệt are behind us. Vicky and Becky wanted to ride alone.

After an initial splash into a dark chamber, we emerge in a brightly colored area with so many animatronics that it's hard to know which direction to look. A bunny lounging against a wooden door carved into a plastic tree trunk catches my attention when suddenly the ride stops, and the music shuts off.

A voice booms over hidden speakers. "To the gentleman in

the white polo shirt: please keep your hands inside the ride at all times."

It takes me a second to register that she's talking about my dad, and I only realize it because I can see that he is reaching forward to touch a fox that is dressed as a man and holding a honeycomb. "Dad! You can't do that," I hiss.

"Why not?" he says with a tone that suggests there are no rules.

"They're yelling at you over the loudspeaker," I say.

"Oh." He laughs and retracts his arm.

About thirty seconds pass before the music returns and the logs continue bumping along their route.

"Such a naughty person." Bác Luy laughs from behind us. "Do you kids know that on this huge ship coming to America, they had all these wild animals: lion, monkey, panda, elephant, everything. And your dad, he thought they were starving, so he started feeding them all their rationed food!"

"They treated them so poorly," my dad says.

"Imagine that, people in Việt Năm were starving for years and he worried about some animals," Bác Luy chides.

"Look, that bear is being hung!" Paul points in horror at a rather happy-looking bear with a rope around his neck.

At first I think he's joking or making it up, but there really is a bear being strung up by a fox. "Was it like that?" I ask, only half joking because I wouldn't be surprised if he said yes. But he says nothing.

The day goes by fast—too fast. We flash through freshly cut lawns, pruned topiaries, colorfully painted gates, and brick walkways leading from cartoonish homes to futuristic rides, and onward through old wood-framed shops with modern gifts on display. Inside a gift shop, Bác Luy gives Becky $50 for souvenirs, and she's thrilled about this until he instructs her to make sure Paul and I get something also. Paul gets a giant lollipop and I choose a floaty pen with a tiny Tinker Bell, who slides up and down when the pen is turned. I wish I could get two, one for me and one for Jackie, but everything is just so expensive.

At dusk, we sit in a row along a gated waterfront, with us girls on one end, Paul and Stephen in the middle, and the parents on the other end. Bác Luy has unfolded a small briefcase into a magician's table, and the No. 2 pencil between his fingers, which had just been straight and stiff moments ago, now flops about as if made of rubber. In awe of this, other kids walk over and fill in the empty spaces at the edge of our blankets to watch as he then easily bends a metal spoon.

More kids gather.

"I can't see," a little girl wearing a blue Jasmine costume says while raising her hand like she's in class.

Bác Luy stands up and massages his left calf as though loosening a knot. It looks painful, like when I stretch too early in bed and pull a muscle. I don't know why seeing this irks me so much, and when I look up Bác Luy catches my eye. He isn't mad, though, more embarrassed. I quickly look away. I hadn't meant to stare. He reaches his full height with a stance just slightly askew and continues with his magic show. First, he makes a coin appear out of thin air, then he walks it through a sheet of paper without creating a hole, he makes cards and a pencil stick like magnets to his open palm, and he causes two paper clips to jump together with the help of a dollar bill.

Vicky, accustomed to her dad's tricks, turns to grab a cookie from the pile of food Bác Nguyệt has put on our blanket, the movement causing her shirt to rise, revealing the bottom portion of an older bruise. She quickly pulls her shirt down. Our eyes meet, but before I have a chance to say anything, a booming voice comes over the loudspeaker: "We now invite you to join Mickey and experience *Fantasmic!*—a journey beyond your wildest imagination."

The lights cut, and everything becomes shadow. In the darkness, a shimmer of light zips like fairy dust over the riverbank, and in a spectacular blaze of lights and exploding fireworks, Mickey himself appears as the conductor of water, lasers, and, well . . . magic. There's a story being told, but I can't quite comprehend it because I'm so distracted by all the theatrics. Images are projected onto a wall of water that continuously dances to the beat of classic Disney songs. Then, as if all that isn't enough, electric boats appear with dancing Disney characters, adding a live-action element to the show. I've never seen anything like it, and I let myself imagine being one of the Disney characters, smiling and waving at people like me in the audience. It's ridiculous, of course, because I don't look anything like these princesses, but just this once, for a few moments, I let myself believe that after college, maybe I could work here. Not as a princess, but maybe I can learn how to operate the lights or be in charge of the pyrotechnics and fireworks. Maybe I'm dreaming too big. But isn't that the point?

On the car ride home, I'm sitting in the middle section, across from Bác Nguyệt. Paul's head is on my lap, his feet strewn across my aunt's, and he's dead asleep. Stephen is in the same position in the back with his sisters. Everyone is tired, but my dad and Bác Luy seem to be gabbing away.

"The way our brains are capable of creating that kind of show is impressive," my dad says.

"Did you see the guy collecting garbage? He was dressed like a gentleman. So interesting," Bác Luy responds.

"Sometimes I think if I were born here, I could have been a space pilot."

I look up expecting both of them to laugh, but they don't. I'm so confused. Is he seriously lamenting the fact that he should've been an astronaut? My whole life he's told me to "know who you are," as in *know my place,* and here he is thinking he could've been one of like three people in the world to walk on the moon? Is he for real?

CHAPTER 12
PHÚC

No one expected to drift at sea for so long—nearly a week had passed. They made it into international waters, which meant one hurdle was over. The two biggest threats now were sharks and Thai pirates. Sharks, not normally drawn to humans, had migrated toward the smell of blood. And Thai pirates were soulless monsters who hunted refugees like it was a game. So when a cargo ship could be seen in the distance, they thought rescue was imminent. The families packed up their belongings in anticipation of the move, but when the boat approached, a red flag was waved at them.

"Too full," the skipper shouted, shaking his head.

The occupants on the cargo ship stood on the deck and avoided eye contact, ashamed for not advocating for their fellow refugees but also afraid of getting thrown off for being any kind of nuisance. They weren't the perpetrators of misery, but they felt guilty because they had been in Phúc's exact position just days or even hours earlier.

But it wasn't until a second boat passed and then a third that the occupants of Phúc's vessel began to worry.

Another two days went by without so much as a sighting of another ship. With thirty-three people on board, they were having trouble keeping everyone not only fed but hydrated. In the absence of food, the social order on the boat began to break down. There were two chickens who used to lay eggs, but since the famine, they, too, were barren.

"Pluck the feathers, and let's eat them," one man said.

"And then what? We could be drifting here for months."

"Or we could die of starvation today."

"You're still alive now, aren't you?"

The constant bickering felt like mental jabs coming from every angle, and Phúc tried hard to concentrate on anything but his hunger. Their debates were exhausting, and he wanted to tell them all to shut up because they were wasting their energy, but he knew none of them would listen to a kid. Trapped and drowning in insanity, Phúc hummed a song to himself as a means of distraction. But the arguments only got louder.

"This coming from a gambling degenerate."

"There is no use. We're all going to die anyway."

"Can we please stay on task?"

"Let me try."

"You've tried too many times."

Phúc retrieved his flute from under his blanket, moved as far away from anyone as he could get—about one foot—and faced the ocean. Closing his eyes, he imagined being back on his hill, surrounded by trees, dirt, and family.

He pressed the bamboo to his lower lip, formed his mouth into a whistle shape, and blew a long note. Missing the note at first, Phúc tilted the instrument just slightly up, took a deep breath, and began to play. The soft notes glided above the sea, bounced on the waves, and disappeared. There was no mountain to play the tune back to him now. Instead of stopping, he played louder and with vigor. Maybe someone would hear him; maybe help would find his song.

CRUNCH. The sound was unmistakable yet altogether impossible. Guava.

There was just no way. But then the smell came. The sweet, musky aroma was pungent. Immediately, Phúc was on his feet. Following his nose, he went down the steps, into the galley, and found a pregnant woman huddled in the corner hiding the precious fruit.

"Làm sao . . ." He meant to ask how but the words got caught in his throat. Phúc wasn't consciously *not* speaking, but he had no friends or family on this boat, which meant he had no one to talk to. Without realizing it, he hadn't used his voice in a week.

She looked at him with sadness and rubbed her belly by way of explanation.

"Đưa đây," he mumbled, and reached for what was left—a thin core and tattered stem.

She shoved it into her mouth, but Phúc's hands were quicker. With one hand on her throat and his other pressed into her cheeks, he forced her to spit it up.

As he walked back upstairs, his hands shook, and his stomach growled. Logically, he knew he needed to use the core as bait, but his body disagreed. It took everything he had not to put the food into his own mouth. Before he lost his nerve, he pressed an available hook into one half of the measly core, then tied it six times for good measure and dropped it into the water below.

Within a minute, there was a tug on the line, and he quickly reeled in a small goby fish. He held it in the air while it thrashed about, gulping for water. Phúc gripped the fish, feeling its spiked dorsal fin and slithery scales gently beat against his palm until finally, it stopped moving. This was the type of fish the others would've left to dry or cooked over the fire, but Phúc drove the hook more deeply into its throat and tossed it back over. He was fishing for something bigger. Something Phúc knew, which the others either didn't or had forgotten in their delirium of hunger, was that fishing required patience, except he, too, was fatigued by hunger, and within minutes the ocean had bewitched him into a nap.

When Phúc awoke twenty minutes later, it was to a great

commotion. He had tried to stay awake for the fish, but the ocean's soft lull rocked him into a dream he could no longer remember. Arms hanging off the side of the boat, fingers occasionally dipping into the sea . . . he fell asleep. But now, just after dawn, the others were so rowdy that Phúc could no longer ignore their loud cheering. On the deck of the boat was a three-foot-long carp, gulping its last breaths, surrounded by a group of starving refugees.

Phúc immediately turned to his fishing line. "Hey, that's *my* catch!"

No one heard him. Or maybe the words never left his dry mouth. Pushing through the crowd, he knelt beside the large fish and watched its gray and yellow gradient of scales shimmer like dominoes on an endless loop—standing then falling, standing then falling—as its gills opened and closed. The action was violent, torturous even, and yet everyone around seemed happy. They had found salvation. At last, they would not starve.

The local butcher grabbed the carp, its tail in one hand and its mouth in the other, and gruffly descaled it against the dull edge of the boat. Iridescent flecks flew like sparks into the ocean. A thin puddle of yellow formed on the ocean's surface—the scales floating like a school of fish moving in unison. Phúc reached down into the center, but as he touched the water's surface, the flecks dispersed evenly around his fingers. He retracted his hand and the gap closed; he stuck it in again and the same thing happened. Using just one finger, he drew a swirl in the water and watched as the flecks banded together into the shape of a water snake. Phúc laughed as the snake nipped at his finger, playing with him like a puppy in a pool.

"Ăn đi," the butcher said, thrusting a boiled fillet toward Phúc.

Phúc took the fillet only to turn around and watch as the tail of the water snake slithered off.

After downing the piece of fish about the size of his palm and a fistful of rice, Phúc was satiated to the point of being tired. He turned to the group and saw that the carp was nearly picked clean.

"Leave a little bit of the meat and the head, then give it here," Phúc demanded. He was afraid they'd eat everything and leave nothing to fish with.

"Who do you think you are? I ought to slap you for your arrogance," the deacon said sharply. He wasn't wrong; Phúc had spoken with force and an undertone of arrogance, but Phúc wasn't in church, and he no longer cared about being reprimanded.

"I'm the one who caught that fish you just ate because I used bigger bait," Phúc shouted, jumping to his feet. As soon as the words left his mouth, he hated how they sounded. Like a petulant child claiming something that wasn't his. Except it was his. He *had* caught that fish.

"Không, that's not right." This, from another larger man, who had two teeth missing on the right side of his mouth. He spoke calmly through his nostrils. Not only did he think Phúc was wrong, but he warned him not to confuse his heroic dreams with reality.

"All you've been catching with your small bait is small sardines," Phúc argued, and pressed his thumb to the third line on his ring finger to show the man how small his catches were compared to Phúc's.

The man scoffed and turned away.

Phúc pressed on, trying to explain that they were going about it all wrong by using such small bait, which of course would only yield small fish. Phúc knew he was acting bullish, but he didn't care. He caught that fish, and he didn't want to spend another five hungry days waiting for them to listen to him. The man ignored Phúc, handing the fish head to the cook, who boiled it until it was soft enough to eat.

While Phúc stewed in his anger, promising to let them all starve before catching another fish, he felt a sensation he hadn't felt in days. He needed to use the bathroom.

One of the few perks of starvation was Phúc hardly ever needed to relieve himself. Which was good because the toilet was the ocean. In the beginning, a few people at a time—ladies with ladies and men with men—would hang off the sides, their bodies halfway in the water, and relieve themselves. But as the weeks dragged on and the salty water both dried their skin and salinized their bodies, people began squatting at the back bow of the boat and relieving themselves that way. Everyone else would, of course, look away, but still, it felt shameful and dirty to be squatting off the side of the ledge. For Phúc, it was by far the worst part of the journey. Not the starvation, not the fear of dangerous creatures in the sea, just going to the bathroom. The lack of privacy was mortifying, but it was also shameful. Phúc grew up poor, but he was prideful. So, he would wait as long as possible—until his insides curled, and he thought he might explode—before dropping into the water. He never could get himself to squat off the stern.

He knew not to stay in the water longer than necessary, but after two weeks without a shower, he savored the bath. While slowly kicking his feet and dreading the strength he'd need to pull himself back on board, he felt a whoosh underneath and looked down to find a school of bluefish circling his feet.

"Give me the net," he shouted upward. "Give me the net. I see fish!"

A group came rushing over, and when they, too, saw the school of fish, Phúc was given the net, which he securely fastened to his wrist. He quickly dove down. Deeper and deeper he plunged, swinging the net in what felt like slow motion and catching nothing. Then:

Thwack! A large mass hit him across the chest with such force that it knocked his lungs back against his spine, and immediately he was out of air. Kicking for the surface as his body burned from his lungs to his fingertips, he tried not to focus on what had hit him. With salt water stinging his eyes, his arms broke the surface just as a white twenty-foot shadow passed beneath him, swaying side to side.

Gulping for air, he screamed, "Cá mập!"

But the boat was nowhere to be seen. He blinked, wiping his eyes with the salty ocean water, which only reignited the sting. Something rough brushed against his bare legs, and suddenly he was very aware of his naked bottom half. Warm tears filled his eyes, effectively clearing his vision while simultaneously confirming his worst fear.

The boat was gone.

He must have swum farther than he thought. Or the other passengers had paddled away. He would never know. Fatigued, his arms hurt, and his legs grew heavy.

He let himself cry a little harder this time, telling himself the tears were necessary for survival. Finally, Phúc's eyes cleared, and he saw just the tiniest speck in the distance. The boat! Or a giant rock. Whatever it was, he needed to get to it. With fervor spurned on by angst, he swam even as he felt another gentle brush of the massive being beside him. He was no match for a shark, and they both knew it. Up ahead, the boat came closer into view. Not only that—it looked as though they were heading toward him. They hadn't forgotten him. Still, he didn't let up.

Phúc opened his mouth to scream, *I'm over here*, but before the words could escape his throat, a wave crashed over him, and his body sank below the surface. With the weight of the ocean now above him, he kicked but only felt himself drop. He stopped swimming and instead just held his breath. The shark won. He was spent.

But then nothing happened. No sharp teeth bit into his

abdomen, chopped off his head, or clamped onto his thigh. Still, his reserve energy was spent.

The rays of sunlight dimmed as Phúc watched the surface recede. His body ached. He couldn't move. All he could do was hold his breath and wait.

The boat was closer now. . . .

Thirty feet . . .

Twenty feet . . .

Ten feet . . .

Five feet . . .

Three feet!

And then he heard muffled shouts from the surface.

"Trời ơi!" What did the sky have to do with anything?

"Chúa ơi!" What did God have to do with anything?

"Cá mập." Oh.

"Cá mập!" So his shark friend hadn't left him after all.

"Chúa ơi!" God help me.

"Trời ơi!" The universe hates me.

Hands splashed in the water, but none of them could reach him. Seawater filled his throat with brackish coughs as gulp after gulp he began to drown.

CHAPTER 13
JANE

Thirteen doesn't exist. It's bad luck.[4]

---

4   Neither should four and fourteen, but I don't know why, so . . .

CHAPTER 14
JANE

It's quiet in the shop this morning. It's been like this since I opened. The boredom is not all that unusual, but everything feels bland after Disneyland. So far, I've only had two customers, and it's nearly noon now. Well, three if you count the kid mooching off our air-conditioning. He's been walking in circles for twenty minutes. I hate this type of customer because instead of being able to read my book, I have to watch him like a hawk to make sure he doesn't help himself to a five-finger discount with our merchandise.

When I'm at the register, I trust no one and assume the worst in everyone. The sweetest-looking kid is just as likely to steal as the thuggish, baggy-pants gangster. I'm not stereotyping this little kid as he stares at the powdered doughnuts. I'm profiling his behavior. No one takes that long to contemplate a choice. Even thieves, the good ones, anyway, know exactly what they want. This must be his first time. Doughnuts are too stupid an item for this to be a gang initiation, which means he must just really want the food. He's young, maybe twelve, with floppy shoes, unwashed jeans, and a navy-blue backpack with pink zippers. A hand-me-down or donation for sure because no middle school kid with a choice would wear that. That zipper alone screams, *Go ahead, steal my lunch money because we both know I can't defend myself!*

"Can I help you find something?"

"No, um, I . . . Do you have anything for eighty-seven cents?" His honesty is shocking, so much so that I find myself stepping back. I'm more accustomed to getting shouted at or being told to mind my own business. The irony, of course, is that this *is* my business—or my family's business, anyway.

"Uh . . ." The only thing he can get for eighty-seven cents is candy, and I'm sure that's not what he's looking for. "Well, I've got a peanut butter and jelly sandwich for twenty-five cents."

The way his eyes light up, you would think I'd just offered him a gold ingot, and that makes me feel bad for charging him anything at all. Except—and I know this sounds terrible—I can't set a precedent that we give away free food. I know this because I've done it before, and then I've had twenty-five little kids asking me for a cheese snack.

"It's up at the register."

I walk to the cashier's box, keeping an eye on him in the corner mirrors to make sure he doesn't ambush me to get to the register. He may have kind eyes, but he's still a street kid, and you can never be too careful. If he's offended, it doesn't show. He keeps his distance, standing at least ten feet behind me, and he stops that same distance away as I unlock the door and step inside. Only after I'm back inside with the door locked again does he approach the counter. He hands me a quarter and I pass him my sandwich.

And then I can't help myself, so I say, "We're having a sale on the chips, just ten cents a bag."

"Any flavor?"

"Any flavor."

He looks at the chips below the counter so carefully that it kills me to take the rest of his money as he shoves six bags of chips in his backpack.

"Thanks," he says as he leaves. I really hope he doesn't return when my dad is here. On the back of his neck just below his hairline I see unmistakable burn marks. If ever there was a reason to hate cigarettes, this was it. It's like all the crappy smokers got the same memo on "additional uses" for their lung-killing devices. I wish we didn't sell them.

Jackie walks in as the kid exits. "Coffee took forever. What'd I miss?"

I unlock the register door and let her in as she hands me a mocha frappe. Apparently this is our new ritual.

"Oh, just you making me soft. I basically gave that kid free chips."

"Good. He wears a backpack that screams 'steal my lunch money,' so he's probably hungry."

I laugh, not at all surprised that she mirrored my same thought. "We've been friends for too long."

"Hey!" she says suddenly. "I have that pen too!"

She digs through her purse and retrieves a Tinker Bell pen just like mine. A wave of relief washes over me. I had been feeling guilty about not getting her one, but knowing that she went and didn't think to get me one either makes me feel less selfish. We hold them side by side and see that they're a little different. Mine has the Disneyland castle in the background and hers has the Neverland landscape. "I didn't see that one," I say, admiring hers while noticing a small nick at the top and a few scratches on the glass.

"Let's do a temporary trade."

"Temporary?"

"Yeah, that way we'll have something of each other's while we're away at school, and every time we see each other we'll switch back."

"Deal!" I say more enthusiastically than I feel. I love this idea, but I've grown attached to my pen and don't want to give it up. Telling myself it's just a stupid pen, I hand it over and grab hers.

She takes her seat on the floor as I savor the chocolate in my mocha frappe. "So . . . have . . . you told Paul yet?"

"No."

She shakes her head and taps my foot. "Kick me your shoe."

I peel off my Addidas sneakers (the fake kind with only two stripes and an extra *d* in the name) and hand them to her.

"You gotta do it, Jane. Tell him he can call me anytime," she says as she begins to draw a checkered design onto my shoe with green and black Sharpie. Jackie's brain is crazy creative. That's why they asked her to paint the class mural during Spirit Week every year. For our senior year, we had an Under the Sea theme, and she painted a giant stingray with every single one of our classmates' faces on fish beneath it. It was so good, they left it up for graduation.

"Make sure you sign those so I can sell them on eBay. I need money for ramen and snacks," I say.

"No one is going to pay for these," she says. "I just don't want you mistaken for a FOB on your first day of college."

"Are you regretting staying home?"

"No. You know school was never my thing. I'm only attending SJSU because I don't know what else to do."

"You're an artist! You should be making art."

"My mom says art is for white kids whose parents have too much money. She has no plans to support me past the age of eighteen."

"Of course not, because we're Vietnamese and why would we want our kids to do anything fun with their lives? But your art is so good. I bet you could actually get paid to do it."

"We'll see. I slipped an art class into my fall course load," she says, examining my shoe for any missing elements before reaching for my other one. I can tell she doesn't want me to make a big deal of it, so I drop the subject.

By the time she's done, my shoes are hardly recognizable. They look like the kind of sneakers hip-hop singers in bright windbreaker joggers would wear in a music video about money and respect (or the lack thereof). "I'm almost afraid to wear them outside because I might get jumped—and by jumped, I mean someone will say, 'Yo, gimme your shoes,' and I will quickly hand them over," I say.

"How is it that you'll chase a guy around the block for a bag of Cheetos but you can't stand up for yourself if someone tries to steal your shoes?"

I shrug because I have no response. No one has ever asked me this.

After Jackie leaves, I sit at the register alone watching Tinker Bell slide up and down through Neverland. I tell myself that Jackie's pen is even cooler than mine because it has Tinker Bell's natural background. And I'm doing my best to ignore the nicks on it when I hear the back door open, and Paul comes in with my dad. Dad heads for the fridge while I unlock the register door for Paul. He steps in, pulls down the blanket from the shelf that we use for extra butt padding, and plops down on it.

"Unpack more beer," my dad says as the door to the fridge slams shut, causing the bottles to rattle. I quickly jump off my stool to refill the chiller. "Everything okay?"

"Yeah, fine."

Uproarious laughter above the hum of folk music wafts in from the shed my dad built behind the store. The uncles have arrived. I peek into the room to see karaoke songs playing on a tiny box television. In the music video, there's an old guy playing a folk instrument while a girl sings in front of a backdrop of rolling mountains and flowing streams—must be Vietnam. Sometimes my uncles talk about Vietnam. Right now, they're talking about their rickety boat engine dying during a late-night fishing expedition. Our family loves to buy broken things and fix them. I don't understand how they're so confident in their abilities. I would never trust myself to fix an engine in the middle of the ocean. But I guess when you come from poverty like they did, you learn to fix what you have. Or learn to live with the broken pieces.

Each of the uncles owns a modest two-story home with gently used furniture and lots of space. A whole lot more space than we have, but instead of congregating in any of their homes, they make the trek over here to tinker, drink, and talk behind our shop in what basically amounts to a shed with two windows. Since my dad can't leave the store unattended, the uncles come to a place where they're treated to mismatched, cracked patio furniture that is so tattered even thieves won't touch it. We never buy new things. New things smell of money, and if people think we have it, they rob us.

"Don't be lazy. Clean up," my dad calls to me as he exits.

I walk to the register, open the door, and say, "Hey, you wanna eat Pocky sticks and quiz me on my biology flash cards?"

"What flavor you got?" This is quintessential Paul. He doesn't really care what flavor, he just wants to play his handheld *Columns* game.

"Both!" I point to a bag beneath the register, where I've stashed three strawberry and three chocolate boxes.

His eyes go wide. "We can eat all of them?"

I hadn't counted on that, but fuck it. "All of them."

He dashes to the bag and peels open one of each flavor.

"I've always wanted to do this." Holding a strawberry and a chocolate stick side by side, he takes a huge bite and chews. "Yep. So good. I knew it would be good."

"Yo. Hand me some." He carefully lines up two sticks for me, and I bite them while he still holds on to the ends. "You're a mad scientist. This is delicious." I mean it too. I'm impressed with Paul because I myself would've never come up with something so fun. My first thought when he ripped the bag open was, *How are we going to keep the packets fresh?* Lame. I know.

Paul and I are different this way. I think it's why schoolwork is so much easier for him. He, like our dad, doesn't look at rules as being absolute; he questions logic if it doesn't immediately make sense to him, and always comes home with a perfect report card. I admire those qualities in him.

I toss the flash cards I made for Intro to Biology at Paul and move to the bathroom to fill a bucket with soapy water. Wheeling the bucket back into the store, I squeeze the excess water out of the mop by leaning all my weight on the wringer handle, and I sweep it over the eternally dirty floors.

Paul can't read most of the words even though he makes a solid effort, so he holds up the cards, and I read them aloud.

"Polar, a molecule with partial charges. It can be mixed with water. Non-polar, a molecule with no partial charges and does *not* mix with water."

As I mop, I repeat the two definitions over and over until they're memorized.

"Alpha-glucose, monomer for starch and glyco—"

In the shed, the uncles are talking in hushed tones. Most of the time, when they drink, they're pretty jovial, talking about the ridiculous mischief they used to get into as kids. Like this one time, I heard Bác Luy telling them about how he used to sneak out of bed at the convent and pass notes to these girls from the neighborhood. The nuns would wait for him to come back, and the second he fell asleep, one of them would be over him with a stick, beating him raw. Beatings are always hilarious to them.

I press my finger to my lips and then whisper to Paul, "That's good enough for now. Go finish those Pocky sticks."

"You don't want any?"

"No, it's all you."

Paul walks away, and before I can tell him not to eat them too quickly, the conversation from outside pulls me back in.

"Such a waste of a life. To jump off the boat that way," one of the uncles says with a regretful tsk at the end of his sentence. They're speaking in Vietnamese. It's Bác Chuyên. I can tell by the way he slurs his words. Back in Vietnam, he was a deacon, but I've always just known him as a drunk. Divorce is still pretty taboo in Vietnamese culture, so he's still married with five kids, but his wife kicks him to the curb so often that he's more of a couch surfer than anything else. He bounces between houses until they tire of him and he goes somewhere else. He's never stayed with us, though. Thank god, because I find him to be obnoxious.

"No one living on a boat that long escapes insanity," Bác Luy says. I don't know what they're talking about. Floating freely in the open ocean sounds like heaven to me compared to this place. I like Bác Luy; he's the closest uncle we have—except he's not actually related to us. I asked about that once, but I don't remember the answer, which means it was either vague or dismissive. What I do know is he's the only uncle who gives us red envelopes for Christmas and Tết, the Vietnamese New Year. And obviously he took us to Disneyland.

"If those Thai fuckers hadn't robbed and beaten us . . . Take money and jewelry, fine. Why break our bones and cut off our fingers? Our bodies were just a game to them," Bác Chuyên spits. No one is more bitter than Bác Chuyên. One Thai boat crossed him and now all Thai people are monsters.

"You got off easy. What they did to some people is too heinous to even speak about," my dad says, and the sentence lingers in the air like ash from a fire only recently extinguished.

"Let it go," Bác Luy nudges. "This story has already passed."

But Bác Chuyên digs in. "What do you know? You saw one shark and fainted like a dead person." He finishes the last half of his beer in one swig and then stands up, asking, "Who wants another round?" And suddenly he's right in front of me.

"Chào Bác Chuyên," I say, jumping backward.

"Chan—e." He's never bothered trying to pronounce my name correctly. "Con lại đây." He sways slightly. I don't want to approach him, but I have no choice, and he laughs as I scrunch my nose in anticipation of what I know is coming. I stand two arm lengths away, but he steps toward me, brings his hand to my face and grabs my nose between his index and middle finger knuckles before twisting it and howling with laughter. While his hand is attached to my nose, I can't help but stare at the nub where his pinky finger used to be. "This face of yours is so easy to hate. I could just slap it," he says in Vietnamese. Believe it or not, this phrase is a compliment according to my dad. It's the equivalent of "Oh, you're so cute I just want to pinch your cheeks!" Both are equally awful. I prefer no one touch my face—like *any* part of it. This is mean, but I take great comfort in knowing that a Thai pirate chopped off his pinky finger during the war. I like to imagine that they did it to wipe the smug look he constantly has right off his face.

I scrunch my nose, which I'm sure is red, and step aside as he heads to the beer fridge, helping himself to some beef jerky along the way. That he's able to carry four Heineken bottles plus the jerky without dropping any of it is probably his only real talent in life.

My dad is neutral about most people, but he despises Bác Chuyên as much as I do, so Bác Chuyên only comes to the shop as a guest of Chú Thịnh, who is my dad's brother-in-law and the complete opposite of him. Where Bác Chuyên walks into the shop like he owns the place, picks the most expensive beer, and offers what isn't even his to the rest of the guys, Chú Thịnh is overly polite. He never helps himself to anything even though my dad obviously wouldn't mind and offers. He's the only uncle I have who doesn't have kids. His wife, my dad's sister O Uyên, is still in Vietnam. I think she's waiting for him to sponsor her coming to America. I'm not sure how you can be married to someone you only see once a year, but they've done it for over ten years. I suspect my dad keeps him around to make sure he doesn't cheat on my aunt and find himself a new wife.

Chú Thịnh's voice is frayed, and he's self-conscious about it. That he was left scarred from the war and Bác Chuyên seems relatively unscathed—minus a pinky, but it's not even a useful finger really—is proof that there is no karmic justice in the world. The war paralyzed Chú Thịnh's vocal cords. I have no idea how. Everyone thought he was going to be mute for the rest of his life, but some doctors injected medicine into his throat, and now he can talk but can't yell. It's impossible to tell if he's angry or ecstatic.

"I would take the ocean over being stuck on volatile land. If it wasn't the mines exploding from below, then it was bullets raining from above. It's a wonder any of us survived," Bác Luy says. "Where were all the doctors? I still can't believe your dad is the one who fixed my arm. It is true that Việt Năm is a small country."

"I don't miss the ocean. Sharks aren't native to Việt Năm but during that time they lurked in the water. I'll never forget the feeling of its skin. I looked down and it was licking me with its body! This shark, big like this," my dad says, gesturing at the length of the room. "I thought for sure it would eat me, but it just pushed me back and forth like a ball." He laughs as though this moment is funny, instead of horrifyingly scary. "If it wasn't for Thầy Lâm, I would've drowned, and then he went and jumped off the boat anyway." He doesn't laugh this time, and that's how I know this Thầy Lâm guy is dead.

No one says anything for a long, awkward moment, until Bác Chuyên leans forward and resumes making the conversation all about himself. No one seems to mind this time. As I press against the door listening, I wonder why Bác Chuyên was on this boat with my dad instead of any of his siblings.

My dad's older brother and his younger sister still live in Vietnam with my grandparents. I've never met them. His older sister, O Linh, lives in Connecticut and I only remember meeting her once before Paul was born. While Mom watched the store, Dad and I drove from San Jose all the way to San Francisco to pick her up at the airport. She had a long layover on her way to visit Vietnam, so we ate bánh mì in the car for four hours and then dropped her back off at the airport. Chú Thịnh and Bác Chuyên were from the same village of Đà Nẵng, and Bác Luy is chosen family, I guess. Because many from my dad's generation resettled in America, they took to calling each other more familial names as a means of building community. Chú Thịnh and Bác Luy are the only two "friends" my dad has (Bác Chuyên doesn't count for many of the aforementioned reasons) despite the many acquaintances who greet him with "My brotha" or "Mi amigo" at the store. They are not his friends. We don't have friends. We have family, that's it.

When the uncles are around, my dad is usually too pre-occupied to pay much attention to what Paul and I are doing. Vietnamese men are odd. They're friendly with one another, but not overtly. I never see them hug; they just kind of arrive and take their seats. The lack of affection isn't machismo, though. It feels more awkward than masculine, like when I've met the same person too many times to not know their name, and I have to clumsily sidestep a half-greeting.

Only with my dad, it's been like this my whole life. When I was a kid, I used to crawl over to the door and listen to their stories, but sometimes they were so graphic they'd give me nightmares, and I'd wake up screaming that I'm drowning. I think my dad knew then, like he probably knows now, that I was listening, but we've never acknowledged it.

This past January, Little Saigon, in Orange County, was on the news because some video store owner decided to hang the Communist flag next to a picture of Ho Chi Minh in his shop. My dad, Paul, and I sat glued to the television, watching it unfold.

Huge yellow banners read HO CHI MINH = MASS MURDERER and HO CHI MINH = HITLER. I saw a lady waving a paper doll cutout of Ho Chi Minh with a noose around his neck. One poster in particular, though, is seared in my mind. It was white with the words: YOU ASK WHY WE'RE ANGRY? THESE ARE HOW OUR LOVED ONES WERE EXECUTED BY HO CHI MINH. Below the handwritten letters were black-and-white photos depicting the murders. My eyes lifted in shock, and I turned to my dad, who was *completely* stoic. We've never discussed it.

CHAPTER 15
PHÚC

"Why is four bad luck?" Paul asks.

"I just said I don't know why."

"But then how do you know it's bad?"

"Because Dad told me. Anyway, why are you distracting me? Don't you want to hear about the shark?"

Paul makes a motion of zipping his lips and falls back into his pillows.

Sandpaper rubbed against Phúc's underside, scratching his bare skin as he hit the bottom of the ocean floor. And yet, there was pressure above him, like hundreds of pounds of water were pressing into him. Phúc hadn't reached the bottom of the ocean. He was actually almost near the surface, but he wasn't swimming. He was being *pushed*. The giant, toothy shark had caught Phúc on its back and was thrusting his frail and bony body upward. His ears throbbed with the quick ascent. Above water, the shark tossed him upward like one might flip a pancake, and Phúc flew through the air. He floated amid an endless blue sky—until he started to fall.

When he dropped back onto the shark, the impact forced the water inside his lungs to return to Mother Earth's giant pool. Then he was out, as in passed out. The world went completely dark. There was no light, no heaven, just nothingness for seconds, minutes, hours, days maybe? In the oblivion, time became fluid.

When he came to, it was to a fit of lung-scratching, torturous coughing—death by a thousand grains of sand. His lungs burned hot with pain until, finally, the convulsions and bloody mucus subsided, and he found that he had somehow gotten himself thrown back onto the deck of the boat. Hoisting himself upright, he checked his body for bite marks and missing limbs. As far as he could tell, every physical part of him was accounted for.

"Mập ơi!" he called, his voice emanating in a whisper. An enemy would have eaten him, whereas Shark, aptly named Mập, which meant both *fat* and *shark*, had been playing with him. No answer. He would find his friend later. Tired, Phúc sat back down.

First, he shivered, then the fever dreams kicked in, and he slipped in and out of consciousness. One moment the sun shone high in the sky, its rays warming him to his core. Next, he lay on his back in the dark, his mouth dry, his lips chapped, and his skin burnt. At some point, a pounding headache sent sharp, searing pains across his scalp, making him dizzy. During his recurring blackouts, he could hear the men and women screaming. But his busted eardrums dampened the cries, causing the screams to sound distant despite the hard kicks and physical trampling of his limp body.

Calm, black oblivion.

Blink.

Black.

Sharp cry. Silence.

Blue.

Eyes open.

The normally vertical world was now horizontal—a purgatory of sorts. A gruff, half-naked man with mean eyes and dark, burnt skin crudely pressed his body into an unblinking woman, the one Phúc had taken the fruit from, who was either dead or stiff with fear.

Silence.

Darkness.

Hushed sounds.

Screaming.

Vibrations.

Silence.

Nothing.

Then a new sound: metal hitting wood, over and over again, dampened only by the occasional metal hitting flesh. Metal, wood. Metal, flesh. Metal, wood. Like a butcher chopping meat.

More quiet. Longer this time. Eternal.

Phúc's eyelids pressed into his sockets like cinder blocks resting on his face.

When Phúc was finally able to peel one eye open, all he could see was blue.

The completely cloudless blue sky.

His chest rose with great effort.

Air.

Breath meant he was alive.

His mouth was dry. He was stuck. Not his whole body, just below the knees. He tried to wiggle free, but his legs could barely twist, and his ears vibrated with static. Phúc attempted to sit up and was met with a piercing pain in his skull that forced him into a fetal position as his teeth gnashed together so hard that his jaw locked.

As a result, when Phúc's jaw loosened and he could finally move his head, he found that his legs were now detangled from the mass of bodies piled next to him. Quickly realizing that not only were they all dead but he was also completely soaked in blood, he scooted as far away from them as possible before curling into himself. Forcing his mind back into darkness, he prayed for a different reality, but the nightmare was real.

Blood crusted all along the side of his body.

At first, Phúc thought he had been spared the details of what transpired while he lay unconscious, but the images he hoped were lost would soon start to find their way back to him. Phúc's first realization was that he wasn't wrong. His shipmates had abandoned him in the water, but they weren't being malicious. While Phúc dove for the school of fish, pirates had appeared on the horizon, and with no fuel, the passengers tried to paddle away from their line of sight. They were no match for these thieves of the sea, though.

More recollections came.

Barbaric. Unflinching. Relentless.

Thầy Lâm's pregnant wife lay flat on the floor, her head thumping against the dry wood as a large, brutish man pressed onto her. Twisting her long, jet-black hair in the palm of his hand, he whipped her head backward while thrusting forward—her hair held like the reins on a horse.

For a woman of delicate features, her forehead was strong. It took several blows before he drew blood. This torture seemed to go on for a long time, until the sun glinted off a shiny piece of jewelry in her left earlobe, and, without breaking his rhythm, the man ripped the tiny diamond-studded earring from her piercing, causing it to bleed profusely. Her tired eyes met Phúc's before closing one final time.

When a lion strikes its prey, it pounces and immediately lunges for the jugular; a quick, swift death is the goal. But war makes people coldhearted. And the Thai pirates, well, their blood ran ice blue.

Blackout. Phúc couldn't handle any more memories. He didn't want to remember.

A day passed, maybe three. No one, including Phúc, knew

how long he drifted unconscious on that boat—how he could have survived the mass murder. The lack of water, followed by days in the burning hot sun, should have killed him. Maybe it rained, and the droplets of water seeped into his mouth, saving his life. Maybe he really was the embodiment of luck. Or maybe it was just the opposite.

When he regained consciousness, he couldn't move. His eyes were open, but the bright sun made it impossible to see. His brain told his hand to shield his eyes, but nothing happened. His brain told his hand to wiggle his fingertips, but he couldn't see his fingers. As his breathing slowed and he waited for death, a hand reached across his face shielding it from the sun. A few minutes after that, the fingertips began to wiggle. He realized they were *his own* fingers. His body reacted so slowly that sunlight and darkness traded places in the sky several times before Phúc could fully sit up.

If his view of the deck floor had been horrifying before, the massacre he now saw was infinitely more abysmal. Blood splashed across the deck. Thick liquid dripped through the floorboards, coating the ship in death.

One by one, Phúc checked the bodies for signs of life. If they looked pale, he left them, but if their skin was blotchy and blue, he lugged them up to the side of the boat using buckets, planks, and other bodies as leverage until he could roll them overboard and watch them float in the water, stubbornly refusing to sink.

With eighteen of the passengers buried at sea, Phúc counted seven left on the ship.

Thirty-three people had boarded, so where were the rest?

He ran through a mental checklist of people but kept getting them confused, never sure if he had counted them already, and when he started confusing the bodies he had just hauled overboard, he stopped trying to remember.

Remembering wouldn't bring them back. Perhaps anyone still alive feared the boat—now full of bad karma—and they chose to take their chances floating in the open water.

Phúc looked at the seven people he hoped were still alive and tried to remember good things about them. If he conjured up good thoughts, their spirits might choose to stay on earth—to stay with him. None of them had a detectable pulse, but their bodies were warm—they still *felt* alive. Thầy Lâm, whose arms he'd had to extract from their firm grip around his pregnant wife's bruised and bloodied head, had taught Phúc's arithmetic class. Phúc hadn't known he was married or that he had a child. His daughter, whose name Phúc didn't know, lay next to him, weak and just as pale as the rest. As he studied her downcast eyes, a memory surfaced. She was younger but had the same large, curious eyes and sunken-in cheeks, and she came stumbling awkwardly into the schoolyard as students were released. Completely oblivious to the hundreds of students rushing past her, she made her way inside, rebalancing herself with every other step until she found her dad.

And then Phúc remembered—her name was Thúy. The little girl's name was Thúy.

"Please don't leave me here alone." *Please don't make me throw you overboard,* he added in his head.

Across from the father-daughter duo was the deacon.

Back home, Phúc hadn't liked him much. He was bigheaded and self-important, and he didn't know shit about fishing, but all of that seemed trivial in light of their new circumstances. The pinky finger on his right hand was gone, and infection ate away at the unsterilized, open wound. Now that he had been forsaken, would he see the wisdom in God's plan?

Another brain-bursting headache ripped across Phúc's scalp—karma or coincidence, he wasn't sure. The scream-ing returned, but this time, he could see its origin—Deacon Chuyên's wife. Their daughter, a girl no more than a few years older than Phúc, had been taken by a brutish, dark-skinned Thai monster. In Phúc's memory, the man's fingers moved across the girl's trembling bottom lip and into her mouth, forc-ing her to gag. Her mother's helpless scream was met with a backhanded slap so hard that she fell unconscious.

The headache subsided. Deacon Chuyên's daughter was one of the seven missing. Did the pirates take her? "She isn't dead yet," Phúc reasoned to himself, even though he had no proof of life. "Don't give up," he whispered, knowing the assur-ance was hollow.

An older woman lay curled stiffly in a crouched position. The village nurse. She came to the house when Phúc's grand-father was dying. Her bag of medicine was small, mostly con-sisting of this pungent green rub (dầu xanh) that seemed to be the cure for every ailment.

Phúc moved to her and frantically began searching through her possessions. There wasn't much of anything. Torn cloth-ing, toothpaste, several shredded plastic bags, and some newspaper wrapping. Crushing his hands around the paper to make sure they were all empty, Phúc's hand came upon something hard. A tiny pouch wrapped endlessly in plastic to prevent the contents from breaking. Phúc could've thrown the bottle across the ship, and it would've bounced lightly around the deck like a rubber ball. It was wrapped so well. Carefully peeling away layer after layer of plastic, Phúc finally discovered a small glass bottle about the length and width of his two fingers. Even with the weight of the jar in his hand, he could hardly believe the dầu xanh was real.

Gently, Phúc pried open the mouths of Thầy Lâm, his daughter, Deacon Chuyên, the village nurse, two siblings half his age (who he knew nothing about save for the fact that they were now orphans), and an elderly woman who seemed to have survived by clutching a rosary to her chest and trusting God to do the rest. He then poured a single drop into each of their mouths and waited for the magic potion to take effect. There wasn't enough medicine to use it properly; dầu xanh is not meant to be ingested, but they were dying and Phúc didn't know what else to do.

Deacon Chuyên spat the liquid back out and said, "Stop wasting medicine on the dead." Grabbing the bottle from Phúc's hand, he doused his gangrenous finger in the liquid before leaving it in the sun to dry. No one else moved, except for maybe Thầy Lâm, but Phúc was so deliriously tired that he wasn't sure if Thầy Lâm's slight shift was real, a result of the boat rocking, or a figment of his imagination.

CHAPTER 16
JANE

I have my piano lesson today. One hour, every other week. During the school year, my teacher, Chú Quang, picks me up on Saturdays and drops me back off, but since it's summer, I have my lessons on Thursdays (the slowest day at the store). Paul's elementary school is just a few blocks past his apartment, the convenient location no doubt a contributing factor in my dad's decision to let me take the lessons, which my godmother, O Vui—her name literally means *joy*—pushed him to let me do. Because of this, I used to think she was my fairy godmother in the Cinderella sense. She's not.

When I arrive at his apartment, he looks disheveled and pensive as opposed to his usual casual demeanor. He lets me in and has me practice my scales for a while. I should mention that I'm not a very good piano player, and that's not me being modest. I just don't have the "gift of ear" that other players have. I know this because every time my godmother drops in for a visit,

Chú Quang tells her, *It's such a shame that she doesn't have a gifted ear*, in Vietnamese. As it turns out, I'm the excuse she needs to throw herself all over him in a pathetic, middle-aged, single Vietnamese woman kind of way. It's embarrassing and kills her credibility as an altruistic godmother, but I'm fine with the arrangement.

Chú Quang and I get along great despite my untalented ears. Don't get me wrong. I've always *wanted* to be one of those players who sees the notes on the page and hears the music come alive. I've also always wanted a million dollars and a different family.

I like Chú Quang because he usually lets me choose my own music. I bring the song and he quickly simplifies it into beginner chords and notes. This week, it's EMF's "Unbelievable," and I'm unbelievably excited.

"This one today," he says, sitting down at the keyboard in his cluttered living room and placing his own sheet music on the stand. I'm disappointed, but I don't argue. It's not a hard song per se; I just normally know the song already and know when I'm supposed to pause or play a little faster. Without that, I'm out of my depth. I try anyway. The song is melancholic with the rhythm of a funeral march, which is a departure from my usual upbeat and fun choices. After the third stanza, I stop.

"What song is this?"

"Hoài Thu."

"Is it supposed to sound like that?"

He laughs, but it's half-hearted. "No." Putting his hands on the keys, he plays it back for me.

I was butchering the song for sure, but I had the tone right. It's somber, and even though we're only playing on the piano, I can almost hear an accompaniment of wind instruments. A rare epiphany for my ungifted ears. During the pauses in the song, I notice his hands shaking but I say nothing. When he's done, he scoots to the side, and it's my turn.

Chú Quang doesn't have a lot of rules, but one of them is if I miss, skip, or play a wrong note, I have to begin again. I don't mind it. The repetition allows me to learn a song all the way through, and I usually leave feeling somewhat like a pianist. Today is no different. I falter through the first three stanzas, playing and replaying the notes again and again.

While I practice, he pulls the đàn tranh—a sixteen-string Vietnamese zither—from the wall. When I inevitably falter and have to begin again, he joins me. Plucking deftly at the delicate strings, he takes the lead and I follow, finally starting to hear the melody.

As I lean into the music, I sense that he isn't listening. He's taken on that same statuesque look I've seen adults get when thinking about a memory they'll never talk about.

"That's good, very good," he says when I finish, and that's how I know something's wrong. This is the first time he's ever given me a compliment, and it doesn't feel right.

I nod, wondering if I should say thanks, but I decide against it. "See you in two weeks?"

"Okay."

The song haunts me as I walk home. I've never really listened to Vietnamese songs. I've heard Vietnamese music. It's usually playing when the uncles are visiting or when Dad is tinkering alone with something damaged. But, like American poetry, they are hard to comprehend. Plus, they're almost always like the one we played: melancholy cries of lost love and broken feelings. My parents were both Vietnamese refugees who fled after the war. Obviously, I know that the journey was horrible, and a lot of people died, both American and Vietnamese, but something about that song. . . . Listening to it felt like being trapped in a cage during a flash flood. I was anchored and engulfed as I choked on all the raw emotion.

Because Vietnam is such a poor country, I just assumed my parents fled for a chance at a better life. I never considered that maybe the refugees never wanted to leave.

I make a mental note to write down what I can remember of the song when I get home. Maybe it's a popular song that I can find the lyrics to. And maybe if I analyze it like poetry, I'll learn about its meaning. Maybe it'll tell me all the stories my parents haven't. Like why Vietnamese protesters equated Communism with murder.

I looked up the Vietnam War before, but everything I read was about how unpopular the war was. There were also lots of horror stories from American GIs. I saw graphic photos, but where were the stories about civilians like my parents?

On days like this I wish that Paul were older. Not older than me, just *older*. Because then I'd have someone to talk to about it all. Someone to—oh fuck.

Paul!

Paul started summer school today and I'm supposed to pick

him up after my lesson. But for the last ten minutes, I've been walking in the wrong direction.

Shit. I stop so hard my toe digs into the top of my sneaker. I about-face and run full speed back in the other direction. Paul's school is only five minutes away from my piano lesson. I had had plenty of time to get there. My legs are moving fast, but not fast enough. Houses, cars, shops, I need them all to *move* faster. The school has a policy that if someone isn't there to pick a kid up within five minutes, they will call home, and if the parent isn't there within another ten minutes, they mark it somewhere in the kid's file. Three of these and the kid gets booted from summer school.

When I turn the corner and see Principal Avitia standing with him in front of the school, I know I'm in a world of trouble.

"Hi, I'm sorry." Catching my breath proves impossible.

"It's no problem. I spoke to your dad, and he's on his way." She looks at me with the idiotic eyes of someone who has no idea what she's just done. To her, this is no big deal. I didn't show up, she called my dad, and he probably very pleasantly told her he'd be right over.

Fuck.

Fuck. Fuck. Fuck.

"Can you call him and tell him I'm here? Save him the hassle of coming down." I'm begging now, though you wouldn't know it by the nonchalant tone in my voice. "It's just that he really shouldn't leave the shop unattended and I'm here, so . . ."

She looks at me funny. "I can call back, but I'm sure he's more than halfway here by now. Do you want me to try?"

"No, just tell him that I came, and we're headed home." I want to explain further, but lies are best kept short. "C'mon, Paul, let's go."

We're about halfway home when Paul says, "I told her not to call. I told her you would be here." He's scared for me, which makes the already tightly wound knot in my stomach cinch even tighter. We both know what's coming.

"It's okay. It's not your fault," I breathe.

I hear our 1984 Ford Taurus with its broken muffler turn the corner. I stiffen my shoulders and prepare for battle. The car abruptly pulls to a stop in front of us. There is no wave hello or warm greeting. I open the back door for Paul, who gets in, quickly buckles his seat belt, and hugs the door as closely as he can. I want so badly to climb into the back seat with him. Instead, I brace myself for the punishment I know is coming. Quickly, I close Paul's door as gently as I can so my dad can't accuse me of slamming it, open the front passenger door, and jump in. We turn the first corner, and I immediately feel it—knuckles against the side of my skull. A small part of me hopes that he'll see that I am sorry based on how small I've made myself, so I wrap my arms around my head and curl into a ball as several heavier fists reverberate off my back.

"How many times have I told you not to slam the door?" Punch. I exhale a cough that is the direct effect of my lungs knocking against my rib cage. "You know how much it costs to fix a door?" I cough again but say nothing.

Silence. Even if I felt like I could speak, I know the words would turn into tears. One bruise. Two. There will be marks to hide tomorrow. I lean as close to the passenger door as I can and wait for the out-of-body experience to kick in. Briefly, I think about pulling the silver handle and letting myself tumble along the side of the road. *He probably wouldn't even stop. I'm such a worthless piece of shit that he'd probably just keep driving.* Thoughts like this invade my consciousness as a welcome reprieve from the physical pain. With my hands over my head, which is tightly tucked between my thighs, I protect the thing that I know is going to break me free from this situation—my brain. I think of Paul in the back seat, his knuckles white from gripping the holder on the side of the door. He's crying, but he's silent. I don't need to hear it, I can feel it. I'm not sure where he learned that—to not make noise when he cries. Probably me. Tears are inevitable. I wish they weren't, but they're uncontrollable in moments like this. The voice box, though, aside from the occasional gasp for air or hiccup, is easily controlled.

Silence and time. These are the only two things that matter in moments like this. It'll pass—it always does.

"Selfish," he spits. "You are always so selfish. Just this little thing you have to do to pick up your brother from school, and you can't do it."

My back aches from the punches, or maybe it's from the tight ball I've rolled myself into. And then we're home.

"Get the stick," he says. I move slowly, mostly because I'm so tense that I have to tell myself to loosen up so I can exit the car. Paul opens his door and runs inside to our room. Good. He remembers what I told him. Hopefully he plugs his ears. I drop my backpack at the entrance of the house and walk to the back, where a thick wooden stick rests in the space at the bottom of the sliding glass door. The stick is meant to keep intruders out, but today it'll be used to discipline me.

"Kneel down."

I hand him the stick and start to kneel.

"Đứng yên." *Stand still.*

I've never understood why he wants me to stand still *after* telling me to kneel, but it actually helps. Being still dampens the pain. This place, the corner between the back door and the kitchen counter, isn't ideal. For one, the hardwood floor is painful to kneel on, and two, if I fall into the door and shatter it or even just crack it, that will prolong the beating. *SMACK!*

"Đứng yên."

The stick meets my thigh with such force that I stumble forward, landing on my wrists rather than my hands. Before I can even get up, I feel another clap of thunder hit my butt. He's found the sweet spot.

"Đứng yên," he repeats, even though I'm as static as the floor I'm now lying flat against. My mind goes numb with each beating. I tell myself not to count. Again. Again. Again. Again. Each one stings harder than the last, and I find myself weeping. Tears are for the weak. I know this, yet I cannot get my eyes to stop. A salty puddle of pathetic sorrow pools beneath me and the punishment continues. Again. Again. Again.

"Get up."

My hands are trembling, but I obey. Pushing myself up to my knees, I feel the stick lash into my lower lumbar, slicing the skin, and I'm immediately back on the floor.

It's okay, I tell myself. Bruises heal and he hasn't hit me on the head yet. That's the important part. Arms, legs, thighs, back, anything below the neck is fine with me. I try to make myself look as pathetic as possible. The weaker I am, the quicker this will be over. Despite the pain, I hear Jackie in my head. *How is it that you'll chase a guy around the block for a bag of Cheetos but you can't stand up for yourself?* And suddenly I know the answer. It's not my natural instinct to run toward danger; I was taught to do it. And I don't stand up for myself because no one ever gave me that option.

Anger burns inside me; I don't know why. I'm not sure who it's directed at. I messed up. I shouldn't have left Paul at school. How embarrassing for him to have the principal call home. How scared must he have been when he begged her not to make the call? Stupid. How could I be so stupid? Why did I walk the other way?

I hear panting. A good sign. My beating is exhausting him. I dare not move. I simply stare at my pool of tears.

"Get up."

I don't want to, but it's not a choice. My hands shake as I press them under the weight of my body and push upward. The second my body breaks contact with the floor, I feel the stings of every blow all over again. I think if he hits me one more time, I won't be able to get back up. It won't be physically possible. He must sense this, too, because finally, he says the words I've been waiting to hear:

"Go wash your face."

When I find my bed an hour later, I know I'm going to be okay. I lay a washcloth across my lower back and toss a bag of frozen vegetables on top, but half the bag misses the landing mark, and the cold instantly causes my back to arch in pain. I quietly curse, turn onto my side, and reposition the bag.

When I open my eyes, I see him sitting at my feet.

"Are you okay?"

Paul. Paul is here.

I open my mouth to say something, but an emotional pressure on my larynx stops me, and I nod instead. The movement tweaks a nerve, and a wave of pain flashes from my throat to the back of my neck, where it settles into a pulsating rhythm of spasms. I try to hide it.

"I made you alphabet soup, but it's cold now," Paul says.

Alphabet soup is the cure to all ailments. When our mom left and cooking became my responsibility, the only things I knew how to prepare were canned foods. The instructions were easy enough: open can, pour into pot, heat until bubbling, pour into bowls, eat. And Paul would spit up everything but alphabet soup, so alphabet soup it was. He liked picking up the letters and playing around with them too. Sometimes, it made a bit of a mess, and if our dad had seen us, he would've gotten angry and made us stop. I would try to get Paul to sound out the letters so he was learning while we ate, but really, it was to distract from the fact that I felt guilty about laughing and having fun. I *liked* the mess. When something shitty happens, it's become a tradition that we make soup, except this is the first time Paul's made it for me. Usually, it's me trying to distract him from my bruises, wincing, or general bad mood.

I force myself to sit up and smile when I see my name spelled out in the bowl. I eat my name, then pull together P-A-U-L, and hand the bowl back to him. He eats the letters and makes the next word: H-U-R-T.

"A little," I say.

He makes another word: P-A-N-D-A.

I nod because even the simplest answer will cause the emotions I'm suppressing to boil over. Paul brings Panda, my stuffed animal, up from the foot of the bed and places her in my arms. I got her when I was six. We were at a carnival, and my dad started playing the ring toss game. He wasn't doing well; those games are a lot trickier than they look, but he kept playing. Toss after toss after toss, my mother and I watched, and with every miss, my hopes of getting a bear got smaller and smaller. My dad, though, he was relentless. He just kept trying until his ring finally landed on the red bottle and the emcee shouted, "We have a winner! Pick anything you'd like." My dad pointed to Panda. Every time I hug Panda, I remember that moment, the expression of love and loss on his face as he held the bear at arm's length for a long moment before handing her off to me. He had such a tender way of holding her that I wondered if he had a Panda himself as a kid. One he lost to the war along with many other possessions. I swore I would protect her for my whole life, and she's been a source of great comfort ever since.

I hug her tight and scoot closer to Paul, who slurps the last of the soup and then climbs into bed beside me. To anyone else, it probably seems lame, but having Paul bring me the soup (even if it is lukewarm) makes the pain almost worth it. He's smarter than I was at his age. He's already catching on to subtext. He knows the soup isn't just food, and Panda isn't just a bear. Because so much is out of our control, we take comfort in the small things and wait for age to free us. While I haven't been able to fully protect him, one thing I've tried to make sure he knows is that he's not at fault for any of it—and that he doesn't deserve it. No one does.

CHAPTER 17

PHÚC

Phúc was drowning again, swallowing water and sinking into darkness, only this time his lungs didn't burn, and though he could see that he was floating, his arms felt dry. *This must be what it feels like to die*, Phúc thought—serene. As he relinquished life in this world, a calm came over him. But before he could fully let go, he felt a thrust from below push him at lightning speed to the surface. He reflexively gasped for air, taking the deepest, most painful breath of his life. A pair of hands grabbed his wrists. With a heave and a jolt, he was pulled on board, where he immediately coughed up salt water and blood. He banged his fists against the floorboard, surprised at his hands' ability to push straight through it, like a bird passing through a cloud—and then he woke up.

Sweating and full of panic, Phúc closed his eyes once again in search of the truth. Who was it that saved him? Who had plucked him from the water? This was the seventh time he'd had this dream. For what felt like an eternity, Phúc was immersed in fever dreams that began and ended just like this one. Afraid and exhausted, he forced himself back into the nightmare, hoping to get to the end this time. Back underwater, he spun like a top, into the familiar chaos of flailing arms and cascading bubbles clouding the water around him. Aware of himself inside the dream, Phúc concentrated on the details. A face in the darkness, the story within the eye of the shark. He repeated his movements until finally, through glassy waves at the calm surface, he saw Thầy Lâm. He would have addressed him as thầy giáo Lâm (teacher Lâm) in class, where every day he'd end up kneeling in the corner because he hadn't bothered to memorize his multiplication tables.

Thầy Lâm had saved his life.

And then he was awake again.

Tears ran down Phúc's face as he crawled over to Thầy Lâm's limp body. No words emerged from Phúc for a long time. So long, in fact, that the sun had set and risen more than once. And in the entirety of this time, Thầy Lâm sat unmoving, a wax figure of pale skin and weakened bone. His body may have been pumping blood, but his mind was gone.

Deacon Chuyên lay asleep next to him with the green vial of medicine tipped over on its side near his broken hand. Phúc grabbed the bottle and poured more of the liquid into Thầy Lâm's mouth.

"Dậy đi, dậy đi Thầy Lâm." But he wouldn't. He wouldn't wake up.

Phúc looked at Thầy Lâm's daughter and poured the rest of the medicine into little Thúy's mouth.

"That's it, that's all I have in the world." And it was. He knew the girl was dead. He could feel it in how stiff her jaw was as he parted her mouth. Good medicine was wasted, but Phúc didn't care.

Deacon Chuyên awoke just then and grabbed at the empty bottle before throwing it at Phúc's head. "You idiot, are you trying to kill me? Can't you see I needed that?"

Phúc was only partly baffled by Deacon Chuyên's response. For being a man of God, he didn't have much compassion for others. But he had always been this way, a hypocrite by nature. Unlike the nuns, who had a devout passion for service, Deacon Chuyên was mainly concerned with his appearance. As an altar boy, Phúc had to iron his outfit and press the sash, something not even the priest ever asked of him. Looking at his finger, Phúc guessed that the pirates cut off his pinky because he refused to give up his gold ring. His vanity had no bounds. As a man ten years Phúc's senior, his lethargy and lack of agency made him more or less dead weight. And as the only other person on the boat with some presence of mind, he made no effort to carry out the acts of living. Instead, he sat there, waiting. For what? Phúc never bothered to ask.

The half-moon became a full moon, and still, the nightmares persisted. Even on nights like this one where the air was tranquil and the breeze warm, Phúc knew that when his eyes closed, the terrors would begin.

Like a jagged knife cutting into the middle of night, bright and vivid turmoil ripped through Phúc's rest. Suddenly he was on the floor with something hard pressed against his head, digging into his ear and crushing his skull. He wasn't able to identify his surroundings even as a large foot stepped into his skewed eyeline. The sun, it seemed, was high in the sky. . . . Or was it low? The world had flipped upside down. Try as he might, Phúc couldn't get his bearings. The brightness blinded him, and respite came only momentarily when a foot or leg passed in front of him. Sometimes this would be all he'd get—flashes of commotion from a disorienting position. A punch to the back of his skull forced his face skyward. The silhouette of a brutish Thai man looked down at him, his eyes full of hatred for a boy he didn't even know.

In another dream, Phúc was lifted off the ground and flung so high he thought for sure he would land in the ocean, but his back hit a pile of bones as he joined the other battered passengers. Luckily, he fell off to the side, escaping the crushing weight of his fellow refugees.

On yet another night, he watched as they pillaged the ship, taking every pot, pan, grain of rice, fish, net, hook, and piece of clothing on the men's and women's backs. Some of the women were seized, too, the younger ones pushed onto the pirate ships. They were the lucky ones. They were being rescued because they had value. That was the only reasonable explanation for why they were taken and Phúc had been left for dead. He was too young to know that what would eventually befall them was a lifetime of torture and indentured servitude. Being left for dead was Phúc's good fortune.

Some nights were filled with blank screams. No faces or imagery, but scratching, clawing, digging, and distraught wailing. Each cry, like a paper cut, slicing deeper into Phúc's ear canals.

The best nights were when Phúc had no dreams at all. But even in daylight there was little reprieve from the vivid images haunting his consciousness. Just glancing at a crack in the wood would trigger a memory, and suddenly he'd be watching a hand mercilessly removed with a hacksaw. A glint of sunlight on a metal grab bar would take him back to the moment Thầy Lâm's daughter was slammed against it—over and over again. And Phúc had to watch as the light in her eyes shifted from a shaking fear to a blank stare, as her body went limp.

Like ghosts with unfinished business, these memories wanted something from him. He tried to tell them that he had nothing to offer. He tried to explain that he could not be the keeper of their presence. He begged them to please just go away. But they refused.

Afraid to sleep, Phúc got to work looking for food. Using a hook and fishing line that he found hidden beneath the floorboard where the now-dead captain used to sit, he sat with his legs dangling over the edge of the boat, hoping to catch food with no bait.

He thought of home. He thought of the Lunar New Year and moon cakes and his mother. He remembered the time he chased and caught Diệp, the prettiest girl in his village, during a game of Rồng Rắn Lên Mây. His hands had only grazed her waist for a second, but he knew then that he wanted to marry her. How trivial his wants had been back then. When memories of home only brought more sadness, he asked himself unanswerable questions. *Why had the pirate left him alive?* It wasn't because he was young; there were children smaller than him on board. Were they God-fearing pirates? Is that why Deacon Chuyên had lived also?

Much later, when Phúc reflected on this moment again, he would conclude that perhaps they simply hadn't wanted to waste a bullet.

He knew he wasn't special, yet the ghosts continued to tug at him, forcing him to remember them. His mind was a spiral of never-ending horrors pushing him to the edge of his sanity.

"Tôi xin lỗi," Phúc apologized. No one answered.

"Không phải là lỗi của tôi ma," Phúc begged. No one told him it was okay.

"Đổi chỗ với tôi đi," Phúc offered. But no one was interested in trading places. They were not at peace, and neither would Phúc be. That was the cost of surviving.

Something brushed against Phúc's back and he turned around to see Deacon Chuyên walking to the opposite side of the ship. Finally, the man had risen from his stupor. Perhaps hunger had propelled him. Phúc swung his legs back inside the boat and did a double take because sitting to his left was Deacon Chuyên. Phúc returned his gaze to the walking man and stared, stunned at the miracle.

Thầy Lâm stood on the opposite side of the bow.

Thầy Lâm was *alive.*

Phúc closed his eyelids tight before opening them again. He had to make sure he wasn't dreaming or, worse, seeing a ghost. For good measure, he pinched his cheeks and slapped himself hard across the face.

This wasn't a dream.

Thầy Lâm stood on his own two legs. Tall and stiff like a birch tree that had once bent with the wind but now stood upright. The spot where his body had lain for weeks was empty save for his shadow, which remained imprinted on the wood. His pants sagged to one side, barely resting on his hips, and, like an element of the wind, his movements made no sound.

Thầy Lâm, Phúc tried to say, but his voice frayed. With great effort, Phúc opened his mouth but only produced a small cough and hiss—a feeble attempt at choking up words. He wanted to express his profound joy at the awakening of his shipmate, especially since this man had saved his life. Unlike Deacon Chuyên, who was an idiot, Thầy Lâm was a teacher; he would have knowledge of survival skills. Together they would figure out how to fish, desalinate water, and propel the boat forward. Phúc's mind spun with all the things they would do together, and a strange feeling washed over him—hope.

Unable to get his voice to cooperate, Phúc knocked on the wooden ledge to get Thầy Lâm's attention.

But Thầy Lâm wasn't looking at him. His mind was elsewhere, somewhere so far in the distance that it might have been the afterlife. The boat rocked, yet Thầy Lâm held himself firm. It was then that Phúc saw the small pair of legs dangling from his arms. With a strength he shouldn't have possessed, Thầy Lâm whispered, "Thúy, con, tha tội cho ba," before taking one step off the side of the ship. Phúc lunged for him, but shock slowed his reaction, and before Phúc could even stand up, they were overboard. Thầy Lâm and the body he was holding hit the water, and a geyser shot upward so fast that Phúc's head swung toward the clouds, expecting to find a prop plane dropping bombs—except the sky was clear.

"Chú!" Phúc croaked. He tripped and stumbled over to where Thầy Lâm previously stood and saw that, unlike the others, Thầy Lâm didn't float. There was a thin stream of bubbles from below, then nothing. Not even a shadow. Staring into the darkness, he looked for an underwater volcano or anything that might explain the massive splash made by a wafer-thin man and his daughter, but there was no landmass in the water. Horrified, Phúc stepped back to survey the deck, to make sure the bodies were gone, to make sure he'd seen what he'd seen.

Pfffffffffffssssssssssst.

Phúc turned at the sound.

Hope. Perhaps that was just a ritual. Perhaps Thầy Lâm just wanted to bury his daughter his own way. Perhaps he was about to emerge anew. Phúc ran across the ship's bow and leaned dangerously over the side in search of a man he hoped would rise from the ocean. *Pffffsst*, again from behind. Phúc spun again as a giant puff of air blasted through the surface, and a gentle spritz of water dusted Phúc's body. Reflexively, he turned away as a single, massive wave of water rained down on him. The splash exploded over him in a starburst of rods that stretched like snakes, disappearing into a star-shaped pool on the deck. The liquid shimmered thick and blue like metallic paint, and Phúc watched as it pooled around his feet and spilled into the cracks between his toes.

Lifting his foot, he found that the slime fell away and left not a trace of residue behind. He wiggled his toes and studied his foot. It was . . . clean. He hadn't realized until this moment just how dirty he was, hygiene not being much of a priority. But looking at his foot, there was a clear and distinct line where his cracked brown skin had turned honey bronze and silky smooth. Even the thin strands of hair on his legs felt soft like fur. Quickly, he jumped into this shallow pool contained by nothing yet somehow *contained*, and he rolled around feeling the grime, the death, the kidnappings, the starvation, and the fear wash off him. When he stood, he felt like a new person. He felt like a man.

Pffffffssst.

Refreshed and magically dry, Phúc stepped toward the sound of spritzing water. A spotted, monolithic gray mass sprang up from the ocean until it was only inches from Phúc's nose. Its giant gray tail covered in barnacles rose like a mountain, and from its top fell the same deep blue liquid that just moments ago had cleansed Phúc. Reaching over with his hand, he rubbed her tail before she, too, went away.

Phúc looked back at Deacon Chuyên to see if he had seen what Phúc had seen, but he sat with his back to him in a depressed slumber where Thầy Lâm and his little girl had once been.

The waves, which Phúc had grown accustomed to, suddenly became eerily still. He scanned the water as his stomach churned the way it did on land after a long day out at sea—except he was still out at sea. Off in the distance, a small figure wearing a pale pink shirt and shorts and a tiny pair of socks surfaced. Blue barnacles reminiscent of giant floating cacti in the ocean glided beneath the child's lifeless body before the entirety of the humpback whale surfaced, presenting the small frame of Thầy Lâm's daughter cradled on its pectoral fin.

The whale moved toward him. Phúc closed his eyes, did the sign of the cross, and when he opened them, the girl was gone. Phúc leaned over close to the giant mass as it glided past. When its fin surfaced, Phúc squeezed it with gratitude and resolution. A smooth, guttural cry emerged from the whale, sounding a universal alarm of sorrow as a large puff of air burst upward and showered the boat with sparkle. And with that, the gentle giant turned on its side, looked directly at Phúc with a glistening eye, and receded below the surface with Thầy Lâm's little girl tightly folded in the nook of her fin as she carried her off to a proper underwater burial.

CHAPTER 18
JANE

The clock always ticks by impossibly slowly after a beating. This early in the night, the bruises haven't quite set in yet. I should be able to sleep, but instead, I'm staring at the red numbers on my alarm clock as the moments tick by one slow minute at a time. I'm wide awake.

"Are you okay?"

So is Paul, apparently.

"I'm fine. Go back to sleep."

"I never fell'd asleep." Of course he hasn't. I don't know why we perpetuate this lie about things being better in the morning. They're not.

Holding my breath, I turn onto my side, and it hurts like hell, but I don't scream.

"I'm fine. See, hands, toes, and intelligence are all intact."

"I could've walked home by myself. I know how."

"I know, but you're only seven, so the cops might think you're lost, and if they pick you up and take you home and see that we aren't there, they'll think you've been neglected, and they'll take you from us."

As I'm telling him this, I remember the time I was followed home by a cop car, and by some miracle, when I got there, my mom was at the apartment. She wasn't supposed to be. She feigned having lost track of time while I pretended to have disobeyed orders and walked home on my own.

Smart kid, the cop had said. If he had been suspicious before, his fears were all but assuaged after that.

"I want to hit him back," Paul says.

"Definitely don't do that."

"Maybe we should run away. I could learn karate."

I start to laugh, but my bruised body snatches the joy and turns it into pain. Karate won't help us find food or shelter, and those are two things we have here in abundance despite everything else. Of course, I've thought about running away. I've even packed a bag, but I've never had the nerve to do it. It's one thing to take off on your own; it's a whole other thing to drag your brother along the road to starvation.

"Let's go, Jane," he pushes. "He won't miss us. He'll probably be glad we're gone."

"Who would help with the store? He can't run it by himself." Why am I making excuses for the person who just beat me senseless? What is wrong with me? I feel an anger surging. I just want Paul to shut up.

"I don't know," Paul admits.

I start to say "me either" but my throat catches, and I end up swallowing the bubbling sob percolating at the base of my throat.

I close my eyes and try to breathe. Paul's not trying to make me feel guilty. Nonetheless, that's the result, and that guilt is making me want to take my balled-up fists and hit the wall. Hot blood really does run in the family. I feel it coursing through my veins, and I'm ashamed to admit that it does feel powerful. I'm even more ashamed to admit that rather than hitting the wall I want to hit Paul. The idea of hitting Paul, someone who has done nothing to me, makes me feel *good*. I hate myself for feeling this way.

And all this is made worse when Paul reaches over and places a gentle arm around me. He's comforting *me*! I want to hit him, and he's trying to make me feel better. I deserve every bad thing that comes to me.

It takes a long while before I feel Paul's arm go limp with sleep. I turn onto my back and breathe softly as silent tears fall from my eyes. You would think that getting hit would make me hate my dad, and as I'm lying here, I do feel some animosity toward him. But I'm not worried about him. I'm worried about me. I think if Paul hadn't stopped talking, I might have actually hit him. I wonder if he sensed it. I can always tell when Dad's blood is beginning to bubble. Sometimes it can be quelled, but not always. What I want to know is, *Did Paul just have to do the same thing with me?* Did he stop asking questions because he thought I might hit him? I know he did.

I have to leave.

Part of me—a very bad part—wonders if hitting Paul will make him *want* me to leave. If I knew he didn't want me to stay, it would be so much easier to go. I know that makes me a coward, but maybe I am a coward.

Jackie's pestering plays on repeat in my mind. *You have to tell him. You have to tell him.*

Lying here next to him, I try to think of how to explain that I am, in fact, running away, only I'm not taking him with me. I'm running away to an institution that will protect me while leaving him to deal with our father's wrath all on his own. I feel sick. There's no good way to say this because there's no explanation that isn't completely and utterly selfish.

If I say it out loud, maybe it won't sound so bad. Things often sound worse in your head, right? I start to say something, but my throat catches on the words again. Paul shifts, and I freeze, but after a few moments, his light breathing assures me he's asleep. I turn to look at him and feel an ache more painful than the punishment. "Paul," I whisper, testing the words, "at the end of the summer, I'm going off to college."

There. Not so bad.

I let the silence hang in the air, unsure of what his real reaction might be. Would he run from our room and slam the door in my face? Yell at me to get away from him? Call me a liar? Tell me that he hates me? Will he care at all?

"Forever?" His voice is so small, I'm barely sure I've heard it. But the moonlight bouncing off his eyes is unmistakable. Paul's awake, and now he knows. I blink away more tears.

"No, not forever. For four years, maybe three, if I study

harder than the other kids. But I'll be back to visit when I can. Like maybe once a month." That last part is a lie. I'm not sure why I'm lying. I know I won't visit that often.

"You're lying. Like Mom lied about coming back." Technically, Mom didn't lie about that. She just never came back. But I know that's not the point. I start to answer, but I find myself full of rage once again. Why am I still suffering for her mistakes? Stupidly, I thought she loved us too. How was I supposed to know she had a strong backbone underneath all of her obedient and subservient Asian wife bullshit? But also, why does everyone else get to act like an asshole while I have to be the perfect big sister?

"Not like Mom did. I told you that to get you to stop crying. I'm sorry she didn't come back. I *will*. Every chance I get. I promise." Why the fuck am I apologizing for her?

He knows I'm angry.

"Okay," he says as he turns his back to me and scoots over to the wall.

Hey, I want to say. *I've been your sister since the day you were born, and I'll be your sister until the day you die. Don't turn your back on me, look at me!* But he's speaking without speaking, and his message is clear: *You're not coming back, and we both know it.* I feel nauseous.

Even when I hear Paul lightly snoring again, I can hardly sleep because I'm hanging on to the faint hope that he'll turn around and hug me. That he'll say all the things a boy his age could never know but that I need to hear.

At 5:34 a.m., where I end up, where I always end up, is understanding that I deserved it. I was caught up in my stupid, selfish daydream, and I completely forgot about Paul. Not that I think daydreaming warrants a beating of any kind. I'm not that delusional. I was careless. I was negligent because it's exhausting being on guard all the time. It's exhausting having to guess at how many different ways I can get into trouble. My mind is always on high alert, and I know it doesn't excuse forgetting Paul, but sometimes I just can't juggle it all.

Oh good, a minute has passed, now it's 5:35 a.m. I don't have to be up until 6:05 a.m., but I've been patient enough and getting dressed is going to take longer today.

The shower is my place of solace. It's where I can cry in private. My shoulders shake and my mind cycles through yet another routine question: *Why does my dad hate me so much?* Though it is not spoken aloud, this question is a blow to my gut, and I lean on the wall for support only to feel a sharp pain as the cold tile presses into a bruise on my shoulder. I know there isn't an answer. If there were one, I would've found it by now. I reach for the shampoo, and a second pain shoots up my spine. Instinctively, I lower to my knees, the only position that minimizes the spasms, and try to catch my breath. My eyes, blurry from a mixture of tears and water, see only patches of white. I don't want to, but I have no choice. The only position that doesn't sting is flat on my stomach at the bottom of the tub—the same position I took during the beating.

For a moment, I think I might not be able to get up. If the tub were plugged, I could drown. I almost long for it. But then time passes, as it always does, and I find myself rising once again.

My towel, usually a warm welcome in the cold morning air, pinpricks my skin like a million tiny daggers. I don't want to press hard but pressing lightly only lengthens the duration of pain. I start with my legs and sip pockets of air as I move the towel up my body. When I reach my face, I press hard against my cheeks and scream. No sound comes out, though, because I'm too afraid someone will hear me.

The process of getting dressed takes three times longer than it should, but once the clothes are on, they become a part of me, and the pain subsides. Except for the jeans. Pulling my jeans on is so excruciating that I have to stop and lean on the sink several times before continuing. When it finally comes time to button the waist, I fight to push past the pain, but I can't do it. The area around my waist is so bruised that the dense fabric touching my skin causes me to recoil. My jeans will have to go unbuttoned with an extra-long T-shirt to cover up.

On days like this, it's impossible to concentrate on anything but how painful it is to sit on the metal stool behind the counter of the register. So, I stand. But because I'm not actually moving much, my feet begin to ache. And because time is such a bitch, the day drags. Every tick of the second hand on the clock feels like a personal jab of retribution from the universe. I must have been a really shitty person in another life. Like a fly to a trap, I can't help but stare at the clock. Sometimes I stare so hard that I swear I'm able to force time to pass a nanosecond faster. Usually, when I can't stand it any longer, I start making deals with God.

"You screwed me. You really did, you know that? I'll play along for Paul, but in my next life, I better come back as a princess." I know. It sounds more like a demand than a deal, but I don't care. I'm a good person. I don't deserve this. He owes me. God owes me big.

I look at Paul curled up at my feet. I dragged him to work with me because I didn't want to leave him at home with Dad. When Dad is unpredictable, he is a nightmare to be around. Usually, he's calmer after a long night of disciplining . . . but not always. Plus, I need Paul to forgive me, and there's nothing like forcing someone to be stuck next to you inside a five-by-ten-foot bulletproof glass box to make them forgive you faster. Yet another thing I've taken from my dad's playbook.

CHAPTER 19
PHÚC

"How come the whale didn't take Dad too?" Paul asks.

"Take him where?"

"To safety."

I consider explaining to Paul that Thúy is dead, but I decide I kind of like his misinterpretation. "I don't know. I guess Phúc wasn't so lucky."

After multiple sunrises and sunsets and still no tugging on his hook, Phúc started to think he might actually starve to death. He didn't have any bait, and though he could see small schools of fish darting about below the surface, he knew that if he went into the water, it would be too easy to let go—to give up. If his nightmares were any indication of what waited on the other side, then death was worse than life. As he thought about this, he felt a tug. The pull was so sudden that he nearly lost his grip and let the line go completely. *Lift and release, lift and release,* he reminded himself. His heartbeat quickened in nervous anticipation as he carefully wound the fishing line around the width of a torn green sandal. *Nice and easy,* he breathed. But his stomach growled, and his mind began racing with how he might prepare this meal, the first in nearly five days.

Then the struggle stopped. Something wasn't right. The line wasn't limp—the hook had definitely caught on something—but there wasn't nearly enough tugging on the other end.

Maybe it's just a really small fish, he hoped. "That would be okay," Phúc whispered to the universe. If he humbled himself, maybe God would have mercy and help him. But he knew that wasn't true.

The line stopped giving. When Phúc pulled, it stayed taut. The hook was caught.

Phúc tugged lightly, afraid he might accidentally break the wire. It held firm. A lot of the line was wrapped around the sandal, and he could afford to pull and rip the line *if* he had another hook . . . but he didn't. Slipping the sandal underneath the weight of an extra-large bamboo basket that was filled with all the random, useless items Phúc had collected on the ship, he set about looking for another hook. If he could find one, he could afford to lose this one—sort of. Having scoured the boat before, he knew the only places a hook might be hiding were behind the bodies. He hadn't dared to move them before. They were his only hope of life. But now he was desperate. Flies buzzed around the rotting flesh, and as soon as he shifted the first body, the stench he thought he had gotten used to blasted his nostrils with a shock wave so fierce he nearly fainted.

He stepped away to clear his senses, took a deep breath, and started lifting the remaining four bodies one by one up onto the ledge. There, he pushed them over the rest of the way. The act itself was physically draining, but, mentally, something shifted. Knowing they were all really dead emboldened him to live. To survive despite the odds. Now only he and Deacon Chuyên remained on the boat.

"Get up," Phúc shouted at Deacon Chuyên. "Help me." But the man simply rolled over, curling back into himself.

Annoyed, Phúc left him alone and began looking for useful tools among the things left behind. Behind the woman who had died clutching her rosary was a messy, tangled ball of tarred hemp rope. Her prayers hadn't been answered, but maybe Phúc's would be. Quickly grabbing the line, Phúc set about detangling it.

Phúc was used to untying knots. In fact, that had been his first job. As a kid loitering at the docks, the local fishermen would pay him 500 đồng to untangle their nets after an excursion. His tiny hands, abundance of time, and low cost made him a commodity. He hadn't thought of it as a useful skill until now.

Phúc spent so much of his childhood mastering the art of detangling that he saw each task as a puzzle only he could solve. As he tugged at the rope's thick cord, it refused to budge. Lumpy tar adhered to clumps of the knotted line, making it impossible to find the end. This rope was about a centimeter thick, much thicker than any fishing net material, so the knots were easy to spot but not easy to untie. Shaking from hunger, it took every mental faculty he could muster to not throw the rope overboard in defeat.

Wiping droplets of sweat from his strained eyes, Phúc concentrated on one part at a time, cutting carefully at the tarred sections with a dull razor blade. Several hours later, with the sun just feet above the horizon, the tangled line finally unraveled.

Then came the hard part. Without an extra hook, Phúc would have to use this rope to tether himself to the boat while attempting to retrieve the stuck one.

After tying a knot several extra times for safety, Phúc tugged on the rope to make sure it was securely attached, took a deep breath, and jumped into the water. The cold hit him unexpectedly, and then his foot landed on something soft. He looked down and screamed, which, in turn, filled his lungs with water. Beneath his foot was the body of the rosary-clutching lady he'd hauled overboard. Empty of air and full of panic, he fought his way back to the surface.

"Hhhhhhh," he breathed, reaching for the security of the boat only to find that the lip of the vessel was much higher than expected.

"Deacon Chuyên, let me borrow your hand," Phúc called. He didn't come. Kicking as hard as he could, Phúc was only able to leap about two feet. Not enough to reach the ledge. "Deacon Chuyên!" Phúc's lip began to quiver, his heart hammered in his chest, and his breathing quickened as his mind raced with images of the zombie bodies below coming after him.

Focus, he told himself. He still needed that hook.

Swimming toward the back of the boat, where he knew the fishing line was dangling, he scanned the horizon for a thin transparent line glinting against the dim pink sky. Once spotted, he swam to it, wrapped his palm gently around it, took a deep breath, and dove down into the unknown.

Salt water stung his eyes, but he forced them open, pushing away thoughts of decomposing body particles drifting into them. Deeper and deeper, he swam.

Stay calm, he chanted as his lungs burned.

Leaving his fears at the surface, Phúc kicked forward. He ignored the thick, slimy seaweed that brushed against his body, even as it engulfed him and a giant sheet stuck to his face. Peeling the slime away, he reflexively expelled a burst of air and was about to give up when a silver sparkle of light caught his eye. There, just a few feet away, was his hook, pierced deep in the center of a yellow bulb.

He thrust himself forward, squeezed his fingers around the metal, and, with a firm and determined grip, pulled the entire branch of kelp toward himself. It came loose surprisingly easily, and Phúc immediately raced upward, exploding at the surface with gasping breaths. Kicking his feet to stay afloat, he made sure to thread the hook through his shirt so he didn't accidentally let it go, and he followed his safety rope back to the boat.

Checking his shirt to make sure the threaded hook was still there, he slowly swam around the boat, looking for its lowest point—which appeared to be the stern. Again, he leaped, and this time he was able to reach the lip, but his arms shook and he couldn't pull himself up.

"Deacon Chuyên!"

Phúc tried again. Then a third time. He came close that third time, but still he fell back into the water. As his failed attempts tugged at his insecurities, he considered letting himself drift away. He even thought, *If the boat gets far enough away, I'll have no choice but to drown.* The edge of the ship was right in front of him, though, and the ocean was calm. Salvation was too close.

Yanking on the slack of his safety rope until it became taut, he wrapped his shirt around his hand for extra grip and pressed his feet against the algae-covered bottom of the boat. With his toes gripped tight, he walked himself up the backside of the vessel. The rope groaned and stretched under the pressure of his weight, but it held—if only barely. Pulling himself the rest of the way onto the boat, Phúc collapsed on the deck with his heart thundering. Feeling something clutching at his feet, he looked down and saw seaweed wrapped around his ankles like a vine crawling up a post. He kicked it away in disgust only to be pulled upright in pain into a sitting position. Noticing blood spilling from his finger, he burst into a thunderous laugh. The hook he was certain he had attached to his shirt was now lodged deep inside the tip of his thumb. He tried to pull it loose, but it only bled more profusely. So, he took a deep breath, gritted his teeth, and pulled both the hook and a chunk of his finger free.

And then an idea struck him. He took the hook, now fitted with his flesh, tugged lightly to secure it, and dropped the line in the water.

Ten minutes passed.

Twenty.

Patience was a boring task. Seconds stretched for hours until his hand lifted with a jolt.

Tug.

TUG.

The line, which was wrapped around his wrist, cut into his skin. He had known this would happen, but he had no other reel locking mechanism. Phúc jumped into action, grabbing his crude fishing rod made using that same green sandal, and he began rolling the line toward himself. Whatever he had caught wiggled and thrashed about like crazy.

Splash.

Wiping his face with his shirt, Phúc pulled himself up to peer over the side, half-expecting his shark friend to be hanging on to his catch, ready for a game of tug-of-war. Had Mập been lurking in the dark blue water, Phúc might've just crawled over and dropped into his jaws. He was done trying. Luckily Phúc's body continued to generate energy despite his malnutrition. It didn't feel lucky, though. Waking up was disappointing. To wake up was to be crushed with the weight of existence. Mập was nowhere to be seen. Instead, he found signs of life tugging at the other end of his line.

Carefully, he reeled in his catch and hoisted it above the water and then onto the boat. A large, brown-spotted halibut flopped, its mouth agape.

The diamond-shaped flatfish with spikes all along its top and bottom was Phúc's favorite. Flash-fried, the spiked rim could be munched on like shrimp chips. But he didn't have a fryer or any oil for that matter. He would have to eat the halibut raw. As hunger knotted his stomach, he picked up the slimy fish and brought it to his mouth. His lips, thick with grime, wrapped around the scaled flesh, but no sooner had his tongue touched the scales than he began to dry heave. Dropping to his knees, Phúc released his grip on the fish, dropped it to the floor, and watched its tail flap helplessly as it thrashed about. Scales flew like shavings being cast from a rainbow-colored ice block until finally, like the trailing end of a song, the beating of life slowed, with each breath followed by a more prolonged stillness than the last . . . and then it stopped moving altogether.

As he looked at the fish, Phúc wondered if this was how he, too, would die. One slow breath at a time—the stillness between one gulp of air and the next expanding—until his body, weak from dehydration and hunger, could no longer muster up the strength it needed to inhale at all.

Phúc sat staring at the fish for a long while. His hand moved along its slippery body. How odd, Phúc thought, that his fingers were not cold or slimy. And then the fish lifted, levitated really, and Phúc watched it move into the mouth of Deacon Chuyên. He looked down. His hands were empty.

Rage filled his body as he lunged for his catch.

"You weren't going to eat it, so why shouldn't I?" Deacon Chuyên spat, grabbing at the spikes, but the halibut slipped from his grasp, and as he reached forward for it, Phúc slammed his foot down on the man's now gangrenous finger. Pain gripped the uncle and he grudgingly retreated.

Keeping his eyes trained on Deacon Chuyên, Phúc brought the fish to his mouth once more, and this time he tore into its flesh with his teeth and ate. One bite, two bites, three bites . . . all of it. Phúc devoured every morsel. There was no way he was going to let Deacon Chuyên have even the tiniest bit of his meal.

CHAPTER 20

JANE

This is the largest family gathering I've ever been to, and the guest of honor is . . . eccentric. Our family is scattered across the US and travel is expensive, so get-togethers are rare, but this is a special occasion. My aunt O Uyên just immigrated here from Vietnam. I guess Chú Thịnh got his paperwork in order after all. My dad's sister is two years younger than he is. She's flashy in the way she dresses, and her husband is a wallflower by comparison. I can't make sense of them as a married couple, him with frayed vocal cords and her with a booming voice that carries throughout the house. O Uyên's dynamic with him is so the opposite of everything Vietnamese that I can't stop watching how she bosses him around, and he just *takes* it. Their two sons speak zero English, and because my Vietnamese is terrible, I avoid them like the plague. I thought Chú Thịnh didn't have kids, but of course, they lived in Vietnam with their mother, so I just hadn't ever met them. Their relationship with their father is even more interesting. It's like they're complete strangers. To his credit, though, Chú Thịnh is trying. He introduced them to everyone and walked them through the buffet, asking what they wanted to eat. To an American, this probably seems normal, but Vietnamese men never serve their wives, let alone their children. It's disrespectful to the natural hierarchy or something.

Fifty or more people are sprawled out in every room of the home, including hallways. It's so crowded that personal space can only be found in the bathroom, and even then, there are people sitting right beside the door. People drove in from Texas, Florida, Tennessee, Michigan, Connecticut, Orange County (down south), and, of course, the neighboring cities of Sacramento, Modesto, and Stockton.

I'm sitting on a stool in the kitchen. I chose it because I'm near the food, and I can kind of pretend like I'm busy shredding lettuce or something. Paul ditched me for Stephen, who took him to some other part of the house. I watch as the adults greet one another with more joy than I thought a Vietnamese person could muster. They're not exactly crying, but it's emotional.

They're hugging too—well, the women are, anyway. The men pat each other on the back or vigorously shake hands. Everyone is in awe of the reconnection. It's as though they didn't expect to see one another ever again. Like they hadn't planned a reunion at all but just happened to run into each other here.

My dad's eyes are glassy. He looks like he's seeing ghosts. I've never considered how lonely he might be with just me and Paul.

"Ey! There's the big shot liquor store owner," Bác Chuyên

says. It's only 2:00 p.m., and he's already wasted. "These guys, they don't have a business sense, but you do. I have an idea."

My dad shrugs the man off like he's a stranger—like he wasn't just shooting the shit behind our store with him, Bác Luy, and Chú Thịnh a couple of weeks ago. He ignores Bác Chuyên and moves into the group of men who all seem to know him. They hand him a beer and he sits on the complete opposite side of Bác Chuyên, who spots me and immediately approaches.

"Chào Bác Chuyên," I say, and lean as far back from him as I can without tipping off my stool.

"Giỏi," he praises as he drunkenly grabs at my nose, twists, and pulls. I instinctively dip away to remove my nose from his grip and have to hold the counter to keep from falling. He finds this hilarious as he turns to grab another beer from one of the coolers on the floor and returns to his seat in the patio.

Across the room is a group of ten or so people. Some older and others around my age or a few years younger than me. Everyone, except for Becky, Vicky, and me, appears to know each other. Of course, no one is more in the margins than me; even my fobby cousins were invited to join the group.

I must be staring because one of the girls shouts "Hey, you!" and she's looking right at me. Like an idiot, I turn around to check behind me. "Yes, you. Come over here."

I awkwardly slide off my stool and approach them with caution. Like a powerful predator sensing easy prey, she bursts into laughter.

"Dude, come over here. We don't bite. Well, maybe John does, but he's mostly bark."

John looks like a gangster. He's got tattoos all up his arms, and the bleached spikes on the top of his head are so sharp they look like they'll prick my finger if I touch them. "Shut up, Thi. You're scaring her. What's your name?"

"Jane."

"Jane, next time Bác Chuyên grabs your nose like that, just slap him," Thi says. I laugh awkwardly because she must be joking. "I'm serious. You're Cậu Phúc's daughter, right?" she continues.

"Yeah." *How did they know that?*

"Your dad hates Bác Chuyên. Actually, pretty much everyone does. Except for Chú Thịnh, who loves wounded birds, and Uncle Jerk Face exploits it," Thi says. "But he screwed your dad when he was just a kid. You know, he sent your dad to work in Hong Kong and collected his wages for two years? Stole his fish too! Such an asshole. Can you believe he used to be a deacon in Vietnam?"

I have no idea what she's talking about, so I ask, "Are we related?" And again, I am met with laughter. She calls my dad "Cậu," which means we are related through her mother, so her mom must be my dad's other sister. Or, she could just be using the prefix as a term of endearment. The adults do that sometimes just to make things harder for us kids.

"Yeah, girl. Look around, we *all* family. Your dad is my mom's younger brother. My mom is . . . there. She's O Linh to you." She points to her mom, and I recognize her as the aunt we ate a sandwich with near the airport. Thi then lists off nearly every adult in the room and how they are related to me. A few of the relations are so loosely related that I question whether or not we should be considered family. As Thi looks around, she spots a man wearing black slacks and a polo shirt who looks like a car salesman ready to make a deal. "He's Grandpa's brother's son. But because he's Grandpa's younger brother, even though he's older than your dad, he has to call your dad Anh." Confusing.

"But, like, your dad didn't mention us at all? I'm offended. Hey, Cậu Phúc, how come your daughter doesn't know who we are?" Thi yells at my dad. My dad ignores her because he's busy talking to the other adults. "Rude." She laughs.

"Becky and Vicky are the only 'cousins' I know."

Thi bursts out laughing yet again. "Oh my god, Jane. They're like your furthest cousins. No offense, girls." They shrug like they're not offended, but I sense a little bit of jealousy that these cool cousins are more closely related to me than them. "I guess it kind of makes sense that you would think that given how long your dads have known each other. They have the same tortured sense of humor."

"Yeah, we have a photo in our house of my dad, your dad, a white guy, and a Chinese guy at the top of some half-built high-rise," Vicky says. I've never seen this photo and am inclined to think she's lying because she wants to impress the cousins. I consider pressing her on it but decide not to lest I should end up looking like the asshole.

"So, how are we all—" I start to ask.

"Don't think about it too long. It'll give you a headache trying to get it all straight. But we're pretty much all cousins." She points to each person around the table and lists off their name and location. "I'm Thi from Connecticut. That's my brother, John, and my sister, Trâm." Trâm waves at me. She's obviously the shy one in the family. "Over here is Mỹ, Thiết, and Khiên. They're all from Denver. Bảo is the wild child from Vegas. And Mike is from Florida. You can tell by his dark skin and stupid hair." Mike's hair is parted down the middle and is so long that when he tilts his head to the side it falls over his eye.

"What? Fuck you, Thi." Mike laughs. "You're just jealous we got sunshine year-round."

"Hey, can you guys slow it down? I can't translate that fast for the boys," Trâm says.

"No. Ân, Xuân, you gotta learn to listen closely," Thi says in Vietnamese.

"That's mean. Just because you had a hard time . . . ," Trâm argues, though her tone is meek, like she already knows her sister isn't going to back down.

And she doesn't. "Who is going to slow down their conversations at school for them? It's bad enough that they're going to get made fun of for being FOBs."

No one says anything because Thi's right. And even though no one knows this about me, I look down ashamed, thinking about how Jackie and I are *those* kids.

"I un-der-stan a li-tle bit," Xuân says, in really good English for a guy who's been here for less than twenty-four hours.

"Boom! See, they're smarter than you give them credit for, Trâm."

Trâm rolls her eyes and tells them in Vietnamese not to listen to anything Thi says. Everyone laughs.

Mike turns to Vicky and me. "How is it that you both live in Cali and don't know how your dads met?"

Vicky and I look at each other, but neither of us says anything. We both know that her family stopped talking to mine after my mom left. No one wanted to be associated with the broken household.

Sensing the tension, Thi says, "This is why we gotta have more family reunions. My parents don't tell me shit either. I hear everything from them." She points to Mỹ, Thiết, and Khiên and whispers loudly to me, "Their mom loves to gossip. She knows everything about everyone."

"That's true," Khiên says. "I heard they just recently realized that Grandpa fixed Bác Luy's arm after he was hit with shrapnel." I'm shocked by this, not by the information because I'd obviously heard it the night he came over, but that somehow my cousins from another state also knew about it.

"Anyway, you're in San Jose, right? Your dad owns the liquor store?" Thi asks, cutting into my thoughts.

"Yeah," I say. *How does she know so much about me?*

"Your dad was calling around asking if anyone wanted to come help him run your shop. He's funny. He was all like, 'You can tell your kids to bring their baggy pants and gangster hair because they'll fit right in.'" The whole table laughs.

"Oh shit, that's messed up," Mike says. If he is offended, it hardly shows through his hiccupping laugh. "When he saw me, he asked my dad why I was so fat. 'No more alligators in Florida or something?' he said. Like we all be running from alligators all the time. Your dad's hilarious."

I'm pretty sure they have the wrong person. My dad is *not* hilarious. "When was he asking people to come work?" I ask.

"Couple months ago, probably. Apparently, you're the smarty-pants cousin. Going to UCLA or some shit, right?"

"Yeah." A couple of months ago, I hadn't even told him about the acceptance letter. But apparently he knew all along. I wonder if he opened the letter and then resealed it, but that's ridiculous because my dad wouldn't bother. Graduation? But how? I touch the gold necklace around my neck. He gave it to me the night of my graduation, but he never mentioned attending the ceremony. I look over at my dad. The adults have gathered themselves into a haphazard circle, and when my godmother, O Vui, sing-speaks a line, we all turn to look.

None of them are very good singers, but they're riffing off each other to sing a story. Each one takes a line in this impromptu performance meant only for themselves.

"In the night the bombs dropped and we huddled in fear."

"In the night the bombs dropped and we ran for home."

"In the night the bombs dropped and we said our goodbyes."

"But I miss our homeland."

"And I miss our homeland."

"And I miss our homeland."

"In the night the bombs dropped and I couldn't breathe."

"In the night the bombs dropped and there was nowhere to go."

"In the night the bombs dropped and . . ."

I've never understood musical theater before—like, why sing what you can just say?—but now I think I might get it. They're saying what they mean but the words could never express the depth of their commiseration—so it has to be sung. This must be why my dad's generation loves karaoke. I stare in disbelief at my dad as he clinks beers with his siblings or cousins or whoever they are. My dad is laughing deep, bellyaching laughs—the kind that draw tears—and it's like seeing a stranger in his body. Nothing about what they're discussing is funny, and he isn't laughing because it's funny, he's laughing because crying is not an option. I know this because sometimes when I'm getting hit for no real reason, I have an insane ache to laugh too.

When I turn back to the cousins, we all kind of stare dumbly at one another until Bảo says, "Forget their trauma. Let's talk about *my* trauma. My dad whooped my ass so hard I couldn't bend over for a week." Bảo's a clean-cut guy with thin shoulders and glasses that give him bug eyes.

He doesn't look like someone who would take a beating well. "I was ditching like every day, and normally I get home before they do, so I can delete the school's voicemail, but for whatever reason, my dad was home, and he actually answered the call. Man, he chased me all the way around the block with a broomstick! But the next day, I ditched again, because I'm stubborn as fuck, except this time I know I'm in deep shit, so I have my friend circle the block and wait for me when I get home. I, like, barely got to the door, and my dad is running after me with a knife!"

"No way," Thiết says. She's wearing a tube top underneath overalls—clothes I wouldn't be caught dead in. She has dark brown lipstick and highly arched eyebrows that make her look mean even though her demeanor suggests she'd take in every stray cat on the planet if she could.

"But he wouldn't have actually stabbed you," Thi adds.

"I didn't wait around to see. I got the fuck outta there!"

"My dad uses the stick—" Mỹ says. She's a tall, athletic girl wearing jeans and a bright pink sports bra under a white tank top.

"—from behind the glass door?" John laughs, jumping in. "Yeah, my dad's broken like five of those across my ass too."

A collective "Ooooohhh" fills the table.

"Oh please, don't feel sorry for him. He's the troublemaker. If you wanna feel sorry for anyone, it should be me. I'm the one who's always getting whooped by proxy," Trâm says.

"Yeah, I feel kinda bad about that," John laughs.

"My dad used to beat us for no freaking reason except that he was mad. After I figured that out, I just did whatever I wanted. I mean, if you're gonna beat me anyway, I might as well have some fun. I felt bad for my siblings, too, though, because when one of us fucked up, we all got the stick," Mike said.

"Where are your sisters and brother?" Mỹ asks.

"Adam is over there playing games, and my sisters are watching the shop. My dad doesn't trust me to do it." He laughs.

I can't believe these people are related to me. They're bold, fearless, and confident—everything I'm not.

I want to hear more stories, but Mỹ changes the subject. "You guys ever get called into the principal's office after being cạo gió?" I laugh, knowing where this going. Cạo gió is a Vietnamese health practice meant to release toxins from the body, but the end result leaves red markings on your back that look like lashings. In English, we call it coining.

"Oh my god. Stupid Trâm. She thought it would be funny to tell them our parents beat us, which is true, except this time, it was the coining, and the freaking principal pulled everyone out of class. Like, not only my siblings but our cousins, too, and they, like, bring us into the principal's office and ask us if we've been abused and shit. In my head, I'm thinking, 'Hell yeah, but not like that!' That shit ain't nothin'." John is laughing as he says this.

I watch Vicky as my cousins are talking, waiting for her to chime in, but she never says a word. Neither does Becky.

Trâm smirks. Trâm has short hair cut in a stylish bob, light makeup that makes her face always look flush, and red-rimmed glasses. "I didn't think they'd believe me. I told them this fat bitch Joanne choked me in the hallway between periods, and they didn't do shit."

"Anyway, my mom had to call our doctor to fucking explain what cạo gió-ing is and how it's Eastern medicine and shit."

"We got hot blood running in our family. That's for damn sure." Thi laughs.

"Not me," Mỹ says.

"Bullshit. Someone steal this girl's Sour Patch Kids and see what happens," Thi counters.

"That's how I stay so zen. I need the sour to counteract the hot," Mỹ says deadpan. I think she's serious too.

"One time, John pissed me off so bad I took my tennis racket and whacked him on the head. Ya know, because of our hot blood." Thi laughs.

John lowers his head to show us a small scar running between his spikes. "True, and I got the scar to prove it."

I think about the rage I feel toward Paul sometimes and wonder if maybe it's genetic. They all go at each other so hard and somehow remain tight. So, maybe this is how our family shows affection? Maybe hitting each other makes us closer.

Bảo speaks again. "Yeah, but our parents be crazy for real. I don't know if it's our blood or what, but they're wack sometimes. Like, before homecoming, or maybe it was prom, I did something stupid, I forget what it was, but my dad threw a fucking hammer at my face. Broke my fucking nose and shit." His dad is starting to sound like a maniac.

"He's got the homecoming picture to prove it too." Mỹ laughs. "I can't believe Nancy still went with your ugly face."

Bảo turns to show us his profile. "You're just jealous because it made me more handsome."

This causes the table to erupt into laughter that lasts for a full minute. I'm laughing so hard my stomach hurts. My cousins are all so different than I am, but the longer we talk, the more like family they become.

There's a silence after the laughter dies down, and many of us wipe tears away from our faces.

"Last week . . ." I hear my own voice speaking before my brain realizes it. I pause, not wanting to say this aloud but also not wanting to miss this opportunity to contribute my experiences. I let it spill. "I forgot to pick Paul up from school"—looking over my shoulder, I check to make sure my dad isn't around—"and I got the *shit* kicked out of me. I got hit so hard I've been sitting sideways for a week."

"Ohhh, did he make you stand against a wall?"

"What kind of stick?"

"Those fuckin' doorjambs, man."

They are sympathetic without pitying me, and this conversation, which I've never had with another person, feels . . . normal.

Behind us, O Uyên is distributing small gifts from Vietnam: silk scarfs for the women, dried squid for the men, and a thin bamboo flute, which she puts in front of my dad. Dad takes the flute and presses it to his mouth. When he blows, it sounds just like I'd expect it to if a child picked it up and tried to play for the first time. But then he adjusts his grip, and a sweet flutter of notes emerges. *Just luck?* I wonder.

"Did you know your dad could play?" Trâm asks me. I shake my head.

Inhaling deeply, my dad blows again, and the first note sounds like a high-pitched whistle. My shoulders relax, and I'm surprised to find myself relieved. Of course he can't play. If my dad knew how to play the flute, *I* would know. But instead of lowering the instrument, he adjusts his posture and tries again. This time, the room is filled with the rounded whistle of a single note.

The bamboo flute is unlike any American instrument. Its

hollowed core sounds like the wind passing through the mountains. It's a sound that fills the room while simultaneously expanding it.

From the wall, another instrument is pulled. It's the sixteen-string Vietnamese zither, the đàn tranh, that my music teacher Chú Quang played that one day. The three-foot-long instrument is placed in front of Bác Luy. I look at Becky and Vicky, but they don't make eye contact.

Bác Luy plucks a note that reverberates throughout the space and silences the house. It sounds like a sitar mixed with a harp. I think back to the landscapes in my dad's karaoke videos and wonder if all Vietnamese instruments come from nature.

When he starts playing, my dad joins in with the flute. Together they sound like a band. As they play, I imagine the walls falling away, grass taking over the carpet, couches turning into moss-covered rocks. In my mind's eye, we've all jumped inside a karaoke video landscape—we're in Vietnam. Leaves and vines complete with swinging langur monkeys sway to the beat of his music as offshoots of greenery crawl along my dad's legs and body. The vines slither around his waist and up across his shoulders until they reach the end of his flute. With nowhere else to go, the plant reaches forth, creating a sweet flutter at the end of every note.

I've never been to Vietnam before, but I suddenly feel drawn to it. Maybe it's like my grandma always says, *Don't go thinking you're American—you're not. Your roots were born in the Vietnamese soil. No matter where you go, Vietnam is a part of you.* I didn't understand what she meant before, but now I think

I might. This song feels like it was created by some extension of myself. For as long as I can remember, I've turned my back on anything remotely Vietnamese. I haven't wanted to see my heritage as being a part of me because I've always associated it with . . . well, everything bad that happens to me.

When the song ends, I look around at the broken smiles held tight by nothing but grit, and something changes in me. The room, now a museum of statues, makes me uncomfortable. Without the music, it's all too raw. It's almost as if I can taste their pain. And I'm not the only one.

With glassy eyes, Thi says, "See, that right there is something only family understands. It's how you can be smacked silly by someone and still love the heck out of them. Try explaining that to your American friends." I feel myself wanting to cry. I bite my cheek. *What the fuck, Jane? Stop it.* If I weren't in a room full of people, I'd slap myself. *This guy beat the crap out of you last week. Your ass still hurts right now because of him, and you're gonna cry because he played a sad song on the flute?*

"Speak for yourself," John says to Thi. "I got enough friends in jail to know I don't wanna be up in there, but believe me, the thought of returning punches has crossed my mind. Especially when he hits my sisters." His defiance grinds our conversation to a halt, and, for the first time, I feel uncomfortable. I don't know whether to laugh or feel guilty for not being as fiercely protective of Paul.

But then Mike says, "I mean, you could also just stop being such a fuck-up," and it cuts the tension immediately. John throws the spiked red peel of the chôm chôm fruit he's just popped into his mouth at Mike, who slaps it away before Trâm scolds them for making a mess.

Somewhere in the back of my mind, I've always known that our family's fondness for suffering came from actual suffering, the kind only children of war can comprehend, but I've never wanted to acknowledge it . . . to acknowledge that my dad has been through some shit, has seen things I don't even want to imagine. And he is broken—perhaps justifiably so. At the adult table someone sighs loudly and humphs, which breaks them from their trance as well, and Bác Nguyệt thankfully ushers in the food.

The adults start eating, the kids go back to playing, and the chatter from before returns.

"Hey, Jane. You know that's how your dad and mom met, right?" Thi says. "She fell for the sweet flutter of the flute." Thi swoons like it's so romantic, and I want to barf.

"All my mom ever said was that they didn't know each other that well before getting married," I say.

"I heard the story because my mom talks to everyone using speakerphone, and your mom's brother's wife, Mợ Bích, was talking about it." Thi looks at her mom, who is completely oblivious to our conversation. "Anyway, they met on that last boat from Hong Kong to Guam before they were flown to the US and separated. And then, some time later, they happened to run into each other at the Asian Garden Mall in Orange, and that's when they decided to get married."

All of this is news to me. "How does your mom know Mợ

Bích?" Mơ Bích is on my mom's side, so it's odd that she knows my dad's sister.

Thi shrugs.

"That was a fucked-up journey, though," Bảo says. "No one believes me, but I remember shit. I was only, like, five at the time, but I swear the images are clear as day."

"Yeah, as clear as hallucinations can be," Trâm says.

"It wasn't a hallucination!"

"Oh, here we go," Thi groans.

"I'm telling you guys I saw this giant manatee come up right beside our boat, and she like protected us until we were rescued. I remember her eyes were as big as my hands, and she was right there next to me. Animals know. They can sense our pain."

"Or, she was waiting for you to fall over so she could eat you!" Trâm laughs.

"No, that shit was magic."

"Seriously, though, that's some PTSD shit. I mean, I don't remember shit because I was like two when we came over, but the war was fucked," Mỹ says.

"It annoys the shit out of me that they only talk about the American side in our history books," Thi says, looking directly at me for some reason.

"You guys were refugees?" I ask. I didn't think kids fled during the war. It's stupid now that I think about it, but I guess I've never really put much thought into it.

"Yeah, girl. Your dad's only like eight or nine years older than me. I just have that forever youthful look." Thi smiles. "But

I don't remember much about the journey because, apparently, they drugged me to keep me quiet."

"Which explains a lot," John says, twirling his finger next to his head.

Thi shoves him. "Shut up. I remember more than you fools. Not the boat ride, but living in Vietnam. Like I remember saving wax because we used candles for light. Oh, and one night before we left Vietnam, O Uyên called me into the courtyard, where she had a bucket of water. She stood me directly in front of it, pointed to the sky, and said, 'You see that moon? Catch it.' I, of course, had no idea what she was talking about, but I'm like six, so I swiped at the sky until finally, she grabbed my shoulders, moved me a foot to the left, and pointed to the bucket, where the moon was reflected perfectly within it."

"That's so cool," I say. I can't imagine anyone in my family being that creative. I wonder, though, if she purposefully evaded my question or if she really has no recollection of the escape.

"It was, until I smacked the water with the palm of my hand and got us both wet. She twisted my ear so hard it tingled for like a week! I must have ruined her suede shoes or something."

I laugh.

Since the adults are drunk, we all camp inside the house. It's my first-ever sleepover.

Somehow a ton of blankets appear, gathered from the house itself and from each of the dozen or so cars parked on the street. I grab the two blankets we have in the rear of my dad's truck, which double as seat cushions because the back seats are more or less just two plastic butt divots with seat belts. Plastic mats and sheets are rolled open, covering every inch of the floor, and we all find a spot to crash. Paul and I huddle between a couch and Thi, who is lying head-to-toe with the rest of the cousins.

Ten minutes ago, I was yawning and could barely keep my eyes open, but now I'm wide awake. I'm wondering why Jackie and I haven't had conversations like this before. Like right now, I'm not even sure how exactly to bring it up to her, and I tell Jackie *everything*.

CHAPTER 21
PHÚC

In the middle of the ocean, the currents are circular; they never push you toward land, they just turn you around and around.

To the left—nothing.

To the right—nothing.

Behind—nothing.

Front—obviously, nothing.

Stuck in the middle of nowhere were Phúc and an incompetent idiot drifting in an abyss with nothing to do but wait for death.

It was laughable how ill-prepared they were to survive at sea. Or maybe they had a plan and could have made do had most of their supplies not been stolen or damaged, but shouldn't somebody have planned for that? Now there was nothing useful on the ship, not even a compass to indicate which direction might lead closer to land. And with no bait, Phúc's resolve to live dwindled.

Days crawled along at a snail's pace, making time bend in unimaginable ways. Or maybe it wasn't time that was bending, but life itself. Phúc started diving deep into the ocean waters searching for something—he wasn't sure what. He would push past the fire in his lungs and dive until he could no longer see sunlight; until, in the totality of darkness, he was no longer sure which way was up and which was down. Sometimes, he had no recollection of how to reach the surface. Sometimes, he didn't *want* to know. Still, his body refused to drown.

Something cold but soft pressed against his neck. The same touch appeared at his wrist. And then suddenly, a face framed by thick, bouncy curls looked directly at him, tickling his skin.

"Whor-mm."

Whormm? What did *whormm* mean? She was speaking a language he didn't understand, and it would be weeks before he learned what she was saying. *Warm.*

Placed on a stretcher made of cloth, he was moved onto a large cargo ship.

Water. Pure, desalinated water moistened his lips and filled his stomach. But just as soon as it went down, he began to cough it up. Thirsty. He was so thirsty. And suddenly, the water was gone. Phúc gulped and choked, taking in heaps of air. Turning over with agonizing pain, he protruded his tongue to drink more water.

"No!" A dark figure stopped him, pulling his face back. But his torturer must have felt mercy—or guilt—because the next thing he knew, a silver spoon brushed against his lips. One spoonful of water. Two. With the third, he spat it all up again.

He coughed again. If not hell itself, this place was close enough. His energy depleted, he turned on his side and shielded his face from the burning sun, but a firm hand forced him upright.

Wetness touched his lips again. A savory juice, not phở but a similar type of bone broth. The texture resembled a rice porridge unrefrigerated for too long, with soft clumps that might as well have been rocks given how stiff his jaw had become. Once swallowed, though, the mixture not only stayed down, it filled his stomach with warmth, and hour by hour, he felt his blood circulate as life returned to his extremities.

By day three, Phúc could crawl about ten feet along the gritty white floor—a surface Phúc normally wouldn't dare put his head on. Vietnamese people never laid their heads on a place meant for feet.

Exhausted from the physical therapy, he rested against a wall, feeling waves of nausea come and go for hours before a door about halfway down the walkway drew his attention. Phúc crawled over to the staircase, scooting feetfirst down into the darkness. About eight steps down, the seasickness he'd felt before vanished. The obscurity felt good—safe. There were hundreds of shipping containers lining the middle of the deck, each one the size of Phúc's escape vessel and probably ten times more valuable, so he wasn't afraid they would sink.

But he was afraid of being pitched forward into the treacherous open water once again.

He had been rescued by a cargo ship carrying merchandise from India to Hong Kong. What he didn't know was that he was being used as a decoy. Captains smuggling contraband quickly discovered that malnourished refugees not only got them into port quicker, but they were also less likely to have to suffer through an inspection.

Other than scanning the food hall when he was inside, Phúc made no effort to look for Deacon Chuyên. If he had survived, they could go their separate ways from here. If he was one of the cold bodies they'd left behind, well, Phúc didn't need his spirit on his conscience anyway. Wherever he was, Phúc saluted his cunning survival skills and washed his hands of him.

About a week in, Phúc heard a scratching noise, followed by hissing and heavy breathing. At first, he ignored the sounds, but then an earsplitting cry that stretched for an impossibly long moment broke Phúc from his nightly routine of staring at the sky. The stairwell below was shrouded in deep darkness, which made the sounds even more menacing. But on his journey thus far, he had already seen things far worse than could possibly be down there—and he was curious.

Descending five levels of stairs, Phúc found himself in an entirely dark room surrounded by a muted cacophony of sounds. With a focused ear, he heard: a light knocking similar to hollow wood hitting metal; heavy breathing from several different directions; the scratching of a chain slithering across grass; the swoosh of a wooden hand fan opening and closing. When Phúc's eyes didn't adjust in the darkness, he reached into the abyss and fumbled blindly for a switch.

Click.

A sterile, bright white light turned on to reveal a zoo. An elephant, a leopard, parrots, finches, snakes, monkeys, an orangutan, penguins, two polar bear cubs, butterflies, bees, centipedes, turtles, jellyfish in tanks, snails, scorpions, and other hidden insects. Phúc peered inside each of the cages, moving past animals he didn't know the names of until he came face to face with a panda. Sedated, her large black eyes looked up at him the same cowering way puppies do after having an accident indoors.

"Ey." Phúc spoke gently, immediately feeling silly. He was, after all, trying to talk to a panda.

Her eyes, so full of earnest hope, blinked slowly as Phúc's gaze tilted, and then she slumped back down to a hibernating position. Phúc stepped closer. And when the panda didn't move again, Phúc reached his now trembling hand through the metal bars. The panda peered up at him but made no effort to come closer.

One of the men shouted an order in Chinese.

Phúc hit the floor.

The voice came from a different direction than the stairwell Phúc had used. Two men, speaking a combination of Hindi and Chinese, entered and Phúc scrambled to get as far to the opposite side of the room as possible and hide. The two men, sloppy-looking in linen drawstring pants and maroon polo shirts with a lion logo emblazoned on the back, began dispensing dried rations—tiny amounts—to the animals. Phúc squatted behind a row of cages and moved carefully so as not to be detected. When the men reached Panda's cell, she leaped onto her paws and jeered at them as the shorter of the two drew a large needle from a pouch. He inserted the syringe at the nape of her neck and gruffly pushed her backward into the metal bars of her cage as she whimpered in her already sedated state. They repeated this injection with every large animal in the room.

As Phúc ducked quietly over to the stairs and fled upward, he heard the electric buzz of a Taser and a crying growl, but he dared not look.

Up top, Phúc waited for the men to surface and stalked them as they moved about the boat, getting food, smoking at the bow, laughing about things Phúc didn't understand. The pair headed for the captain's quarters, where, apparently, they had a small section to themselves—a luxury location compared to the rest of the ship's stray occupants.

The captain was a stern-looking Indian man, not much taller than Phúc but stout with round facial features that made him look like a super-serious eight-year-old. He ignored the two animal wranglers, who, unfazed by the loud captain, settled down into their cots and fell fast asleep. The men slept until dark, and Phúc, who was peering at them through a window, fought to keep his own eyes open.

When he awoke a few hours later, Phúc peered through the window into the captain's quarters and saw that the two men were gone now. This was their routine. They would feed the animals at sunset, sedate them, and clean their kennels after the drugs took effect. During the day, they slept.

As a guest, Phúc was treated well; he could sit or sleep anywhere on the vessel that didn't interfere with the crew. In the morning, he had his breakfast of eggs, bread, and broth soup, and then he descended the stairs. As he walked the aisles admiring the animals, he found himself drawn to Panda. She wasn't beautiful or even particularly cute, and unlike the other animals, who were curious about him, she lay stubbornly at the back of her cage with a snarl.

He reached his hand in and she raced at him, ripping a light gash into his arm as he fell away from the cage. Phúc had no idea pandas could be this aggressive, but of course, this was his first time seeing a panda in real life. In photos, they always looked serene, perched on trees eating bamboo. Still, Phúc couldn't get past the way her sad eyes drooped yet held his gaze as he stared right back at her. Opening one of the two dozen freezers of food, Phúc found packets of airtight frozen meals. He dipped his head inside and had to lean over the edge to reach a bag of something green. Tearing it open with his teeth, he discovered a bag of peas. Bamboo would've been better, but peas would have to do.

Returning to Panda's cage, he considered how to feed her. The frozen pebbles broke apart easily in his hand, but he knew better than to put his hand into her cage this time. Instead, he threw a pea pebble at her, hoping she'd catch it in her mouth. It hit her square on the snout, and rather than accept the gift, Panda rushed the gate and took another swipe at Phúc. This was obviously not the way to go. Standing outside of Panda's reach, Phúc considered his options.

Taking a single pea, he rubbed it between his fingers to defrost it before rolling it like a marble toward Panda. It hit her paw. She sniffed it, licked it, and sat up. Phúc now had her attention. He stepped forward but stopped when she growled at him.

"Okay. I'll just sit here," Phúc said, and rolled several more peas her way. Panda happily ate, never taking her eyes off him. "You don't trust me. I get it, but I'm not like those guys. I'm just a . . ." What was he exactly? A captive? Technically, he hadn't consented to being put on this ship, but he was hardly in a cage, and he was definitely not being mistreated. He settled for ". . . boy," unsure why it even mattered.

Panda stared at him, her expression of contempt unmoved. One after another, Phúc rolled the peas toward Panda, waiting until she flattened her round body into a lazy eating position on her stomach.

When Phúc's hand slipped and a pea knocked against the cage, landing halfway between them, he considered reaching in to retrieve it but watched instead. Panda lifted her body like she was a cumbersome beast three times larger than she actually was and moved toward him. Phúc sat perfectly still as her eyes narrowed at him. However, to his surprise, when she reached for the pea, she ate it and then laid herself down at the front of the cell instead of retreating again.

Over several days, Phúc moved closer and closer to her, gaining her trust an inch at a time, until one day, he held forth a shaking hand full of peas, and she ate from his palm. He giggled at the tickling sensation of her sandpaper-like tongue scraping across the inside of his hand. In his haste to connect, he reached to pet her, only to be met with a snarl.

"Okay. No touch," Phúc said, and quickly pulled his hand away. For a moment, she looked like she might retreat backward, but instead, she laid her snout between the bars of her cage as Phúc poured another handful of peas. As she ate, he very gently stroked her chin, patiently waiting for her to press her neck into his palm and allow him to pet her. He rubbed as gently as he could until she rolled over on her back, and he more playfully rubbed her belly. In this position, Phúc saw how striking she was, how majestic. He realized that as long as he reached for her with his palm up instead of down, she allowed him to touch her. She even seemed to enjoy it.

That morning, Phúc followed the caretakers as they made their rounds, watching for where they kept the keys. He expected they wore them on their belts or hid them somewhere locked and guarded, but no. The giant ring of keys dangled, unsecured, above the light switch on a carabiner that hooked to the loop of a screw eye. Simple.

CHAPTER 22
JANE

The tiny register room smells of chemicals. Jackie's painting my toenails a cobalt blue while her own hot-pink toes are drying.

"Stop moving your foot," Jackie says.

"Stop tickling them." I try my best to keep still.

"There," she says, finishing. "Make sure you don't knock into anything while it dries."

"I've never felt more like a hostage."

"So dramatic. What's going on with you today?"

"What do you mean?" I say, even though I know exactly what she means. I've been trying to bring up the things my cousins talked about all morning.

"You're acting weird."

"I'm totally acting weird," I admit. "So, last weekend, we had this big family reunion. The first one I've been to since my mom left."

"Oh, crazy. What was the occasion?"

"My dad's younger sister just immigrated here with her two sons."

"Oh my gawd, I hope they didn't make you show them around. I had to do that with my fobby cousins when they first came, and it was hella embarrassing. We went to the mall and they just would not stop talking in Vietnamese. Like, hello, you're in America. Practice English."

"Right," I say reflexively, even though I'm not sure I agree anymore. I think it's kind of sad that they're in this new place without any friends and we're making them feel bad about themselves.

"Is that why you're acting weird? Are they coming today or something?"

"What? No," I say, remembering what I was about to tell her before. "Okay, so when I was at my cousin's house, one of them talked about how their dad chased them around the house with a knife. Another cousin had his nose broken with a hammer. . . . And it was just so . . . I dunno, nice?"

She looks genuinely confused. "What do you mean?"

"Like, they talked about it like we talk about using a mirror to shove a tampon up your you-know-what. No embarrassment or judgment."

Jackie looks at me wide-eyed, like she's just now comprehending what I'm saying. "Jane, that's not normal. Has your dad hit you like that?" Before I can stop her, she lifts my shirt and sees the remnants of the bruises from weeks ago on my back. "What the fuck, Jane?" she says in almost a whisper.

And in this moment, I know I've made a mistake. My

tongue twists in a knot that stretches into an ache that reaches my stomach.

Slowly, like she's approaching a stray dog that she thinks might bite her, Jackie says, "Jane, I've never been hit like that in my life and neither should you." She looks at me like she's seeing me for the first time, like really seeing me, and realizing just how sad and pathetic I am. "Is this why you sometimes used to change in the bathroom during PE? How often does this happen?" Her tone is gentle, but I hear the accusations, and the shocked look on her face makes me feel both embarrassed and ashamed.

"Stop," I say. "Please, just stop. It's not a big deal." I can feel my hands beginning to tremble.

"Why are you so okay with this?"

Because we're Vietnamese. It's what Vietnamese people do, I want to shout. But it's obvious now that Jackie's experience is not like my own. I stare out the window.

"I'm sorry. I don't mean to make you feel bad. This isn't your fault, but we have to tell someone. This is not okay, Jane."

She's not saying any of the right things. What is she talking about? Tell someone? I'm not abused. This is cultural. This is our history. Why is she acting so . . . American? "You're overreacting," I say with a laugh, hoping she'll drop the subject.

"My aunt is a social worker. I'll tell my mom to ask her what you should do."

"No. Stop. You don't get it."

"What don't I get? Jane, this isn't right. If not for yourself, what about Paul?"

If she was looking for my nuclear button, she found it. "*What about Paul?* You of all people know how much I've given up for Paul. Fuck you, Jackie."

"Fuck yourself. You're being selfish and you know it." That stings and I feel the tears pool in my eyes.

"You don't think I know that? You don't think I feel guilty about that every time I think about leaving? You're the one who kept pushing and pushing, saying, 'Jane, you have to go to college. Jane, don't be a loser. Do this for you.' And now you're making me feel like shit." I wipe my face, swallow hard, and wait for the tears to dry.

Jackie doesn't say anything for a long while. I think maybe I've gotten through to her and she's finally seeing things from my perspective, but then she says, "I didn't know. If I knew this was happening, I wouldn't have said those things."

And I. Just. Snap.

"Well, it's a little late for that," I yell. "All our lives I thought I was the sheltered one, the one who didn't know how the real world worked, but I was wrong. You're delusional. You don't know shit."

Before she can defend herself, the door to the shed opens and my dad comes in. He looks tired and slightly angry. "You have to go home," he says to Jackie.

"Good, she was just leaving anyway," I say.

Jackie stands up, and for a second, I think she might say something, but she just bows slightly, says "Dạ," and leaves while I keep my eyes trained on the floor.

I avoid looking at my dad, afraid of what he's going to say.

Had he heard the conversation? No, there's no way, not from outside.

"Go home. Put on black clothes. Get Dad's suit," he says in Vietnamese. Black? Do I even own a black dress? Now I'm anxious. Respectable black clothing can only mean one thing: a funeral.

That my dad doesn't feel the need to tell me whose funeral it is, is not surprising. But I'm bothered by it. Jackie's reaction has me feeling all kinds of things about my dad. Part of me wonders if she's right. If Paul and I would've been better off without our dad. If I would be a different, more confident person had I been raised by someone who didn't have anger issues and allowed me to question his authority.

I don't remember being explicitly told not to ask questions, but I must have learned this behavior from somewhere. Of course. My *mother*. There is a stern inflection that takes over my dad's voice when he refuses to be challenged. My mother knew it, I know it, and so does Paul.

But when did we all relinquish control? Well, not we. I never had any control.

In the bathroom stalls at school there are yellow stickers that read "Abused? Call 1-800-799-SAFE." I've heard stories about abused kids being in denial. And now I have to wonder if I am one. Maybe I'm worse. Maybe Jackie is right, and I'm a straight-up coward.

You go home and get the clothes, I imagine saying. I test it out, knowing I wouldn't ever dare to actually speak it. And the truth is, I don't mind being told to go home because I *like* being at home. There, I don't have to worry about squaring my shoulders during a verbal fight I know I'll lose if it turns physical. Just walking through the door of the store makes my body stiffen, and this is a place where I've spent most of my life.

At home, I take my time gathering our things even though I know he's waiting. Paul's suit is two sizes too small lengthwise, so I pull the threading on his jacket and pant cuffs and iron out the creases. Luckily, he's skinny, so the girth still fits nicely. I don't bother with his shirtsleeves since they'll be covered by his jacket. When he puts it on, I can't help but feel proud of how good he looks—even in morbid black meant to signal grief. While I'm doing all this, he remains silent. It's now been a full three days since he's spoken to me. The kid can hold a grudge. He's mad at me because I made him read a book instead of letting him watch TV. Ever since I told him I was leaving for college, he's been testy. He hasn't come right out and said it, but his attitude and challenging eyes basically say, *And who is going to make me when you leave?* He has a point, but I'm still here, so for now, *I'm* going to make him.

I don't have a black dress, but I'm able to find a black skirt and black cardigan to pair it with. The outfit is demure, but that's the point, right? Besides, it's all I've got. Flared and made of cotton and nylon, my skirt is shorter than it used to be, landing a few inches above my knees. I try pulling it down, but the cardigan isn't long enough to cover my stomach, and that's definitely worse than the skirt being a little short. Still, as I stand in front of the mirror, I can't help but admire my own reflection. I look almost . . . *adult*.

Paul lifts me out of my reverie when he comes in with black shoes that no amount of de-threading will make fit onto his feet. I momentarily panic until I remember the black Oxfords in the closet that I had found three months ago at a thrift store. They fit perfectly. I slide on my black velvet pumps that are in every Payless ad and head to my dad's closet.

"I'm almost ready. Go get in the car."

In my dad's closet, I move a little more quickly. I take down a black button-down shirt, slacks, socks, shoes, a jacket, and all four of his ties because none of them are black and I don't know which one he wants. As I move clothes aside, my hand knocks into metal. Lifting the shirts, I see an old cookie tin. The rusted lid is difficult to pry open, but I dig my nails beneath the lip, and it eventually gives.

At least twenty gold bars are neatly stacked inside with our Social Security cards and passports. We have passports? Why? We've never even left the state, let alone the country. I open them to look and see that they're actually all expired. Figures. A couple flimsy pink papers that look like legal documents are stuffed in the side. Beneath all of that, though, are a few creased, faded black-and-white photos. One of my grandmother, Bà Nội, and one of my grandfather, Ông Nội. They look stiff and unhappy. My grandpa is the aged image of my dad; they both have the same prominent forehead.

"Jane?"

"Coming!" I slam the lid shut, replace the undershirts, and run downstairs to find Paul waiting at the front door. "In the car, buckle up. C'mon, let's go."

"Duh. I've been waiting out here for like an hour. What took you so long?"

I smile. He's talking to me. That's a start.

I pull up to the shop as Dad is unlatching the iron gate to close it. Leaving the engine running, I get out to help him.

"Write a sign and tape it to the window."

On the ground is a black Bic pen and a piece of spam mail from AAA towing. I turn the paper over and write the word C-L-O-S-E-D. "That's it? Just closed?"

"Close for family emergency."

I add the rest and use the Scotch tape to tape the page to the glass door. I'm barely done placing it when he pulls the gate closed and quickly padlocks it.

"Let's go."

We hop back in the car, and he speeds off driving twenty miles over the speed limit. I say nothing, and he doesn't either. Instead, I peer out the window and wonder who died.

Bác Luy's house is quiet out front, but as soon as we walk inside, I can see that things are already in motion. Women cook, men drink, and the kids play with one another. After adding our shoes to the pile by the door, we walk past the living room, which is empty save for an elderly woman praying the rosary. Then I see it. The ancestral altar with Bác Luy's photo front and center. *Bác Luy is the one who died?* He seemed so healthy last weekend at the family reunion. I look around for Becky and Vicky, who are nowhere in sight. It's probably a good thing since I'm not sure what to say to them. I swallow hard and look skyward, hoping to push back my ridiculous tears. Why the fuck am I crying already?

Dad leads us to the altar, where he stands in silence for a long time. I keep my head facing forward but my eyes scan the pictures on the wall. The number of family photos on the wall is impressive compared to the bare walls in our apartment. Wedding photos, the girls' baptisms, First Communions, even a few sporadic school photos from elementary school, and trips they'd taken to Las Vegas and the Grand Canyon. I stare in awe at a few older photographs of Bác Luy and Bác Nguyệt wearing wide-legged bell-bottom jeans and matching blazers, which must have been the style at the time but somehow feels like seeing Vietnamese people playing dress-up in seventies American attire. I stop. Holy crap, Vicky wasn't lying. Inside a gold frame is the photo of Bác Luy and my dad standing next to each other amid an unfinished concrete construction project, each wearing dirty, ill-fitting jeans and hard hats. The background shows a sprawling cityscape below. It must be Hong Kong. There's a second photo with two additional people, a white guy and a Chinese guy, and all four of them awkwardly stand for the camera in an attempt to pose together as friends.

When my dad is done paying his respects, he presses on the back of our heads until we bow.

"Is this you?" I ask as he starts to walk toward the voices of other men talking.

"Uh-huh," my dad says, looking at the photo.

I count the levels in the photo and say, "You stood at the edge of a thirty-two-floor building?"

He nods. "Thirty-seven floors."

I shake my head, pretty sure I counted correctly. "No, there's only thirty-two."

"In Asian culture, they skip number 4, and in Hong Kong, they skip 13 too. Bad luck."

Thirteen, I understand. "Why the number 4?" I ask, but before he can answer, my aunt comes around the corner and calls for us to come join them. He and Paul follow her, but I hang back just a bit to stare at the image. The guy in the photo certainly looks like my dad, but it's hard for me to imagine him as a teenager. Let alone a teenager in a foreign country standing at the top of a skyscraper.

The front door opens, and a family I've never seen before enters. The parents and kids look at me, and when the dad smiles, I bow my head slightly in acknowledgment of them. The dad nods back before ushering his family into the main room. With more people likely to arrive, I follow them through the hallway and find a place in the other room, a large open area that is a combined kitchen and family room.

On the floor of the family room, a group of kids around Paul's age play *Super Mario* on a Nintendo 64 system. Paul slides in easily. "You gotta jump up top!" he shouts. This is the only game we have at home, so we both know all the secret passages for skipping levels and getting extra lives.

Through the open sliding glass door, I see a man pat my dad on the shoulder, and I swear it's Bác Luy himself, but this man is chubby with a potbelly, and he's nearly bald—must be his brother. I didn't know Bác Luy had a brother, but, of course, I wouldn't know that. I don't know 90 percent of the people here. The rest of the men take turns greeting my dad with gentle smiles, pats on the back, and beer. Three of them offer him a Heineken simultaneously. He takes the one nearest to him. Bác Luy is the closest thing to a brother that my dad has in America, and I guess they all know this because they gather around him like he's a wounded bird.

I'm awkwardly standing alone in the middle of the living room, so I turn toward the kitchen. I'm hoping someone will give me a job peeling shrimp or something. Bác Nguyệt is the busiest of anyone. She isn't joyous by any stretch of the imagination, but she's not hysterical in the way I would expect a widow to be. Around the kitchen, she moves with purpose, and when the other women tell her to sit and rest, she brushes them off. Like a chef in a busy restaurant, she lists off orders for her make-shift kitchen staff. The whole operation is so big that they've set up additional hot plates in the garage for all the deep-frying that is about to take place. Women I've never even seen before clean and chop vegetables and roll egg rolls at the kitchen tabletop. I take a seat on an empty couch halfway between the kids at the Nintendo and the women working in the kitchen.

"Is that Anh Phúc's kid?" O Ngữ asks. That she refers to my dad as Anh means she's younger than him. I guess she sort of remembers me too. O Vui nods without looking at me. I think I make her uncomfortable because she rarely speaks directly to me.

"No news from Ngọc Lan?" O Ngữ continues. Ngọc Lan is my mother's name. They must think I don't understand Vietnamese.

"I heard she's in Vegas," O Vui says.

"What does a girl become without a mother? Look at how she dresses."

"Don't worry about her. She's smart. She's going to a famous college soon down in Los Angeles. And she understands Vietnamese." I look up at Bác Nguyệt, who drops supplies for the women beside them and then heads back outside to monitor the deep-frying.

I don't dare look at the women, but I can sense them looking at me. Without moving too much, I start to pull down on my inappropriately short skirt when Becky emerges from upstairs.

She is immediately swarmed by women asking if she wants something to eat. She nods. The previously cluttered countertop is cleared, and a bowl of hot noodles is placed in front of her. She takes a couple bites, but the act of feeding herself drains her energy, and for what seems like a long time, she stares off into space—which happens to be directly at me.

I'm staring back at her, and though one might think I'm gawking at the bereaved, what I'm actually doing is much worse. I, the guest, brought here to comfort her, am hoping that *she*, the daughter of the deceased, will save me.

"You want some?" she finally asks.

"No, thanks." The response is reflexive and not at all what I truly want. She doesn't offer again, though I expect her to because it is common in Vietnamese culture. When someone says no to food, you make a bowl and encourage them to have just a little.

Don't get me wrong. I'm not blaming her; I'm just really uncomfortable and now really hungry.

We continue occupying our spaces in silence.

I want to say something to console her, but everything feels trite. *I'm sorry for your loss*—too formal. *I'm sorry about your dad*—too comfortable. *I'm sorry*—not enough of anything. And the longer I let the silence linger, the more difficult it becomes to speak at all. After a while, she gets up and walks off, her bowl of noodles still steaming on the table. The uncomfortable stillness in the room must have been suffocating. Or maybe I made her uncomfortable.

"I haven't looked at tickets yet," I hear my dad say. I wonder if he's planning to send me to college on the bus. A blender roars to life in the kitchen, and I miss out on the next few minutes of conversation.

"Long says that with each passing day Grandpa gets weaker," my dad says when the blender stops. They're all speaking in Vietnamese. Bác Long is my dad's brother. I've talked to him a couple of times on the phone. He usually just says hi, then lets the conversation die until my dad takes the phone back and they start talking.

"You need to go now. No matter the cost. Otherwise you will regret it. Your father was a good man. He saved a lot of lives.

If you don't go now, your kids will never know him." I turn my head to see who's talking, but the conversation has gone silent.

"Long . . . He's a dragon, all right. He doesn't understand respect," Bác Chuyên says. His voice I'd recognize anywhere because it sounds like he has bubbles in this throat when he talks. Also, my nose has trained me to hear him so I can run the other way and save it from getting twisted. My dad doesn't answer.

"Bỏ đi," someone else says, waving the topic away, and I realize that what I had mistaken for apathy on my dad's part is actually something more akin to anger because there is tension there.

"No, this subject I cannot let go of. Find a stick, use a broom. The kind of man who uses a chain . . . and then to look your father dead in the eyes and not know to use a light hand."

Is Bác Chuyên saying that my uncle in Vietnam beat our grandpa? With a chain? The idea seems both impossible and completely probable.

"Ey, shut your mouth," another man says. "Were you there? No. Shut your mouth."

"Their house was full of noise. The whole town heard it. You only need to look at Ông Đoàn's scar to know it."

Yeah! I think. *Mind your own fucking business.*

Bác Chuyên glares.

"Hearing is not seeing," my dad says. I wonder if he was there. If my dad watched my uncle hit my grandpa. I consider going out to the patio and just pulling up a chair, but I know they'd shoo me away.

"When do Anh Hòa and Chị Bích start?" This question

comes from a man with a distinct, nasally pitch and the conversation takes a stilted turn. This is why I've always pretended to ignore their discussions. They never finish their stories. They speak in broken fragments that might as well be Morse code.

"Next week," my dad says.

This both relieves and scares me. It takes some guilt off my shoulders about the shop closing, but it makes me nervous because it means he'll be home with Paul a lot more. Knowing this makes my stomach ache.

"You have to go home," the man urges. He means home to Vietnam. For someone with such a childlike voice, the dude sure is bossy. In light of today, though, I guess it makes sense that they're thinking about our grandparents in Vietnam and how none of us grandkids in America know them.

Silence. Then someone brings up the recent wildfires that started in Oregon and have spread to us in NorCal, and this sparks a debate about American incompetence.

I've only spoken to my grandparents a handful of times on the phone. I can have a conversation in Vietnamese, but don't ask me to write a letter. So, language isn't the problem; the problem is, I never know what to say. Grandpa would sometimes try out American phrases that he repeats over and over, *Hello. How are you? My name is Vũ Đoàn Thái*. It's strange to hear my grandpa refer to himself by name. In Vietnamese, family members address each other by title, not by name—the latter is rude. *What is your name? I'm fine. Thank you*. Grandma, though, she's mean. She'll ask if I'm fat like the Americans she sees on TV, and though I'm not "fat" by American standards, I am on the chubbier side of the Vietnamese spectrum, so I usually fall silent.

"Those hamburgers make you fat. Make sure you eat Vietnamese food." To which the only response I give is: "Dạ."

To be honest, I'm sort of glad I haven't met my grandparents in person yet because I'm not sure I like them.

Before dinner is served, there is prayer. Becky, Vicky, and about fifteen other teens emerge from upstairs, and I'm suddenly aware of how the cloistered group has left me out. None of the cousins I had connected with are here. They couldn't afford to travel back so soon, so they are having their own East Coast prayer service in Florida. I think I recognize a few others, but I'm too busy staring at the floor now to really know.

"Let us pray," Bác Nguyệt says, starting the service.

We all turn to the makeshift altar, where the solemn portrait of Bác Luy stares at us. Although he's young, he isn't smiling and doesn't look particularly happy in what looks like a military uniform. The bright red-and-yellow-striped flag on his lapel is adorned with several gold stars and pins, and a flurry of ribbons hang off his shoulder. I lean in closer. It's hard for me to believe that this soldier, who probably shot and killed other Vietnamese soldiers in the war, is the same man who showed us magic tricks at Disneyland.

Beneath his photo are three bowls, one with rice, one with tea, and a larger bowl containing chả and sweet rice wrapped in banana leaves. On either side of the food is a fistful of incense from which each family member draws three sticks. Then we bow three times before the altar and step aside.

Dad, Paul, and I do it together. Since there's no music playing, the room is eerily quiet. In the middle of our third bow, a gasp and shriek pierce the air behind us. I start to turn around but catch my dad's eye and continue to stare fixedly at the altar. When I'm finally able to look, I see that both Becky and Vicky are sobbing uncontrollably. Seeing them cry makes me tear up as well, which in turn makes me feel dumb. I am sad about Bác Luy's death, but I think my tears are actually for the girls. The pain on their faces is so obvious that their sadness has leapfrogged over to me, causing my body to react in a way that my brain can't quite make sense of.

As we move back to our standing place, Paul reaches for my hand and holds it as he wipes a tear from his face. I'm glad we're not fighting anymore.

Over the years, I've imagined my dad dying a million different ways. Every time he gets angry, snaps at me, or even just shifts his tone in that vengeful way that tells me I'm in trouble, I imagine a life without him—by sometimes graphic and very unpleasant means. But as I listen to the girls cry tears so fierce it's almost as though their bodies are forcing them to gasp for air they don't want to inhale, I get it. Becky and Vicky love their dad. They love him despite the bruises and lingering pain, and it doesn't make sense, but that's the truth. I know this because I feel the exact same way.

CHAPTER 23
PHÚC

"Maybe when I grow up I can have a pet panda too."

"Pandas belong in the wild," I say.

"Maybe I'll live in the wild."

"Hmm, then I guess you just have to find a panda willing to put up with your stinky breath!" I tickle him until his sides hurt.

Even though the keys came in such varying sizes that Phúc could eliminate most of them on sight, it still took a while to decipher which one opened Panda's cage. He was beginning to feel like he'd already cycled through the keys twice without finding the right one. Still, he persisted until he felt the metal teeth click and the lock popped open. Carefully, he opened the cage and let himself in, but Panda didn't come to him. Instead, she sat back with gnashed teeth, her eyes full of suspicion once again. This time, Phúc knew to be patient. Sitting pressed up against the door of the cell, he rolled frozen longan fruits to her the same way he'd rolled her the peas. Each day, Phúc stayed put and let her move closer and closer until he woke from a nap one day to find her snout resting in his lap. Not wanting to wake her, he watched her back rise and fall, and he sank into the comfort of her warm breath blanketing his legs.

When she awoke, she rolled onto her back and looked up at Phúc adoringly. Her mouth parted, and she wriggled her head side to side, nuzzling deeper into Phúc's thigh. She was the puppy Phúc always wanted but couldn't have because dogs were a burden during the war.

Panda's paw pressed into his chest as she gently sniffed around his head, her breath tickling his face—this was the first real connection he'd made since leaving Vietnam.

Panda's paw was larger than Phúc's hand, but she was always gentle. In the dark, she'd squeeze her head through the hole between his arm and thigh, roll over on her back, and paw at Phúc until he rubbed her belly. Sometimes, when she heard the gate squeak open, she would move to it and tumble into him before he could even fully enter. When she was feeling energetic, she used him like a tree, climbing up on his shoulders and hanging on tightly to his head as he tipped over on his side and rolled around with her on the cold steel surface of the cage. Long used to play with Phúc like this; he would prop Phúc up on his shoulders, hang on to Phúc's feet, and run through the forest. Phúc could remember the distinct chattering of his teeth as he bobbed up and down, half laughing and half screaming. His brother was the source of the most fun he ever had.

Panda nuzzled Phúc's neck, licked his face, and pulled him from his reverie for belly rubs.

Jumping to his hands and knees, Phúc bent his neck and began somersaulting around the cage, with Panda chasing him close behind. He giggled as they bumped into one another and bounced backward lightly, tumbling into the bars surrounding them. And then Panda rolled so hard, she ended up upside down in a corner, forcing her to shimmy her butt to free herself. This sent Phúc into a laughing fit so intense his stomach ached with joy as he lay back and clutched himself with glee.

Phúc's laughter filled the typically quiet room as it echoed against the cold steel walls so that when he stopped to catch his breath, the room returned to its normal state of sedated silence—the quiet now all the more pronounced. Somewhere nearby, Phúc could hear the faint tap-tapping of spidery legs spinning webs or whatever it was they did in the dark. Phúc hated spiders. A shiver ran down his spine just thinking of the creepy crawlers. Where Long could be loving, he could also be cruel, and he used to catch spiders around the house and toss them down Phúc's shirt.

What are you so afraid of? Look how big you are and how tiny the spider is! Long would say. Long.

Despite everything, Phúc missed his brother.

Settled now from their laughing stupor, Phúc sat up. Panda climbed onto his shoulders and gripped her legs around Phúc's neck as her paws covered his eyes in a game of peekaboo/ freeze tag. Every time Panda lifted her paw, Phúc jumped forward and pretended Panda wasn't on his shoulders but rather hidden somewhere. He'd move this way and that to Panda's delight until his eyes were covered once again and Phúc stood still. Panda could happily play this game for hours at a time.

Suddenly, Panda shook violently and fell from his shoulders. Phúc tried in vain to catch her but found himself disoriented by a blinding light.

Just beyond the cage stood the zookeepers. They bickered with one another about who left the cage unlocked until they saw that the keys were still in the lock itself. One of them, the younger and more sinister one who looked like an Indian Jack Nicholson with a balding head and crazy eyes, realized that Phúc was the culprit. "What are you do-oing?" he yelled, gesturing wildly with his hands.

"Mày nghĩ mày đang làm gì vậy?" the other one said. He was shorter than his colleague and about a decade older with a pockmarked face and a scruffy, half-gray beard. It took Phúc a moment to realize he was speaking in stunted Vietnamese because the accent was garbled. But then he saw something flicker across the younger one's face. Not much larger in stature than Phúc and only slightly older, his stiff demeanor and icy eyes held something far more sinister and dangerous than his partner—jealousy.

Quickly scrambling to his feet, Phúc puffed up his chest as he'd seen in Western movies, widened his stance, and geared up for a fight. "I just play," Phúc said in broken English. "She's my friend," Phúc added in Vietnamese, hoping the older man might show some mercy. The words were as stupid as they sounded.

Click. The padlock pressed shut, its key removed, and Phúc was officially locked in. "Wait! Let me out," Phúc begged. Ignoring him, the men stepped back.

"Heeeeelp!" Phúc yelled, calling to anyone who could hear.

Indian Jack Nicholson spun around and grabbed Phúc's throat through the bars. "Câm miệng," he warned as his concrete grip pressed into Phúc's larynx—he was Popeye-strong. Phúc struggled to breathe as the man dissolved into a fit of laughter. With a final squeeze, the man let go.

And before Phúc could even take in a deep breath, he found his body twisted in an involuntary convulsion while every part of him vibrated with electricity. Both men began chanting, "Fight, fight, fight!" one speaking Hindi, the other Chinese. Then the searing heat coursing through his nerves abruptly halted. Panda, who was also shocked, came to him and curled up into a whimpering ball at his side.

"Fight, fight, fight!" they pressed, but Phúc didn't understand. Panda, unfortunately, did, and with a pang of sadness in her eyes, she slapped Phúc, tearing a gash in his shirt. *Bzzzzz.* Her body convulsed once again from the Taser. Using Panda as a shield, Phúc hid behind her in a crouching position—the same position he sat in while he watched his brother beat their father. The men shot their Tasers once again, but Phúc scrambled to the back of the cage, just out of reach. Lowering their Tasers, the two men walked away and shut the light off behind them.

Phúc breathed a sigh of relief.

Bzzzzzzz.

The men hadn't left, they'd merely shut off the lights.

Flashes of electric current ripped through the darkness, casting a flicker of stop-motion images. The jolt forced Phúc to grab hold of Panda in painful desperation before they each slid back toward the opposite sides of the cage. Blood streaked across the interior of the cage as the two men stood directly behind it, their fists knocking against the metal enclosure. Forced into action, Panda now growled at Phúc.

Confused, Phúc reached into the darkness, but instead of being met with kindness, Panda's paw ripped across Phúc's stomach and the arm he'd raised in defense. The marking wasn't deep, but in all their play fighting Panda had never once scratched him, not even a little, and Phúc knew then that something wasn't right. The men were obviously hoping Panda would slap Phúc down the way she did when they entered the cage to sedate her.

Bzzzz. The Taser knocked Panda to the floor as Phúc devised a plan. He would strangle Panda to the point of unconsciousness, scream that he had killed her, and then sneak past the guards as they raced to revive her.

"Ow! Okay, asshole, let's go!" Phúc shouted. If they wanted a fight, he would give them a fight.

"Fight, fight, fight . . ."

Urgent.

Fierce.

Angry.

"Fight, fight, fight . . ."

Feeling his now tattered shirt rub against his open wound, he ripped it off.

Bzzzzzz. Light. Only this time, they missed. Phúc listened as the Taser head clanked and scraped along the cage floor as it was reeled back into the hands of his torturers. Crouched in the corner, he waited for the next burst of immobilizing shock.

When it came, Phúc lunged at Panda and wrapped the remnants of his shirt around her neck as he dragged her to the back of the cage. Shrouded in shadow, Phúc whispered, "Stand still." He wanted her to play dead.

But she didn't stop. "Stand still, just for a minute," he directed with urgency. But Panda didn't understand. She thrashed against him, banging his body into the metal bars of the cage with each gulp of breath she was able to take.

"Stand still," Phúc shouted.

Finally, Panda's body went limp. Her paws pressed outward, the soft fur on her body turned prickly, and her lungs deflated. As Phúc loosened his grip, Panda twitched three times in succession, stopped, then twitched one last time before she stopped moving altogether.

"Fight!" This was met with silence. "Hey!" Still nothing. A flashlight beamed into the space. This time it was Phúc's turn to watch. He stared at the stunned men and watched their eyes travel from his own face, down his arms, to Panda's unmoving body and the tight grip Phúc had around their prized animal's neck.

She wasn't moving. "No," the pock-faced man gasped, and Phúc looked down in horror and released his grip altogether. Panda was supposed to be unconscious, but unconscious people still breathe, and Panda wasn't moving. Quickly, Phúc moved to do chest compressions, but before he could even press down once, he felt his body being flung backward. He watched wide-eyed as the men worked to resuscitate her. But Phúc knew death's stare. Scrambling to his feet, Phúc closed the gate, locked the men inside, and ran back up to the deck, where he puked off the side of the ship.

This panda was traveling across the ocean because someone paid a high price for her, and Phúc murdered that sale. As he turned toward the captain's quarters, Phúc winced, feeling for the first time the cuts Panda had left across his body. Sitting like a lifeless statue on the bobbing deck, Phúc let the blazing sun turn his cuts into scabs that would eventually become scars. The blinding heat burned like peroxide as his blood crusted over and his flesh sutured itself back together. Amid the throbbing pain, Phúc listened to the distant screams of the men trapped six stories below, content with the knowledge that they, too, were suffering.

Night gave way to day, and somewhere in the distance, a shape began to emerge—land. The tiny, irregular peaks at the horizon line weren't a figment of Phúc's imagination. Soon, the others would wake and come up to the deck too, but at the moment, the ship was quiet. Phúc's hands tingled with the sensation of death. He rubbed his palms together until they turned red, hoping to scrub away the feeling, but it persisted. The phantom feeling of Panda's fur would linger on his hands, haunting him for the rest of his life. *Ngứa tay*, his mother would've scolded. But she would have been wrong; his hands weren't itchy, they were on fire. Squeezing his fists around the railing until his knuckles turned white, he slipped his legs through the gaps, allowing his feet to dangle off the side, and he watched as the mass of land grew taller and wider with each passing minute. His body had made it to Hong Kong, but his soul was broken.

A large dock came into view with giant cranes lined up like trophies at the finish line of a long, heartbreaking race. Sea lions clapped and cheered loudly on red metal buoys, encouraging them along the final stretch. Seagulls glided effortlessly around the ship's perimeter, occasionally landing on the railings and welcoming them. Metal cranks and gears screeched to a halt, bumpers dropped, ropes flew through the air, the off-ramp opened, and serenity turned to chaos.

Phúc and his fellow refugees spilled forward, not knowing what awaited them but sure they wanted to be first. Quickly, and albeit unsteadily, Phúc made his way down the ramp until his bare feet hit concrete. As soon as they did, he fell to his knees and pressed his forehead to the ground. *Ground.* He had finally made contact with earth. His hands trembled in disbelief as they scraped across the dirt and pebbles. Grateful footsteps shuffled past, making their way toward Chinese men in dark green camouflage fatigues with HONG KONG embroidered above their left breast pocket.

Still collapsed on the concrete, Phúc remained in his praying position. At first, tears streamed down his face, but then, suddenly, he was overcome with laughter. As if the whole experience had been a hoax he'd survived. Pulling himself upright on his knees, Phúc surveyed the scene before him. Men in uniform sat at rows of cheap plastic folding tables, and beyond them, throngs of refugees crammed into a massive tented space that looked cobbled together with a combination of scrap metal and tarp. If it rained, there would surely be leaks. When he finally stood up, a wave of nausea washed over him, and suddenly the earth began shifting underfoot.

Be still, he told himself.

But everything refused to stop spinning. Even with his eyes clamped tightly shut, he felt his body rise and fall with the flow of the ocean. He bent at the waist, then the knees again, and eventually, he stumbled over to a grassy patch and curled into himself with his forehead pressed into the dirt.

He squeezed his eyes shut, forcing his brain to focus on the sound of chatter, footsteps, an engine blowing steam, water lapping against the dock, and metal clanking against metal. He concentrated on being still.

Lifting his forehead again, Phúc took a deep breath and wretched forward, his body reflexively pumping his stomach. As his shoulders pushed upward and his throat opened, he choked up air one, two, three times before his body expelled a spoonful of vomit. A napkin was thrust in Phúc's face from an unseen person, and he gratefully wiped his mouth. Unpleasant as it was, throwing up recalibrated his system, and when he stood again, the owner of the napkin was gone, and Phúc had regained his land legs.

Inside, they were stripped of their clothes. Their dignity was less of a concern than the health risks they posed to the larger population of Hong Kong. As Phúc stood naked, a man on a stepladder combed his hair for lice, then made him raise his arms spread like Jesus on the crucifix while he checked his armpits, nose, and pubic area. Once it was determined that he didn't have lice, Phúc picked up his clothes and carried them to the next station.

Dousing himself with a splash of cold water, he quickly shut off the valve, lathered himself with soap, and rubbed and rubbed, peeling away layers of dirt. Using his thumb, Phúc pushed into his damp feet until friction peeled away tiny spools of gray skin. Stopping only when his fingers were numb with fatigue, he turned the water back on and watched as weeks of filth pooled at his feet. And still, his body burned with guilt.

On the other side of the intake tent were rows and rows of triple bunk beds with thin mattresses, on top of which sat rolled-up bamboo mats, equally flat pillows, and pieces of fleece fabric—a sheet, pillow, and blanket. Set just a foot apart from each other with three feet between rows, thousands of refugees lay scattered like prisoners in an overpopulated, minimum-security facility.

At the edge of the encampment, he found a small patch of vacant dirt, pulled a blanket and pillow from one of the empty beds, and laid it on the floor. He placed his wet clothes on one end and lay flat on his back on the other half. If he squinted his eyes, he could almost ignore the encampment on his right periphery, the chain-link fence on his left, and the guard tower off in the distance. Back home on especially humid days, he would lie down in front of the door. With his shoulder up against the ledge, he liked the feeling of being at home but also a part of the larger world. Far from home now, he pictured being back on the tile floor just beside the doorstep at home.

On his stomach, he imagined the faint pressure of Bà Nội's foot as she pretended to step on him as she left for the market. He grabbed her legs, not willing to let go, this time with an urgency he hadn't felt before. It felt good to touch her again. To know that no matter what happened, her steadfast determination would force everything to be okay.

Phúc awoke the following morning to pieces of paper being shoved toward him and a stern voice demanding his documentation. The man, a Vietnamese refugee with a Southern accent and deep craters covering the bottom half of his face, towered over him as he still lay on the ground. Phúc didn't have documentation. Carefully, he searched his pants even though he knew there was nothing there. He figured it best to make a show of looking rather than appear defiant, but he had spent three months in a boat with nothing but these clothes, and he knew every millimeter of them by feel. Within the inner seams and all through the bottom cuffs were thin gold chains. But he dared not feel for them for fear that someone might notice. Hundreds of people had come to his mother to have these secret pockets sewn into their clothes, and some of these people were probably here at this camp now. Afraid that the slightest breeze or even his own thoughts could cause the faded and beaten cloth to spill its contents, Phúc tried not to think about the gold at all.

There were no papers anywhere on him, though. He didn't know this at the time, but his documents were "lost" on purpose. South Vietnamese documentation would've gotten him in trouble. If the Communists had caught him, those papers would've been the only proof they needed to kill him. It would've meant death by gunfire.

Phúc shook his head no.

"Fill this out," the lava-faced man barked at Phúc. He was a refugee as well, but he could speak English, which made him more valuable—and he made sure Phúc knew it.

Phúc was brought to a small office trailer, where he was handed new papers to complete. He wrote his name, date of birth (somewhere in the haze of escape he'd aged up to fourteen), country of origin, city . . . Not sure what to put under occupation, he wrote down *mechanic*. Technically, he had repaired bikes, so he figured he could do that here also.

When he was done, the papers were taken by an American woman who had to be at least six inches taller than him. At her desk, she typed his information onto card stock that she manually fed through a typewriter. Just like that, with no background check or any kind of in-depth analysis, he was given his identity back. An identity he would soon change.

Seventy-eight days passed with Phúc doing the same routine. He woke up, ate, walked the perimeter of the camp, showered every other day, walked some more, and slept. But on his seventy-ninth day, Deacon Chuyên found him.

"Stand up," Deacon Chuyên said, smiling at Phúc jovially and kicking him with a hardness that said he was anything but. Next to him stood a tall Chinese man who had shoulders like a Lego figurine, thick and square.

"Phúc Vũ," the tall Chinese man said, eyeing him skeptically before mumbling something to a translator who stepped up from behind. The short man kept his head hung low and his body slumped so that he looked more like an attaché case than a person.

"Is this right? You are a mechanic?" the attaché asked Phúc while giving him a slight nod yes.

"Yet." Phúc nodded, not yet able to pronounce the s.

"Papers?" the man asked, his palm open. Phúc produced the document he had been given earlier. "It says here you were born in 1964. You're fourteen?"

Before Phúc could answer, Deacon Chuyên grabbed the document. "Typo. The four should be a one."

"How old are you?" the Chinese man asked.

"Tell him that your age is seventeen?" Deacon Chuyên translated. It was an instruction framed as a question.

"I one seven," Phúc said, gesturing the number 17 with his fingers. He was scrawny for a seventeen-year-old, but so were actual seventeen-year-olds—malnourishment had that effect.

"You want to work?" The Chinese man sized him up.

Phúc nodded emphatically as he remembered Bà Nội's words: *If someone asks you to work, you work. It doesn't matter what. You do it.* Bà Nội knew Phúc could be lazy, so she made sure to remind him to say yes to any job.

The Chinese man pointed to a beat-up beige truck with wheels that were slightly too small for its frame. Twelve other men were corralled in its bed, where Phúc squeezed himself in too. When he turned to ask Deacon Chuyên what kind of work they would be doing, he found that he was alone. With a jolt, the truck lurched forward and crossed through the encampment to a gate that rolled open as they approached. And just like that, Phúc was allowed to leave the refugee facility.

Huge skyscrapers and industrial buildings whipped past so fast that before Phúc could take in any of the details, they were behind him. In Đà Nẵng, the tallest building was three stories high and made of stucco. These gigantic steel structures covered in glass gave him vertigo as he bent his neck back, searching for the top. *Weren't they afraid of the glass breaking and falling hundreds of feet to the ground? What a pain it must be to work at the top of the building. How long would it even take to climb all those stairs?* Phúc wondered. In all of his fourteen years, he had seen a lot of things, but Phúc had not yet encountered an escalator, never mind an elevator. So, he imagined thousands of steps zigzagging to the top with hundreds of men in suits and wax-shined shoes making the daily climb.

The architecture wasn't the only thing that was different about this country, though. The people wore button-down shirts, bell-bottoms, and skirts in vibrant colors—a stark contrast to the elastic-waist pants and long-sleeved, button-down silk shirts they had back home. And here, the women walked with clusters of men as equals—not behind them. This, he found distasteful.

For a while, he watched the scenery pass, feeling like something was amiss. And then he realized what it was. The streets were *too bland.* Where was the flavor? How were there no stalls selling candy, skewered meats, coffee, ice cream, and yogurt? These beautifully paved cement pathways were devoid of any vendors. No sticky rice burned in clay pots. No baguettes with pâté being made by squatting and hunched-over women. There was no life, no culture, no style. The whole city was concrete and steel.

Phúc longed for home.

CHAPTER 24
JANE

This isn't real.

Except it is real.

Nothing about this experience *feels* real.

Not the packing. Not the twenty-seven hours spent on airplanes and in airports. Not the shiny new passports made with our school picture "samples" that we obviously returned sans a photo or two. Not even this very moment, right now.

I'm here, but I'm having a hard time believing it. My feet are touching Vietnamese soil. I want to crouch down and touch it with my hand, but the airport is crowded, and I don't want my family to think I've gone crazy. Plus, I don't see soil anywhere. But my brain is suspended in disbelief. Fourteen hours ago, we were in San Jose, and now we're here—on the other side of the Pacific Ocean.

We've come with three large suitcases and three duct-taped moving boxes full of old clothes, medicine, and cheap plastic toys for the kids. One of the boxes is full of yellow and brown bags of M&M's. (Apparently, they don't have those here.) Oh, and school supplies—pencils, pens, notebooks, and erasers—all from the dollar store. Paul and I have seven pairs of underwear, each with zipper pockets sewn into the back for the two gold bars that we are each smuggling into the country. When my dad first gave them to me, I was annoyed at how uncomfortable it would be to have them pressed against my lower back for twenty hours, but they're actually so unnoticeable that I find myself continually reaching back to make sure they haven't disappeared.

Two days before we left, Cậu Hòa and Mợ Bích showed up at the store. I guess Cậu Hòa lost his job or something, so my dad's call was somewhat of a relief to them. And now we (well, he and my dad) are business partners. With more time together than we had when they came for dinner, I noticed that Cậu Hòa not only *looks* like my mother but he has some of the same mannerisms too. They both arch one eyebrow when curious, flare their noses when angry, and flex their fingers when bored. He dresses in oversized button-down silk shirts and pleated khaki pants. They drove from Colorado with all their stuff, moved in down the street from us, and are watching the store while we're gone for the week.

After passing through security at the San Francisco International Airport yesterday morning, we stopped in a secluded corner, where my dad gave me two gold bars to tuck into my zipper, and he placed the other two bars inside Paul's underwear. Mợ Bích told me that the pickpockets are so good here that you don't even feel them reach in and take your wallet—from inside your jeans!

Now that we're here, I'm so nervous about meeting my grandparents that my legs won't stop shaking. It occurred to me after my dad told us about the trip that his family's idea of discipline and punishment must be similar to my dad's—apple not falling far from the tree and all that—and I'm scared to be spending so much time stuck in their house.

As we exit the terminal, a little elderly woman emerges from the crowd, and a look of recognition comes over her face. Suddenly, I'm engulfed in a hug that includes deep sniffs of both my cheeks. It's startling but loving and com-*plete*-ly unexpected. She stands eye to eye with my dad but somehow seems taller, with kind eyes and a sturdy demeanor—like a tree that has weathered many storms.

"Chào Bà Nội." My dad's hand pushes at the back of my head, reminding me that I need to bow as I greet my grandmother.

I fold my hands across my stomach like I was taught as a child and bow while saying in Vietnamese, "Dear Grandma, I have just arrived." I've used this phrase awkwardly a thousand times before, but this time it feels appropriate. It sounds really formal when translated into English, and maybe it is in Vietnamese, too, but I think it's more of a respect thing than a strict adherence to archaic etiquette. I like saying it to her.

She lifts her chin in a deep laugh and looks a lot like the Halloween skeleton in the *Nightmare Before Christmas* movie.

"Grandma thought you wouldn't know how to speak Vietnamese. Good!" She laughs. I don't know why she thinks I can't speak Vietnamese when I've talked to her on the phone, but I let the dig slide. Plus, the animated thumbs-up she gives makes me laugh, and then she's hugging me again, only this time it's a side hug as she turns to Paul.

"Dear Grandma, I have just arrived," Paul repeats.

Paul bows so far he loses his balance and is forced to take a step forward. Grandma repeats her loving hug-sniffing with Paul and then abruptly announces, "Let's go already. The car is waiting!" Um, we have a car?

"Where is Grandpa?" I ask.

She tells me he's resting, but there's something somber in the way she speaks that suggests his tiredness couldn't be helped. Although she is looking at me as she says this, I get the distinct feeling the message is meant for my dad.

Our taxi, a small, flat-faced pickup truck, looks like it only fits two passengers, but somehow all five of us squeeze in. No seat belts. I don't even see them. "Relax," Grandma says, patting my hair. She must sense how stiff my body has become, but I can't relax. We drive like this on bumpy dirt roads until we reach an alleyway that is too small for the truck to fit through. We all vacate the car. The driver and my dad grab our three suitcases, and all of us walk about halfway into the alley, passing many wrought iron fences that open up into courtyards before we stop in front of a two-story, light green house.

The driver opens a latch, and we spill into the sizable dirt courtyard. There are stacks of plastic bins in one corner, a few bicycles scattered about, and two motorbikes parked parallel to each other on the right.

"Ông ơi!" the driver calls.

A stout, elderly man with a heavily wrinkled dinosaur face emerges in the doorway. His head and mouth resemble an apatosaurus, but his body is reminiscent of the T-rex. And perhaps his most startling feature is the giant scar ripping across his face from cheek to temple.

"He-lo. How. Are. You?" Ông Nội says, becoming all at once familiar. As he awkwardly pats me on the shoulders rather than hug me, I see five subtle but distinct lines crack across his left cheek and neck. Deep crevices within which many secrets flow. Grandpa is vibrant, but I can tell he's sick because where Grandma is sturdy and firm in her stance, he is shaky and soft.

"He-lo. I am good," I respond, bowing my head.

My dad clicks his tongue. "Disrespectful. Dear Grandpa, I have just arrived."

Grandpa nods impassively. "Hungry yet?"

My dad tells him we haven't eaten since the small meal they served on the airplane.

"Ey," he says, and leads us through the foyer, which is just a wall with ancestral photos. I notice that his feet shuffle more than walk, but he doesn't use a cane. We pass another room with the same linoleum flooring and move to the dining area, where a round wooden table sits surrounded by mismatched plastic chairs—all under a tin roof not fully attached to the house.

Maybe I gave my dad too much credit for picking the ugly

chairs for the store that I was certain no one would steal. I can see now that he probably thought they were perfectly good chairs, so why *wouldn't* we sit on them? The floor here is dirt like the courtyard, but it's so compact that it's not at all dusty. On the far side of the room, a woman tends to the stove, preparing the last of several dishes. It's a feast. There is rice, hot and sour soup, crunchy noodles with sautéed vegetables, and two different kinds of fish, fried and simmered.

"Please, sit!" Grandpa says, gesturing for us to be comfortable as he unbuttons his cuffs and rolls up his sleeves. With everyone seated, there is still one empty chair, which I assume is going to be filled by the woman cooking—an aunt perhaps? Except no one has introduced us to her.

Instead, through the doorway comes a tall man with long arms, a friendly gait, and the Communist gold star on the lapel of his collared shirt. He's the spitting image of my dad—maybe an inch taller, but otherwise they could be twins.

"Oh my, Phúc!" The man embraces my dad tightly, and they laugh together. "Long days, long days," he continues, squeezing my dad's shoulder. "Who is this?" He's asking about me, but the feeling is mutual. Who is *he*?

I am introduced as Jane, the elder daughter, and Paul is introduced as his second (male) child.

"Chào Bác Long," our dad says. Paul and I both bow our heads and repeat, "Chào Bác Long."

He then asks the inevitable question of why we don't have Vietnamese names. My dad explains as he has a million times that it was my mother's idea to try and make me American through and through. But they learned from their mistake with Paul, who got Quốc as his middle name.

My uncle turns to me very seriously and asks what name I want.

Before I can answer, a pair of geckos chase each other along the perimeter wall and I yelp, "Ah!"

Paul, of course, makes a dash for the reptilian creepy crawlers, but I grab his shirt collar. "No!"

My uncle laughs. "A girl as big as you, and you're scared of a lizard?"

"Let him go," Grandma says. I release Paul's shirt. "Go ahead." She gestures, and Paul walks cautiously toward the duo. As he approaches, they immediately scatter.

"I'm gonna kill you if they jump in our food," I say in English.

Grandma swats at me. "Ey, leave him alone." I don't know how she knew what I said. "You know, when your dad was a kid, I used to let him run amuck. Bombs would be dropping here or over there, but I let him go because your feet, they have to touch the soil with your bare skin to know the land. To know it in a way no foreigner ever will."

Bác Long stands suddenly, moves to the wall, and swiftly catches a gecko in his hands. "Come here." He gestures to Paul, who immediately bolts over. I cringe as the reptile is placed inside Paul's hands, but at the same time, I'm in awe of how gentle this man seems to be with my brother. I've never known Vietnamese adult males to be anything other than stoic or dismissive of children.

"Heee!" I yelp as the furry paw of a golden retriever lands on my lap.

"Down," my grandma hisses. But the dog doesn't listen.

I laugh and rub his soft head. "What's his name?"

"Chó." Grandpa laughs. He's a dog. What else would he be called? *Chó* literally translates to *dog*.

"Don't let him eat too much. He's already too fat," Grandma says, but Chó doesn't look fat to me. I tear a piece of beef off the bone and feed it to him.

"Ey!" My dad slaps my hand. "Do you know how expensive meat is here, and you're feeding it to the dog?" he says in English.

I don't know if my grandpa understands or if he can just intuit based on tone, but he tells me to go ahead and give the dog the bones—they're his favorite part anyway. I peel more meat away and look to my dad for approval, except he's taken to ignoring me. Gently, I put the bone back on my plate.

"Good. Except, do you know who is older in age than your dad?" Grandpa asks. I try unsuccessfully to suppress my smile. I mean, he is technically more senior to my dad, but I've only just met him, and I'm not comfortable shifting authority this quickly. Sensing this, Grandpa urges me on. "If Grandpa says you can give the bone to the dog, you can go on and give it." This twist of fate is fun. Grandpa is pulling rank, and I consider it, but I also know who disciplines me, so I shake my head and smile.

Grandpa is relentless, though, and he presses my dad. "Tell the girl to give the bone to the dog already."

"Who you saving the bone for?" my dad barks at me in English. Shit. I'm in trouble now.

"No one," I reply, wishing I could just swallow the bone myself to get everyone off the topic.

"Chó," Grandpa calls, and the dog's head perks up. "Eat it." To my dismay, Chó swipes the bone off my plate in one swoop and disappears into the kitchen.

And then something occurs to me. "Grandpa, do you eat dog meat?" My question is earnest. I really do want to know if Chó will be eaten at some point. I've heard the rumors. I've been teased at school for it. Immediately, my dad slaps the back of my head, but Ông Nội roars with laughter, which then makes the whole table erupt in bellyaching amusement. Honestly, I can't tell if they're laughing with me or at me. Given my family's sense of humor, they would find it equally funny that (a) I think they eat dog, and (b) I am horrified at the prospect of unknowingly being fed dog stew. I mean, we *do* eat a lot of weird animal parts.

In between laughs, Ông Nội jokes that Chó's too old to taste any good, and then, as if on cue, Chó howls from his spot inside the door. This makes even Paul and me laugh, and just like that, the tension from earlier is gone. My grandpa is funny, my grandma is nice, and my uncle, he seems pretty okay too. I don't understand it. Also, that aunt no one introduced me to is not an aunt. Bác Loan, a simple woman in her sixties who wears her hair in a tight bun and is always in casual silk pajamas called áo bà ba, is their live-in maid. She greeted my dad warmly when he arrived, which means she was around when he was a kid.

Grandma orders her around, but not in a condescending or bossy way; it's more matter-of-fact, like a customer ordering items at a merchant counter. So strange.

After lunch, my grandma even tells me to leave my shoes on. No Vietnamese household allows someone to leave shoes on inside. So, I ignore her and take them off but instantly slide and fall smack on my ass. "I told you to keep your shoes on," Grandma laughs. She's not angry, though. She doesn't even yell. She simply walks to the closet, grabs a pair of house slippers, and hands them to me, but not before mocking me. Slap-rubbing my butt, she tells me I'll be fine because I'm young and my butt is made of hamburgers.

"Come here. Grandma wants to tell you a story," she says.

I move to sit beside her, no longer afraid she might discipline me. The living room is painted a slightly paler green than the exterior of the house, and there is an altar in one corner displaying black-and-white photos of ancestors I've never met. There isn't any furniture, just shiny rugs woven together using thin pieces of plastic and arranged in such a way that the alternating monochrome colors create a floral design. There isn't much in the way of padding, and I flinch when my tailbone lands hard on the floor.

Taking my hand, my grandma runs it along the dirt floor just beside our mat, and when she sighs, I know to listen closely because she's about to tell me a story.

My dad was still a child. A bomb rocked the night. This time, the whole house shook, and dust and sand rained back down to earth. Massive fires pierced the darkness, creating the illusion of sunlight. But it was not daytime. Dirt from the courtyard had been displaced, and the very next day, without much fuss, Grandma and my dad went about putting it all back together. Trip after trip, my seven-year-old father would bike with three full buckets—two on the handlebars and one tied to his stomach while it rested on the back half of his seat. Alongside him, my grandmother walked, carrying an even heavier load across her shoulders on a bamboo stick.

I touch the dirt floor again, and this time it feels warm. Like the heat from an explosion decades ago still lives in the soil.

She tells me my dad wasn't always so serious, that he used to be a dreamer—a kid who wandered about the destruction with blinders over his eyes. He was a talented musician, and when he climbed high into the hillside, he could settle the entire town with his songs. The soulful sounds that flew from his flute reminded Đa Nẵng's people of the beauty that their homeland was capable of producing.

Before this summer, I would never have guessed my dad could play the flute. Loud, booming drums? Maybe. But a delicate pipe in which musical notes fluttered through and emerged gracefully? Impossible. Except I know it to be true. I saw it with my own two eyes.

That night, the war came to her literal doorstep. It scared my grandma, and all these years later, the fear still lives in the deep creases around her eyes. Those wrinkles, made of soft skin, hold the tears she has carried with her since the end of the war and the beginning of our familial separation.

"The night was cold and eerily quiet," Grandma begins, and the roof opens to a bright night sky lit up by orange and yellow sparks. The ground beneath us shakes in broken staccato as bombs break with the natural rhythm of the land—they don't belong here. We arrive in 1971. My dad, a skinnier version of Paul, lies next to his brother, teenage Uncle Long, and Grandma. They huddle together in this same broken corner of the house, shaking with fear. In her mouth, she can taste the particles of metal in the air. And then *BOOM*!

A bomb falls in the alleyway, destroying not just their courtyard but the neighbor's as well, plus the two houses in front of them. Dirt resettles, but concrete kills. Her hands shake as she motions the dropping of bomb after bomb after bomb—a relentless barrage of destruction. The families in nearby houses are gone, just like that. And in the courtyard, where the two motorbikes now stand among the shrapnel, is a large piece of bombshell with the remnants of a faded and cracked American flag undeniably visible—they were American bombs.

The very next day, Uncle Long escaped to the North and joined the Communists. But the seeds of dissent were present long before this moment.

Grandma's sister, Bà Huỳnh (the one whose death prevented us from going to Disneyland one time), was the mother of Việt Cộng soldiers. Nine years Grandma's senior, Bà Huỳnh had lived in the North when the war began in the 1950s. Because she lived there, her family became Communist. The Communists were clever. They built underground tunnels and figured out how to rally support from within South Vietnam. Uncle Long was one such convert. So when Uncle Long and Bà Huỳnh's son, Uncle Giang, connected during the war, they built an unshakable bond.

I think about the maze of underground tunnels and wonder if this is how they did it. If this was how they kept in touch.

My dad, though, was loyal to Grandma, who believed in the Republic of Vietnam. And after the war, well, the two brothers had their differences. I wonder what my takeaway from this is supposed to be. The war was complicated. I know that. But is she making excuses? Does she even know what my dad is like now? Should I be the one to tell her he's not the soft kid he was before the war ended?

"The chain on your neck, your dad carried that across the ocean when he crossed over," Bà Nội says, then points to the back of my jeans. "This pocket in the back of your pants, I taught your dad how to make that."

I reach for the secret compartment in my underwear, which I had forgotten about, unzip the pocket, and give her the gold bars. Her outstretched hand shakes as they land in her palm. I wonder if she thinks they were worth it. If sending her son on a boat to America, leading to twenty years of separation, was worth two measly gold bars.

I knew our family to be huge, but the parade of different faces that come through the house in just a few days is startling.

They're introduced to me as aunts, uncles, cousins, and older or younger men and women delineated not by our respective ages but by the ages of our parents in relation to each other. The wave of new people is so overwhelming that I can hardly tell one from the next. And truthfully, all I want to do is spend more time with Grandma. Our suitcases and the boxes we brought stand open in the living room, and as people come visit, they each take some of the items. I've never known adults to get so excited at the sight of M&M's. Uncle Long, who has been diplomatically dispensing the items, tears open a pack of candy and tosses a giant plastic spider at my dad, who flinches as he catches it in one hand.

"A grown person as big as you scared of a little spider," Bác Long says to my dad before turning to me. "When your dad was small, I used to catch these little spiders and drop them down the back of his shirt to watch him dance like a monkey." I can hardly believe my ears, and I must have a look of horror on my face because he points at me and starts laughing. "Like father, like daughter!"

The spider down the shirt is horrifying for sure, but that's not really why my mouth is agape and my face has contorted into awe. I'm shocked because that whole "You are a big human scared of a tiny spider" is the exact same thing my dad says to me when I yelp and call for help when I find one in the store. If it's just a daddy longlegs, he'll pick it up and thrust it at me before letting it go outside. The other, more gnarly spiders are deftly squished with whatever shoe or sandal is on his foot. That's right. He will step on a spider in sandals! As I watch my dad laugh and scare the other little kids with the plastic spider, I wonder what he was like at Paul's age.

"There is one extra bag left," Bác Long says. "Who wants to play for it? I'll be the Doctor, Phúc will be the Dragon. If I win, I keep this bag for myself. If the Dragon wins, the kids get to eat this candy now." Eight or nine of my fifteen or so cousins leap to their feet to play. Uncle Long points at the ones still sitting. "Don't cry when they win and you have no candy," he warns, and they, too, get up.

Paul and I look at each other. We have no idea what game they're playing.

"Come here," my dad says, and he lines up the kids from shortest to tallest.

"What are we supposed to do?" I ask.

"Hold on this shoulder, and don't let go," my dad says.

And that's literally all the instruction we get. Everyone else jumps into place. Fingers press tightly into my shoulders. I hear my dad shout "Bắt đầu!" and the line I'm in starts running. Because the line is so long, I can't really tell what's happening as our "dragon" weaves this way and that. I think I'm keeping up, when suddenly I start to feel my fingers slipping. I let go.

Uncle Long jumps for joy—something I've never seen a grown Vietnamese man do—and I laugh. He picks up the giant bag of M&M's and starts kissing it while rubbing his belly like he's really going to enjoy eating it all by himself. This makes me laugh harder, until I realize my cousins are staring at me, and they're not happy.

Crap, I just lost us the game. I start to apologize but don't have the words, so I just kind of stand there dumbly watching.

"Okay. Okay. Đừng khóc nữa," Bác Long says, making a mocking gesture of wiping his tears. He opens up the large bag filled with mini packages, and he walks around us. Taunting everyone with his bag of candy, he offers to trade. We get candy if we let him búng lỗ tai.

He starts with my dad, who laughs and turns his ear toward Uncle Long, who, with great joy, pulls on my dad's earlobe and gives it a solid flick.

"Ow!" my dad says, grabbing his ear in laughter. He's handed a bag of candy.

As Uncle Long moves down the line, the little kids squirm, but he only flicks their ear lightly before giving them their reward. When he gets to me, he asks if I've ever had my ear flicked before. I shake my head no, and a huge grin crosses his face. I notice my cousins all smirking too, but seeing as how I broke the chain, I'm not about to bail on the punishment.

"Chuẩn bị chưa?"

I nod yes and close my eyes because I'll never be ready, and I feel the quick flick of his fingernail hitting my earlobe. It stings, but the anticipation was far worse than the actual punishment. When I open my eyes to check and make sure that was it, he and all my cousins burst into laughter. Apparently, watching their Việt Kiều, aka overseas Vietnamese cousin, get her ear flicked brings them all great joy. Of course it would, because Vietnamese people love suffering. I'm not mad about it, though. It's better than having them all hate me for losing the game. And now that I think about it, by flicking my ear, Bác Long kept me from being the "American enemy" among my family.

I don't know if it's jet lag or adrenaline, but I haven't slept much since arriving, and I'm not at all tired. Which is why it's 4:00 a.m. and I'm sitting at the dinner table eating a fourth meal that the poor maid had to make for me. I hadn't meant to be a burden, but Bác Loan must have heard me enter because as I rummaged in the fridge for a snack, she pulled on my arm gently, escorted me to the table, and made me a cup of hot tea, rice, and eggs with scallion.

"Finish eating, and then Uncle Long will take you to see Việt Nam." His voice is so shallow and quiet that I think I must have imagined it, but when I turn my head to the doorway, my uncle is standing there waiting. He doesn't look patient, and he doesn't budge from where he's standing, so I quickly down my food and follow him to the motorbikes.

Moonlight casts a dim gray glow across the sky as we enter the courtyard. "Wait there," Uncle Long says, and gets on his bike. He turns the ignition key and kicks the engine into gear. The bike roars to life. Uncle Long then gets off the rumbling bike, opens the gate, hops back on the bike, kicks up the stand, and tilts it to the side so I can get on behind him—no helmets.

"Watch the exhaust pipe," he says, pointing to a metal cylinder near my foot—it's shiny and hot. Taking my wrists, he wraps my arms firmly around his stomach. I am uncomfortable for about two seconds until he revs the engine, and we shoot forward into the alley.

The city is quiet but not empty. Storefronts creak open, and street vendors park in place, but we don't stop here. We pass through all of that and head up a steep hillside. As the city falls away, lush green foliage takes its place, and the smell of exhaust is replaced by lemongrass. We aren't going that fast because he has to navigate around potholes and muddy trenches and because he probably isn't used to having an extra 110 pounds on the back of his bike. But he seems to know exactly where the obstacles are, and we speed through the straightaways. Mesmerized by the passing scenery, I'm not really paying attention to where we're going until he suddenly veers right—straight into some bushes. We stop.

Uncle Long looks both ways to be sure no one else is around. He revs the engine, and we shoot forward. Like Moses parting the Red Sea, the bright green foliage recoils to the side, revealing a path. He slows and tugs at a branch. "This is called a shy plant. When you touch it, the leaves clamp shut." I reach for an undisturbed part and touch it like I'd pet a cat. It closes, and Bác Long's eyebrows shoot up. He looks at me mischievously and he whispers to the plant, "Don't worry. This Việt Kiều has our blood. Open wide to welcome her home." I smile, thinking this is my uncle's way of telling me I belong here, when suddenly the leaves fold open in a flutter. My jaw drops. I've never seen a plant react with such humanlike emotion. My uncle revs the engine and we continue.

This can't be real. We stop and park at the edge of Tarzan's jungle, except this isn't animation—it's real. Water rushes from a ledge just a few feet above my head and cascades down into the open valley below. Vines hang everywhere as if we've fallen into the epicenter of the world's rain forest. Birds crisscross past one another, and dragonflies zip about like schools of fish in the mist-filled air.

From up here, Đa Nẵng is a mere microcosm of a much larger ecosystem made of trees, flowers, vines, roots, and all the species in between, including us.

"Come here." I walk to where he's standing at the edge of a dirt cliff. "That over there is Đỉnh Bàn Cờ," he says, pointing to a huge mountain on our left. "And far that way near you, Thái Bình Dương," he says, pointing toward the Pacific Ocean. "There is no place on earth like Việt Nam."

Taking me by the shoulders, he turns me around. His command is gentle, unlike the firm tone my dad has, which makes my whole body stiffen. Behind us is the strangest tree. It's thick-rooted and bushy, providing ample shade, but it also has roots falling from its branches. And as I stand next to Uncle Long, a man who admittedly scares me, the tree takes on the shape of a wise man's beard.

Uncle Long tells me that this tree has stood here for over 800 years—the life span of eight people. It has weathered wars, famines, and typhoons. Impressive. Next, he walks me into the cave of roots and shows me a set of initials carved into the bottom. *P.V.*—Phúc Vũ, my dad. Pulling a small Swiss Army knife from his pocket, he hands it to me and nudges me forward. Beneath my dad's initials, I add + *J.V.*

"When he was real little, your dad came here a lot," he says, laughing to himself. "He thought it was his secret spot, but anyone who lives here knows about it. He had the gift of ear, though, so people liked to hear him play." I let the dig slide. Imagining my dad as an emotional teenager with a secret hideaway spot like this is difficult, but my uncle doesn't seem like the type to exaggerate.

I don't know how to answer, so I avoid eye contact and stare at the tree. This beautiful place suddenly makes me sad, and I have no idea why.

Bác Long speaks poetically, and I gather I'm supposed to read between the lines. But my Vietnamese isn't strong enough to fully grasp the meaning. I think he's telling me about how the region and water are connected and from that water something pours out. Spirits maybe? He looks at me and I nod, silently praying that he doesn't ask me any follow-up questions. If I can't decipher English poetry, I sure as shit cannot elicit meaning from Vietnamese poetry, proverb, or simple conversation. I smile dumbly and listen because it's the best I can do.

While he talks, I imagine what it would've been like to grow up here. To wake up to the sounds of bombs, to smell whatever it is explosions smell like, to run from gunfire you hear but can't see, to be a child of war. It's all so foreign to me.

My uncle, who must have sensed my wandering mind, tsks his tongue. "Sometimes there is no choice between good and bad, only between bad and worse." I look over to let him know I'm listening and wait for him to say more. My American History book barely touched on Vietnam, and maybe that's what he means—that although we're a small country, we matter. But he offers nothing more. Maybe he thinks I wouldn't understand, and the situation was far too complicated for my simple teenage brain. It could also be he has regrets. Or he feels righteous indignation about his choices; his side *did* win the war, after all. I want to press him for more information. I have so many questions, like how he could have abandoned his family. And did he really believe in the Communist cause?

"Con . . ." My Vietnamese is failing me. I don't know how to ask anything that's springing to mind. I try to think of the right words, the respectful phrases I need to open and close my audacious questions, and the humble tone to show him that I'm not accusing him of anything. "Tại sao Ông Nội có—" I want to know about Grandpa's scar.

He cuts me off, and I flinch, prepared for him to strike me. But he just says, very matter-of-factly, "Don't believe that shit they write in your textbooks about Việt Nam. This is a beautiful country."

There's no way one conversation can explain a complicated family history spanning twenty-plus years, let alone an entire war. And although deciphering his words feels a bit like understanding poetry, he's told me more about the war in the last hour than my dad has told me my entire life.

Back at the house, everyone is eating breakfast when we arrive. Two bowls and chopsticks are promptly placed on the table as we sit.

"Where have you been?" Paul pouts.

"Bác Long just took me to see the countryside on his motor-bike."

"Why didn't you wake me? I want to see too."

I don't have an answer for that because the thought hadn't even crossed my mind. "Sorry, I will next time."

Despite having a housemaid, Grandma is constantly in motion; she never sits still. Even when she's eating, her chop-sticks move about the table, rearranging food to make it easier for Paul and me to reach or deboning the fish so we don't choke. Grandpa, though, spends most of his time upstairs resting. Dad spends a couple of hours up there every night, but he never invites us, which I think is odd, but then again, I wouldn't know what to say, so I guess I'm kind of relieved.

As the maid clears my bowl from the table, she shakes my shoulder and points to my muddy legs. "Đi tắm đi!" she says, and ushers me toward the shower. It's a simple tiled room with a large plastic bucket filled with clean water and a smaller plastic pail with a handle. There's no plumbing here and also no privacy. I quickly lather and rinse, still not used to the lack of running water.

"Mosquitoes love your hamburger blood." Grandma laughs, pointing at my legs. "Finish bathing and come see me." Back home this would have startled me, but now I know it's just how things are in Vietnam.

I find her and Paul on the living room floor with a rag, bucket, and bottle of water. Paul has an arm over the bucket, and she's rubbing it with a towel as he tries not to flinch. Even with the mosquito netting wrapped around our beds, we both look like we have a bad case of chicken pox. Paul sucks in air through his teeth, and Grandma laughs, rubbing harder.

"People pay a lot of money to drink this, and here we're rubbing your arms and legs." Paul scrunches his nose. He understands her, but his Vietnamese is even worse than mine, so that's about all he can do.

Then it's my turn.

Paul scoots over and lies on his back, spread eagle and stiff like he's afraid that so much as a twitch will revive the pain.

"Ah!" I yelp as Grandma laughs and pats the vodka, *not* water, into my arm to help ease the stinging. And as soon as the wet rag meets my skin, I understand why.

"Join me in my misery," Paul grumbles, and then winces.

Bà Nội slaps him on the leg, "Speak in Vietnamese." He winces and says, "Chị đau với con," which translates to *my older sister hurts with me*—not bad. Grandma laughs. Had this exchange happened over the phone, I would've thought her cruel, but I can see now that there is virtually no situation in which she cannot find humor.

"Why does Bác Long live here, but my dad lives in America?" I ask in broken Vietnamese. I get that Uncle Long is a Communist, so of course, he would stay, but why did his brother have to flee then? My question is basic because my Vietnamese is bad, but it's loaded, and I think Grandma gets it.

"Umm." Bà Nội nods. She contemplates this a moment before saying, "First, you should know, war was not a choice. Not for ordinary citizens, anyway. For our family, the war was as simple as this: We lived in the South, heard Southern propaganda, and became soldiers in the South Vietnamese army. My older sister lived in the North and heard Northern propaganda, and her sons became soldiers for the North Vietnamese. Each side felt the bombs, witnessed the destruction, and believed in their cause."

I don't know if she is so caught up in the narrative that she's scrubbing more gently or if I'm so preoccupied with her storytelling that I no longer register the pain.

She tells me that Communist propaganda spoke of unification, but that's not how it felt. No one trusted each other, not even family. Bác Long, Grandma's own flesh and blood, was not to be trusted. And even though he was a senior colonel, he could not guarantee that Phúc wouldn't be drafted for the next war. The uncertainty meant that many people fled, and many more were gunned down. Who do you trust if you can't trust family?

"Is it right that Ông Nội's scar is because of Bác Long?" I ask.

"No," Grandma says. "But that scar is why I sent your dad to America."

I nod again, but I don't totally understand. I think she's saying there was distrust within the family, yet she denies that Uncle Long caused the scar. Uncle Long also seemed to say no when I asked. And Grandpa could've gotten that scar any number of ways. War causes all kinds of disfigurement. Then I remember

Uncle Chuyên talking about the chain and I don't know; the evidence seems pretty damning against Uncle Long.

Still, I have a hard time picturing my uncle, a man who plays children's games with such fervor, being this callous. But then I remember my own beatings and I think, *Is a man capable of hurting his own family? Absolutely.* So maybe Uncle Long wasn't so much denying it but saying that nothing is as simple as it looks. Like he had to do it because it was better him than someone else?

Grandma sees me struggling with this information, and she laughs—further proof that she can find humor in *any* situation. "Here's something no one tells you: when a war ends, guess who cleans up the mess.

"Ordinary people.

"War is chaos. We want to believe there are charts and strategic organization, but there aren't. There are just people roaming freely, who end up stepping on land mines. X marks the spot is a fantasy. There is no X there; it's all just chance.

"If you're lucky, you'll miss it by an inch. If you're lucky, you'll only lose a leg. If you're lucky, you'll escape.

"I put your dad on that boat alone because each child having a fifty percent chance of survival is better odds than all three of them having a single fifty percent chance of survival."

"But if they traveled together, they could help save each other," I say. Weren't families supposed to stick together?

Grandma shakes her head. "The only result there is that everyone drowns." The way she says it, there's no room for interpretation; it's a fact.

"You think you have choices because you were born into

a democracy. War is not democratic. War is about power, and when you don't have any, your only job is to survive. This is how it happened for us.

"So many treacherous things happened in the ocean. But good news traveled faster than bad news because the living can speak while the dead disappear. As news of more and more families finding refuge in Malaysia, Indonesia, and Hong Kong spread throughout the country, citizens grew more confident about the journey.

"Do you know why I named your dad Phúc?" I shake my head no. "I had three miscarriages before he was born. When he survived birth, I knew he was lucky, and because of that, I knew he would make it. I knew."

Bà Nội pats my arms and legs, causing them to tingle, and gives me a thumbs-up. "Don't scratch, or it will scar," she says, making a scratching motion and wagging her finger at me. Pointing to the bottle, she says, "Doesn't look like much, but this will keep your skin from having marks. We can't send you back to America disfigured!" I kind of doubt that this will work, but the itching has subsided. And the mosquitoes don't appear to like the smell, since I haven't gotten any new bites, so maybe mosquitoes don't like getting drunk.

It's our last night in Vietnam. Dad and Bác Long have completely taken apart a motorbike in the courtyard while Grandpa and Paul lie side by side in a wide swinging hammock.

Grandpa and grandson don't have the language skills to speak to one another, but neither of them minds as they glide side to side in what looks like quiet meditation. Just inside the doors, Grandma and I roll the ingredients for bánh tết. This dish is usually only made during the Lunar New Year, but when I told Bà Nội that it was my favorite food, she insisted on teaching me how to make it properly. We spent four hours yesterday preparing the filling, and today we're assembling the ingredients before they cook. The process consists of taking three pre-cut square pieces of banana leaves, laying down rice, sticking the pork belly and mung bean filling (made yesterday) inside, and then coating it evenly in rice. I am sure mine will be lopsided, but I do my best to copy Grandma.

"Do you know why your dad knows how to fix that motorbike?" Bà Nội nods toward my dad and uncle.

"School?"

She laughs. "No. Ông Nội was a boat mechanic, and your dad used to help him."

"I thought Grandpa was the person that"—I pause and try to find the word for combat medic—"fixed people who were hurt during the war?" Wasn't that what Bác Luy said?

Grandma nods. "Before. During the Anti-French Resistance War, he learned to reset bones. After the war, even now, people still come here to have him straighten broken bones, but his job, what he did for money, was to fix boats. He used to take your dad down to the docks with him. That's why he can do all that."

To be honest, I'd never really questioned how my dad knew

anything, but it's true. He never consults books but somehow knows how to fix the fridges, freezers, and all our cars. In my head, I equate being cheap with fixing things. I figured he learned because he didn't want to pay for anything new.

"Vietnamese people are highly adaptable. Survival is about grit. Millions of Vietnamese were stranded at sea for weeks or months. Think about it, how did they survive?" She looks at me, but I have no idea, so I just stare at her until she continues. "When something breaks, fix it. If you lose something, find it. If you drop something, dive for it. You do whatever it takes, and sometimes that means doing things or eating things you don't like. Like dog." She smirks at me now. She's trying to make light of the lesson, but I sense she's saying something else too. "Your dad was lucky, but that doesn't mean he didn't have to fight to live, do you understand?"

"Dạ," I say, and I think I actually do. Nothing is black or white. War forced people into gray spaces. As a result, my dad is many shades of gray. He's not all good, and he's not all bad. He's both.

"I can't be mad about it, though, because he could've been one of the half a million dead bodies floating in the sea, whose lives stopped mid-sentence. I know it in my head, but I don't keep it in my heart," she adds, poking me in the chest.

"Dạ," I repeat, not wanting to be poked again because it kinda hurt!

CHAPTER 25
PHÚC

When the truck finally pulled to a stop, Phúc found himself standing in front of a warehouse with several large, open doors the size of semitrucks. Inside, heavy machinery squeaked and clanked and crunched. As he passed by bolts that were the size of jumbo tires, it dawned on Phúc just how far away from home he had traveled.

The group was led deeper into this futuristic cavern, where each of them was matched with a pair of safety goggles, a bright orange or yellow vest, and a hard hat. None of the gear fit, making the petite men look like children pretending to be adults—all besides Phúc, of course, who at fourteen, actually *was* a child.

"Keep on at all times!" the foreman shouted over the noise as he tapped on his hard hat. He was an abnormally tall man with perfectly straight teeth and a sharp demeanor that belied a relaxed nature. Phúc understood the tapping of his hat, the two fingers pressed against his goggles, and the tug of his vest to mean that he was to wear his uniform every day.

Off they moved together, a cluster of bright colors amid a sea of metal, rust, sawdust, and dirt. As they continued into the warehouse, the machinery swooshed and crunched overhead and on all sides, warning them not to disobey the rules. They walked and walked and walked some more until they came upon a small office in the back. Each worker received a long, cream-colored piece of card stock and a pen.

At this point, a shorter white man came and stood next to the tall foreman. "Viết tên của bạn," the man said, and it took them all a second to realize he was speaking Vietnamese. Jamison—whose name they would learn later—was a good-natured guy with a thick neck and muscly arms. When he spoke their language, it came with an English accent, and he enjoyed watching the men react. He waited as their expressions turned from confusion to recognition, and then they erupted in friendly laughter before continuing. Not long after that, the crew gave him a Vietnamese name: Chú Sơn. Also, his real name was hard to pronounce.

Chú Sơn translated as the foreman held up his card and slid it into a metal box where teeth clasp shut, and a date and time appeared within the designated boxes on the punch card.

From here, everything moved much faster. Chú Sơn pointed at each of the twelve men and asked, "Tên, nghề nghiệp." Chú Sơn's English accent over-sharpened the *t* sound and completely missed the vowels when pronouncing *nghề nghiệp*, but the men surmised that he meant "Name, occupation."

Mến Hoàng, a fisherman, became a sorter along a huge conveyor belt. In Hong Kong, sorting fish translated to sorting pipes.

An Ngô, a dentist, was asked about a cavity and then skipped over. In Hong Kong, they needed dentists too!

Trúc Hồ, a jewelry maker, was placed before a massive foundry. In Hong Kong, melting jewelry translated to forging brass.

And then it was Phúc's turn. "Phúc Vũ, mechanic."

Chú Sơn looked skeptical.

"Bicycle." The group laughed collectively because *every* kid in Vietnam was a bike mechanic. When the foreman got the joke a moment later, he laughed too, then led them off in yet another disorienting direction. Glancing past Phúc, he pointed to another man.

Bình Dương, a lawyer, was also nearly skipped over. His was the only truly useless skill on the site. But Bình Dương didn't accept this. He stepped forward and explained that most of his job was pinning pages together with brass tacks. Chú Sơn considered this, then assigned him the job of screwing pizza-sized nuts onto the enormous bolts.

Following the lawyer's lead, Phúc puffed himself up, walked to one of the oversized bolts, and began awkwardly screwing it onto a cylinder. The action made him look even smaller than before. "I am fast. Faster than these old men," he said in Vietnamese, ignoring the glares from his countrymen.

Chú Sơn was amused, but he waved Phúc off. "That job is taken."

With only a handful of men left, they walked through a set of heavy double doors and emerged at the edge of a giant pit. Here, Phúc was paired with a Chinese man in his early twenties named Tom. Tom spoke British English but no Vietnamese. If he had a problem with Phúc's youth, he made no mention of it.

Amid the dirt, steel beams and rebar poked up from the ground, reaching heights greater than Phúc thought possible. It reminded him of the bamboo forest that grew along the Đỉnh Bàn Cờ mountain. The arm of a metal crane swept across the sky like a fighter jet but without the screaming noise, and Phúc instinctively ducked as a wooden box of cables passed nearby. Tom laughed as the shadow rolled over them and the arm extended into the metal forest.

"This is gonna be fun." Tom smiled, and Phúc nodded, keeping his face serious. Whatever it was they were building here, Phúc wanted in. He wanted to learn. He would do whatever it took.

A truck with a large, slowly rotating container attached behind it pulled up beside them. Quickly leading Phúc around the truck, Tom pointed to various knobs, switches, gauges, and a small water tank just behind the driver's-side door. For every knob, Tom would say a word and turn to Phúc to make sure he understood. Phúc nodded yes to everything, but Tom wasn't dumb.

"Say it. Hydraulic transmission system."

"Okay."

"Hydraulic transmission system," Tom repeated.

"Yes."

"Hydraulic transmission system." This time Tom pointed to his mouth. "Hy-draul-ic trans-miss-ion system."

"Hy-dol-lic tan-missen sis-tem."

Tom approved. "Good."

They spent that day and the next learning and relearning phrases corresponding to knobs, buttons, chutes, and mechanisms. Tom made Phúc learn the name of every part of the concrete mixer before letting him into the driver's seat. Whatever Tom did, Phúc mimicked, and so the lessons went. This copycat direction took longer than it would have if Phúc had spoken English or Chinese, but for whatever reason, Tom didn't appear to mind.

Phúc nodded back curtly, like a robot ready to complete its next task.

"Relax, man, it's just a job," Tom said, but Phúc only stiffened more. He wasn't here for fun; he was here to work and had no interest in making friends.

In a week, Phúc became a cement pouring expert. His eye for depth and measurement, coupled with the shorthand sign language between him and Tom, meant they were done with their job by noon nearly every day. This must have been why Tom was so patient. They were in no hurry. Once the cement was poured, it needed to dry before the next level could be added.

When the project manager decided to expand their job, he added Nick and Luy to their cementing team.

Tom and Nick shook hands and bumped fists, excited to be working together again. "This is Luy," Nick said. "Pronounced like Louie. Watch him, though. His sleight of hand is slicker than a card shark."

Luy shook Tom's hand with his right and produced Tom's wallet in his left. Nick burst with laughter, patting Luy hard on the shoulders in applause.

"What the—" Tom said, taking his wallet back but not before checking to make sure its contents were all there. When he saw that they were, he shook it at Luy, laughing. "I'll be watching you." Pushing Phúc forward, Tom said, "This is Phúc, not to be confused with *fuck*. He's a serious kid, but I'll get a smile out of him yet." Nick and Phúc shook hands. Phúc bowed slightly in deference, but he stepped away from Luy. He didn't want to be associated with a thief.

"*Phúc* rhymes with *duke*. I can remember that," Nick says, shaking Phúc's hand.

Nick and Luy had been working together on another part of the building for months. Tom and Nick, both expats, had been coworkers and drinking buddies for more than three years. Together the four of them worked quickly and efficiently. Tom and Phúc operated the trucks while Nick and Luy smoothed and evened the molds using flat-edged hand tools. Then they spent the rest of the day drinking, playing cards (Bác Luy and Phúc taught Tom and Nick how to play Tiến Lên), or taking naps. Nick, like Tom, enjoyed mentoring, and when he noticed the slight dip in Luy's gait and the scabbed scar across a calf not yet healed, Nick did his best to give Luy the sections of cementing that had him kneeling rather than standing. They never talked about the wound—they didn't need to. Phúc could tell Bác Luy was grateful.

Unlike other kids his age, Phúc liked beer the instant it touched his lips. He didn't know that drinking during the day would make him sleepy, that the alcohol would relax his muscles and draw him into a deep dream. Or that the carbonation would bubble through his veins and surface in his mind like hot lava.

That first day, as he lay drooling on the pavement next to an unfinished floor, his eyes twitched, his fists clenched, and his knees kicked at the air as he dreamed of the cook from his escape boat lying helplessly on an open deck amid pools of watered-down blood sloshing from side to side. She threw her arms up in front of her, shielding herself as a five-gallon pot of boiling rice soup splashed down upon her. The skin melted off her bones and into the crawling soup, but Phúc, as horrified as he was, couldn't help himself. In a sickening attempt at survival, he reached toward her to scoop a handful of spilled broth with cupped hands.

He awoke to a bottle of liquid pouring into his mouth, but the image chased him into reality, and he threw up the three bottles of beer, dried squid, and crispy, deep-fried fish bones he had eaten earlier. Prickly, undigested bones tickled his neck as they came back up like a cactus pushing through his esophagus.

"Drink." Tom was standing over him with a fresh bottle of beer.

Phúc waved him off. Beer was the last thing he wanted right now.

"*Drink,*" Tom insisted. When Phúc still didn't accept, Tom pointed to Luy. "Tell him to drink."

"Uống đi. Cho ấm bụng." Luy was a seasoned drinker, so he understood that even though it was counterintuitive, the beer would warm his stomach and make him feel better. He, unlike the others, also understood that Phúc was being tormented by demons far worse than alcohol poisoning.

Phúc took a sip. He wasn't afraid of vomiting; he was afraid of falling asleep again. His nightmare wasn't real. The stomach-churning soup made of melted skin wasn't real. But the terror persisted because deep down, Phúc knew if it meant survival, there wasn't much he *wouldn't* do.

For weeks they carried on like this, Phúc always cordial and never friendly.

"Why is your face always wrinkled in a frown?" Luy asked Phúc in Vietnamese. Phúc turned away. "Tom seems to like you, but you have a really bad attitude for someone lucky enough to be given a job here."

"Says the thief," Phúc hissed.

"Back home, yes, but who didn't?"

Phúc scoffed.

"I made a deal with God. If he let me live, I swore I'd never steal again. Now I just do it for entertainment. Magic tricks."

"Magic is for kids, and we're not here for fun."

Luy raised an eyebrow at Phúc. "You think I'm stupid? These men might not be able to tell, but I know you're not seventeen." Luy saw fear creep up in Phúc's eyes when he said this, and he instantly felt bad. "I'm not going to tell. We've suffered enough, don't you think?"

Phúc nodded.

"Your hands. Em bị tật khi nào?" Luy asked, but Phúc didn't have a disability so much as he had a haunting. His idle hands prickled, and though the itching was phantom, the scratching was real. Red marks of his own making streaked across his palms. He knew something was wrong; he just hadn't expected anyone else to notice. Shoving his hands into his pockets, he didn't answer.

CHAPTER 26
JANE

I am never late.

If it's my first visit to a place, I give myself twice the amount of time it should take to get there, and I always leave a forty-five-minute buffer. Always. I drive exactly the speed limit, not a mile above or below, and I keep both hands on the steering wheel at the proper ten o'clock and two o'clock positions. On this schedule, I typically arrive at the coffee roaster's between 6:54 a.m. and 7:15 a.m. They open at 8. This buffer is in case my piece-of-shit, puke-brown, 1979 Corolla Liftback (which I secretly love because its four wheels will take me places) decides to fall apart.

On this particular morning, though, I got sidetracked by what I thought would be a quick Yahoo! search of the Vietnam War because my uncle was right. Everything about the war seemed to be from the American perspective. Every article was about Vietnam veterans who were not Vietnamese but rather American. I speed-read through articles about how unpopular the war was and how famous people like Jane Fonda drew criticism for visiting North Vietnam and being quite vocal against the war. Whatever their stories, I didn't care—I wanted to find something about Vietnamese people, *my* people, who lived amid the chaos, fought in the war, or fled like my dad. Yet, page after page revealed nothing helpful. I started trying different keyword searches until I noticed that it was already 7:24 a.m. I officially had zero buffer time and ran out the door. But I remembered I needed to unplug the internet line and replug the phone line, which I did, and then I rushed to my car, which now . . . won't start. Fuuuuuuuck.

The wholesale shop where we buy our ground coffee and condensed milk is twenty-two miles across town. It takes between thirty-six and forty minutes to get there on an average day. I make this trek once a week, twice if need be. Luckily, needing to go twice is rare, because it also happens to be right in the middle of the Vietnamese shopping district, the only part of town where driving rules and etiquette seem to fly out the window. You either learn to drive like the other Vietnamese people or you'll never get a parking spot. It's worth the hassle, though. Our coffee is our best-selling product and probably single-handedly keeps our store afloat because it costs us fifteen cents to brew and we charge $1.99 per cup. So, right now, I need my puttering car to get its shit together.

I turn the key again, pumping the brakes, and as luck would have it, the engine turns over. I check all the gauges; nothing seems to be amiss. It must be the starter or alternator. I make a mental note to go scrapping for that part later. I take off, careful not to press the gas too hard as I drive exactly the speed limit, brake a full three car lengths behind the car in front of me, and beg the engine not to stop.

"We're almost there. . . . Halfway there . . . Easy . . ."

I should've named my car. If I were a typical teenager, that would've been the first thing I did, but I know better than to get too attached to anything. Nothing that is a noun belongs to me. This mentality has saved me from a shit-ton of disappointment. My first lesson in the practice of non-ownership happened when I was six. I had this awesome jean jacket with a giant sparkling unicorn sewn on the back. I loved that freaking jacket. One day I went to the park with my mom, and while I was running around in the jungle gym and monkey bars, it just disappeared (someone stole it). It was never replaced.

When I was done crying, I wiped my tears, determined never to speak of this moment again. I don't know if I thought my desire to brag about it jinxed my luck or if I intuitively knew that if I cried about it at home, my parents would laugh at me or, worse, *punish me.*

Something in the engine begins to rattle. I tell myself it's not my car, but instead of moving on with another vehicle, the sound stays with me.

"C'mon, c'mon . . . ," I beg, gently gripping the steering wheel.

Then I see it: the uphill section of Overland Boulevard that I just know is going to kill the engine. But the light is green, and I beg it to stay that way because my car will die if I have to stop before reaching the top. I'm only a quarter of the way up, and I can hear the engine sputtering in a laughable, cartoonish, putt-putting sort of way. As I press the pedal to the floor, my tires spin in place and spew that awful skunk-like stench before the engine lurches and dies altogether. Quickly, I angle off the road and drift into the Chevron gas station on momentum alone.

Not only does it *not* work, but there's also a grinding sound accompanied by a mild vibrating of the key in the ignition. Shit. Somehow, I've made it worse.

Using the pay phone, I call home. It rings and rings. No answer. Dad must have left to open the store already.

I return to the car, where my blinking hazard lights reflect off the steel frame of the gas pumps. I pace back and forth, considering my options, but there aren't any. I'm too far to walk. I release my hands, which were clasped tight on my lap, and stretch my fingers wide. There is simply nothing I can do. I am no doubt in trouble for the car breaking down. I don't know how, but I will be found to be at fault.

As the futility of my situation sinks in, I kick the rim of my back tire, injuring my toe far more than the car. "Ow!"

"Need some help?" I spin around and come face to face with Jackie. She now has long, layered hair dyed light brown with highlights. It's so shiny that it appears to bounce even though she's standing still. She's even prettier than I remember.

"Not unless you got a mechanic degree I didn't know about." I hear the snark in my voice and instantly hate myself. As friends, this sarcasm would've been funny, but as ex-friends or whatever we are, it's obviously petulant.

"Maybe I do. You don't know," she says.

"What are you doing here?"

"I'm heading to Eastridge to meet Mirabelle. Just stopped to get gas and saw you beating up your innocent car."

I want to continue bantering and just pretend like our last conversation never happened. But we haven't spoken in weeks, and the mention of Mirabelle irks me. Why were they suddenly hanging with each other? She must sense my question because she says, "Her and Carly got into a fight over Carly's new boyfriend. I guess he said something about Mirabelle's weight."

"That's messed up," I say, knowing how sensitive Mirabelle is about her size. "Carly should've stood up for her or put her boyfriend in his place."

"Totally," Jackie says. Then, after a moment, she adds, "I tried calling you. Your aunt, I guess, picked up and said you were in Vietnam?"

Hearing this surprises me. "Yeah. My dad took us to see my grandparents. I guess he wanted us to meet in case they die or something."

"I was worried about you. I didn't know what might happen to you. There are no rules over there. What if they chopped you up or fed you dog meat?" she exclaims.

I smile. A month ago, this would've been funny.

We fall into a kind of awkward silence until finally, Jackie says, "I told my mom about what's happening to you." She puts both hands up in surrender. "Before you freak, I'm sorry. I didn't know what to do, but you'll be happy to know that she told me it was none of my business."

I look at her, unbelieving. Never in a million years would

I have thought that Jackie would betray me like this. Mostly I'm angry at myself for trusting her. For thinking I could tell her anything. Jackie seems to know this, too, and takes a deep breath. "She got really mad at me actually, called me spoiled, and told me that I don't understand anything about the world. Whatever that means."

"She's right."

Jackie doesn't react. "She said a lot of unthinkable things happened to refugees. She told me that she was raped. Several times."

I look up at Jackie in horror. She stares off. "I've spent so much time wondering about all the boys at school. Why they don't want to date me, why they do want to date me, and ugh, it makes my stomach churn to think of any guy touching me now."

"I'm sorry," I say. "I'm pretty sure it happened to my mom too." Part of me says this because I selfishly still don't want to let her off the hook. And it *could* have happened to my mom.

She nods. "I'm not trying to make excuses. I'm sorry for what I did, but I still just think if we don't address it, how will it ever change?"

"I am addressing it in my own way," I say.

"My mom said I was lucky because my dad is a real gentle soul. Most men who came over are like your dad; she said battered women are an ordinary story, children too. And that every family has to navigate through it on their own—without judgment. I'm not judging your dad. I just think he's wrong, and if someone told him so, he might stop."

"How is that *not* judging? I feel like what your mom said just went right over your head."

"Because it doesn't make sense. My parents went through the same thing, and they don't treat us like that, so maybe your dad is just an asshole. I don't understand why everyone feels the need to defend him."

"That's because you think everything a person does is either right or wrong when sometimes it's both."

Jackie doesn't say anything, and at this moment I know that things have really changed between us. She would never say it, but the way she looks at me now, it's the same way we both used to look at the FOBs navigating the lunch line at school—with pity and gratitude that we aren't one of them.

Reaching into the car, I open up my purse and locate the Tinker Bell pen we swapped before. "We should probably trade back," I say.

"What? No. This meet-up doesn't count. It wasn't planned," Jackie says with pleading tears in her eyes.

I look at her for a long while. We both know that's not what I meant. I'm not exchanging the pen so we can continue our planned ritual. I'm returning it because if I don't, we'll end up keeping each other's—and I want mine back.

"Okay," I say, putting the pen into my purse while cursing my stupid crying eyes. She seems to take this as an olive branch, but I know our friendship is over. I don't hate Jackie, but for the first time, I'm seeing how different we are. When we met, I thought she was so confident and cool, two adjectives I didn't believe could be associated with a Vietnamese person. It wasn't that we had a lot in common as much as I wanted to *be* Jackie. I thought of us as this duo of Vietnamese girls rebelling against our cultures, but Jackie was never rebelling. Her family already fit the mold of being well-assimilated American citizens. So actually, it's not Jackie who changed, it's me. I don't hate being Vietnamese anymore (though I wouldn't say I love it either), and I think my fobby cousins are kind of brave for starting over in a whole new place. If it were me, I know I'd be freaked out.

A motorcycle roars by with country music blaring from hidden speakers, and I remember where we are.

"People are going to think we're complete weirdos," Jackie says while delicately wiping her eyes.

"We *are* complete weirdos."

"I've really missed you," she says, and I start to reply, but before I can say anything, a Cambodian man walking toward us starts yelling at me.

"You can't stay parked there all day," the man—presumably the owner, in a neatly pressed but faded Chevron polo shirt—shouts.

"I know. I'm sorry. My dad is on the way." I get back into my car, pretend to try starting it again, and look at him dumbly until he concedes that I'm not going anywhere and goes back inside.

"I should go," Jackie says.

"Yeah," I say, feeling my throat catch. We don't make plans to see each other again. As she walks away, my heart aches for the friendship I've lost. But it's not a real friendship if one person looks down on the other, and I can tell that Jackie will never be able to look at me without thinking about my bruises.

I watch her green BMW Coupe pass through one green light

and then another before she turns right and disappears. After she's gone, I walk back to the pay phone to try the store again.

"Liq-or Store."

"Ba, the car died on me. I'm at the top of Overland at a gas station. What should I do?"

"Stay there." The line goes dead.

I hang up and wait.

Ten minutes.

Thirty minutes.

An hour and fifteen.

Two hours.

The Chevron owner is staring daggers at me through the store window. I do my best to shrink into my smallest form. Every moment that he's not helping some other customer, he glares at me disapprovingly. I get it. My crappy car is sitting broken in front of his business. If the tables were turned, I'd be glaring at me, too, from inside the window. I glare back. I mean, what am I supposed to do?

When my dad finally does arrive, he's in a chipper mood. The thing with my dad is, I never know what will be considered a mild annoyance and what's the end of the fucking world until the moment is upon me. Seeing that it's the former, I relax.

"What happen?"

"I was driving, and all of a sudden, I felt the engine die, so I pulled in here, and now it won't start."

He tries starting it, but the car remains idle. Much to my relief, that grinding sound doesn't happen again. Maybe it was just the way I turned the ignition?

He pops the hood and walks to the front. "Every couple of months, you need to check the engine fluids. You see this here? This is the oil." Pulling out the dipstick, he cleans it off, reinserts it, and yanks it up again to show me. "Between this two lines is okay. You need maybe another quart in here." He holds the silver stick closer to me so I can see. It sits inside the scarred dip in his thumb. When I was little, he used to tell me the devil came at night and removed this chunk of skin because that's what the devil does to naughty kids.

"Did you ever think maybe the devil cut your finger so it could fit the dipstick?" I ask.

My dad laughs.

"How did you really get that hole in your finger?"

"I hook it on the fishing line, and I don't know, so I pull really hard." He makes a tugging gesture with his hands as his face cinches in familiar pain. "A fishhook, you know, it has an extra hook at the top, so the fish can't get loose, so when I pull it . . . Man! Blood everywhere." He laughs at this like he's telling me a story about tripping over his shoelaces instead of accidentally mutilating his hand.

"Ew, why didn't you just leave it in?"

He just shakes his head in resignation and doesn't answer. Maybe he thinks I'll never understand.

"I told you, the devil make you do crazy things," he says, shoving the dipstick back in its place.

Not wanting to hear a lecture on the devil, I change the subject. "How come I've never seen you play the flute before?"

"What flute can I play?" he says, opening his palms in a gesture of empty hands. "When they pick me up, I didn't even know where I was. I had the shirt and pants on my body and everything else was gone."

"Why didn't you buy a new one?"

He shakes his head. "Not the same. You see the flute here is metal; it's not like the bamboo in Việt Năm. The sound is totally different."

"No, the Vietnamese one. I've seen it in the stores."

He laughs. "Those are just toys. The real one is special make. Only the old-time people know how to do it." His answer is so simple and basic. He got to America, they didn't have his flute, he stopped playing. It seems to me like he didn't really try all that hard to get a new one, but I don't dare say that. After adding oil, he pulls the dipstick out again and shows it to me. "Here, this is full."

I nod. "So is this why it died? Not enough oil?"

"No. That should be enough for the car to run okay. Here, the water need to be above this line. And the washer fluid here— make sure it above this line. Over there, the transmission fluid, you have to reach under to get to."

"Was it the transmission fluid?"

"No. Not that either." From the bed of his truck, he locates a new battery and, using a wrench, proceeds to swap it for the old one.

Once the battery is changed, he has me try to start the engine again. It turns over.

"Is it fixed?"

"Temporary. Take my truck and go get the coffee." He hands me the keys to his car. I grab my things and hurry off to the truck before he can change his mind. In the two years I've been driving, this is the first time he's ever let me get behind the wheel.

"Thanks, Dad."

"Okay," he answers, not looking at me.

I look at my watch. I've only got thirty minutes to get to the warehouse before they close for the day.

Sitting in the cab of the truck, I start the engine and slowly merge into traffic. As I join the other cars, I get my first brush with independence. In a week, I'll be sitting in a dorm without anyone to answer to and no Jackie to lean on. I'm scared of how alone I'm going to be—how lonely. And I have to tell myself to grow the fuck up. If my dad could leave home and take care of himself at the age of twelve, I, for damn sure, could make it through college.

CHAPTER 27
PHÚC

Paul yawns. "I'm getting sleepy."

"Sit up straighter."

"Can we make some popcorn? I always imagine better with popcorn."

I exhale a frustrated breath, but honestly I'm feeling a little tired myself. "Okay."

Paul jumps up and runs to the kitchen. He pulls the popcorn from the pantry and I toss it in the microwave. We listen as the kernels pop.

"Is this why Dad always makes me eat the fish's eyeballs?"

His question startles me. "Huh?" I say.

"Because he's worried that we'll starve?"

"Oh, maybe." I hadn't thought of that as the reason. I always thought he did it for fun because he liked to watch us squirm.

Ding.

"Okay. No more interruptions. Promise? I'm almost done."
Paul nods, one emphatic yes with his eyes ogling the popcorn.

We return to the bed, and I continue with Paul's question
lingering in the back of my mind.

As Phúc continued to drink beer, the vivid nightmares invaded more than just his sleep. A recurring presence in his dreams was Thầy Lâm's little girl in her pink sweater and pants. Tonight, he chased after her along the deck of the boat as she wildly swung from the railing, as though she were playing on monkey bars over sand rather than hovering thirty feet above the open ocean. Panda did somersaults alongside her like they were old friends. Thúy's laughter felt sinister against the backdrop of danger, and with every passing moment, his anger mounted.

"Stop," he yelled, though the words choked in his throat because his tongue was numb. "You're going to fall in," he warned. "And I'm not jumping in after you!" They ignored him, laughing at the game of chase in which he was an unwilling participant. Then, just as he'd gotten close enough to protect Thầy Lâm's daughter, Thúy's eyes went wide with fear before she let go and plunged into a crimson ocean with Panda following gleefully behind. His body jerked awake.

The dreams varied only slightly in the time of day and how the boat was set up, but everything else remained the same. In other dreams, Panda jumped first, and Thúy was like a fearless daredevil, running along the gunwale of an old frigate with ornately carved railings. Tipping her head side to side to match the beat of a nursery rhyme, she was naively calm despite the ship pressing forward against thunderous waves. But again, just as Phúc got close, she'd arch her back, stretch toward the sea, and fall into the breeze.

Sometimes Phúc jumped in after her and woke up in a cold sweat. Sometimes he watched her fall only to be startled awake when jostled from behind. The only constant was that Phúc couldn't ever change the outcome. No matter what he did, Thúy and Panda always jumped, and he'd wake up in a helpless panic knowing he had failed yet again.

Despite the nightmares, Phúc didn't stop drinking because he wasn't yet seasoned enough to know it was optional. He was paid to work from 6:00 a.m. to 3:00 p.m., which meant that when Tom handed him a drink, and Luy cheered "Một trăm," Phúc also raised his glass in cheers.

Every day, after three beers, Phúc would fall asleep drunk, wake up in a nightmare, and find reality again in a pool of vomit.

Finally, after a week of witnessing Phúc's spiraling routine, Tom patted Phúc on the back and said, "C'mon, I want to show you guys something." Technically they weren't allowed on the upper floors of the structure, but Tom was the boss, so Phúc, Luy, and Nick followed.

"Don't worry. It's completely safe." Tom winked.

Together the four of them stepped into a metal, open-faced lift that operated on a pulley system. Unlike an elevator, this red metal box had a single lever for up and down. There weren't floor numbers yet either because, apparently, the bosses were still arguing about whether or not to include the unlucky fourth, thirteenth, and fourteenth floors. Tom lifted the metal lever upward, and with a jolt, they started ascending.

One floor . . .

Two . . .

Three . . .

Seventeen . . .

Nineteen . . . Thirty-two. STOP.

Tom released the lever and manually pulled open the gate, and together they walked onto a cement platform that would eventually become the building's most senior executive suite. Exposed metal beams pierced through holes in the flooring that ran hundreds of feet to the ground below. Without any walls, windows, or guardrails, the openness of the space, though technically safe, was unsettling.

"You okay?" Nick asked.

Having never been this high off the ground before, Phúc could see his feet planted firmly on the ground, but his body would not stop swaying. Even though the building was utterly still, Phúc couldn't find his balance.

He sat down.

Luy, who was several years older than Phúc, boldly walked the perimeter, albeit at a safe distance of about five feet from the edge. Tom and Nick, however, walked right up to the edge and sat with their feet dangling thirty-two (or thirty-seven, depending on who's counting) stories in the air.

"Qua đây." Luy beckoned to Phúc. Luy was unrelentingly

kind no matter Phúc's coldness toward him. Phúc followed. From here, they had a 360-degree view of the city, and as Luy continued to walk in circles around the perimeter, he pointed to landmarks: the port they arrived at, the camp where they stayed, a colorful red-and-gold building that he called "the lucky red envelope," and what looked like a hundred small ships crowding the harbor. An invisible barricade prevented the vessels from docking. Countries neighboring Vietnam hadn't planned for the mass exodus—least of all Hong Kong. The British-ruled country didn't think the boat people were strong enough to make it that far and, thus, didn't know what to do with the massive influx of immigrants. These boats were forced to remain at sea for weeks before the administration did whatever they did to decide where to put them. All Phúc could think about when he saw them, though, was how many dead pandas were hidden below deck.

Stand up! Phúc commanded himself as he leaned back onto his calves in an attempt to stand, but his arms and thighs were already shaking so badly that he resigned himself to crawling. As he inched toward the edge where Tom and Nick sat, he picked up a discarded, hollow pole with a hole on one side. And even though the scrap metal, left over from the pipe installation, was cold to the touch, it grounded him, quelling the imbalance of his stomach. Even the stinging of his hands had subsided.

The view was stunning. A large river cut across the city, separating the two equally industrial halves. Every square inch of the land had been paved over, built on, and organized into clean, geometrical systems. The mechanics were impressive. That Phúc could stand this high off the ground in a building built by men was unimaginable just months ago. But the lack of greenery was alien to him. In Vietnam, it had felt like the wind, for instance, had been one with his breath. And though Phúc took the same breaths in Hong Kong, the oxygen that filled his lungs tasted heavy and full of concrete. The city was as lifeless as Phúc felt.

As Phúc lay with as much of his body touching a surface as he could manage, he searched the horizon for anything that looked lush and green. Then, slowly, he sat up, crossed his legs, closed his eyes, and held the metal bar out into the wind. He listened as a hollow whistle passed through the circular tube. It wasn't quite as sweet and soothing as the warm air that passed through his bamboo flute; instead, there was a sharpness to the measure, like a finger circling the top of a wineglass. Suddenly, the sound was gone.

Sitting up, Phúc ran his finger along the metal's surface before bringing it to his lips. Rather than producing a feather-light note, the sound dropped like a brick sinking to the bottom of the ocean—muffled to the point of not existing.

Undeterred, Phúc pulled himself up on his wobbly legs, held the pole to the side of his mouth, took a deep breath, and blew a few more notes before finding the makeshift flute's sweet spot. And finally, when he exhaled one long, confident note, the world at thirty-two floors above Earth abruptly froze. There was no wind, no shuffling of feet, no rustling of trees, no laughter, nothing but a shrill ring that hung in the air long after it left Phúc's metal rod.

For a moment, Phúc let the silence hang there before taking another breath and blowing again. This time he ran his index finger along the shaft, and the sharp note curved into a wave. A self-taught musician, Phúc played music that no one recognized or could sing to—but he wasn't trying to write a song. He was expressing a feeling.

At first, Tom, Nick, and Luy sat still and listened. And slowly, Hong Kong came back to life, merging with Phúc's tune. Nails being hammered into wood down below began knocking in the measured ticks of a metronome, and Phúc looked to his comrades to join him. Luy found a loose grouping of colorful electric wires and split them into thin strings pulled taut around a discarded board that was lined with nails on its sides. And when he plucked that first string, he became the band's sixteen-string zither, the đàn tranh.

Nick found a broken saw and mallet. With the broad end of the saw tucked between his legs, he bent the skinny end into an s-curve and gently hit the saw, creating a distorted warping sound that shifted the note as he curved the saw upward and downward. The wobbly effect sounded like an eerie gust of wind on a cold October night. The three of them fell into song with Tom sitting idly nearby and swaying his head, content to just listen.

When the music ended, Tom jumped to his feet and held up his finger, signaling them to hold on. He then *dropped off the side of the building.* His fingers, white from the weight of his body, clung to the edge where just two seconds before he had been sitting, and then they, too, were gone. Phúc rushed over, momentarily forgetting his fear of heights, but stopped short five feet from the edge. He had already witnessed one suicide. He didn't want to see another.

"Toooooom!" he yelled, his metal flute clattering against the floor as he dropped it.

Silence.

Then from directly beneath them came a thump. *Thump. Thump, thump, thump.* Moving away from the edge, Phúc continued hearing the drumming and followed it to the center of the floor, where an unfinished portion of the construction left a four-foot-wide hole that extended like a funhouse mirror into oblivion. Clustered in the center of this hole was a thick bunch of rebar that Tom was climbing like a kid in a jungle gym. He had two empty five-gallon paint buckets on each of his arms and one clutched between his gritted teeth. As he neared the top, Nick took the bucket from his teeth, and Tom hopped out of the hole like a rabbit from a magician's hat.

This time, Tom and Nick took the lead, quickening the tempo. The band now had drums, and as the keeper of pace, Tom wasn't interested in Phúc's melancholy reminiscing of his past. Instead, he pushed them to explore happier melodies. After a few minutes, Phúc and Luy retook the lead again and drew the group back into the sounds of loneliness and nightmares. Back and forth it went with every song.

And in this quiet way, Phúc and Luy forged a deep friendship.

For over two years, Phúc, Luy, Tom, and Nick carried on like this. Life was quiet. But it couldn't stay that way forever. Phúc was a refugee, this camp was temporary, and America was calling.

One day, a female soldier came to Phúc's makeshift bed at the edge of the encampment and asked, "Are you Phúc Vũ, from Đa Nẵng, born on January 1, 1961?" He almost said no, but he had no idea where that lie might lead him, so instead, Phúc nodded yes.

"You've been granted immigration to San Jose, California, in the United States. Do you wish to accept?"

Once again, Phúc nodded.

"Yes or no," the woman said.

Although he still didn't understand much English, *United States* and *yes* were the two phrases he'd learned.

"Yet." Phúc looked her straight in the eyes and tried to enunciate better. "Ye-sss. Plee, ye-ss."

CHAPTER 28
JANE

I hate cleaning day. Every once in a while, Dad will decide that the apartment needs a deep clean, and today is that day, I guess. Instead of working at the store, I'm scrubbing the kitchen floors with a bucket of bleach mixed with vinegar. It smells like shit. *I* smell like shit. Paul is in the living room watching a cartoon like I told him to. I figured there's no need for both of us to be suffering, and he rarely gets to watch TV, so I'm happy to do it . . . well, as happy as one can be as an indentured servant. It's 3:00 p.m., and I've already wiped down the shelves, scrubbed every part of the bathroom, and moved all the furniture away from the walls so I can vacuum. *The Fresh Prince of Bel-Air* comes on at 5:00, and I really want to be done by then.

I'm cleaning old food from the fridge when I open the trash can and find it full.

"Paul!"

Silence. I can hear the chatter of cartoon characters. "Paul!" I repeat. Still nothing.

Ugh. I wash my hands in the sink and yank the trash bag out of the bin. It gets caught on something and rips open, spilling its contents all over the floor I *just* cleaned. Great. I get a new bag, pick up the trash with my bare hands because we don't have gloves, and then hold my breath to reach deep into the can to get the crap stuck to the bottom. Now I'm pissed. I take everything to the backyard, where I dump it in the large bin, spray the can clean, and leave it upside down to dry.

"Thanks for the help, Paul," I shout sarcastically at his astonished face as I pass through the living room.

"What?"

"I called you to come help me. I've been cleaning all day, and I ask you for fifteen seconds of help, but you couldn't get up?"

"I didn't hear you."

"Yeah, because you weren't listening!"

Without a word, he makes his way to the back door to see what I was doing. I watch him pick up the trash can and bring it inside. "Who asked you to do that? I left it there for a reason."

Paul does exactly as he's told, but when he returns, I block him from coming back in. I'm bolder than I've ever been with our dad. Paul steps toward me, his hand reaching into the doorframe before I slam the door shut. It all happens in a split second.

"Ow!" he screams, and begins to cry, wailing at the top of his lungs. The shock turns into a guttural cry of pain.

Even as he clutches the hand I just smashed in the doorframe,

I make no move to soothe him. I just stand there. Watching him cry. Waiting for him to stop. I don't know how to react. The problem is, I saw his hand there. I was angry, and I slammed the door on it. I knew what I was doing. I should be sorry, but it's like I somehow skipped over guilt and went straight to anger. I'm so indignant that instead of letting him back inside, I close the door on him.

Paul deserves an apology. But that's not how it works in my family. Elders never apologize. And I am Paul's elder. He messed up, and now he's suffering the consequences. I shouldn't feel bad. It's not like I hit him for no reason. He should've listened to me.

It's quiet now. Paul must have stalked off. My closing of the door made him leave. And so he did. He walked away from me the same way I've walked away from my own beatings. But surely this wasn't as bad. I didn't *keep* slamming the door on his hand. That's at least a little better, right?

Paul is fine. I've dealt with worse, and I turned out fine. This is good for him. He needs to toughen up anyway because once I'm gone, he's next in line.

What would an apology accomplish anyway? Nothing.

I can't even imagine my dad uttering those words. *I'm sorry.* Actually, it would probably be really off-putting. I would probably hate it. Because then I'd have to say, "It's okay," even though it isn't. And maybe that would lead to me saying *I love you . . .* ? No, no way. Not *ew* exactly, just . . . uncomfortable. We're not mushy. We don't apologize. We just . . . be. We be, and then it blows over, and things go back to normal. *That's* our normal.

But I shouldn't have done it. I know that.

For some reason, Jackie pops into my mind. I wonder, if she saw what I just did, would she call the cops on me? The thought makes me feel both guilty and relieved to not have her in my life anymore.

Without looking for Paul, I open the door and leave it ajar, returning to the kitchen to finish my chores, and I only know that he is back in the apartment when I hear the TV shut off and the house go completely silent. I think about my cousins. Did they influence me to finally let go, to cave to my anger? Is that a good thing? It doesn't *feel* good.

I'm tagging inventory with sticker price tags. Usually, I'm meticulous, making sure that every bag is marked, but right now, I'm skipping a few here and there, hoping to just get through the tedious task. Paul's been avoiding me, and I know this is shitty, but he's stuck with me for the next ten hours. I leave for college on Tuesday, and if anyone can hold a grudge for four days, it would be Paul.

I haphazardly finish sticker-tagging and bring a bag of Flamin' Hot Cheetos into the cashier's box, where Paul is sitting on the floor. "Want some?"

"No, thanks." He doesn't look up at me as he unveils a king of diamonds, which he needed to unblock another row of cards in his game of Solitaire.

I wait, observing him move the rows and solve the entire puzzle in what seems like thirty seconds. If he can feel my stare, he doesn't let on. If he's mad at me, he isn't acting hostile. Why are we like this? Why doesn't he throw something at me? Or kick and scream like that brat at Disneyland? Is he afraid of me? Am I just like Dad?

"You wanna play Thirteen?" he asks, and sighs. I jump at the olive branch, only to feel instant shame at how acutely his actions mimic my own. He's still mad, but he's also afraid. This offer isn't him forgiving me; he's placating me because he knows it's easier than being difficult and running the risk of me possibly hitting him again. I hate that he thinks of me this way.

"Sure, deal 'em up," I say.

Thirteen is a Vietnamese game that is mostly strategy and partly based on memory. Four players are each dealt thirteen cards. Unlike American card games, the lowest card is a three, and the highest is actually a two. Suits follow the standard poker tiers of spade, club, diamond, then heart at the top. The goal is to get rid of all your cards first. The person with the lowest card (three of spades) sets the pattern by laying down the first hand, and that becomes the thing to beat, whether it be by a single, pair, triple, sequence of three or more, et cetera. We get pretty competitive about it, and it's slightly harder with only two players because it's more difficult to guess what the other person has.

Paul shuffles. Even though he's been practicing for the last couple of weeks, he can't fully complete the shuffling dome. Still, he's good for a seven-year-old. After dealing, he sits up to hand me my set before lying down flat on his stomach. I can see his cards from where I'm sitting. The earnestness of his actions is almost too much for me, and I can feel the words *I'm sorry* bubbling in my throat. Instead, I ask, "When I'm gone, you're gonna need to make your own lunches and wake yourself up for school in the morning. You know that, right?" It still seems unreal to me that in a few days, I'll be living somewhere else. My routines will be different. I'll be free to do as I please on my own. I had all summer to get Paul used to the idea, but I only brought it up that once on accident, and instead of building trust, I all but shattered our bond yesterday. Maybe he's glad I'll be leaving now. If I were him, I would be.

"I know."

We play several rounds, and Paul beats me fair and square. And then, somewhere in the course of the game, things actually do return to normal. I can't pinpoint an exact moment; I just know that at some point, his laughter turned genuine.

I take a deep breath and say, "I'm sorry, Paul. I shouldn't have slammed the door on your hand."

He looks up at me, surprised. His little eyebrow is raised so high and it makes me kind of want to laugh. Then he smiles and says, "It's okay. It didn't hurt that bad."

I let out a laugh, and he joins me. And that's how I know I made the right choice. I'm never going to turn into our dad. This is us breaking the cycle.

I'm so distracted with glee that it takes me a minute to deliberate my next move, and a quick check of the clock reveals that it's already 9:30 p.m. "Last round, you need to eat something. When you come back, we'll play some more," I say.

Paul is silent. I drop my head to his level and see that he's fallen asleep. I'm familiar with this kind of exhaustion. It's a weight that hangs on my shoulders after every beating too. A gray cloud full of questions that I know I'll never get answers to. Gently, I pull his cards from his fingers and place them face down on the counter next to mine. We'll have to finish the game later. I tuck a pillow behind his neck, roll him onto his back, cover him with a blanket, and return to the shelves to properly tag the rest of our inventory.

Dad is arguing with someone in the shed, and the store is unusually quiet, which makes it hard to ignore. Also, I'm kind of curious because the two people who are typically on the receiving end of his anger are in here.

"Screw you, asshole. You didn't live with the Việt Cộng. You have no idea." It's a male voice shouting in Vietnamese. I'm pretty sure it's Bác Chuyên, but his words are even more slurred than usual.

There is silence before my dad finally tells him to just go home. The man is drunk, and maybe my dad is too. I know even just mentioning the Việt Cộng will cause riots here in America. But the history is complicated, and it's not my dad's or my uncle's fault that the country went and cut itself up. In the bathroom, I fill a mop bucket with soapy water and pretend to mop the floors. Metal slides across asphalt, and the drunk uncle slurs something about not caring if Uncle Long is my dad's older brother. Something, something, then if he ever comes across a Việt Cộng, he will shoot them all. I drop the mop.

I peek my head around the corner at the man accusing my dad of . . . of . . . treason, I guess?

Yup. It's the nose pincher, Bác Chuyên, who confronted my dad at the funeral.

I move away from the door, but I don't stop listening.

"Cậu ơi," my dad urges. "Go home." This time my dad's voice is even-tempered, but Bác Chuyên is belligerent. He's so angry that he's spit-screaming. And even though I'm now at the far side of the store, I can still hear everything.

Smacking his lips at the end of every phrase, he shouts, "You think about what you're saying. Think about all those people who died. Remember it!" In that last jab especially, his tone is more pleading than angry, even though instead of the direct prefix for *brother*, he used the one for *you*, which, in Vietnamese, is insulting.

"Shut up. You are no better. *Deacon* Chuyên," my dad scoffs. "If God could see you now."

"You don't know what you're talking about. You were just a small kid," Bác Chuyên shoots back.

"I remember everything. On the boat, you stole my catches; in Hong Kong, you stole my wages. Did you think I didn't know? I knew. I just let it go like you need to now."

"You lost some fish and some measly wages, and you think you know anything? You don't know shit until you've smelled the burning flesh of your family in a fire lit by the Việt Cộng."

Dad is silent. I guess he didn't know.

I can't help myself. I return to the door and peer at them. Bác Chuyên looks haggard and exhausted, which makes sense,

I guess. Death is tiring. He is the same person, but he looks different to me now. I can see that his sunken face carries in it a daily sorrow so heavy that the simple act of breathing appears difficult. But there is something familiar about him too; he looks like so many of the broken men I've kicked off our doorstep in the morning. If I didn't know who he was, I'd say that he was crazy, but he's not. Just like the others, I imagine his memories are real and probably pretty frightening.

Standing here, I collect another piece of the family history puzzle. I have the framework and a few big portions of the image put together, but there are missing and tattered parts—even still, I'm starting to realize that, actually, I know more than I thought. Through conversations like this, I've been privy to these stories all my life.

I've started writing down fragments of descriptions I've heard over the years. And even though I mostly have broken pieces, it's not nothing.

The hook that scarred his finger. That wasn't stupidity, it was desperation.

Sharks circling the boats waiting for people to jump . . .

Thai pirates. No one talks about what they did in detail, and that's how I know they were the worst.

Knowing what my family has been through, I feel kind of bad now for having spent so much time wishing for a different life.

During especially painful beatings, I would imagine being struck with such a force that the first blow—*smack!*—cracks the floor with my body; the second—*thud*—shatters open the ground with seismic force and sends a jagged lightning bolt of a fault line racing out on either side of me as far as the eye can see; and the third—*smack!*—pushes me through hundreds of layers of earth and water and molten lava until I emerge on the other side of the world in France. My home there is fancifully filled with Rococo-style furniture and different parents—parents who read old newspapers and drink aromatic tea in delicate-looking cups. The walls would shake and rattle with every hit, but in my fantasy, as I lay on the floor coloring or painting, we, together, would endure the earthquake with dignity and poise.

For as long as I can remember, I've wanted to be a different person from a different family with a different history. Maybe my dad has too.

"What are you doing just standing there?"

Huh? My dad's question cuts into my thoughts. "I was getting the mop."

"Well, hurry up. Don't just stand there looking like a mute," he spits in Vietnamese.

Normally, the insult would fester in my brain as I listed off all of his faults, but today I let it go.

Quickly topping it off with soapy water, I roll the clunky yellow mop bucket over to the chip aisle. I swish the mop around, place it in the strainer, and press down lightly, knowing that I can mop the entire store in one full sweep this way.

"Ey, look down. You drip everywhere."

He grabs the mop from my hands, and I tense, but instead of striking me, he returns it to the strainer and presses down, causing a rush of foaming water to cascade into the bucket. He does this twice and with force. Thrusting the wooden handle toward me, he reaches into his pocket for his cigarette pack before leaving me to finish.

He didn't hit me and yet my neck is stiff, my shoulders tight, and my leg trembles slightly. The signs were all there: the tone, the correction, the anger. Physical pain, I understand. The emotional sadness I just saw flicker across my dad's face, though, I do *not* understand. Standing here, I feel as though someone's grabbed hold of my lungs, and instead of taking regular breaths, I'm forced to sip the air. *Breathe. You're* fine. Holding the mop with clammy hands, I find that my heart aches for the little boy who, born in a different world or time, could have become someone completely different. Without the pain and trauma of war, I have to wonder if maybe he could've been the astronaut he believes he should've been.

CHAPTER 29
PHÚC

Two days after his name came up on the US government's list of qualifying refugees, Phúc was brought into a much smaller tent of quarantined individuals. And for the second time, he was stripped naked and checked for traces of disease—so much as a cough, and the immigration process would begin all over again. Next, he was interrogated about his allegiance to Vietnam, America, and even Hong Kong. What did he think about America? What were his experiences with the US Army during its occupation in Vietnam? Were any of his family members killed in the war? Did he have family in America already? How did he think he could contribute to the American workforce when he arrived?

Phúc didn't yet know if he hated America or Americans. How could he hate a place or people he had never met? What he did hate were the terrors that plagued his sleep. The nightmares, which began during his drinking hours, persisted through the night and haunted his mind like a fog that refused to lift. He'd be walking down the street, see someone dressed in shorts and a tank top, and stop dead in his tracks at the person's resemblance to one of the many Thai pirates who had invaded his boat. He didn't even have a clear image of what they actually looked like; it was more a feeling.

These flash memories were reminders that he had many sins to atone for. Many dead faces to pray for. Many souls to light incense in honor of. Many spirits who he knew were not at rest.

Although Phúc recognized alcohol made his nightmares worse, he didn't stop drinking, though he never let himself get to the point of being drunk either. Sobriety was the coward's way out. If the demons wanted to haunt him, he deserved to be haunted.

There were no long goodbyes with Tom or the rest of the crew. He wanted to tell Tom that he wouldn't be returning, but as soon as Phúc agreed to leave, his paperwork was processed, and he wasn't allowed to exit the camp. "Someone else will take your job," he was told, and that was that. With so little information, Phúc did what he was told and waited.

Two months passed with Phúc stuck in a claustrophobic, sequestered tent before they were finally led back to the same dock where Phúc had been so grateful to land two years earlier.

The colossal cargo ship, which originated in India, would,

over the course of thirty days, transport Phúc across the Pacific Ocean. As he boarded the ship along with two hundred other refugees, he was told to find a spot and get comfortable. This would be their home for the next month.

While docked, the ship felt no different from being on land, but as soon as it pushed toward open water, Phúc shot for the railing, and his body expelled itself of his morning meal of rice, cabbage, and pork. His stomach now empty, Phúc calmed, and when he looked to his left he found a row of other people also throwing up. If Phúc hadn't felt the puke lurch through his esophagus again, he might have found the trail of bile to be pretty. It looked like an enormous, floating, light-pink coral reef. The smell, though, was something altogether different. Despite the breeze and the ship's forward momentum, the aroma of rotten fish and sour pickle (or maybe just papaya) filled the air.

Déjà vu. Here he was once again on a large cargo ship being transported like a product rather than a person. He rubbed his hands raw against his jeans, wishing he could peel off the layer of stinging skin. Peeking down the stairwell, he was relieved to find that there were no animals. Below deck was nothing but large steel containers stacked in neat, tightly packed rows that sank into a dark abyss. There was nowhere to go below deck this time. This was fine with Phúc, though. Far less crowded than the previous boat, this one was headed to Guam.

The ship, carrying military cargo, had one of two types of people aboard: Vietnamese refugees and American soldiers.

Besides the obvious racial differences, they were different in so many other ways. The Americans were clean-cut, strong, tall, and uniform in the way they dressed, walked, and spoke. As Phúc sat squatting at the edge of the deck, he studied the way they moved about with their backs straight, their shoulders back, and when not being called to attention, with a stupid-looking gait. The Americans looked not only happy but proud. They moved with purpose and poise, and Phúc decided he would too.

Instead of squatting, Phúc stood up, and, using the wall, he straightened his spine, pulled his shoulders back, and lifted his chin so that he stood at a perfect ninety-degree angle to the floor. Up and down the walkway, he practiced this stance.

Unbeknownst to him, sitting on the upper deck of the ship was a girl about his age. She watched from her perched bird's-eye view as he practiced moving about the world like a man. Smiling to herself, she kicked her legs lazily against the boat's frame. The familiar sound, not too different from bullets knocking against a wooden boat, caused Phúc's head to make a sudden and sharp turn upward, and they locked eyes.

The attraction was immediate, but Ngọc Lan was coy, and Phúc was inexperienced, so it took four additional days on the ship before Phúc finally walked upstairs and sat down next to her.

"What is your name?"

"Ngọc Lan."

"Phúc. You are from Quảng Bình?"

"Yes. You too?"

"No. Đà Nẵng. But my dad treated a lot of soldiers from Quảng Bình."

"Your dad is a doctor?"

"Yes," Phúc lied, turning away. His dad didn't have a license or anything, but he healed just as many of those soldiers as the actual doctors did, and Phúc resented her for asking such a stupid question.

Ngọc Lan was demure in both features and personality. She wasn't pretty, nor was she ugly, and so she often went unnoticed. But she was kind and, despite having fled her homeland also, she had hope of better things to come. Ngọc Lan left in a refugee boat the same way Phúc had, but her boat was one of the lucky ones; they made the entire journey without encountering any Thai pirates, fever, sickness, or suicide. All thirty-four passengers on her vessel had made it to the Chinese cargo ship with an hour left of fuel. An hour!

To Phúc, her story could hardly be considered tragic or painful, but he listened as she talked for hours and hours about how scary it had been, how every moment on the water felt like an eternity, how she was certain she would die. But she hadn't died, and as far as Phúc could tell, she hadn't really suffered either, not by comparison, anyway. Not by a long shot.

Despite his bitterness toward Ngọc Lan, he let her fawn over him. She was brought up with traditional values of deference toward men—he could tell this in the way she handed him his food, with both hands. He had been responsible for teaching his own sisters this; at seven years old, Uyên sat beside the rice pot, attentive to his need for a second helping, and he was allowed to slap her hand if she dared return his bowl using one hand instead of two. Knowing that it was her place to care for a man, Phúc let Ngọc Lan sit up all night and wait for his nightmares to manifest so she could wipe the sweat from his forehead and comfort him.

Aboard the ship, his nightmares returned with vigor and without the help of alcohol. He found himself only sleeping in three-hour spans, after which he'd wake up disoriented, shaken, and unsure if he had fully returned to reality. The dreams were so bad that he'd wake up in a pool of sweat but have no fever. The smell of the ocean, which had at one time made him feel free, now blanketed him with nausea, and the waves, which he had once jumped over with joy, now made him long for sleep.

"Tell me about it," Ngọc Lan would say, only to be met with a blank stare. It frightened her to see him this way, but it also strengthened her resolve to want to help him. What was broken by man could be mended by a woman. She believed she could wrap him in love, and if she squeezed tight enough, she could suffocate the demons out of him.

And maybe Phúc believed it, too, because he bit his tongue when she cried about her lost home.

"Ba và Mẹ, they gave me everything they had. They traded all of their savings to get me on that boat. And the whole time, all I could think about was what a waste it would be if I died. This is the burden of being the only one left. Anh Hòa was caught by the Việt Cộng, and Chị Diễm is lost. There is no one else." She sniffed. "What are they going to do without me?

Who will feed the dogs and joke with Ba? Or walk with Mẹ and shoulder the groceries?

"I have so much fear," she would say, repeating her crisis like a broken record, her hands shaking every time.

She wore her heart on her sleeve. Exposing it like that . . . well, it was just asking for someone to break it.

To prevent himself from doing something stupid, Phúc got up without saying a word and walked away. He speed walked around the ship twice, then did jumping jacks in place, and in the middle of his attempt to lunge around the ship, an American soldier stopped him.

"You're not doing it right." The man was in his early twenties and had a perfect military cut and eyes so green they looked like emeralds. He dropped down into a squat.

Phúc did the same.

"No." Shaking his head, the man walked over to Phúc, gently pulled his shoulders back, and then pressed down so that his thighs were parallel to the floor. Phúc's untrained legs immediately began to shake. "Good! Yes." The man laughed. "More," he said, gesturing for Phúc to continue.

As Phúc set off, the man followed, and soon there was a train of American soldiers doing squats in a circle around the ship. At first, the other Vietnamese refugees on the boat found this hilarious, like some kind of absurd clown show led by a cat. Phúc just looked so small compared to the American men. But then, slowly, they, too, began to join. Their legs and joints had begun to hurt, so who cared if they looked stupid in the middle of the ocean? Their bodies needed the movement, and the silliness of it all brought them to a place of joy they hadn't felt in years.

This was a turning point in Phúc's refugee journey, a moment of cautious optimism and hope for better things to come—in America. For the first time since leaving Vietnam, Phúc began to think about the future, one that didn't involve him dying or starving or living in immense physical pain. When all was said and done, he might actually get to live the American dream. If he worked hard, he might be able to buy his own car and have a house with a wife and kids. He might be happy.

So when he stumbled upon Ngọc Lan in the middle of yet another one of her self-pitying monologues, he nearly walked away. She was holding court with her circle of girlfriends, her legs bent up to her chest and her chin resting on the tops of her knees. But then he heard his name. That was her first mistake.

"And I didn't even have a journey as rough as Phúc's, poor guy. My heart hurts for him, for the loss he endured, and all those people who died . . ."

Approaching her quickly, Phúc grabbed her wrist and yanked her toward him. "Let's go." Then, when they were far enough away that he thought no one could hear, he chastised her. "Why do you talk about me? Why do you talk about any of this stuff like you know?"

"Anh ơi, let go of my hand," Ngọc Lan begged, her eyes welling with tears. Caught so off guard by his reaction, she apologized. "I'm sorry, I'm sorry, Anh-a." And that was her second mistake.

He grabbed her by the shoulder and, using his right hand, slapped her face so hard it sounded like a firecracker. The manic gesture surprised him, not because he felt remorse but because he didn't. Hitting her lit his hand on fire, and he craved the heat, not because he hated Ngọc Lan, but because he knew he deserved to burn.

CHAPTER 30
JANE

I need to wait for the spray of the shower to turn on. Seconds crawl by like minutes. Standing in the doorway to our bedroom, I can see my dad lying, open-mouthed and twitchy, on his bed. Across his torso, the five shallow scars rise and expand with every breath. He's snoring lightly, but there's also something else. His throat ekes out a few murmurs, like he's yelling at someone in his sleep but can't find his voice, and right when he seems on the verge of finding it, his eyes pop open. I jump back into my room and wait.

The pipes hiss to life; it's 5:09 a.m. The shower door rumbles as it bounces rather than rolls shut. I have three minutes—maybe less.

Inside my dad's bedroom, I'm nervous. I've never snooped around my parents' things before. Was he drafted but fled because he was too much of a coward to join the military? Does he despise the Americans for losing the war? Or for not helping enough? But then why, after someone steals from us, does he sometimes say, "Americans gave to us when we came here. We have to give back"?

My fingers tremble as I peel open the tin. Our new passports have replaced the gold bars, the pink slip is a vehicle registration, and then I find it—my dad's refugee card. About the size of an index card and just as thick, it reads:

Family Name *(Capital Letters)* PHÚC THỊNH VŨ	First Name	Middle Initial	B-250	
Country of Citizenship Vietnam	Passport or Alien Registration Number R23-922-855	Permit Number 092 20 11		
United States Address *(Number, Street, City, and State)* 334 S. Pine Valley Ln, San Jose CA 95112				
Airline and Flight No. or Vessel of Arrival ICEM PA 197	Passenger Boarded at Guam			
Number, Street, City, Province *(State)* and Country of Premanent Residence Vietnam				
Month, Day, and Year of Birth January 1, 1961	PAROLED PURSUANT TO SEC. 212(d)(5) OF THE I & N ACT TO: Indefinite VN Refugee			
Province *(State)* and Country of Birth Da Nang, Vietnam	PURPOSE: ALRP CAT I/IN 10068A			
Visa Issued at Visas Falcon Cleared	EMPLOYMENT AUTHORIZED			
Month, Day, and Year Visa Issued November 17, 1979	(Port) DIS20 1980	(Date) JPY 1543	(Officer)	FORM I-94

SURRENDER THIS COPY WHEN LEAVING THE UNITED STATES—SEE REVERSE

There's one for my mom too. And there's a photo of the two of them, both dressed in bell-bottom pants, my dad standing on a large rock, my mom sitting on one below, the ocean in the background. They look like a couple—it's not romantic, and I wouldn't say they look necessarily happy. They're just . . . together.

The shower shuts off. I quickly return everything to the box and bolt from his room into mine.

I slap my face a few times before exiting to make my cheeks red and then enter the kitchen. I sit, anxiously waiting for Dad to make his morning coffee.

"I'm not feeling too good," I say when he appears.

He doesn't even look at me. "Take Tylenol. I need you to watch the store."

Damn it. I slapped myself for no reason. Unless I'm on my deathbed, there is no way I'll ever get out of watching the store.

I wake Paul, get him dressed, make our lunches, and pop two Tylenols even though I feel fine.

At the store, my dad immediately walks the perimeter, picking up trash with one hand while he smokes with the other. I begin my morning routine of checking the shelves to see what needs restocking. Everything looks good until I notice that the cans and bottles inside the refrigerators are sweating. I open the door, and my fears are confirmed. The cooler is broken. I take a deep breath and go find my dad.

"The cooler is broken," I say.

"What?"

"The cooler for the drinks. It turned off or something. Everything is warm."

"Siet," he says—that's *shit* with a Vietnamese accent. Every time my dad curses, which isn't often, I have to resist the urge to laugh. It's hardly threatening when it's butchered so bad, but

I know better than to react at all. He stubs his cigarette in the yellow parking pole and follows me back inside.

First, he opens the door to make sure I'm not a moron, and when he confirms that it's broken, he gets his tools and goes to work.

"Go buy a bag of ice and put some drinks in a bucket for the customers," he says. "Nhanh lên," he adds as if I might stop and get my nails done on the two-block walk to the store.

I can't get the image of my parents out of my head. My mom must have been just a year or two older than me, maybe my same age. I used to think I looked more like my dad, but now I can see where I have my mom's round eyes, flat nose, and plump cheeks. Despite my desire to cut ties with all things Vietnamese, I've always been somewhat curious about what being a refugee means. Especially after my tenth-grade American history teacher, Mrs. Dannenberg, mentioned I was the daughter of the refugees we were studying. I remember the class looking at me in awe like I had made the perilous journey myself despite being born in San Jose, California, and growing up alongside them in school.

Guilt. I left class that day feeling guilty for not knowing my own history. But when I got home and found myself hovering near my dad, who was fixing the coffee machine, I told myself it didn't matter. That whatever they went through in the past shouldn't have affected how they treated me. We weren't that kind of family. We didn't talk about trauma, we didn't admit to fear, and we never said "I love you." I lived by these unspoken rules my entire life, and I'd been too afraid to break them. I might have even told myself they deserved whatever happened to them because Vietnamese people were assholes.

Vietnam was unexpected in a lot of ways, but now I see that I was wrong about so many assumptions. Having seen the shack-like buildings, I see where my dad gets his "scrappy" mentality. Vietnamese people are nothing if not practical, so I imagine that after it rains, they find something flat and sturdy, create four posts, and *bam!* They have shelter. And maybe the next time it rains, they notice a leak, so a tarp goes over the top. When confronted with a problem, they don't look to anyone else; they just fix it. Now I know why my dad keeps fixing the fridges when they break; in his mind, there is no other option.

I'm so lost in my own thoughts that I barely remember putting the two hefty ice bags in my cart or paying for them. My pondering stops when I turn the corner and spot a crowd around our store. I speed walk that last block, the bags dripping with every step. Squeezing past people, I duck under the yellow tape strung between the light poles and go inside. I technically crossed under their boundary but only to cut around the people blocking our entrance.

"Stay inside," an older officer warns me. He's been around as long as we have. I don't know his name, but he's always so warm and friendly that I've imagined living another life where he's my dad.

"Yes, sir."

With the entrance blocked by gawkers, the store is empty except for the officers. When I finally spot my dad, it dawns on me. I didn't even consider that *he* might have been hurt. That the reason the cops had surrounded our store could've been because he was bleeding to death on the floor after being robbed and shot.

"Stay inside," my dad instructs as he follows the officers to the crime scene.

"Okay."

I think in order to work here and not be afraid, we convince ourselves that it's a completely safe space. That if we're inside, minding our own business, no one *wants* to kill us. People might steal from us, vandalize the place, or throw a punch or two; but kill us? No way.

A tall—like, absurdly tall—officer walks in wearing a vest that makes him look more like a giant robot than a person. "You guys notice anything strange when you opened up this morning?"

"No, but my dad sent me to go get ice as soon as we arrived. Our fridge is broken again."

"Anyone loitering or anything around the property?"

"Not that I know of."

Another officer walks in and nods at me. "Your dad says you can show us where the cameras are?"

I walk them to the office, where we keep the video camera system. Behind me, the two of them tower over me. "It just downloads to this box that saves it for seven days and then deletes it."

"Can you make us a copy of it?" the first one asks.

"Uh, I don't know how to get it off the box." My dad hates it when the cops ask us to do their job for them. We used to show them videos all the time when we would get broken into, but the justice system is shit, and we've never gotten anything returned. After a while, we stopped trying.

The second cop steps in front of the computer and moves the mouse around, scrolling through the feed. "Okay. We'll send a technician over here to copy it then." He hands me his card, which reads LIEUTENANT GEOFF TROWE. They leave, and my dad comes back inside.

"What's going on? Why are there so many cops here?" I ask.

"Someone got killed."

"Who?" People die in our neighborhood all the time, but it's still shocking to hear. And it's not often that it's on our property. I wonder if it's someone I've seen before.

"I told her last time she got beat up. But she didn't listen. This is what happen."

"She was a customer?"

"That's why I tell you to stay away from those people. You want friends like that girl? No. Friends will kill you."

I don't say anything. Strange as it may seem, my dad is not actually yelling at me. I mean, he *is* yelling at me, but it's more out of frustration at the world.

"You think I'm strict, but I'm not. I'm easy. You want to be like these girls. Go ahead, see how you do."

I like these conversations. They're the closest thing he and I ever have to a heart-to-heart. He rants, and I listen. And this time, I really listen because now I know that my dad has seen some things, things that can really change a person; it makes me consider that maybe he's not yelling at me for no reason but rather because he worries about me, like the time he followed me to school.

Alone in the store, we scrub through the footage of the

murder ourselves. It's the kind of thing you expect to see on TV, and we don't see her getting stabbed or dying because the dumpster blocks the angle, but we don't need to see it to know how it happened. A part of me wants to go outside, to sit with her. When I first sat down at the computer, I only saw the live video feed, where plain-clothed cops carefully took pictures and stepped around the white sheet covering her body. Watching the crime happen in real time is surreal. Even though I know she's gone, there's a part of me that thinks we can still save her. It seems really unfair that she should die like that and then have to lie in the same uncomfortable position all alone in the cold while strangers move around her looking for evidence. Is it too much to ask for a blanket? Not just some sterile sheet to cover her, but something warm. Something human.

My dad is silent as he watches the playback, and I wonder what he's thinking about. If he's remembering things he saw during the war. "Is this what it looked like when people died in the war?"

He shakes his head and looks at me like I asked if the moon was blue. "This is nothing. During the war, it was really bad. Just imagine one body here and one over there and ten, twenty more . . . everywhere. And those people weren't soldiers. They were just regular people." He shakes his head again in a gesture of pity. But it's not pity; it's weariness. "That's why Việt Năm has a lot of ghosts." He laughs and walks away.

CHAPTER 31
PHÚC

"Ngủ dậy."

Nudge.

"Ngủ dậy!"

Shove.

Open. Close. Open. Phúc blinked in reverse as beams of yellow against a bright orange sun pierced his eyes. Cast in shadow above him was the old cook, her face freshly melted from the pot of boiling rice that the Thai pirate had drowned her in. Close. His throat was dry, his mouth chapped and cracking on the edges. His body ached with the limp fatigue of a fever. His eyelids, weak and crusty, were so tightly sealed they might as well have been suction-cupped together. Even with full concentration, he couldn't pull them apart. Using his hand, which hung heavy with the phantom weight of a brick attached, he pressed down on the skin above his eye and pushed upward. *Pop.* With his eyes now open, Phúc's leg kicked the air, and he jerked awake. The sky, now a star-filled black, was static—indifferent to the rapid beating of his heart.

For just one night, Phúc wished the ghosts would leave him alone.

He wasn't drifting alone at sea any longer; he needed to remind himself of that often. But the safety of the cargo ship did nothing to counter the visitors frequenting his imagination. These memories were the kind that rested somewhere deep in one's mind and sprang to life at the slightest provocation. But never were they more vivid or long-lasting than when he was on this cargo ship.

At breakfast, the Americans and the Vietnamese refugees became more familiar. There were language barriers to overcome, but they were all bound for America, so they figured they might as well try to get to know one another. At Phúc's table were Ngọc Lan, her friend Bích, Bích's adopted sister Thảo, and a handsome American soldier, Colin. Colin was eighteen years old and new to the US Navy; Phúc could tell this by the way he was constantly being yelled at while standing at attention. This morning was no different.

Sergeant Red, a tall, redheaded man with a beak-like nose and pointed chin, walked up beside Colin, who immediately stood at attention. "Sir, yes, sir," Colin said, and saluted.

"Sit up straight, Boot. Sailors do not slouch!"

Colin, whose posture was already stiff, adjusted only slightly and replied, "Yes, Sergeant," and the man walked away, a smirk on the edges of his lips. It wasn't just Sergeant Red who did this either; any officer who walked by might come upon Colin and insult whatever he was doing.

Colin didn't seem to mind getting yelled at, though. Sergeant Red could have been reciting a prayer at him for all that Colin reacted to his shouting, and the girls giggled with delight every time.

None of them had ever seen a man shake off humiliation with such ease.

Across the room, a group of sailors began a game of snake jump rope. A crowd formed as a long rope slithered along the floor. The first jumper double-hopped to maintain her balance as the boat rocked. She was short for an American, with thick thighs and huge, muscular calves. But her most defining feature was her focus. In full concentration, she lifted her feet and followed pace with the rope. A man joined, also focused on the rhythmic wriggle of the snake. The two men controlling the rope sped up or slowed down to add difficulty, but the two jumpers kept going until the woman jumped out. The sailors encouraged refugees to give it a try. A couple of Vietnamese teens around Phúc's age jumped in but quickly stepped on the rope when the boat lurched or the pace changed. Then Ngọc Lan got up—this was a bold and unprecedented move for a Vietnamese girl.

She watched for a long moment, her gaze concentrated on the placement of the other jumpers' feet. Something about the way she approached the game shifted the atmosphere in the room, and the crowd leaned in closer, supporting her attempt.

Nodding, she jumped.

One foot, the other foot. Up. Up. Up.

To everyone's surprise, including her own, she seemed able to keep up. With every second that she didn't trip, the crowd grew quietly intense. But months of inactivity made Ngọc Lan's legs weak. They were thin and bony, and after a minute, they began to wobble. Still, she pushed herself, making it through a few more leaps before the rope caught her ankle, and everything stopped.

The group exhaled a collective, disappointed sigh.

But Ngọc Lan wasn't sad; she was euphoric even as she panted. An older woman, thin with charred black teeth, a potbelly, and cracked feet, nudged Ngọc Lan and handed her a wad of elastic fabric. Again, Ngọc Lan laughed. The woman wanted *her* to show the Americans how Vietnamese people jumped rope.

Releasing the band, Ngọc Lan called her friends over, and each took a side. Then it was the Americans' turn to watch as the girls demonstrated Chinese Jump Rope. The game, which focused on balance, was made more difficult by the unpredictable bobbing of the ship. For the girls, though, this only added to the fun. Starting with the band around their ankles, the two girls stood opposite each other and created two parallel lines with the rope. Then Ngọc Lan demonstrated the skill. The main objective of the game was to make it through the routine without messing up.

Then it was the Americans' turn.

"Jump into the gap. Both feet to the sides. Both feet in. Jump out to the side. That seems easy enough," Colin said, stepping up to the plate.

To help, Ngọc Lan stood inside the rope, facing Colin as he fumbled his way through the exercise.

All around the room, both the Vietnamese and the Americans appeared to be cheering Colin on. Everyone except Phúc, who scowled at Ngọc Lan's hubris and exited the room.

Outside, Ngọc Lan found Phúc sitting alone with his feet dangling over the side of the large vessel, his heels kicking hard against the metal exterior.

"Why aren't you happy?" she asked, standing awkwardly next to him.

Phúc shook his head at her. "You. You spend a few months away from home, and you've lost all your principles. Jumping up and down in there like an American. You are not American, and Vietnamese girls do not act that way with strange men."

Ngọc Lan tried to laugh it off. "What could I possibly have been doing wrong? In front of hundreds of people?"

"Exactly, in front of hundreds of people. Embarrassing. You embarrassed yourself."

"I'm sorry, Anh. Don't be mad, huh?" Ngọc Lan urged, and sat down next to him. She had no way of knowing that when he looked at her, all he could see was Panda—a dumb animal that allowed itself to love and trust too easily.

"Forget it," he said as he pulled himself up, and walked away.

Asleep on the deck, twitching like he did every night—Vietnamese ghosts were relentless—he kicked and begged in small motions trying to escape the spirits. And when he managed to wake himself, he found his head nestled in Ngọc Lan's crossed legs as she stroked his hair.

"Why are you here?" he asked, making no effort to remove himself from the comfort of her touch.

"Everyone in your life has left you. I will not be one more person to leave you behind."

If she wanted to stick around to do things for him, Phúc wasn't going to stop her, but he knew, in turn, that he would give her nothing. Phúc made no effort to comfort her or apologize. There was no need. Vietnamese men didn't do that. At dinner that night, when he was done eating, he simply wiped his lips with the napkin she provided and left his tray for her to clean—dishes were a woman's business.

Outside, on the lower deck, Phúc found a sailor with a pack of smokes and stood beside him until he was offered one. Taking the cigarette to his lips, he watched as a bright, shiny Zippo lighter flickered to life and lit up the end. He inhaled deeply and expelled a reflexive cough. The sailor, an older man in his mid-forties, laughed as he patted Phúc firmly on the back.

"First time is always like that," the man said before tossing his butt into the water and returning to his post upstairs. At sixteen, Phúc didn't know why men smoked. What he did know was that men loved beer, dried squid, and cigarettes, despite how the smell clung to their clothes like a campfire doused in pepper. Inhaling only half as deep the second time, his body took to the nicotine with ease. A calm washed over him. And for the rest of his life, he would inhale tobacco in the hopes of chasing this singular feeling of peace.

His body, suddenly limp with fatigue, melted to the floor. Laying his head in a place meant for feet barely bothered him anymore. He relaxed his shoulders, pressed his back against the gritty surface, and watched the sun begin its descent toward the horizon. For miles upon miles, he lay there watching wisps of cloud drift slowly across a vibrant blue sky.

Later, Phúc and Ngọc Lan would disembark together, walk through customs separately, and not see each other again until over a year later. He wouldn't bother searching for her. If she came back, she came back, and if she didn't, that was fine too. For Phúc, not caring was the truest kind of freedom.

Their chance encounter at a Tết festival sometime later, which led to a two-week courtship resulting in marriage, would do nothing to change his broken outlook on life.

But for this one evening, before they docked in America, before he knew how difficult his life would become as a resident alien, Phúc had a dream.

Whoosh.

Fabric flapped in the wind. Phúc listened as the sound whipped this way and that until finally, the massive, bright

American flag came into view. The captain of the Navy ship had raised it to full staff as the national anthem blared through the ship's intercom. Phúc sat up.

Day turned to dusk, and far off in the distance was a twinkling of lights. The United States of America—Guam, to be exact, but American soil nonetheless. It would be here that he'd be processed before being flown to San Jose, California, for resettlement.

Ngọc Lan, having finished her dish duty, brought Phúc a foam cup of lukewarm water.

As she sat beside him, she, too, looked up at the majestic red, white, and blue star-spangled banner floating across the orange-and-yellow sky. And Phúc considered that his dream of having tea with the man on the moon might really happen.

He had been bouncing a ball against the wall of the courtyard when the neighbor began calling people over to the only television in the village. This long, rectangular box with a twelve-inch screen sat at the back of a crowded bottom-floor room of the only three-story house in town. The first floor was an empty room the size of a two-car garage with a door on the far right, which opened to a stairway leading to the main house. No one was allowed upstairs, but everyone was welcome to loiter below. As the only house in the neighborhood with a television box, it was a natural gathering place for social events. People brought their own mats or plastic chairs and congregated in groups determined by age more than anything else—except for this one night, where every single eye was glued to the screen.

Static webbed itself across the screen as the antenna struggled to pick up the signal. The black sky and light-gray, crater-filled landscape had everyone afraid to blink. Then the man inside a puffed-up white suit climbed down the steps of his spaceship and, taking one solid, slow step after another, bounced across the moon carrying the American flag.

The moment was bigger than America, though. The bright white figure, which stood against a gray, lifeless moon, united the whole world. This rocket ship carrying people had reached the actual moon. And the occasion was so monumental that a country so divided, a country that had been fighting itself for over twenty years, actually stopped. The relentless gunfire and chaos ceased for one long, unbelievable day. That was the true miracle.

The ship's horn blared loudly, cutting into Phúc's memory, and he stood up—it felt rude not to.

For the second time in his life, Phúc arrived in a new country. The first time he hadn't felt much besides relief, but this time was different. This time he was filled with limitless possibilities. He was filled with *hope*. Maybe he could become an astronaut if he wanted to. Why not? He hadn't been the best student in Vietnam, but he could change that here. Just as he had done with his forged documents in Hong Kong, he could reinvent himself here too. He would be the man he could never have been in Vietnam.

Large splashes of ocean water kicked up the sides of the boat as it pressed onward to Cabras Island and the Port of Guam, trailing a sun that had halfway melted into the horizon.

Down below, dolphins shot up from the water, chasing the boat or perhaps racing it to see who might make it to shore first. Colorful schools of fish drifted toward and away from the ship in unison. Phúc waved at the fish like a soldier being welcomed home after a long and hard-fought battle abroad. Then he blinked, and the sun was gone. Looking down at the shimmery surface reflecting off his cup of water, Phúc noticed a bright white reflection bouncing around inside. As the boat moved with the current, the spotted white image would lose its shape and then re-form as it splashed against the sides of his cup. Stiffening his stance, he held his hand as still as possible so as not to shatter or spill the delicate object. With the same gentle grasp he might use to catch a firefly in the night, Phúc caught the moon.

CHAPTER 32
JANE

"Adam told me Mom is in Las Vegas, and she's a cocktail," Paul says as we walk to the store to pick up dinner. It's not really framed as a question, so I have half a mind to ignore it or change the subject. . . .

"Who's Adam?" I flare.

"You know that guy you were talking to with the hair that goes like this?" Paul uses his hands to gesture that the hair parts down the middle and is floppy.

"Mike."

Paul shrugs; he doesn't know his name, but there was only one person with hair like that. Mike is our cousin who lives in Florida and loves cars more than his mother—Thi's words, not mine. We've talked on the phone a few times since we met, but I already feel the conversation waning. After "what's new" is followed by "nothing much" several times, the calls start to feel pointless. "His younger brother. He told me when we were playing Thirteen online. Well, he told everyone, actually, in the chat room." Paul has kept in better touch, apparently, over a card game no less.

Our trip to Vietnam ended three weeks ago, and since our return, nostalgia has gripped our parents. We're constantly having family gatherings. I don't get to see my out-of-state cousins like Thi, but everyone who lives in NorCal congregates at Bác Nguyệt's house on Saturday nights. With Cậu Hòa and Mợ Bích working at the liquor store now, we seem to have a lot more free time, which has turned into family time.

Family or not, though, I want to punch this Adam kid in the face. Who does he think he is, talking about things he knows nothing about? The camaraderie I had felt with my cousins begins to wane. I shouldn't be surprised that my extended family talks about my mother—it's good gossip for them, even if it still stings for me.

Four years. She's been gone four years, and it simultaneously feels like yesterday and eons ago.

"She's not a cocktail. She's a cocktail waitress, I think." I heard the whispers from my aunts who thought I couldn't speak Vietnamese. They weren't malicious about it; they were pitying, which is worse.

The frigid breeze of the air-conditioned grocery store washes over us as we walk inside. Home, shop, grocery store—this is my life. We head for the fruit and vegetable section, where I grab a couple of tomatoes and an onion.

"Do you remember her?"

Yes. I remember lots of things. I remember too much. I remember long walks in a huge forest. I remember things that will break Paul's heart. I remember things that I don't want to remember. I remember the last time I saw her with such vivid detail that just a flicker of that memory makes my jaw tighten and my eyes well. I remember the way she left the dishes undone, the laundry unwashed, and her kids behind without a second thought. I remember checking the mailbox for an unmarked postcard, a secret letter, a box with money, and directions on how to find her. I remember being an idiotic dreamer.

"Some."

"Maybe we should find her in case . . ."

My throat suddenly dries. I turn my head and narrow my gaze, hoping this will convince my eyes not to cry. Why am I on the verge of crying? I didn't cry the day she left, so why am I gonna cry now, four years after the fact, when I couldn't care less about her? *Stop it, you stupid fucking eyes.*

"No, Paul." I'm walking faster now, afraid he'll catch up and see how much I'm affected by this. I'm bagging things I don't even want or know how to cook: jalapeños, squash, red lettuce, anything with a giant sale sign. I bite the insides of my cheeks. Does he honestly think she would take better care of him than I have? Does he not care that I put my teenage life on hold to be his mother? I'm getting angry now. "If she wanted to be a part of your life, she would've come back. If she wanted to be our mom, she would've said so. Don't hang your dreams on her."

"But who's gonna take care of me?"

Hot tears drip down my cheeks, and I stare at the ceiling

covered in long white fluorescent bulbs. I'm sure I look ridiculous, but if I look at Paul, I'll lose the little amount of composure I have. After a moment, I drop my head, letting my hair cover my face, and I blink hard. If I wipe my face, he'll know I'm crying, so I open the freezer door and just stand in it with my head tilted downward as though scanning the choices on the bottom shelf.

The icy air quells my tears. I reach down and grab ten Banquet meals: four Salisbury steaks, four chickens, and two chicken potpies. Then I take a light breath, step back, and let the door bounce shut.

"C'mon. Let's get home before everything melts."

In the kitchen, I finish putting the last of the groceries away and start packing. I take one knife, fork, spoon, plate, and bowl. Do I really need these? I put everything back, take a pair of chopsticks and a soup spoon, then close the drawer. I'm signed up for a meal plan, so I don't know why I'd need that stuff. Chopsticks and a spoon for the ramen I'm bringing are all I need. I don't want to get too hopeful, but I leave for college tomorrow, and despite my efforts to take as little as possible, I have about half a trunk worth of things. I was able to find everything on the packing list except for extra-long sheets and a shower caddy, but I'll make do. My pile in the corner of our room is modest but not quite the single suitcase I thought I'd be carrying for my arrival at school. I was careful not to take anything that Paul and I share, like the toothbrush holder and the one blanket we have that feels like being hugged by a teddy bear.

I told my dad the move-in day was on August 17, and he said, "Okay." That's it. That was the entirety of our conversation.

So, everything is set—except that I have yet to reconcile with Paul about leaving.

While he takes a bath, I sit on the floor between my pile of stuff and our bed. I've been thinking about this tale I'm about to tell for some time now. This story, our history, is both true and made up. It exists like this because I only have the framework of a puzzle. And as far as I can tell, the adults have tossed, burned, forgotten, or refused to acknowledge that certain pieces ever existed. So, I'm telling Paul a folktale, knowing that certain details will never fully be revealed.

I've been wondering something a lot lately that I think Paul wonders too. Why don't I hate my dad? I mean, I don't adore him or anything stupid like that, but I don't hate him either. I pick up Panda and realize she's the only gift Dad has ever given me—her and the gold chain dangling around my neck, which I've only had for three months. She's still soft even after all these years of being crushed between my arms on lonely nights. I hold her at arm's length and wonder what she knows.

I can still hear the sounds of balloons popping, water shooting across runways, and bells dinging. I remember the carnival lights. I also remember a look—it was just a flicker, quick as a blink, as Panda passed from him to me. My dad held her with a tenderness that only children possess, and secrets passed between them. I knew she was special then, but I hadn't known why—I still don't, not entirely. I squeeze her tight now, half-expecting stuffing made of truth to spill out, but nothing happens. Perhaps she knows that they aren't her secrets to tell, and in that way she is magic. I had planned to take her with me, but now I know that she belongs here—at home. I stuff her in one of Paul's drawers for him to find tomorrow.

I've never had to explain to anyone our family dynamic, but that thing Thi said about getting thrown into a wall and still loving someone really resonated with me.

So, here's what I think. I think war breaks people. And to overcome it, strength manifests itself in strange and sometimes ugly ways.

There is so much about my family's history that will die with my parents' generation because we kids don't know how to ask, and they wouldn't know how to answer. And even if I somehow gained the superhuman power of gentle yet incisive questioning, I still wouldn't understand their responses. I don't know what the Vietnamese words for rape, murder, or insufferable claustro-phobic conditions even are. But there's also something else that's stopping me.

I'm not sure I can handle knowing the real horror.

This past summer has taught me too much already. I have only charred fragments of this story, and already I can feel myself changing. Maybe Paul can feel it, too, and that's why he's asking about Mom. He thinks that I've crossed over to her side; he sees my leaving as a betrayal.

I haven't lost my resolve, though. In fact, nothing is scarier to me right now than allowing forgiveness—my own forgiveness—to make me stay. Forgiveness might propel me toward an even deeper understanding. And if I truly understand the insanity, I might understand *his* insanity. And then I'll feel bad for him, and I won't go.

But I cannot stay.

I also can't leave Paul in the dark.

I stand up and move to the bathroom, where Paul has run a bath and is diligently soaping his hair, scrubbing his shoulders, and scratching himself under the armpits. His back is to me, and I can see the reddish-blue hue of a bruise under his shoulder blade that has not yet healed. He seems older now. Different in some way. I think about how I was exactly his age when I started working in the store.

I came out of it okay. He will, too, but only if he listens.

Grabbing his towel off the rack, I hold it open as he stands up and wraps himself inside the stiff fabric that is in need of a proper wash.

"Get dressed and get into bed."

He pulls an old T-shirt over his head, and I walk to the kitchen to make us some hot chocolate. Normally, I wouldn't let him drink this stuff so late in the day, but something tells me we're in for a long night.

I scan the small two-bedroom apartment where I've spent my whole life, and a wave of nostalgia passes over me.

On the table sits *Tiger Finds a Home*. The story is simple. A tiger named Tiger is caught in a cage, put on a boat with other animals, and then released into a wildlife sanctuary where he knows no one. It's a lonely journey that ends with a willingness to explore his new world. Tiger is a lot like us—sheltered. And he's also a lot like our dad, forced to venture into foreign territories. Having stood in my dad's childhood home, I see now how similar my dad is to this tiger.

The bubbles of boiling water return my attention to the stove. I fill two cups with powdered cocoa and hot water and walk back into the room, where Paul is tucking himself into bed.

Using his pillow, Paul wedges himself into the corner with his stuffed bunny, Mr. Rogers, who fits neatly into the curve of his elbow. Before Mom left, Paul had been obsessed with having a little brother. I guess because *I* had a little brother. So, I told him Mr. Rogers could be our little brother, and the three of us have been pretty tight ever since.

I hand him his cup. "Can you hold it there and not spill it?"

"Uh-huh." He's already sipping it with delight.

"Are you comfortable?"

Paul doesn't respond. Instead, he sits up, straightens the sheets, and pulls the now slouching Mr. Rogers up so that his neck is above the sheet line. He manages to do this without spilling a drop of liquid onto the sheets. Paul is going to be okay.

I can't say the same for myself. I'm nervous. I've spent so much of my life despising anything Vietnamese: the people, the culture, the lessons. But now I'm about to try to convince Paul that he should do the exact opposite of what I've done and try to embrace our history. Paul could easily close his ears to me. What I do know is that I can't hide from it any longer, that I was wrong about a lot of my assumptions, and that I still feel extremely conflicted about all of it.

I used to think my family didn't talk about feelings, but it does. The intense and difficult topics are disguised in humor. *Dark humor* is what it's called, I guess. And that's our therapy. We laugh about things our American counterparts would find horrifying, like being chased around the house with a hammer. We joke, and we get through it as a family. Not with therapists.

My father does not have friends. He has family and those who escaped Vietnam with him. To call his fellow refugees "friends" would be categorically wrong. They've built self-contained communities in order to re-create some semblance of Vietnam in America. Marriages were forged, and as we spread across the United States, we cling to one another. Sometimes I think my parents' generation tries to maintain tenuous relationships just to remind themselves that what happened to them was real, that the journey wasn't just a figment of their imaginations. Others witnessed it, too, and together they survived it.

As Paul spends more time with Dad, maybe this story will get him to pay attention in a way I never did. Maybe he'll learn things I didn't know, and over time, we'll begin to really understand why our elders act the way they do. Even if he doesn't, maybe that's okay too. Because maybe it's not our place to make them relive a history they want to forget. We'll take what they can give, and we'll imagine the rest—it's the best we can do.

Taking a deep breath, I tell myself not to rush as I think back to all the collective memories I've overheard: the stories, the anecdotes, the snippets of information I pretended to ignore.

"Sit still. Both of you. Mr. Rogers needs some blanket too."

"You're acting weird," Paul says.

"I need to tell you a story, and it might take a while, so get comfortable," I reply.

"Why? What's the story?"

"Can you please sit still? Every time you shift, I lose my concentration, and if you break my concentration, I'll miss key details and then you won't understand what I'm trying to tell you. It's about Dad."

"Can't we just watch a movie?"

"Shhhh. There is a small town in the center of Vietnam called Đà Nẵng. That's where our family is from. . . ."

GLOSSARY OF CHARACTERS

Adam—Jane's cousin from Las Vegas. Little brother of Mike.

Ân—Jane's cousin who just immigrated to the United States.

An Ngô—Fellow refugee working in Hong Kong.

Principal Avitia—Paul's school principal.

Bảo—Jane's cousin from Las Vegas.

Becky—Bác Luy and Bác Nguyệt's daughter. Jane's non-cousin cousin. Sibling of Vicky and Stephen.

Mợ Bích—Cậu Hòa's wife. Jane's aunt (her mother's sister-in-law).

Bình Dương—Fellow refugee working in Hong Kong.

Carly—Jane's high school classmate. Mirabelle's close friend.

Bác Chuyên (Deacon Chuyên)—Phúc's uncle. The only other surviving shipmate on Phúc's refugee boat. Jane's great-uncle, known for his missing pinky and nose-twisting greetings.

Colin—Sailor on the United States Navy cargo ship headed for Guam.

Chị Diễm—Ngọc Lan's older sister.

Diệp—Phúc's childhood crush.

Geoff Trowe—Officer who speaks to Jane after the murder.

Uncle Giang—Bà Huỳnh's son, Phúc's and Long's cousin.

Cậu Hòa—Jane's uncle (her mother's brother). Husband of Mợ Bích.

Bà Hương—Quốc's grandmother.

Bà Huỳnh—Bà Nội's sister. Jane's grandmother's sister.

Jackie Nguyễn—Jane's BFF.

Jane Vũ—Phúc's daughter. Paul's sister. Jackie's best friend.

John—Thi and Trâm's brother. O Linh's son. Jane's cousin from Connecticut.

Khánh—Boat refugee.

Khiên—Jane's cousin from Denver.

Chú Khoa—Quốc's dad. Bà Hương's son.

Thầy Lâm—Phúc's schoolteacher and fellow refugee. Father of Thúy.

Cô Lệ—Quốc's mother.

O Linh—Jane's aunt from Connecticut. Phúc and O Uyên's older sister. Bác Long's younger sister. Thi, John, and Trâm's mom. Friend of Ngọc Lan.

Bác Loan—Family maid in Vietnam.

Bác Long—O Linh, Phúc, and O Uyên's older brother. Jane's uncle.

Bác Luy—Jane's uncle with no actual blood relation. Phúc's friend from his days working in Hong Kong.

Mến Hoàng—Fellow refugee working in Hong Kong.

Mike—Jane's cousin from Florida. Son of O Ngữ. Adam's older brother.

Mirabelle—Jane's high school classmate and ex-friend.

Mỹ—Jane's cousin from Denver.

Ngọc Lan—Jane's mom. Phúc's girlfriend. Cậu Hòa's little sister. Friend of O Linh.

O Ngữ—O Vui's sister from Florida. Mother of Mike and Adam.

Bác Nguyệt—Bác Luy's wife. Mom to Becky, Vicky, and Stephen.

Nick—Luy and Phúc's boss in Hong Kong.

Bà Nội—Jane's grandmother. Phúc's mother.

Ông Nội—Vũ Đoàn Thái—Jane's grandfather. Phúc's father.

Panda—Phúc's only true friend.

Paul Vũ—Jane's little brother. Phúc's son.

Phúc Vũ—Jane and Paul's dad.

Chú Quang—Jane's piano teacher.

Quốc—Phúc's classmate and shipmate on first escape boat. Son of Chú Khoa and grandson of Bà Hương.

Raven—Jane's classmate. The one Sarah and Zoe chose over her.

Sergeant Red—Colin's superior.

Mr. Rogers—Paul's stuffed bunny.

Ronan—Jane's kindergarten classmate.

Samar Mhaskar—Jane's high school classmate who sells colored contact lenses.

Sarah—Jane's classmate. Zoe's twin.

Chú Sơn (Jamison)—Foreman's translator at the Hong Kong construction site.

Stephen—Becky and Vicky's younger brother. Bác Luy and Bác Nguyệt's son. Jane's non-cousin cousin.

Thanh—Boat refugee.

Thảo—Mơ Bích's adopted sister.

Thi—Jane's cousin from Connecticut. O Linh's daughter. Sibling of John and Trâm.

Thiết—Jane's cousin from Denver.

Chú Thịnh—Jane's uncle. O Uyên's husband.

Thúy—Thầy Lâm's five-year-old daughter and fellow refugee on Phúc's boat.

Tom—Phúc's boss in Hong Kong.

Trâm—Thi and John's sister. O Linh's daughter. Jane's cousin from Connecticut.

Trúc Hồ—Fellow refugee working in Hong Kong.

O Uyên—Bác Long, O Linh, and Phúc's younger sibling. Jane's aunt.

Vicky—Bác Luy and Bác Nguyệt's daughter. Jane's non-cousin cousin. Sibling of Becky and Stephen.

O Vui—Jane's godmother. The one who shamelessly flirts with Chú Quang.

Xuân—Jane's cousin who just immigrated to the United States.

Zoe—Jane's classmate. Sarah's twin.

AUTHOR'S NOTE

This story is inspired in large part by events that have occurred in my life. As such, I strived to be as honest and authentic as possible.

Drawing from the narratives of my parents, grandparents, aunts, uncles, and other Vietnamese Americans, I have woven together a story that is both imagined and speculative. Jane is a wholly unreliable narrator because she, like me, doesn't have a full or complete grasp of Vietnamese history.

The reasons for this are nuanced and complex, but I'd like to share a few simple ones. First, I am "flawed." I speak conversational Vietnamese, but I cannot read legal documents in the language. Second, most historical accounts are dominated by the perspectives of military elites and American GIs, which do not represent my family's experiences. Third, I'm Vietnamese American, so I learned about Vietnamese history in my *American history* class. That's right. Chew on that for a minute. And lastly, my parents rarely talk about what happened to them. As a teen, I was too timid to ask. As an adult, I understand that it's not my place to ask them to relive their traumas if they prefer to leave the past in the past.

Jane's story is not a complete or perfect chronicle of events; it's not meant to be. Sometimes we don't get answers to all the questions we want to ask, and we're forced to bridge the gap with whatever tools are available. Mirrored after my own life, Jane's story is ultimately a search for a connection to the past so she can curate a sense of belonging in the present.

Okay, now for some truth talk: writing authentically meant not deleting things like colorism and microaggressions that I knew wouldn't sit well with many readers. First, I must say, I am not an authority on racism within my or any other community. The hows and whys of racism among Vietnamese Americans are varied and difficult to simplify. I wrote an unfiltered and honest point of view knowing that once this book fell into the hands of readers, these characters would be judged. I hope they are. There are so many things I admire about my people and our culture, but I felt that it would not be truthful to tell this story without acknowledging the ideologies and prejudices that are very real and very present within our society.

For me, writing has always been about putting my stories into a collective pot of knowledge. How we interpret and process the narrative is not up to me. It's up to you, the reader.

I sincerely thank you for coming on this journey with me and look forward to meeting you again in the next book, about Paul and his mother.

ACKNOWLEDGMENTS

This book would not exist without the harrowing journeys that my mother, Nancy Ha Hoang, and father, Richard Men Hoang, had to endure as Vietnamese refugees. Thank you, Mom and Dad, for the sacrifices, punishments, and everything in between. Similarly, this story wouldn't be what it is without my siblings, Dr. Kimberly Kay Hoang, Andrew Quoc-Viet Hoang, and Lillyan Thuy-Tien Hoang, and our shared experiences. The suffering, the "Hoang-efficiency," the laughter, fights, tears—they're like a million knots, big and small, woven into this giant safety net that I know I'm very lucky to have.

Thank you, Jennifer Weltz, my warrior agent, for taking a chance on a random query nestled deep within your inbox. You nurtured my story and me as a writer, and I am forever grateful.

To my editor, Phoebe Yeh: you connected so fiercely with this book and lit the torch that would lead it into the world. Thank you for your sage advice, thoughtful feedback, and boundless enthusiasm. I am eternally grateful to the team at Crown Books for Young Readers, especially Trisha Previte, Megan Shortt, Tisha Paul, Melinda Ackell, Alison Kolani, Christine Ma, Janine Barlow, Mary McCue, Joey Ho, Adrienne Waintraub, Daniela Cortes, and Teresa Tran, for all the work you do behind the scenes. Marcos Chin, I have nothing but admiration for the way you peeled Jane from my imagination and made her real by lending your deeply emotional yet delicate artistry to the cover.

At the center of this book is family. I have a lot of cousins, but there are a few of you in particular to which this book owes a massive debt of gratitude: Lynneara Hoang, Kym Oanh Solancho, Mai Dinh, Linh Nguyen, Nguyet Reilly, Khannie Bueno, Kim Nguyen, Patricia Hoang, Bao Nguyen, Dang Khoa Nguyen, Kristine Hoang, Gimy Nguyen, and Kevin Nguyen. Some of you called me out on my BS after reading an early draft, others helped me with regional Vietnamese spellings or lent me your personal experiences, a lot of you fed me while I was broke, and every single one of you has influenced my life, and therefore this story, in some way.[5] We have a complicated and sometimes painful shared history; we're connected in many of our experiences, and I hope this book clarifies and deepens those connections.

Long before *My Father, the Panda Killer* held any promise of publication, it was an idea and hundreds of thousands of words tossed onto pages in a jumbled mess. Shirley (mom-in-law) Stimac and Ed (dad-in-law) Eslinger, Sara Taylor, Shawn Muttreja, Eric Gee, Katie McElhenny, Ian Robert Simpson, and Daniel Bayer—y'all are the true heroes here. Without plugging your noses, you sifted through piles of garbage to help me mine the gems. I am fortunate to have your time and support, and I promise to pay you back in tacos.

Thank you also to Nu-Anh Tran and Quan Tran for your knowledge and guidance.

---

5   If I have abstained from mentioning you and you find yourself offended, please call Kimberly—she'll tell you what you did.

Mai Nguyen Ha: I would not be a writer today had you not said (with ridiculous conviction) that I could do it. Thank you for believing in me before I believed in myself. Jessica Ng, Stephanie Tang, Mikey Ngo, Adam Vaun, Indigo Wilmann, Shakir Baruka, Dr. Ed and Chi Thuy Rhee, Ellen Burns, Gina Hendry, Amy Meyerson, Lina Sahai Wood, Nicole Noonan-Miller, and Katie Suh, you have enriched my life in more ways than I can count. Thank you for coming on this wild journey with me.

Ryan Eslinger, my husband, you believed in my potential when my sentences were practically incoherent. You are the backbone of every book I've written. Somehow you knew when to prod, when to push, and when to let go. Because of you I get to live every day in the pursuit of my dreams, and really, there is no greater gift than that.

Taschen, I started writing this book before you were born, but when I think about who I wrote it for, it is you. I'm sure there will come a time in your life when you'll wonder where your mom's neurosis comes from. This book does *not* have all the answers, but it has some. You'll have to ask me for the rest, and don't you dare do it over text.

And finally, to you, the reader, thank you for reading this book. With my hands clasped tightly in front of me, I bow to you, not only for opening the book but for continuing to turn the pages.

With so much love,

ABOUT THE AUTHOR

JAMIE JO HOANG is the daughter of Vietnamese refugees and grew up in Orange County, California (not the rich part). Jamie left for college at UCLA under the pretense of becoming a doctor or lawyer, but returned with a degree in Theater, Film, and Television—sorry, Mom and Dad! After working for MGM Studios and later as a docuseries producer, she quit her job and moved to Houston to pursue her real passion: writing. Her adult novel, *Blue Sun, Yellow Sky*, was a personal master class in storytelling and paved the way for the young adult novels that she's been holding in her heart for over twenty years. When Jamie's not writing, you'll find her wandering, pondering, and chasing experiences. She blogs about her life and travels at medium.com/@heyjamie and tweets at @heyjamie. She posts pretty pictures on Instagram as @heyjamiereads.